# Pride & Prejudice
# with a Side of Grits

by Jane Austen and Mary Calhoun Brown

Wentworth & Collins, Publishers

Published by Wentworth & Collins
Email: publisher@wentworthandcollins.com
Visit the publisher's web site at www.wentworthandcollins.com


ISBN-13: 978-0615675831 (Wentworth & Collins)

ISBN-10: 0615675832


For additional copies, please order at www.wentworthandcollins.com.
Wentworth & Collins books are also available at Amazon.com, in Kindle
format and at your local bookstore upon request.


Front cover photo licensed by iStockphoto.
Author's photograph by Janet Wise McCormick.


PRINTED IN THE UNITED STATES OF AMERICA

Pride and Prejudice with a Side of Grits is a work of fiction and descriptions of
events and characters are fictitious creations of the authors' imaginations.

This one's for Cam

# Chapter 1

Jest 'bout ever'body 'round here knows that if'n a feller's got two cents to rub t'gether, he's a-lookin' fer a right-nice girl to git hitched to.

Not too many folks've figured out jest what's a-goin' on in his noggin' when his pickup first rolls into town, but they's a-sure of one thang, their daughter's got dibbs on 'im, be'cuz she seen 'im first.

"Hey, Benny," screamed Flo from the back stoop while she wuz shellin' pole beans. "I heard someone done rented that big ol' doublewide on the other side of the Park N Shop."

Benny rolled right over on the couch, scratched his butt and didn't pay no never-mind to a word she said.

"Well, I knows it fer sure," she said. "Miz Long hollered to me on her way to the Piggly Wiggly."

Benny put a pillow over his head.

"Doncha wanna know who done let it?" asked his wife.

"If'n you wanna tell me so bad, then jest go ahead. Dadgumit!"

This wuz enough of an invite fer Flo.

"You had better know. Miz Long says the doublewide's been rented by a Nashv'lle feller who tricked the gob'ment into givin' 'im both welfare AND disability, but he's jest as spry as any young man oughtta be. He rolled into town and up the holler in a candy-apple red, four-wheel-drive Ford pickup truck with a CB antenny as long as a fishin' pole. He reckoned he liked that trailer right away, and told ol' Morris he'd take it. He's s'posed to move in b'fore the demolition derby comes to town, and he's even hired 'im a girl to clean the damned thang fer 'im."

"What's his name?" Benny perked up a little and shoved the pillow back under his head.

"Buford."

"If'n he hired a cleanin' girl, he ain't got no ball and chain."

"Oh, he ain't hitched fer sure. Imagine that! A single feller with a couple of checks from Uncle Sam every month! Our girls'll be as anxious as a one-eyed cat watchin' two rat holes."

"Why should they give a never-mind?"

"Darlin' Benny," replied his wife, "you're dumber 'n a sack full of hammers! We gonna unload us a daughter on that Buford feller. I don't care if'n he's so ugly he has to tie a pork chop 'round his neck to git the dog to play with 'im."

"You figure that's why he's settlin' here?"

"How can he be schemin'? A-tryin' to talk to you is like a-tryin' to nail jelly to the wall! That new feller's gonna plum fall right in love with one of yer daughters, so you better be fixin' to visit 'im jest as soon as his U-haul turns up the holler."

"I ain't a-goin', Flo, darlin'. You can go, or hell, put the girls in some halter tops and cut-offs and send 'em up there on their own. But now don't you be wearin' that shirt you won the wet t-shirt contest in last night, or young Buford'll be on you like flies on a pile of dog shit."

"Oh hell, Benny! I look old enough to scare the buzzards off a gut-wagon. I done lost my looks years ago. When a woman's birthed five daughters, she quits thankin' on her own looks."

"The only time a woman says that is when she's uglier than the southbound end of a northbound donkey."

"Alls I got to say is you better be takin' Buford up a six pack of Bud, or at least some of my prize-winnin' cornbread, lickety split."

"I ain't doin' it, Flo."

"You're so tight, you squeak when you walk! What's a six-pack of Bud to you! Thank of yer damn daughters. One of 'em's gotta git hitched. I cain't afford to feed 'em, and I'm worried one of 'em's gonna git knocked up b'fore long. Billy and LuLu Lucas will be goin' without a doubt, and they's averse to meetin' strangers. Now, you know you've got to go. We jest cain't go less'n you go first."

"Quit yer worry wartin'. I'd be willin' to bet this Buford feller'd be right glad to meet you, and I'll send over a coupon fer a free oil change and a note on the back sayin' he can run off with whichever of my girls he takes a likin' to. But I reckon I oughtta put in a special word fer my Lizzy. She's so sweet sugar won't melt in her mouth."

"The heck if'n you will! You're so dumb, there's a tree stump in a Looziana swamp that's smarter 'n you! Lizzy ain't no better 'n any of the others. Compared to Janie, she's uglier 'n home-made soap, and she don't dress near's good as Lydie. Jest last week Lydie had on them jeans she bought at the thrift shop, and they wuz so tight if'n she'd a had a nickel in her back pocket, we could'a told you if'n it wuz heads or tails. Now that girl knows how to dress! But you's always givin' Lizzy preference."

"Aw, Sugar! Not one of 'em has much to recommend 'em," Benny replied. "They's all so stupid they couldn't pour water from a boot with instructions on the heel, but that Lizzy has somethin' special. She knows more 'n a Philadelphia lawyer."

"Shut yer trap, Benny! How can you go on like that 'bout yer own children? You jest like to bug me."

"Git over yerself, woman! You go on like this ever' time some new buck rides into town."

# Chapter 2

Of course Benny didn't let grass grow under his feet b'fore he visited Buford. He rode up there on his four wheeler on account of he couldn't git the engine in the old Chevy to turn over. He kept his visit to himself, though, so's to vex Flo later on.

That night as the tv shined blue into the faces of each family member, Benny leaned back in his Lazy Boy, released his substantial gut from the confines of his belt buckle, and took a long drag off his cigarette as he watched his second daughter bedazzlin' the pockets of her jeans. "I sure hope Buford likes them pants, Lizzy."

"How the hell 'r we to know what Buford likes," her mother spat, "since we ain't never gonna meet up with 'im?"

"Oh, Momma! None of us need yer bull tonight. Miz Long done already told us she would introduce us down at the revival assembly."

"Miz Long ain't gonna do no such thang. She's got them two nieces she's a-tryin' to marry off so's she won't have to raise any more of other people's babies."

From out'a the blue, Benny asked, "Lizzy, when 'r you goin' to another one of them dances of yers?"

"Two weeks from tomorrow."

"Well shit!" cried her mother. "And Miz Long ain't goin' to be back from Myrtle Beach 'til the day b'fore the dance so they's no way she can introduce Buford to us b'fore then. How 'r we goin' to git dibs on 'im? Ah, well. He's prob'ly so dumb if'n he had an idea it would die of loneliness."

"Well, I wish I'd ha know'd that b'fore I took 'im over some of our fresh eggs. I could've ate 'em fer supper," replied Benny.

A look of consternation crossed the faces of the girls. Benny grinned his lopsided grin and his eyes smiled so hard they squished up into little slits as he said, "Flo, you better close yer mouth. Yer catchin' flies."

At that, Flo began a thirty minute tirade as to why she had suspected Benny'd pull through fer 'em all along. The rest of the evenin' wuz spent speculatin' how long they should wait b'fore askin' 'im over fer some of Flo's famous pinto beans and cornbread.

# Chapter 3

Now that Flo and her daughters knew their Daddy had seen Buford, it wuz all they could do to pry information out'a 'im, some with the tact of a crowbar, and others with innocent questions asked with a grin so big they looked like a goat in a briarpatch. Benny wuz 'bout as useful as tits on a daddy turtle, so the girls had to depend on their neighbor LuLu to paint 'em a picture of the handsome stranger.

LuLu reported that Buford wuz jest the bees' knees. He wuz like a long, cool drink of water. As they listened to LuLu's description, Flo's daughters wuz as quiet as a mouse pissing on cotton. With rapt attention, each girl heard what she wanted to hear, but all five girls beamed when LuLu said that Buford loved to two-step and square dance. He planned to go to the next dance with a whole bunch of folks, and jest 'bout ever'body knows that if'n a man likes to dance, a country girl with a short skirt can two-step her way into his heart.

"If'n jest one of my daughters can git her foot in the door on the good side of the tracks," said Flo to her husband, "then it won't be long b'fore we can git rid of the rest of 'em. Then, I can die happy."

A few days later, Buford skidded into the gravel driveway in a cloud of dust and opened up a cold one with Benny. He arrived pretendin' to return the empty egg basket, but anyone could tell he wuz a-lookin' 'round fer Benny's daughters. Word travels fast in the country, and Buford'd been told at least a couple of 'em wuz lookers. Buford kicked the dirt, disappointed when Benny told 'im the girls wuz out, but he perked up when Benny invited 'im back to supper.

Needless to say Flo wuz beside herself, runnin' 'round like a chicken with its head cut off preparin' fer their guest. She'd already dug a side of deer from the deep freeze and had it laid out to thaw when she got the news that Buford had to scoot out'a town fer a bit. She thought that wuz a fine howdy-do and wondered if'n he might be a crazy ol' coot, always flyin' in and out'a town and never settlin' in at his doublewide on the good side of the tracks.

LuLu quieted Flo's fears when she reported Buford'd gone to carry back twelve gals and seven fellers fer the upcomin' hoe-down. Benny's girls wuz wound tighter 'n a new girdle 'bout so many gals a-comin', but then word got 'round he wuz only brangin' his two sisters, one of their husbands and another young feller.

Buford wuz easy on the eyes, handsome as all git-out. His manners wuz tolerable, and he carried his liquor wrapped up in a brown paper poke. So of course, ever'body wuz wonderin' what he wuz drankin'. His sisters looked right as rain with their noses pointed up, walkin' slower 'n a bread wagon with biscuit wheels. Buford's brother-in-law, Harley, wuz spread out like a cold supper and sweatin' like a stuck hog. But his friend Dutch wuz smack-down gorgeous. Every eye watched 'im as he strode in wearin' his Sund'y-go-to-meeting clothes. He wuz a tall drink of water with a sour expression on his face like a bulldog lickin' cat piss off a stingin' nettle. Ever'body could tell Dutch wuzn't too happy to meet up with 'em. Ever'body thought he wuz jest too big fer his britches and decided not to like 'im right then and there. Somebody said he wuz shittin' in high cotton, but no one there cared much 'bout his money if'n he wuz goin' to act like that. His big farm in Lexin'ton couldn't even've saved 'im from the hard feelin's spreadin' 'round the room faster 'n green grass through a goose.

Buford soon chewed the fat with most of the folks who turned out fer the dance. He wuz a real hoot, and cut the rug with the best of 'em. He wuz hot that the dance ended so soon, thought it wuzn't quite right, so he decided to throw his own shin-dig out back of his house as soon as he wuz settled. Well, hide-near ever'body yee-hawed at that notion, and Buford stood out as ever'body's favorite. His friend Dutch, however, wuzn't so lucky. He wuz marked as the proudest man anyone had ever seen, and he wuz generally hated fer being such a snooty stuck-up Richy-Rich. And the woman with the wickedest tongue against Dutch wuz Flo, who had jest recently been told how Dutch had snubbed one of her daughters at the dance.

Lizzy, as it turned out, had been obliged by the lack of fellers to sit out a couple of dances, and durin' that time Dutch had been standin' close enough fer her to hear his conversation with Buford who wuz a-tryin' to goad his friend into square dancin'.

"Aw, come on, Dutch," he said. "Git on out there and dance. I cain't stand to see you over here lonelier 'n a divorced widow woman."

"Hell no! You know how I hate jukin' less'n I know the girls real well. At a hoe-down like this one, it looks like people ridin' who ain't never rode b'fore. Yer kinfolk 'r cuttin' a rug right now, and there ain't another woman in this room who ain't got lice or some kind of fungus. Hell, half of 'em 'r dippin' snuff."

"Whoa there, Nellie," replied Buford. "I never seen such purty girls in all my life."

"You're two-steppin' with the only tolerable girl in the room," said Dutch, a-lookin' at the oldest of Benny's daughters.

"If'n I'm lyin', I'm dyin'. She's sugar in my hand, fer sure, but one of her sisters is sittin' over yonder. She seems purtier 'n a stump of grandaddy long legs. I'm sure my partner would hook you up."

"Whichever one 'r you talkin' 'bout?" And he turned and spied Lizzy. She locked eyes on 'im and gave 'im the stink-eye. He turned back 'round to Buford and said, "She's tolerable, but I don't want nobody's re-ject. If'n nobody wants to dance with her, why should I bother? Why don't you go dance with yer purty little missy? Yer wastin' yer time here with me."

Buford side-stepped to the dance floor with his thumbs tucked in his front pockets and his elbows flappin' out like chicken wings. Dutch rolled his eyes and walked off. Lizzy could've spit nails at 'im, but she decided to make fun of 'im with her girlfriends instead. She wuz smart as a tack and laughed so hard as she retold the story that Dr. Pepper jest 'bout came out her nose.

B'fore long the party broke up. Flo'd been watchin' her oldest daughter all night as she danced, and she noticed Janie had caught the eye of the new folks. Buford had chosen her fer the slow songs, and as they'd danced, Flo noticed you couldn't have slid a piece of paper b'tween 'em. Buford's sisters with their mall-bought outfits seemed to like Janie jest fine, and Janie seemed happy with all the attention, though she wuz shy by nature.

Lizzy could tell Janie wuz happy as a pig in mud, and the other sisters wuz happy campers, as well. Mary, who had peculiar ways, talked funny and didn't mix well, had been called "accomplished" by one of Buford's sisters. Kitty, who wuz the knee-baby of the family, and Lydie never set down all the night long. They practic'ly had fellers lined up to dance with 'em. So the family returned to their tiny shotgun house full of Cheez-Whiz and stories where they found Benny passed out drunk with the tv on and a copy of the National Enquirer layin' across his gut.

"Wake yer ass up, Benny!" Flo hollered. "We had a kick-ass time at the hoe-down. You should'a come. Buford wuz all over Janie like flies to shit. Ever'body said so. He stood up with some of the other girls in town, but they 'r jest white trash and ever'body knows it." And with that, Flo started describin' all the girls Buford danced with and what they wuz wearin'.

"Like I care what ever'body wuz wearin'!" Benny spat back at his wife. "Shut the hell up and leave me alone. I wuz asleep!"

"Hell fire and damnation!" continued Flo. "That Buford is a hottie. You never said how strong he is. Why, he had his sleeves cut out'a his shirt, and I could tell he lifts himself some weights or somethin'. And he smelled so good. Janie said he must wear some kind of man perfume or somethin'. I told her that I don't like a man who smells loud, and she said it might've been his friend Dutch who smelled so good."

Here she wuz interrupted again when a pillow hit her upside the head. Benny told her that listenin' to her wuz like watchin' grass grow.

"Well, that Dutch," Flo continued, "he thanks he's hot snot on a silver platter, but we all know he's jest cold boogers on a paper plate." And with this she began her retellin' of Dutch's snubbin' Lizzy at the dance while Benny nursed his now lukewarm Pabst Blue Ribbon and pretended to listen as he stole glances at the tractor pull on the tv.

# Chapter 4

Out in the lean-to Janie and Lizzy chewed the fat as they normally did after a party. Janie wuz scared of her own shadow most of the time, but she always got on all right with her little sister.

"Besides bein' easy on the eyes, Lizzy, Buford's as funny as a fart in church. And do you know what he had inside that poke? It wuz a brown bottle of IBC Rootbeer. Nuthin' else. He told me he don't drink in public, liquor or beer or nothin'. Can you imagine?"

"He's sweet on you, Janie," Lizzy replied, "and I know this ain't yer first rodeo, so you better take it slower 'n a snail drunk on molasses crawlin' up an ice hill in January. He ain't gonna buy the cow if'n he can git the milk fer free."

"Lawdy, Lizzy!"

"I'm jest sayin' be careful. You thought Peter Bob Widell wuz jest the bee's knees, and he used to knock you clean into next week and then some. And then there wuz ol' Rupert Clonch. He wuz so stupid he couldn't hit the broad side of a barn-- even from the inside-- with the door closed, but I seen you moonin' over 'im like he wuz the king of Sheebah. You never do see the fault in other folks. What did you thank of Buford's kin folk? I didn't take to 'em much."

"By the time I got over thar to visit with 'em, I wuz so dad-blammed tar'd and sweaty from dancin', I felt like a mashed bug. They seem right nice, though, and the skinny one is gonna stay with Buford and help 'im keep house."

Lizzy listened but couldn't help but thank Janie wuz so full of shit her eyes wuz turnin' brown. Those sisters of Bufords's wuz stuck up higher 'n a light pole and meaner 'n quarrelin' cats in a gunny sack. On the surface they looked like fine ladies in their lacy shirts and cowboy boots, but underneath Lizzy suspected their hearts wuz cold enough to freeze the tits off a frog. They wuz s'posed to be related to some state senator or another, and they told jest 'bout ever'one they came across 'bout their high relations. They had plum fergot their Daddy wuz a workin' man jest like ever'body else.

Neighborhood rumors aside, Buford'd inherited money from his Daddy when his Daddy ended up dead as a doornail at the factory. Nobody knows what happened, so the company shelled out the cash to prevent lawyers from gittin' mixed up in it. His Daddy'd always wanted to buy his own house and quit rentin', but died b'fore he could make his American dream come true fer his ownself. Buford wanted a house to call his own, too, but seein' as he could rent the doublewide at such a good price, he decided to put off makin' any decisions fer a while.

His sisters wuz hell bent on Buford gittin' a house of his own, and thought rentin' wuz below 'im. Tammy, the single sister, wuz more 'n happy to stay with her brother and eat at his table of the evenin's. Patty and Harley would shack up there as long as they could seein' as how their daughter raised huntin' dogs and their house smelled like wet dog and pee. Plus they owed a couple of months back rent, and they wuz avoidin' the landlord.

Buford and Dutch wuz thick as thieves. They'd started out as huntin' buddies and got along mostly be'cuz they wuz jest so diff'rent. Buford wuz easy-goin' and lackadaisical, which should have driven Dutch plum crazy, but fer some reason it didn't. Dutch wuz smart as a whip and had more money than a monkey on a train. His family had been walkin' in tall cotton since Napoleon wuz in knee pants. He wuz tighter 'n a fiddle string with his money. He'd been to the cotillion when he wuz younger, so he knew which way to hold his fork. Dutch wuz so stubborn he could argue with a wall, and he walked like a banty rooster with his shoulders pressed back and his chest pushed out.

Dutch and Buford's rehash of the hoe-down wuz in keepin' with their personalities. Buford thought all the girls wuz jest as purty as puddin' pie, and the older folks wuz pleasant enough and right welcomin'. He thought Janie wuz jest purty as a picture, and no one could hold a candle to her. Dutch, on the other hand, thought the town folks looked dumber 'n a box of rocks, and the girls wuz so rough that maybe the dog had been keepin' 'em under the porch to chew on. He wuz kind enough to admit to his buddy that Janie wuz a far cry from ugly.

Patty and Tammy liked Janie and called her "that sweet girl," which their brother took as permission to thank 'bout her however he wanted.

## Chapter 5

'Bout a stone's throw from Benny's house lived Billy and LuLu Lucas. Billy had owned an autoparts store a few towns over and served on the town sanitation board. He wuz all puffed up 'bout that and took on airs. Benny overlooked his airs, and they wuz always t'gether under one car or another with grease under their fangernails.

LuLu wuz goodhearted but dumb as a stick. When God wuz passin' out brains, she got stuck behind the door and didn't git any. She could whip an egg, and she wuz always passin' out chocolate chip cookies to the neighbor kids. LuLu and Billy had a whole herd of kids, fat as lard every one of 'em except their oldest daughter Charlotte, who wuz so skinny she had to run 'round in the shower to git wet. She had great big bug eyes and a mouthful of horse teeth, and that's prob'ly why she wuz twenty-seven years old and had never been hitched. Charlotte and Lizzy both taught the ankle biters in Sund'y school and wuz close friends.

"You had a right nice start at the dance, Charlotte," said Flo with jest a speck of sarcasm. "Buford asked you to dance b'fore anyone else. I'm guessin' that's on account of yer height. Law, child! If'n you git any taller, I'm gonna have to put a rock on yer head."

"I reckon he liked his second choice better."

"I declare! You must mean Janie. Yessirree! He only had eyes fer her after they tore up that dance floor t'gether. I heard tell you wuz standin' close enough to overhear what Buford said to Willy Crabtree?"

"He looked Willy right in the eye and told 'im flat out that the purtiest girl in the room wuz Janie. There's no two opinions on that, he said."

"My word! Well now, he wuzn't talkin' out both sides of his mouth there! It might all come down to nuthin' though. We gotta keep our wits 'bout us with this one."

"My ears had perkier overhearin's 'n yers did," said Charlotte. "Seems ol' Dutch ain't worth a listenin' to as his friend, is he? Poor Lizzy!"

"You jest need to shut yer yappin' trap right this instant. Lizzy ain't gonna be vexed by the likes of Dutch! That man makes me madder 'n a wet hen. If'n he came near me I'd knock 'im into next week! Miz Long told me Dutch sat next to her fer near by half an hour and never once opened his durn mouth, not even to say 'howdy-do.'"

"You said yer peace, Momma. Now I wanna say mine," said Janie. "I seen Dutch talkin' to Miz Long with my own eyes."

"That's only on account of her askin' 'im how he liked the double-wide. He had no choice but to say somethin'. She said he talked back to her like she wuz stump-hole ugly and duller 'n dishwater. Those wuz her exact words."

"Tammy, Buford's sister, told me," said Janie, "that Dutch don't fancy yammerin' on and on less'n he's right acquainted with folks. He's s'posed to be happy as a dead pig in the sunshine to talk to his friends."

"You lie like a rug, Janie dear. If'n he wuz such a 'nice guy' he would've had a sit-down with Miz Long. Ever'body is sayin' he wuz rude be'cuz her car's broke and she had to ride to the hoe-down on her John Deere lawnmower."

"I don't care if'n he's quiet as a church mouse 'round Miz Long," said Charlotte, " I jest wish he'd a' given Lizzy the time of day."

Flo replied, "Lizzy, I don't care if'n he asks you to dance later on. I wouldn't give 'im a second look if'n I wuz you."

"I thank we can spit-shake on that one, Momma. I wouldn't dance with Dutch if'n he wuz the last man livin' on earth."

"I cain't blame 'im fer his pride," said Charlotte. "He's rollin' in dough, hotter 'n Billy Ray Cyrus back in the day, and he has ever'thang goin' in his favor. He oughtta thank highly of his ownself. Don't git yer panties in a twist, but I thank he has a right to be proud."

"Yep," replied Lizzy, "and I could forgive 'im his pride if'n he hadn't embarrassed me so bad. I turned fifty shades of red right there in front of ever'body."

"Pride," said Mary, who always talked fancy and b'lieved that her thoughts wuz worth hearin', "is a very common failing I believe. By all that I have ever read, I am convinced that it is very common indeed, that human nature is particularly prone to it, and that there are very few of us who do not cherish a feeling of self-complacency on the score of some quality or other, real or imaginary. Vanity and pride are different things, though the words are often used synonymously. A person may be proud without being vain. Pride relates more to our opinion of ourselves, vanity to what we would have others think of us."

The room wuz silent fer half a beat after Mary finished talkin'. She wuz always using her uppity words, and not a soul could understand her. Mostly they jest blinked at each other 'til one of the Lucas boys rolled in the room, covered in mud and leavin' tracks on the plastic runner that wuz used to protect the high traffic areas in the Lucas's lodge-style family room.

"If'n I wuz as rich as that Dutch feller," he said, "I suwanee, I'd be as high falutin' as I want. I'd keep a pack of bird dogs and drink Mountain Dew all day long."

"Well, yer teeth would rot out," said Flo as she adjusted her dentures a bit. "And if'n my shadow crossed yer path, I'd take that Mountain Dew away quick as a whip."

The boy declared he'd like to see her do it, and she kept sayin' she would do it in a  heartbeat, and the argument didn't stop 'til their visit ended.

## Chapter 6

The sisters made their way down past the Park N Shop to pay a visit to Tammy and Patty, and not long after that Tammy and Patty stopped by to say howdie. Janie wuz startin' to grow on Buford's sisters, but Mrs. Benny wuz as useless as a sore thumb. They didn't wish one of her visits on their worst enemy. The sisters couldn't tolerate Janie's trail of little sisters any more 'n her mother, but they wuz right friendly to Janie and Lizzy. Janie couldn't git enough of their attention, but Lizzy could tell they wuz a-lookin' down their noses at ever'one. Lizzy couldn't like 'em come hell or high water. She knew they only gave Janie the time of day be'cuz Buford wuz sweet on her. It wuz clear as daylight. He brightened up and tucked his shirt in his britches every time Janie came into sight. More'n once she seen 'im chuck his chaw into the bushes so Janie wouldn't have to look at it all brown in the side of his jaw. Janie, being shy and all, didn't let on that she wuz smitten, but Lizzy could tell. She mentioned her hunch to Charlotte.

"I thank she should seal the deal, if'n you know what I mean," Charlotte said with a wink. "I know she likes to play coy and the like, but some girl's gonna lay down with that man b'fore long, and then he won't be interested in watchin' Janie bat her eyelashes at 'im. Men's brains is like teeny-tiny little peas rattlin' 'round in their big ol' heads. They don't thank with their brains, Lizzy. They use their peckers."

"She's flirtin' with 'im jest as much as her nature will allow. He's got to be an idjit if'n he cain't see it. She's not a-tryin' to hide her feelin's fer 'im. I thank he'll figure it out."

"Maybe he will if'n he's 'round her enough. I jest thank they need more 'alone' time. Hell's fire! They's always surrounded by they's kin, and that's half the holler on Janie's side. She jest needs to make the most of every half hour they have t'gether. I have a new over-the-shoulder-boulder-holder if'n she wants to wear a low-cut shirt. It ain't comfortable to wear, but it pushes the girls t'gether to make a right nice cleavage. I've gotten some hoots and hollers wearin' it. Buford'll be so mesmerized by her boobies, he'll propose without even knowin' it."

"Yer plan is a good one," replied Lizzy, "if'n alls Janie wants is to git hitched, and if'n I wuz schemin' to git a rich husband, I'd prob'ly take you up on yer offer. But Janie's pure hearted. She's not goin' to try to trap 'im into marryin' her. She's honestly smitten. She's only known 'im 'bout two weeks. They've been to a couple of dances, she's been over to his house once and they've been out to the Dairy Queen four times."

"Well, good Lord, Lizzy! You make it sound like alls they did wuz chew their food. Four times at the Dairy Queen includes ridin' in his truck there and back. You can git to know a man real good when yer ridin' in his truck and settin' close."

"I thank they decided they both like fried taters better 'n tater tots. I cain't say they've talked 'bout much more 'n that."

"I wish Janie well. If'n she wuz married to 'im tomorrow, I'd thank she had as good a chance of happiness as if'n she'd studied 'im from the booth at Dairy Queen fer a year. Stayin' married is jest a roll of the dice anyways. I thank it's better to learn to hate 'em after yer married instead of a-knowin' they's faults ahead of time."

"You split my sides, Charlotte! You know that dog won't hunt. I swear you don't have the sense God gave a goose."

Busy as she wuz watchin' Buford moon over Janie, Lizzy didn't have the foggiest notion that thoughts of her wuz spinnin' 'round Dutch like a thousand fruit flies to a ripe, sticky Georgia peach. At first Dutch thought she wuz so ugly she'd make a freight train take a dirt road, but that wuz all due to the stink eye Lizzy wuz givin' 'im. The next time he laid eyes on her he wuz in a mood to criticize. But no sooner had he convinced himself that she wuz like the gift of a white elephant, (Nobody wants one of those in their Christmas stockin'!) he began to muster up the idea that her wide, Mabelline mascara commerical eyes hinted at uncommon smarts in these parts. He nearly got a woody thankin' 'bout the way her hips moved when she walked, and even though he thought she wuz one step away from white trash, he wuz caught up in her playfulness. Of course, Lizzy wuz plum ignorant of his thoughts.

Dutch had a hankerin' to git to know Lizzy better, so he took it on himself to listen in on her conversations one night at Billy Lucas's barbeque.

"Dutch must thank I've only got one oar in the water if'n he thanks I didn't see 'im listenin' in on me talkin' to Lieutenant Dan," Lizzy said to Charlotte.

"Why doncha go on over thar and call 'im on it?"

"He's so puffed up! If'n I don't go over thar and give 'im the 'what fer' right away, I'll regret it, I'm sure."

Not long after, Dutch sallied up close to the friends without a notion to say a word. Charlotte looked at Dutch, then back at Lizzy and mouthed, "I dare you," which wuz all Lizzy needed.

"Dutch," she began, "did you thank I sounded like a plum fool when I asked Lieutenant Dan to throw a square dance down at the VFW?"

"You didn't sound like much of a fool to me. Girls 'r always wantin' someone to throw a dance." He grinned like the Cheshire cat.

"Well, shit fire and save matches," wuz all Lizzy could squeak out when she seen his look.

Charlotte decided to help out when she seen the look on Lizzy's face. "I'm goin' to pull out my fiddle, Lizzy, and you know what that means."

"You're colder 'n a well-digger's butt! Some friend! Wantin' me to fiddle and sing in front of ever'body. I cain't sing my way out'a a paper bag if'n my life depended on it, 'specially in front of all these Nashv'lle folks. They prob'ly hear Garth and Reba live and in person in a big city like that." Charlotte wouldn't let up, so Lizzy added "Well, all right. If'n I cain't git you to shut up, I might as well play a little." She gave Dutch a cool glance and said, "There's a sayin' 'round here-- 'keep yer breath to cool yer porridge,' and I'll keep mine to swell up my songs."

Lizzy wuzn't no Charlie Daniels, but she played right well. After a couple of songs, her sister, Mary, took the instrument and switched the tone from slap-yer-knee fiddle music to the longer, drawn out sounds of the violin. Mary worked hard to try to fit in with other folks and liked to show off when she could.

Mary had a tough time of it, playin' violin songs to a fiddle crowd. Her sawin' away at the strings wuz done jest perfect, but ever'one preferred Lizzy's fiddle even though she wuzn't half as good. Half a dozen love birds stood up to dance to Mary's playin', swappin' spit and swayin' t'gether like four-legged monsters.

Dutch stood stiff as a board in the corner, lost in his own thoughts, not realizin' Billy Lucas wuz attemptin' to jumpstart a conversation.

"I jest love me a good party. Don't you, Dutch? There ain't nuthin' like a good throw down on a fine evenin' like this. Makes me feel like the king of England."

"Every savage can dance."

Billy only smiled. He didn't like to talk 'bout Indians. It wuz a sore subject fer 'im, seein' as how his sister had to work fer 'em at the casino, and she often as not had a black eye to show fer it. "Buford's got some moves out there, I'd be willin' to bet you can cut a rug with the best of 'em, too."

Dutch checked his cell phone even though there wuzn't any service this far out. 'Bout that same time Lizzy wuz walkin' over to git a cool one, so Billy thought he'd tease her a bit, fatherly to her as he wuz. So he called out to her, "Hey, Lizzy! Why ain't you dancin? I've got a partner fer ya, rightcheer. Dutch cain't refuse a lady so fine as yerself."

He caught her hand as she passed and drew her up close, then twirled her 'round toward Dutch, who wuz in a mind to accept her hand fer the dance.

Lizzy pulled away, stumblin' slightly. "No sirree, Billy Lucas! I ain't plannin' to dance right now. I sure do hope y'all didn't thank I came over this way to beg fer a partner."

Billy Lucas said, "You's the best we got in this town, Lizzy. You cain't deny me the pleasure of watchin' you cut a rug!"

Lizzy gave Billy a look that said, "You're crazier 'n a loon!" And sashayed away. Her reluctance to push up against Dutch on the dance floor didn't make 'im thank any less of her, and he didn't mind watchin' her walk away or the way her hair brushed against her waist as she moved.

He wuz thankin' on this when Tammy stumbled over in a cloud of perfume. He smelled her b'fore he seen her. "I bet I know what yer thankin'," she said.

"The hell if'n you do."

"Yer thankin' jest how awful it'd be to spend very many nights 'round people like this. These folks 'r real white trash, if'n you ask me. They thank they're high class, and it jest cracks me up to high heaven. I'd be right pleased to hear yer opinion on 'em."

"Yer barkin' up the wrong tree, Tammy. You must be three sheets to the wind. I wuz thankin' on how some girls 'r jest as purty as a speckled pup."

Tammy's eyes flew open like two milk saucers and asked 'im which girls he wuz referrin' to. Dutch replied, "Lizzy."

"Lizzy!" repeated Tammy with a slight burp. "Git out'a town! How long have you been sweet on her? You thankin' on gittin' hitched?"

"That's jest what I 'spected you to ask. You could start an argument in an empty house! You went straight from me likin' the way some gal looks to gittin' married."

"Well, I'll be! If'n yer so serious 'bout it, I'd like to give you a pat on the back fer havin' the best mother-in-law in five counties. I'm sure she'll wanna hang out at Pembrook Farm with you fer a month of Sund'ys, four times a year."

Dutch listened to her, but he never paid her no nevermind. She jest kept yammerin' away at the mouth, and he felt right safe from her teasin'.

# Chapter 7

Benny wuz so poor he couldn't jump over a nickel to save a dime. Fer that reason he wuz tighter 'n a bull's ass at fly time. Flo said he wouldn't give a nickel to see Jesus ridin' in on a bicycle. In fact, money wuz so dear he had to git one of his kin to make the mortgage payments on his shotgun house, and he had to promise the feller that when he kicked the bucket, the house, land and ever'thang belonged to him.

Flo wuz no help in that department. Her people didn't have no money, neither. She had a sister, Fern, who'd been lucky enough to snag the Assistant Manager of the Piggly Wiggly, and now he managed the place. They also had a brother who sold appliances in Nashv'lle. He did right well.

Flo and Fern lived jest a skip and a jump from each other, not a mile of dirt road b'tween 'em. As you might expect, Benny's girls wuz close to their Ain't Fern and took a shinin' to walkin' to Fern's three or four days out'a seven. There wuz a Dollar General Store in that direction, and Kitty and Lydie liked to window shop in every aisle. There never wuz two bigger airheads ever born. They took a likin' to pickin' up gossip along the way, and they'd jest learned that the Army National Guard wuz gonna be camped out at the fair grounds fer the whole winter.

With the thought of fresh meat on their minds, Kitty and Lydie visited Ain't Fern more reg'lar, and they started siftin' through the rumor mill to learn more 'bout the fellers who'd be hangin' their hats in the neighborhood. Ain't Fern fluttered in and out'a the fair grounds, givin' them boys some southern hospitality, and in return she kept her nieces up to speed on what wuz goin' on in the camp. The only thang them girls could thank 'bout wuz soldiers and officers, and they rolled their eyes at their mother's rants 'bout Buford's wads of cash.

After he'd heard jest 'bout enough, Benny said, "You girls don't know shit from shinola. I thought you wuz stupid fer a while, but now I know you are."

Kitty felt scolded and dug a speck of sausage out'a her front teeth. Lydie, on the contrary, kept goin' on and on 'bout a feller named Carter who she wuz eyeballin'.

"Benny, you make my ass itch, you little cotton picker! How could you trash talk yer own daughters like that?"

"The truth hurts, don't it?"

"You better give yer heart to Jesus, 'cuz yer butt's mine! These girls is smart in their own way, ever' last one of 'em, and don't you say nuthin' diff'rent."

"You don't know yer butt from a hole in the ground. You can git glad the same way you got mad or die unhappy."

"Well, they ain't a-dults, Benny. What do you 'spect, that they'd have the sense of they's folks? When they's our age, they won't be thankin' on no soldiers any more 'n we do. Back in the day, I liked to snuggle down with boys in camouflage, myself. My poor heart skips a beat when I see them boys in uniform, and if'n one of 'em knocked on the door and wanted to carry away one of my girls, why I'd let 'em. I thought Lieutenant Dan looked smokin' hot in his uniform the other night. If'n I wuz younger, I'd tap that."

"Momma!" cried Lydie. "Ain't Fern says that Lieutenant Dan and his buddy Carter wuzn't talkin 'bout you when they wuz plannin' to go out the other night. They didn't even know you wuz in that wet t-shirt contest. Git over yerself."

Flo couldn't git a word in edgewise on account of the phone started rangin'. They let it go to message jest in case it wuz a bill collector or somebody a-tryin' to sell somethin'. Janie listened to the message. "Who the hell wuz it, Janie? What's a-goin' on? What's it 'bout? Good Lord, Janie, has the cat got yer tongue?"

"It's Tammy. She and Patty ain't gittin' along so well, so they want me to come and have lunch with 'em over to their place. Says her brother and Dutch 'r takin' lunch at the fair grounds with the National Guard."

"With the National Guard!" cried Lydie. "I jest cain't b'lieve Ain't Fern didn't say nuthin'."

"Eatin' out," said Flo. "That's 'bout as unlucky as findin' a penny wrong-side-up."

"Can I borry the truck?" asked Janie.

"Hell no. Take the dirt-bike. Them clouds over yonder look like rain's a-comin' You'll have to stay over thar til the rain lets up."

"How do you know they won't jest send her back home?" Lizzy asked.

"If'n 'em boys 'r down at the fair grounds, they'll have Buford's truck and Harley and Patty ain't got no proper vehicle. They rode into town in that junky ol' rust-wagon, and it up and quit on 'em half a mile up the road. They had to carry they's grips all the way to Buford's from the edge of the county line."

"Come on, Momma. I'd rather go in the truck so's my hair doesn't git mawmucked up."

"Yer Daddy needs the truck fer work today, Janie. Don't give me none of yer back talk."

Janie wuz then obliged to go to lunch on the dirt bike, and her mother jest wouldn't shut up 'bout the possibility of a storm a-brewin'. Flo's prayers wuz answered when not a lick after Janie took off, the skies opened up, and it started pourin' the rain. It wuz a real gully-washer, and Janie's sisters wuz worryin' themselves into a tizzy on account of the back tire on that dirt bike wuz as bald as Uncle Phil, and it tended to fishtail in high water. Their mother jest grinned like a fox in a henhouse. It rained all the day long and into the night. The creeks wuz risin', and Janie couldn't come home without fearin' fer her life.

"I'm as lucky as a man in a woman's prison with a fist full of pardons!" exclaimed Flo 'til ever'one wished she'd jest shut up. She acted like she had a hand in makin' the rain. Night fell and b'fore the rooster crowed the next mornin', the phone rang, wakin' up ever'body but Lydie who wuz still drunk from the night b'fore. Out'a habit, Benny's clan let the call go to the answerin' machine to avoid trouble.

The message said Janie had come down with near new-monia, and her head wuz hotter 'n blue blazes. As it turns out she wuz sweatin' like a pregnant nun. Tammy and Patty practic'ly blocked her from the door, sayin' she best be restin' there with 'em than a-tryin' to ride that dirt bike back through the flooded roads.

"Dadgummit, woman!" said Benny to his wife when Lizzy had told 'im 'bout Janie. "I s'pose if'n she's dead as a doornail tonight, it would all be on account of a-tryin' to git her claws into Buford under yer watchful eye."

"Oh my! She ain't gonna die, you dipshit. I jest hope she don't look rougher 'n ten miles of bad road with snot a-runnin' down her face in front of that man."

Lizzy wuz feelin' right anxious 'bout her sister among them strangers. She couldn't git the truck and the dirt bike wuz gone, so she decided to walk to Buford's doublewide, even though it wuz on the other side of town.

"You're an idjit, Lizzy. You cain't walk that far in the mud. You're gonna look like hell when you git there."

"I don't care what I look like, Momma. I'm gonna take a gander at Janie and that's it."

"Are you hintin' 'round fer me to try to fire up that rusty ol' tractor on blocks out back?" Benny asked.

"No sir. I'm not a-tryin' to avoid the walk. It's not that far, three miles. I'll be back by supper time."

"I admire the activity of your benevolence," said Mary, "but every impulse of feeling should be guided by reason; and, in my opinion, exertion should always be in proportion to what is required."

"I didn't understand a damned thang you jest said, Mary," said Kitty and Lydie, "but we'll foller you down past the fair grounds if'n you like, Lizzy." And the three sisters set off t'gether avoidin' the deeper of the muddy ruts in the lane.

"If'n we go quick as a whip," said Lydie, "we might could catch the sight of Carter b'fore he heads packin'."

In the shade of the grandstands next to the weed-infested horse track, the girls split up. Lizzy walked on, avoidin' the flooded streets and cuttin' through the fields on her way to Buford's trailer. She avoided mud and cow patties when she could, and b'fore she knew it, the shiny metal of the genuine aluminum siding stood smack dab in front of her. She wuz covered in mud to her ankles, had ripped the leg of her jeans on some barbed wire, and she wuz sweatin' like a stuck hog.

When she knocked on the door, somebody hollered fer her to come on in. Ever'body but Janie wuz stooped shouldered over their bacon and grits, jest a-spoonin' it in. They wuz surprised she'd walked all that way jest to check in on her ailin' sister. Tammy and Patty gave a look to each other that said they'd disapprove of Lizzy even if'n it hair-lipped the Pope. The girls wuz polite but fake as three-dollar bills. Buford seemed genuinely happy to see her. Dutch didn't say much, and Harley didn't stop eatin' the whole time. Ever' once in a while he jest stared out the window with blood-shot eyes that hinted at a headache bigger 'n Texas. He looked like he might throw up right there in his fried eggs.

Nobody could give Lizzy a straight answer 'bout how her sister might be doin'. Gittin' 'em to say much 'bout Janie wuz like a-tryin' to plait live eels in a bucket. Finally one of 'em said Janie had tried to sleep on the pull-out sofa in the back. She wuz hot as a biscuit and didn't feel much like stirrin'. When Lizzy and Janie finally seen each other, they wuz both relieved. Janie wuz still most of the time, saying she wuzn't asleep, she wuz jest checkin' fer holes in her eyelids, but Lizzy knew the truth.

After breakfast, Tammy and Patty came 'round to check on 'em, and Lizzy wuz quick to tell 'em how much she 'preciated 'em not shooin' her off the stoop while Janie wuz ailin'. Buford had run down to the pharmacy and said it wuz no wonder she came down with a cold, bein' out in the weather like she wuz. The pharmacist said she should lay low fer a few days 'til she wuz spry enough and on the mend. Buford'd picked up some Gatorade and Kleenex, and promised to heat up some Campbell's Chicken Noodle soup fer dinner. Lizzy never quit her side, and Tammy and Patty hung 'round on account of they didn't have nuthin' else to do.

At three o'clock, Lizzy felt she needed to head on back home so's to git there b'fore dark. Tammy offered to carry her over-home in the truck, and she didn't have to twist her arm too much b'fore Lizzy wuz agreeable. But Janie wuz feelin' weird bein' left alone in her skivvies with near strangers, so she begged Lizzy to stay with her, and they telephoned their parents to let 'em know they'd both be sleepin' over.

# Chapter 8

At five o'clock that evenin' Tammy and Patty finally decided to shower fer the day and put on their faces, and at six-thirty Lizzy wuz called in to supper. Ever'body wanted to know how Janie fared, and Buford seemed 'specially concerned. Truth be told, Janie wuz no better 'n she wuz that mornin'. Tammy and Patty kept repeatin' how agrieved they wuz, almost like they didn't know what else to say. Lizzy got the sense them girls wuz afraid Janie's cold wuz a- catchin', and they didn't want no part of it.

Buford wuz clearly vexed 'bout Janie, and he kept a-goin' in there to see her, whether to check on her health or try and steal a glimpse of her in her step-ins, Lizzy couldn't tell. Janie wuz embarrassed by the whole thang, and if'n she didn't sleep so much, she'd prob'ly have called somebody to come pick her up and take her home. Tammy follered Dutch 'round like some kind of little lost puppy sniffin' out fer bacon. Patty went out on the stoop to smoke a cigarette, and Harley wuz playin' online poker and throwin' back Jack Daniels like there wuz no tomorrow.

Directly after supper, Lizzy went back to Janie's bedside, and Tammy began flappin' her lip even b'fore Lizzy wuz out'a earshot. She declared Lizzy's face wuz as long as a wet week; she wuz as useless as a broken leg, and she could make a preacher cuss. Patty nodded like a bobble-head doll to the entire tirade, then she added, "She ain't got nuthin' to recommend her but being an excellent walker. I dee-clare! I won't forgit how she looked this mornin' fer a coon's age. She looked like a wild woman!"

"You ain't jest whistlin' Dixie. She looked like she hadn't combed her head nor warshed her face. She looked jest like Edna Mae Hockenberry!"

"Oh my gawd! And did you see the hem of her jeans? There had to be at least six inches of mud on 'em. I wuz afeared she'd track it on the rug. And them Wranglers had been let out. You could see the crease at the bottom where she ripped out the seam."

"You might be shootin' straight, Patty," said Buford, "but it wuz lost on me. I thought Lizzy looked fine and dandy when she showed up this mornin'. The mud on her jeans didn't pass my mind."

"I'm sure as shootin' Dutch seen it," Tammy stage whispered. "I bet you a dollar it has made you thank less on her Maybelline eyes."

"Don't be ugly, Miss Tammy. I thought her eyes wuz lit up with the exercise."

With that, Harley hauled himself up on his feet and announced to the room that he "had to go see a man 'bout a horse."

Patty answered, "Turn the fan on in there, Harley. None of us wants to smell yer bizness." And then she added, "I'm right fond of Janie. She's such a sweet girl, bless her heart. I wish she wuz settled. With a Momma and Daddy like that, I thank she's gonna struggle."

"Didn't I hear they have relations not far from here?"

"Yep, an uncle. And they have another uncle that lives somewhere near Nashv'lle selling used appliances."

"Oh my!" answered Tammy as she let out a loud snort of laughter.

"If'n they had appliance salesmen comin' out their ears," cried Buford, "I don't thank it would make 'em less agreeable."

"It must be a stretch fer 'em to git on in the world without money or good relations," said Dutch. "They'll prob'ly have to marry some poor local fella whose either tighter 'n a gnat's ass or crookeder 'n a Looziana politician."

Buford stretched out on the Lazy Boy and his sisters wuz agreeable 'til Patty let out a loud yawn. The game wuz comin' on the tv, so the sisters dug down deep to find some affection fer the ailin' and left the front room to sit with Janie 'til they wuz hankerin' fer some Hostess cupcakes. Lizzy didn't like store-bought pastries, so she stayed with Janie 'til much later. When Janie'd dropped off to sleep, snorin' lightly, Lizzy tip-toed out'a the room and found Buford and his guests playin' five-card-stud at the coffee table. They made room fer her on the davenport, but Lizzy told 'em she hadn't played poker since God wuz a child. She picked up a book instead.

Harley stared at her with his yellow and red eyes, mouth open. "Are you tellin' me you'd rather read than play poker?"

"Lizzy hates cards," Tammy said. "She's edumakated and thinks we're below her."

"Git off my back, will ya?" cried Lizzy. "I don't read all that much and I don't thank I'm better 'n all y'all. I like loads of thangs." She walked over to an open box where there wuz more books and a few old Nascar magazines worn at the edges.

Buford stuttered and said he wished he had more of a variety as he kicked the box of old magazines behind a table. "I'm an idle fella. I wish I had more fer ya to look at. I'm not much of a reader, myself."

Lizzy told 'im she wuz right happy with the book she had in her hands.

"Where in blue blazes 'r all of Daddy's video tapes?" asked Tammy as she pulled VHS tapes out'a a brown paper poke. "These cain't be all of 'em." She turned to Dutch. "I reckon y'all have shelves full of movies at Pembrook Farm, doncha Dutch?"

"I reckon I've got a few. When the video store down from the farm went under, I bought up ever'thang I used to rent from 'em."

Patty said, "I hope when you git yer house, brother, that it's half as nice as Pembrook Farm."

"Ain't that the truth."

"You oughtta use Pembrook Farm's house plans and make one jest like 'er. There ain't no house like it no-where."

"There ain't no way to copy that there farm. It'd be easier to buy it away from Dutch, but it's jest too dear."

Lizzy spent more time listenin' to the back n' forth 'n she did to her book. Finally she set it down and cozied up to the card table b'tween Buford and Patty to watch the game.

"Is Suzanna still growin' like a weed?" asked Tammy. "Last time I seen her, she wuz gittin' so skinny she'd have to stand up twice to cast a shadow."

"She's gangly on account of she eats like a bird, but she's growin' up fast. I'd say she's 'bout as tall as Lizzy there. Maybe taller."

"I jest cain't wait to lay eyes on her again. I never met nobody who cracked me up half so much. Her jokes is jest so funny, but she doesn't even use swear words or nothin'. That girl's headin' somewhere. Plus, I hear she's playin' the dulcimer and the fiddle?"

"I jest cain't git over how these young folks do." said Buford. "They's better 'n we wuz when we wuz that age. All I thought 'bout wuz chasin' skirts."

"Better 'n we wuz? What in the sam hill 'r you talkin' 'bout?"

"Well, they know how to do jest 'bout ever'thang. Why, they can cut hay and put it up in the barn, they take woodshop and home ec in high school so's they can use a hammer and make biscuits and gravy. They teach 'em up at the Vo-Tech how to fix computers and run speaker wire. And I even hear they have to take a foreign language to gradyate from high school."

"You got most of that right, Buford," said Dutch, "But I never did see half a dozen girls who could make proper chicken n' dumplin's."

Tammy added, "When I applied fer junior college, the list of classes I had to take included math and hist'ry and Spanish. I jest wanted to learn how to type and use a word processor, so's I jest decided college wuzn't fer me."

Lizzy slipped out'a the room and came back only to say Janie wuz feelin' poorly, and she would stay with her fer a while. Buford offered to go back to the CVS, but Lizzy said they oughtta wait til mornin' to see if'n she wuz farin' better. Buford spent the rest of the night worryin' whether or not Miss Janie would want some ice cream from the Dairy Queen.

# Chapter 9

Lizzy spent the chief of the night in the back room with Janie and telephoned her Momma the minute she opened her eyes. She wanted her Momma to peek in on Janie to make sure she didn't need to go to the Urgent Care. Well, nobody never had to ask Flo twice to visit over on the good side of town, so quick as a cat she darkened their door and who wuz a-taggin' along but her two youngest daughters, nosy as they wuz.

Janie wuzn't so sick that she needed to spend money on a doctor, so Flo wuz plum tickled 'bout that. But seein' as how she wuz laid up in the home of a right fine looking feller, Flo didn't want her to git well lickety-split. She made up some excuse 'bout the seatbelts being broke in the car and not wantin' to take any chances when Janie said she thought she oughtta go on back home. Lizzy knew they never used no seatbelts anyhow, but she kept her lip zipped 'bout that one. After spendin' a gnat's minute with Janie, Flo, Kitty and Lydie went out to where ever'body wuz eatin' breakfast. Buford asked how Janie fared.

"Lawsy-mercy!" Flo screeched. "She's far too ailin' to carry her home. I know they say fish and visitors smell after three days, but I'm a-goin' to have to trespass on yer kindness fer a little bit longer."

"Carry her home!" cried Buford. "Don't even thank on it. If'n you try, I'm gonna jerk a knot in yer tail. Why, my sister'd tan my hide if'n we sent her home in the state she's in."

Tammy gave Buford a look that said, "Don't piss on my leg and tell me it's rainin'." Then to Flo, she said, "Don't you fret a minute 'bout Janie. I won't leave her side. I'll be all over her like stink on dog shit 'til she gits better," her tone as cold as a witch's tit in a brass bra.

Flo went 'round in circles with her thank you's and 'preciate ya's. "They's no doubt if'n it wuzn't fer high class friends like all y'all, she'd be worse off by now. Even through her snifflin' she's right pleasant comp'ny. She wuzn't no trouble as a baby, and her disp'sition is fine and dandy even though she's so poorly. You got a right nice view out that big winder, Buford. It's nice the way 'em trees over yonder block out the loadin' dock at the Park N Shop. I hope you's a plannin' on hangin' 'round here a bit, settlin' in fer a while?"

"Whatever I do, I do it faster 'n a knife fight in a phone booth, so if'n I should decide to skip town, it'd be fast as lightnin'. You could blink and miss it. I'm like that, but I'm settled fer the time bein'," he said as he discreetly spit somethin' brown into an empty Mountain Dew can.

"That's 'bout what I 'xpected," said Lizzy.

"You figure me out already, have you?" he said, turnin' toward her.

"I sure have. Yer a playboy is what you are."

"I'd like to thank yer a-tryin' to puff up my ego, but somethin' tells me yer talkin' trash. I can see right through you." He spit again into the can.

"If'n it looks like a duck, and it quacks like a duck and it walks like a duck, well, then, I reckon it's a duck."

"Lizzy!" cried her mother. "Watch yer manners. Remember yer place. You cain't go on over here like you do at home."

"I had no idear," continued Buford with a lopsided grin and a wink, "that you's payin' such close attention to my behavior. I'd better watch my p's and q's 'round these parts. You must git a real kick out'a it when new folks come into town. I reckon it gives y'all somethin' to talk 'bout besides the weather."

"Sure as shootin'. But the more complicated somebody is, the better. I git a big hoot outa that. I could watch 'em fer days."

"Out here in the country," said Dutch, "cain't give you many folks to study. By nature, when you live over yonder in the edge of nuthin' way out in the sticks, you end up watchin' the same folks over and over."

"Folks is so diff'rent from one day to the next. There's always somethin' new goin' on with ever'body. The drama 'round here is better 'n reality tv."

"Surely, surely," squeaked Flo, gittin' her feathers ruffled by Dutch's way of puttin' down country folks. "they's jest as much to do in the country as there is in a big city like Nashv'lle."

All the jaws in the room dropped open, and Dutch gave her a look that said, "Somebody needs to knock some sense into you." Then he turned his back on her. Flo thought she'd won that round and grinned so big you could see more gums than teeth.

"I thank Nashv'lle's not got nuthin' on the country, exceptin' the shoppin' and the country music stars. The country's much more pleasant, ain't it Buford?"

"When a body's in the country," he replied, "it wants to jest soak in the sunshine and go fishin'. And when a body's in town, you jest wanna go jukin' and clubin' and stayin' out all night. They's both right nice. I could take either one without complainin'.'"

"Aw, darlin' that's be'cuz you gots yerself such a good heart. But that feller over yonder," she glared at Dutch, "seemed to thank the country ain't nuthin' at all."

"Momma, you're 'bout as dumb as a bucket full of rocks," said Lizzy, blushin' fer her Momma. "You could argue with a stop sign. Dutch only meant to say there ain't as many folks out here as there is over yonder. You cain't say he's wrong 'bout that."

"Hells bells, Lizzy. Nobody said they wuz as many folks out here as there are over in the big cities. He jest needs to git out and mix more with folks. Any idjit could see that they's bunches of folks to mix with out here. We got folks comin' out our ears."

Buford wuz startin' to git ticked off at the way Flo wuz talkin' with his buddy, but he kept it under his hat on Lizzy's account. Tammy couldn't help but smile at her brother like the cat that swallered the canary. Liz tried to change the subject by askin' her Momma if'n Charlotte had paid a visit while she wuz gone.

"She came by yesterd'y with her Daddy. We jest love Billy Lucas. Not a finer man in these parts, I'd say. His words could make the sun shine on a rainy day. That's what I call good breedin'. People that keeps they's mouths shut all the time could learn a thang or two from 'im."

"Did Charlotte sit down to supper with y'all?"

"Naw. I thank she had to go make some pies fer the cake walk down at the church on Saturd'y. They's raisin' money fer to send some kids to camp or somethin' like that. She's such a good egg to help out like that. A good girl, I tell you, but bless her heart she ain't much to look at."

"She seems all right," said Buford.

"Well, bless her heart, she's jest a dear. It's jest too bad she's so plain. LuLu even says so herself. I thank she's jealous of Janie. I don't like to go braggin' on my own child, but you jest don't find too many girls put t'gether as nice as my Janie. I know I'm partial to her. When she wuz jest fifteen years-old they wuz a feller at my brother Guthrie's place down in Nashv'lle, and he wuz jest taken with her. My sister-in-law, Tildie, thought he wuz gonna try and knock her up so he could marry her. But then we came to find out that he wuz thirty-two years old, and with her jest bein' fifteen, we jest couldn't let that happen. Benny went after 'im with a shotgun, and that wuz the last we seen of 'im. Maybe he thought she wuz older than she wuz, but we never heard from 'im again. He did write some verses on her, and they wuz right purty, they wuz."

"And that's all we're gonna say 'bout that," said Lizzy rudely.

Dutch smiled at her. The room wuz silent fer a bit, and Lizzy worried her Momma would open her big trap again. She tried to thank of somethin' to say, but the cat'd caught her tongue, and she couldn't stir up nuthin'. Flo started back with her thankin' Buford fer his kindness and hospitality to Janie and apologized fer troublin' 'im with Lizzy. Buford wuz polite which made Tammy polite. Tammy wuz clearly put off, but Flo didn't seem to notice much. After a bit, Flo threw her keys at Kitty and said, "Go jump start the Chevy, darlin'."

With that, Lydie nearly jumped out'a her shoes. She and her sister'd been whisperin' back and forth through the whole visit, and they decided they'd press Buford into havin' the big shin-dig he promised.

Lydie wuz 'developed' as they say. Flat-chested ladies pay good money fer the ninnies God gave Lydie. She washed her face with Noxema every night to keep the zits away, and she flirted like a ten-dollar whore. She wuz by far her Momma's pet, and Flo treated her more like a girlfriend than a daughter. With her boobs as big as they wuz, and the low-cut shirts she liked to wear, she attracted the attention of the soldiers ever' time she passed the fair grounds. She wuz practiced at gittin' men to do her biddin', so she had no trouble askin' Buford to throw his party. His answer to this ambush wuz ever'thang they wanted to hear.

"Hell, yeah, I'm ready to have a throw-down, and when Janie's better, you can pick the date."

Lydie had to use her fingers to count the days 'til some of her favorite soldiers would be back in town as she, Kitty and Flo drove away in a blue cloud of exhaust.

# Chapter 10

The day had passed jest like the day b'fore with Tammy and Patty spendin' some time with Janie who wuz on the mend, and Lizzy joinin' 'em fer supper. Nobody pulled out the card table fer five-card-stud, though, and Dutch wuz over to the computer typin' away to beat the band. Tammy wuz pert near right on top of 'im and wuz readin' over his shoulder, movin' her lips as she read. Harley and Buford wuz playin' blackjack on the couch, and Patty wuz a-watchin' 'em.

Lizzy took out her bedazzler and started in on the points of her collar, but she wuz listin' to Dutch and Tammy's conversation. Tammy jest couldn't say enough 'bout how fast he typed and how good he wuz, not needin' to use the spell check and all. She wuz all agog at the length of his letter, and he did his best to ignore her.

"Suzanna's gonna be grinnin' from ear to ear when she receives this email."

Dutch didn't say a word.

"Yer so fast at typin'. Yer like a duck on a junebug."

"I am not. You're jest slow."

"How many emails you reckon you send a year? I bet y'all send a ton of 'em, 'specially business emails. I'd hate that."

"I guess I'm jest lucky that I have so many to send."

"Lordy, tell Suzanna that I'm itchin' to see her."

He ignored her.

"I thank that sound's turned down too low on that there computer. Do you want me to fix it fer ya?"

"I'll mend it myself."

"How do you know when to start a new paragraph? It always confounds me."

He didn't respond.

"Tell Suzanna I'm right proud of her improvement on the dulcimer, and I'm over the moon 'bout her plans to put up wallpaper in her room."

"Can you not shut up fer a minute while I write? I don't have time to be scratchin' down every thought you ever had."

"Never mind. I'll see her b'fore long anyhow. Do y'all always write so long to each other? How sweet!"

"They's usually long, but I don't know 'bout sweet."

"As a gen'ral rule, I thank if'n you can write a long letter, it cain't be a bad one."

"Quit butterin' up Dutch, Tammy," cried her brother. "He needs to concentrate so's he can come up with 'em 25 cent words, doncha Dutch?"

"I write diff'rent from most folks, that's fer sure."

"Oh my heavens!" cried Tammy. "Buford couldn't write two words without havin' to look one of 'em up in the dictionary."

"I git the cart b'fore the horse most of the time," Buford said. "My brain works faster 'n my fangers do. Folks cain't decipher my meanin' even when they try."

"I ain't never had that trouble," Dutch said.

Lizzy looked up at Dutch and with a laugh, she said, "Lord, it's hard to be humble, when yer perfect in ev'ry way."

Buford asked, "Can we talk 'bout somethin' else?"

Dutch smiled at her, but Lizzy thought he wuz madder 'n a polecat that'd jest lost its tail, so she tried to keep her face blank-like.

"Arguin' sticks in yer throat like a hair in a biscuit, don't it, Buford?" asked Dutch.

"It's true I don't care fer it, so if'n you and Lizzy wanna mix words, you can jest go on outside."

"I don't care to fight with Dutch. He oughtta finish that there letter to his sister, anyhow."

Dutch banged away at the keyboard in silence. When he wuz finished he asked Tammy to git out her fiddle fer some music. Tammy offered fer Lizzy to go first, but Lizzy figured it wuz so's she could make fun of her, so she let Tammy go first. Tammy played and Patty sang along, but Lizzy couldn't help notice that Dutch's eyes stuck to her like a fart in a phone booth. She couldn't figure why he would be watchin' her so close. She wondered if'n she had food in her teeth or somethin' in her hair to make 'im stare so. She really didn't care what he wuz a-lookin' at, she jest wished he'd stop.

After a while, Tammy wuz playin' some real toe-tappers, and Dutch came up behind Lizzy to ask if'n she wanted to two-step.

She smiled and kept quiet. Dutch repeated the question, figurin' she didn't hear 'im the first time.

"Hell," she said. "I heard you the first time, but I couldn't thank of a thang to say. You wanted me to say 'yes' so's you could make fun of me, so I jest decided to keep quiet to spoil yer fun. Now I guess I'll say 'no' so you can hate me even more.

"I wouldn't dare."

Lizzy wuz expectin' 'im to be nasty at her, and she wuz shocked he wuz so nice. She gave 'im the fish eye and began to wonder 'bout 'im. Dutch had never been so smitten in all of his born days. He wuz beginnin' to thank that if'n she wuzn't such white trash, he might be in danger of takin' a fancy to her.

Tammy's eyes threw daggers across the room at 'em. She wuz plum et up with jealousy and wished Janie better so's to git rid of Lizzy faster. She wuz always a-tryin' to provoke Dutch while Lizzy wuz off tendin' to her sister, singin' 'im the schoolyard song that ends with "and then came Dutch with a baby carriage."

"I'm as happy fer y'all as a sissy out to sea," said Tammy the next day as she and Dutch wuz movin' the old bathtub out'a the way so more cars could park in the driveway. I don't know how in the world yer gonna git yer mother-in-law to shut the hell up at the family reunions. I sure do hope those sisters won't drag every Tom, Dick and Harry through yer house. And yer wife! She needs to learn some manners."

"You got any more marriage counselin' fer me?"

"Law, yes. Make sure you git good pictures of her relations to put next to yer folks' pictures up at the farm. Set the frames smack down next to the picture of yer uncle shakin' hands with the Mayor of Lexin'ton. They's in the same bizness, yer uncle and Lizzy's Uncle Phil, ain't they? Phil's the manager at the Piggly Wiggly and yer uncle manages 'em uppity folks at the country club. As fer a picture of Lizzy, you could go right down to the Sears & Roebuck and have one taken, but I don't know if'n they'll be able to catch the expression she always gives you with those Maybelline eyes."

"You couldn't be more right if'n you wuz three lefts, Tammy. I'm quite sure them folks at Sears couldn't catch her eyes with their color and shape and the way she makes 'em up with that purple and blue eye shadow. It'd be tough."

Right then, the screen door banged shut behind Lizzy and Patty, both loaded down with garbage bags, headin' out back to toss 'em over the hill.

"I didn't know y'all wuz fixin' to come outside," said Tammy with some confusion. She wuzn't sure if'n she'd been overheard.

"Yer spoilt," said Patty. "You know'd we wuz cleanin' up inside, and you snuck out like a haint." She handed her trash bags to Lizzy and helped with one end of the bathtub.

Lizzy walked by herself with all four bags of garbage, filled mostly with empty beer bottles and Mountain Dew cans half-up with snuff spit.

Dutch said, "We don't need three people to tote this bathtub out'a the way. One of y'all need to go help Lizzy with the trash."

But Lizzy wuz wantin' to git away, so she said, "Y'all go on with that there bathtub. You make a picture there, and I don't wanna spoil it. This trash ain't no bother." And she hurried happily 'round the side of the house, hopin' to be back home b'fore long.

# Chapter 11

The boys wuz fixin' to watch wrastlin' on the tv after lunch, so Lizzy went back to check on Janie. She felt up to goin' down the hall to watch The Biggest Loser on the black and white set with the girls. Tammy and Patty wuz pleased as punch to see their friend up and about, and Lizzy had never seen 'em in such a good mood as they wuz b'fore the boys came in a-lookin' fer 'em. Them girls jest loved to make fun of the contestants. Lizzy thought it showed they wuzn't raised right.

When the boys thundered down the hallway, Tammy wuz on Dutch like a fox on a chicken. He couldn't git a word in edgewise. Dutch jest talked over her, sayin' how much better Janie looked. Harley staggered a little and belched out somethin' 'bout her not being so pale. Buford on the other hand jest went on an on with his praises. He said she looked healthy as a horse and purtier 'n a painted carousel pony. He sat her down right next to the gas logs and turned 'em up on high, inspite of the cost of natural gas. And when she seemed flushed from the heat, he led her across the room to the other side. He took up the spot next to her on the love seat and paid no never-mind to nobody else in the room. Lizzy sat bedazzlin' in a chair across the way and watched 'em like a hawk.

After a snack of buffalo wangs and pork rinds, Harley offered to pull out the card table, but Tammy told 'im he needed to go in the corner and sober up. She'd heard Dutch say he wuzn't in the mood to play poker. He kept after her, though, and finally Tammy spat out that nobody wanted to play and he should jest shut the hell up. With that, Harley stretched himself out on the sofa to nap, though if'n he wuz an inch taller, he'd be round, so there wuzn't much stretching fer Harley. Dutch picked up a Field and Stream Magazine and so did Tammy. Patty wuz paintin' her fangernails green to match her tank top and listenin' to the conversation.

Tammy spent more time a-lookin' over Dutch's shoulder at his magazine as she did a-lookin' at her own. She kept askin' stupid questions 'bout the pictures on Dutch's copy and leanin' down over 'im, pushin' her ninnies against 'im fer emphasis. He wuz concentratin' hard on an article 'bout fly fishin', and she wuz havin' no luck whatsoever. B'fore long Tammy got tired with her magazine. She'd only picked it out be'cuz Dutch wuz readin' an earlier issue. She yawned so wide she looked like the Grand Canyon and said, "Ain't this nice, jest a-settin' and readin' of the evenin' instead of watchin' that ol' squawk box. I de-clare there's nuthin' like readin'. When I have a house of my own, I'm gonna subscribe to all kinds of magazines so's I can read all the time."

No one made nary a peep. Then she yawned again, tossed aside her copy of Field and Stream and looked 'round the room fer somethin' to do. When she heard her brother mentionin' throwin' a shin-dig to Janie, she turned to 'im and said, "Buford, 'r you shootin' straight with all this talk of a party? I thank you oughtta ask some of us if'n we's interested. I thank one or two of us'd consider it more of a punishment than a treat."

"If'n you's talkin' 'bout Dutch, he can go on to bed b'fore it starts, but as fer the shin-dig, it's as good as done. I jest gotta git some more chicken wangs and figure out how I'm a-goin' to let folks know."

"I jest thank the music's too loud at most parties, and you jest cain't have a conversation with nobody."

"I s'pose we could skip the music, but then it wouldn't be much of a dance, now, would it?"

Tammy didn't say nuthin', but soon got up and started swayin' 'bout the room, pacin' like, a-tryin' to git Dutch to notice. Now she had a figure on her. No one could deny that. But it wuz all lost on Dutch. She wuz gittin' perterbed and said, "Lizzy, why don't you stretch yer legs a bit and come over to look out this winder at the view. You been settin' a long time."

Lizzy wuz pop-eyed at the request, but stood up anyway, and when she did, Dutch looked up. He closed his magazine to watch the two girls, wonderin' what  Tammy had up her sleeve. Tammy invited 'im to join 'em as they looked out at the stars, but he said he ought not. "Y'all jest doin' that so's I can see yer butts better, and if'n I'm standin' next to you, I won't be able to see 'em at all."

Tammy wuz doin' her best to look surprised at Dutch. "I wonder what in the hell he's talkin' 'bout?" she asked Lizzy.

"I have no idea," answered Lizzy, "but I can promise you one thang, he means to be hard as nails in his judgin' us. The best thang fer us to do is jest ignore 'im."

Hard as she tried, Tammy jest wuzn't up to ignorin' Dutch and told 'im he best jest explain himself right then and there. He jest winked at the girls and said nuthin'.

"Dutch is not one to tease, Miss Tammy," Lizzy said. "He jest wants to make fun of us. I'd like to hear 'im, though. I need a good belly laugh."

"I ain't makin' fun of none of y'all. I never claimed to be a comedian," he said as he dug 'round a molar with his toothpick.

"I ain't a comedian, neither," said Lizzy. "Alls they ever do is make jokes 'bout their private parts, anyhow. I can still laugh at 'em, mind you, but I'm sure you'd be offended."

"Anyone can laugh at that kind of thang. I try to be better 'n that. My Momma raised me better," he said.

"Well, I never! You're full of yerself! They ain't no conceit in yer family, God love 'em. When it came to vanity, you got it all."

"Vanity ain't no good, I agree. But pride, well there darlin', when pride comes from hard work and improvin' yer mind, it ain't a bad thang."

Lizzy turned her head to hide a smile. She jest loved messin' with him.

"I reckon yer done with yer assessment of Dutch," said Tammy. "And what do ya thank?"

"I thank Dutch is the ultimate guy. He'll tell you that his ownself."

"I said no such thang," said Dutch. "I've got faults, but not when it comes to hard work and improvin' myself. Fer one thang, I git soppin' mad right often. One time I turned over a chifferobe jest 'cause I couldn't find my wallet. I jest cain't forgit it when somebody does me wrong. I keep score on the wrongdoin's of others. Some folks might say I'm resentful and hold a grudge. Once I hate ya, I hate ya forever."

"Oh my word!" said Lizzy "You're all mawmucked up. Holdin' a grudge is a character flaw, but I cain't make fun of you fer it. You might jest hold it against me."

"I thank ever'body has their faults and defects; even the best education cain't learn it out'a you."

"And yers is to hate ever'body."

"And yers," Dutch said with a killer smile, "is to misunderstand 'em on purpose."

"Let's watch some tv" said Tammy, tired of not bein' included in the back and forth. "Patty, do you mind if'n I wake up Harley?"

Her sister helped move Harley off the couch and back to the bedroom, and the remote wuz found. Dutch wuz happy to watch a little reality tv to git his mind off of Lizzy's jeans and her darlin' sense of humor.

# Chapter 12

After Janie woke up the next mornin', Lizzy called their Momma to beg fer someone to pick 'em up that day. But Flo had been countin' on the girls stayin' with Buford fer a few more days, which would finish up a full week of Janie bein' under his roof. She flat out refused to send anyone over with the truck. Lizzy wuz wantin' to sleep in her own bed under her Daddy's roof, but her Momma wuz not gonna listen to her lip. Lizzy wuz stubborn as a mule when she got somethin' in her noggin', so she asked Janie to see if'n Buford would carry 'em home in his pickup truck. He wuz happy to oblige, but wanted 'em to wait 'til mornin' since Tammy needed to use the truck that night to return some britches at Kohl's. They wuz agreed, and Tammy could've jest kicked herself in the ass fer bein' the cause of Lizzy stayin' another night in their house. As much as she liked Janie, she hated Lizzy with the heat of a thousand suns in the desert with no shade to be found.

Buford seemed genuinely blue that Janie would be leavin', but she wuz determined to git back home where she belonged.

Dutch wuz never so happy to hear anythang in his life. Lizzy had been under roof long enough. When she wuz in the room, it wuz like he wuz drunk on her, and he couldn't thank on nuthin' else. He could feel the heat off of her skin when she stood close to him, and he had to thank of baseball to keep his little buddy under control. He wuz embarrassed by how much Tammy teased him 'bout Lizzy, and he wuz havin' to try harder and harder every time she wuz 'round to hide his feelin's. He wuz right proud of how controlled he had been 'round her. He felt jest like the Marlboro man in them commercials. That last day, Dutch didn't say but ten words to her the whole time. He wuz sure that if'n he'd sent any vibes out to Lizzy hintin' he'd taken her bait and wuz hooked, his silence that last day had surely made her thank again. At one point they sat at opposite ends of the davenport fer a full half hour, and he never said a peep, jest kept a-lookin' at his magazine as if'n it wuz the most interestin' thang in the world.

The sooner the time came fer Lizzy and Janie's drive home, the nicer and nicer Tammy started bein' to the girls. And as Buford took his time helpin' Janie into the cab of his truck, his hand lingerin' on her backside a little too long, his sister said how nice it would be to have supper over at Janie and Lizzy's house some time real soon. She even hugged Janie and shook hands with Lizzy, who jest couldn't help but smilin' 'cause she wuz crackin' up with laughter on the inside."

Their Momma almost didn't open the door fer 'em when she seen 'em a-knockin'. Flo wondered why on earth they'd come home so soon, and she hollered at 'em fer bein' an imposition and askin' Buford to drive 'em all the way across town. Benny, on the other hand, wuz tickled pink to see 'em and had really missed 'em while he wuz stranded with his loud wife and her spawn. He couldn't make hide nor hair of what those girls wuz talkin' 'bout. He much preferred his older daughters.

They found Mary, as usual, deep in study. She went on 'bout human nature and threadbare morality 'til Janie's eyelids wuz at half-mast. Kitty and Lydie yammered on and on 'bout all the thangs they'd done and the boys they'd met. Liddy let slip that rumor had it Lieutenant Dan had up 'n got himself a fiance.

# Chapter 13

"Darlin'," said Benny to his wife as they sat over their eggs and bacon the next mornin', "I hope you's plannin' on somethin' better 'n Hamburger Helper tonight. I got reason to b'lieve we got comp'ny comin'."

"What in the hell 'r you talkin' bout, Benny? Ain't nobody comin' 'round here less'n Charlotte's plannin' to stay over. My suppers 'r good enough fer her; she eats like a damned bird anyhow."

"You jest act like you know the world. It ain't Charlotte. It's a feller, a stranger to y'all."

"It's a man and a stranger? It's gotta be Buford. They's no two ways 'bout it. Janie-- you never said a word 'bout this you little vixen. I never git tired of a-lookin' at that Buford. But, good Lord! I ain't got not fish or nuthin'. Lydie, girl, come here right this instant. I need you to run down to the market fer me."

"It ain't Buford," said her main squeeze. "It's a man you ain't never seen b'fore in all of yer days."

Well, let me tell you, that got ever'body's attention right now, and Benny wuz dodgin' questions left and right from the women folk. After a while he explained," 'Bout a month ago I got a letter from a feller, and well, I jest didn't wanna say anythang to upset none of y'all, so I didn't say nuthin' 'bout it. I answered his letter a couple of weeks back. It's my cousin Cooter, who when I kick the bucket, can turn right 'round and kick all y'all out on yer asses, I'm sorry to say.

"Oh. My. Heavenly. Stars!" cried his wife. "Don't you say a word of that again. I cain't bear to hear it. Don't you dare mention that spiteful man. The fact he owns most of this house is bad enough. If'n the tables wuz turned and I wuz the man of this house, I'd have tried to do somethin' or 'nother 'bout it."

Janie and Lizzy tried to explain to Flo 'bout the recession and the economy and that their Daddy's got bills like Ain't Nellie's got pills. They had tried b'fore, but it wuz somethin' Flo couldn't understand if'n somebody opened her head and stuffed it right down into her brain. She kept on spittin' her vile and cussin' Cooter up one side and down the other 'bout his cruelty toward his purty little cousins. How could he take house and hearth away from five little girls. Why, she wuz sure she wuz as nervous as a whore in church to meet up with 'im.

"I know it ain't fair," said Benny, "and ain't nuthin' can be done 'bout it, but if'n you'll jest hear me out maybe you'll feel a little better, darlin'."

"I ain't gonna feel better 'bout this come hell or high water. I thank it's ballsy of him to write to you. Why, he's two faced, pretendin' to be kin like that. He should jest continue the family feud you've been havin' with that uncle of yern. Hell, I always thought yer family tree wuz short a few branches!"

"I thank he wants to make up with us, Flo. Jest listen." And he pulled out the dirty, folded paper and handed it to Lizzy to read.

*"Dear Cousin Benny, I'm jest sick to death of this feud 'tween you and my Daddy. I always felt bad 'bout it, and that's why I gave you that money fer the bills. Now that my Daddy's dead, I wanna make amends with all y'all. I waited 'til after the funeral out'a respect and all. My mind's made up now.*

*"I been preachin' of late at a little Baptist church outside of Knoxv'lle, and there's a parishioner there named Prudence Majestro who's Daddy donated the money fer the parsonage where I live. She has been awful good to me, and she leaves me fresh produce right out'a her own garden. She presses a fifty-dollar-bill into my hand every Sund'y with a wink, and by now I know she purty much owns me. I wanna do what's right by the church, but with money comin' in like that, I have to make a few compromises, and Miz M lets me know reg'lar what those compromises are. Of course I don't mind, but she tells me when the grass at the parsonage is half an inch high and when the shrubs need trimmed. She calls me weekly to remind me to dust the furniture, and when I leave the lights on in more 'n one room, she calls me to tell me I'm wastin' God's precious resources, bless her heart.*

*"I'm much obliged to Miz M fer takin' such good care of me. She lets me know when there's fightin' in the private lives of folks in my church and tells me to stick my nose in it and how to stop them hard feelin's. With that in mind, I wanna try fer the same kind of peace in my own family with you and yer kin. I thank Miz M will give me a thumbs-up fer my efforts with y'all, and maybe she'll slip me an extra $20 from time to time. I know what I'm a-tryin' to do is the right thang to do, 'specially since I practic'ly own yer house. I hope you won't hold it against me that you 'r beholden to me and my money. I cain't help but thank on yer poor daughters and how they must feel 'bout me. I know with yer history of heart disease and un-Godly addiction to cigarettes and corn liquor, they must worry 'bout where they might live if'n you should up and die. I hear they're real lookers, and I hope to make thangs right by pairin' off with one of 'em. I hope you won't mind my shackin' up with y'all fer a while 'til I make up my mind which one I want. I'll be in yer area on Mond'y by supper time, and I*

*hope you'll show me that Southern hospitality I know our family is famous for. I checked with Miz M and she is copacetic with my stayin' on at yer house fer my vacation. Yer Cousin, Cooter."*

"He means to be here by supper time," said Benny as he folded up the letter. "He seems nice enough, and I do owe him a bundle, so I thank we should make 'im feel at home, 'specially since this Miz M has padded his pockets like he says."

"I thank it's right nice he wants to kiss and make up with the girls. Jest thank of that, kissin' cousins! I won't discourage 'im."

"I wonder what in the world he means to make up his mind 'bout," said Janie. "Does he really thank any of us would have 'im?"

Lizzy wuz puzzled by his expressions of love fer Miz M and that she didn't mind 'im takin' a vacation this soon to the start of his job. Surely someone in their congregation would need to be married or buried or baptized while he wuz gone.

"He's got to be some kind of an oddball," she said. "I cain't figure 'im out. He seems like a pompous asshole to me. And what does he mean by apologizin' fer ownin' our house? If'n he didn't want it, he could jest let us keep it. I thank if'n leather wuz brains, he wouldn't have enough to saddle a junebug."

"Liz, I thank you hit the nail right on the head," said her Daddy. "Stupid is as stupid does. One minute he seems like somebody who'd brang you a cold one while yer under the car, and the next minute he wants you to pat 'im on the back fer it. I don't git 'im. I'm anxious to lay eyes on 'im."

"In point of composition," said Mary, "his letter does not seem defective. The idea of the olive branch perhaps is not wholly new, yet I think it is well expressed."

Kitty and Lydie looked at Mary like she wuz signin' the surrender. They didn't care how well their kin wrote. Alls they cared 'bout wuz them boys in camouflage, and neither girl had snuggled up close to one in a coon's age. As fer their Momma, Cooter's letter had smoothed down her feathers, and she could be heard whistlin' Dixie out in the garden.

Cooter showed up right on time, and ever'body used their best manners when they howdied and shook. Benny didn't say much, but the women folk wuz ready enough to talk. Cooter didn't need a whip to git 'im to join in, in fact he prob'ly would need one to git 'im to stop. He had tongue enough fer ten rows of teeth. He wuz as round as a millstone, and he'd be a foot taller if'n his feet wuzn't so big. His expression wuz serious as a heart attack, and when he said his s's, you could tell he wuz wearin' false teeth. He wuz butterin' up Flo with talk of her "fine daughters" and said he'd heard they wuz the purtiest girls in five counties. He said that after layin' his eyes on 'em (and his eyes had been all over 'em!), they had to be the purtiest girls south of the Mason-Dixon line. He wuz quick to let Flo know that with looks like that, they'd be sure to catch a man and be dancin' in high cotton b'fore they wuz too much older.

Lizzy whispered to Janie, "He's as full of wind as a corn-eatin' horse." Janie nodded, but, of course, Flo wuzn't a person who turned away compliments, so she kept 'im a-goin'.

"Well ain't you jest as sweet as a mushmellon!" cried Flo. "I'd like to see 'em all hitched b'fore long. I thank our money situation is like a lost ball in high weeds. Hopeless. The way thangs 'r jest ain't right."

"Are you talkin' 'bout the mortgage money I've been payin' fer Benny?"

"Yessirree. We're so poor we go to Kentucky Fried Chicken to lick other people's fangers. Well, it ain't so bad as that, but right nearly. I don't hold nuthin' against, you, Cooter. Law! I'm not sure what would've happened if'n you didn't float Benny that loan. Shit happens, and don't I know it."

"Truer words ain't never been spoke, Miz Flo. There's somethin' I could say that'd make you feel better, but that'd be gittin' the cart b'fore the horse." He gave Janie the once over and caught her eye. "Maybe when we git to know each other better."

Janie shuttered like a haint had jest stepped over her grave. Jest a-lookin' at Cooter made her wanna take a shower, and the look he had jest given her, well, the less we say 'bout that, the better.

And speakin' of hungry, 'bout that time, the buzzer let 'em know the roast wuz done. As they headed in to supper, Cooter had nice words fer everythang from the framed Nascar clock on the wall to the new linoleum to the mounted eight-point buck's head that stared down at the venison roast they wuz now eatin'. All his compliments would've warmed Flo's heart if'n she didn't thank he wuz thankin' it wuz his own property. Cooter trailed on 'bout how tasty the deer meat wuz and how the gravy Flo had made hid it's game-y flavor. He wanted to know which of his fair cousins had shot the deer they wuz eatin', and Flo set 'im right as rain, sayin' that Benny wuz perfectly able to kill enough meat fer his own table, and the girls wuz not expected to provide in that way. Cooter begged her pardon six ways from Sund'y, and she declared that she wuzn't offended a bit, but he kept up his sorryin' fer another fifteen minutes at least.

# Chapter 14

As they ate their supper, Benny didn't open his mouth less'n it wuz to put food in it, but once they'd pushed back from the table, he decided to git Cooter talkin' 'bout this "Miz M" he bragged 'bout in his letter. He started by sayin' Cooter must be right pleased to have a parishoner who wuz so loaded. Cooter couldn't say enough 'bout her kindnesses and her hoity-toity manners and how she wuz always watchin' out fer 'im. As he spoke, he took on a serious face, sober as a judge. His eye twitched when he told of her "special" visits to the parsonage, and ever'body wondered what he wuz doin' to earn that extra cash on Sund'ys. Miz M had approved of every one of his sermons and had even invited 'im over to play cards one night to make the teams even. Some folks thought Miz M wuz slicker 'n owl shit and meaner 'n a wet panther, but she had only been gushin' kindness with 'im. He said she talked at 'im like she would talk to anybody else, and she didn't mind that he went out drankin' on Frid'y nights. She thought he should date 'round and git hitched at some point, but it had to be the right gal. She offered suggestions on everythang from the way he ran the church to the shelves in his upstairs closet. (Wonder what she wuz doin' up there?)

"Sounds fine as frog hairs," said Flo. "I wish we all had a Miz M. Does she live close by?"

"They's a garden and a dirt road b'tween her house and the parsonage. She grows roses with buds as big as yer fist. The kids 'round there call her house the Rose House."

"Did I hear you right when you said she wuz a widow woman? Does she have any kin nearby?"

"She's got a daughter who'll git her house and all the woods behind it when she's six feet under. 'Bout thirty acres."

"Ain't she a lucky duck!" cried Flo shakin' her head. "She'll prob'ly end up shackin' with a gambler who'll give all her property away. Is she a looker?"

"She's a sweetheart. Miz M says she could win the Miss Tennessee title in a heartbeat on account of her inner beauty. Miz M says that's what's most important, and of course, she's right. You can tell by the daughter's hands that she's never had to work a day in her life. Her nails 'r real long and curved. She paints 'em red as a fire engine and puts glitter hearts and flowers on 'em. They's real fancy. I thank if'n she didn't wear so much eye shadow she would look nicer, but I'm not one to judge. She reads them fashion magazines reg'lar, so I suppose she knows what she's doin'. She told me she wants to git a butterfly tattoo on her back, and I told her I thought that wuz classy. She's so pale, I'm sure the colors would turn out. She doesn't git out much on account of her Momma has her home schooled by some fancy tutor. That-a-way she won't take a chance on breakin' one of her fangernails on a pencil at school. She's right proud of them fangernails, I tell you."

"Does she go out with boys?"

"It's hard fer Miss DeeDee to do much at all with her fangernails as long as they are. Plus, I heard one of the local boys sayin' he wouldn't want her hands anywhere near his privates fer fear that she might poke 'im with one of her nails. That's a shame, I say. Them boys 'r idjits if'n you ask me. Her hands 'r so soft. Sometimes I jest sit and thank on 'em. When I told Miz M that, she liked it. I could tell. I like to throw out compliments 'bout DeeDee to Miz M." He coughed. "She really likes it."

Benny blushed fer Cooter. "You're doin' right by Miz M. Women folks like to have their daughters complimented. Say, I wuz wonderin', do you make up yer compliments on the spot or do you plan what yer gonna say in advance, like?"

"Mostly I make thangs up as I go along, but when I'm alone in my bed at night, I thank on thangs to say and when to say 'em. I always try to say stuff so's it seems like I haven't planned on it, though."

Cooter answered the way Benny thought he would. When the Lord wuz passin' out brains, Cooter'd thought He said "trains," and he passed 'cause he don't like to travel. Benny listened to his kin, trying to swaller a grin. This wuz better than reality tv. He took a gander at Lizzy from time to time to see if'n she wuz enjoyin' the show as much as he wuz.

After makin' a dent in Flo's famous apple-rhubarb pie, Benny and Cooter went out back to smoke on the screened-in porch.  One smoke wuz 'bout all Benny could take of Cooter, and like a stuck duck in a dry pond, he looked to his family fer help. They asked Cooter to help 'em pick out a video from the cardboard box in the corner of the room, and he wuz joyful as a junebug to help out. As he neared the bottom of the box, he jumped back like he had been bit by somethin' fierce. He gave a knowin' wink to Benny and said, "Um, I'm not much in the mind fer a movie. Maybe we can see if'n there's somethin' good on the tv." He grasped the remote with both hands and landed on the preachin' channel. Little did he know but those spicy videos he had stumbled across belonged to Flo. But what he don't know won't hurt 'im.

B'fore the first commercial break, Lydie spoke up louder than the tele-evangeler as he wuz healin'. "You know, Momma," she said, "Uncle Phil says he's gonna switch cell phone carriers. He said he jest don't git enough bars when he's up in the holler. And if'n he does, Ain't Fern tells me Lieutenant Dan says he's gonna switch too. Ain't that somethin'?"

Lydie wuz shushed by her older sisters, but Cooter took the hint and switched off the tv. "I've noticed young girls jest ain't as interested in the Lord's work as they used to be. Most of the Lord's lessons pertains to 'em d'rectly. Nothin's quite so good as a godly woman. But I'm not here to preach or impose my values..."

Then turning to Benny, he offered to play 'im at a game of horse-shoes out back. Benny wuz willin' to put five bucks down on the game and wuz glad to git some fresh air. Flo told Cooter that she wuz fixin' to whup Lydie so hard she couldn't sit down fer a week fer all of her interruptin'. Cooter said there wuz no harm, no foul and picked up a horseshoe to throw.

# Chapter 15

Cooter didn't have the sense God gave a goose. And he hadn't improved much with education or comp'ny since most of his twenty-five years he'd spent with a Daddy as crazy as all git-out and tight as a gnat's ass. Cooter'd gotten his preacher's degree from an online school where if'n you pay yer fee, you git yer "B." And since his Daddy had been so hard on 'im, whippin' 'im with a switch every chance he got, Cooter'd grown up humble-like. But now that he had fists full of Benjamin Franklins to spread 'round like butter on toast, he had his nose stuck up in the air so far, he'd drown if'n it started to rain. He wuz lucky to 've been hired on to the Baptist church where he worked, and luckier 'n that to have hooked up with the uppity Prudence Majestro and her cold hard cash. The combination of money, his job, his relations with Miz M, and his high and mighty thoughts on himself had made 'im intolerable. He'd rather talk 'bout himself than any other subject.

Now that Cooter wuz settled in the parsonage and had some money to blow, he decided to put on that old ball n' chain so's he could have some reg'lar sex without folks at the church gossipin' 'bout it. And to try to smooth thangs over with his kin, he thought he'd up and marry one of his purty little cousins. This wuz how Cooter figured he could end the family feud, and he wuz right proud of himself fer thankin' on it.

After a-lookin' 'em over like prize pigs at the fair, he decided on Janie. Since she wuz the purtiest and the best pick of the five, he would git down on one knee and propose. He pulled Flo aside after breakfast the next mornin' and reminded her of his parsonage in Knoxv'lle and trailed on 'til he announced his plans to git hitched to Janie. Flo told 'im the younger four girls wuz fair game, but she thought Janie wuz rubbin' up against the new feller, Buford, and wouldn't agree to it fer nothin'.

Even though he wuz slower 'n molasses in January, Cooter switched from Janie to Lizzy in the time it took Flo to walk across the room to move the rain bucket from under a drip since it wuz so darn dry outside all of the sudden. She nearly skipped across the floor, thankin' she might have two daughters married off and two less mouths to feed. She thought maybe she'd turn on QVC to window shop with the money she'd be savin'. And to thank, she'd wanted to spit in Cooter's vittles jest yesterd'y.

Lydie had a bee in her bonnet to go by the fair grounds, and all her sisters 'cept Mary decided to tag along. Cooter figured he'd go seein' as how Benny kept after 'im to go. Benny wuz used to havin' the remote control to himself, and Cooter had no sooner swallered his last bite of biscuit than he grabbed hold of the remote and yammered on while he flipped channels, not stoppin' at any of the fishin' channels. Benny liked to flip through the want-ads, spend some quiet time with the tv and recline in his Lazy Boy after meals. Cooter'd taken the paper to the can with 'im earlier that mornin' and had taken the Lazy Boy as his own since arrivin'. Benny couldn't git rid of 'im quick enough.

B'tween wheezin's, Cooter talked the girls' ears off on the walk to town. Lizzy thought more 'n once that the trip would be more pleasin' if'n they stuffed a rag in his mouth and rolled 'im down the street like a bowling ball. Sweat ran in rivers down his red, puffy face. He dabbed at his face with a damp piece of Wendy's napkin, which wuz leavin' little yellow bits stuck to his forehead. Once they made it all the way down to the fair grounds, Cooter couldn't keep nobody's attention, what with all the strappin' boys in uniform and the window dressin's at the Dollar General.

The weather wuz so dry the catfish wuz carryin' canteens, so when the girls seen an unfamiliar hottie walkin' up toward 'em, kickin' up dust with his boots, they thought he wuz a damned mirage. All of 'em stared with their mouths open. He swaggered like some kind of a cowboy, and he wuz wearin' leather pants so tight you could see his religion. Lizzy felt quite sure he wuz stuffin' socks down there, if'n you know what I mean. He whistled as the girls walked by, and Kitty and Lydie turned and walked right up to 'im, standing too close fer good behavior. The feller walkin' with 'im wuz acquainted with the girls and introduced the stranger to 'em as Joe Wickham. Joe said he wuz an undercover narcotics agent fer another state's police department, and said he'd come down to the fair grounds to train the National Guard in some hand-to-hand combat. The girls could've melted smack dab into the sticky Tennessee heat. All Joe Wickham needed to make 'im perfect in their eyes wuz a uniform. He had bad boy hair all the way down to his shoulders, colored like the sand down in coastal Looziana. A girl could imagine her hands runnin' through that tangle of hair. The motorcycle boots he wore gave 'im a good two extra inches of height, and all told he wuz prob'ly six feet two inches without the boots. By the size of his arms, the girls could tell he'd lifted a keg or two in his day. Joe wuz good with the ladies, and Benny's daughters fell fer 'im hook, line and sinker.

They wuz still gittin' to know Joe when Buford and Dutch pulled up in the pick-up. They moved slow as to not kick up dust 'round the girls, and they started in with their howdies. Buford and Janie locked eyes as they talked. Buford'd jest then been on his way to see Benny to ask how Janie wuz farin'. Dutch confirmed it with a nod and wuz tryin' not to look at Lizzy when he got all pop-eyed a-lookin' at the stranger. Lizzy watched his expression change when he seen Joe Wickham, and she seen Joe's face turn white as a sheet hung out to dry. After a beat, Joe nodded at Dutch as a howdie. Dutch jest watched 'im. Lizzy couldn't help but wonder what the sam hill wuz goin' on.

Within a minute, Buford pulled ahead. He didn't seem to notice the spit-fire b'tween Dutch and Joe Wickham.

The girls walked with Joe and Cooter down the street to their Ain't Fern's house, and begged 'im to come inside fer some sweet tea. He wuzn't havin' any, even after Ain't Fern threw up the front window and nearly begged the feller, on account of he needed to git on back.

Fern wuz always glad to see her nieces, and she wuz pleased as punch to see the two older girls since they hadn't been by in a good while, what with Janie's ailment and all. She and Cooter howdied and shook, and they wuz all polite-like with each other. Cooter went on one of his long-winded speeches 'bout how sorry he wuz to jest show up without hollerin' first and how impressed he wuz with his purty little cousins. Fern didn't know what to say to 'im except 'thank you kindly' b'fore she started in with what she knew of Joe Wickham. Folks said he wuz from another state where he worked undercover to arrest folks who ran meth labs. She'd been watchin' 'im through the front window when he pulled up on a Harley Davidson motorcycle, and she'd still be watchin' his tight little ass in them leather pants if'n she could. Lydie and Kitty stared out the window hopin' to catch another look-see, but the only folks they could see wuz the National Guardsmen out in the field doin' pushups in the heat. Ain't Fern said she wuz plannin' to invite some of the boys over fer supper and cards the next day, and she figured she'd invite Joe and the girls along too. You couldn't keep the girls away fer all the tea in China. They bear-hugged their Ain't Fern, and Cooter apologized fer bargin' in on their visit seven or eight more times 'til Fern jest told 'im to give it a rest.

On the long, hot walk home, Lizzy told Janie 'bout the look Dutch'd given Joe Wickham. "He wuz as angry as a horse chewin' on bumblebees." Janie thought Lizzy wuz wrong, but Lizzy said, "If'n I said a rooster dips snuff, you best be a-lookin' under his wing fer the can."

Back home, Cooter went on a tear 'bout how nice Ain't Fern'd been and how nice her house wuz and how the peanut butter cookies she wuz offerin' wuz the best he ever had. He said that exceptin' Miz M and DeeDee, he had never met with such a fine lady. Not only had she given 'im a big hug on the way out the door, but she'd also included 'im in the supper invitation fer the next night. He said he'd never been treated so fine in all his days.

# Chapter 16

Benny pinched Flo's butt as he told the girls and Cooter that he had no problem with their supper with Ain't Fern. He told 'em he wuz already stiff as a poker, and he couldn't wait fer some "alone time" with Flo. He tossed over the keys to the Chevy and told 'em to take their time over to Fern's.

Gittin' five girls and their cousin Cooter in the Chevy wuzn't easy, but no one complained 'bout bein' squished, 'specially not Cooter. He made sure he wuz pressed up against Lizzy. She turned her face the other direction to avoid his breath, which smelled like the dead critters their dog wuz always draggin' up on the back stoop. The minute they opened the door to Ain't Fern's front room, they learned Joe Wickham wuz already there.

Cooter oogled all his surroundin's, and kept up a steady stream of "whoo-wee's" when marvelin' at how real the faux stone looked on the fireplace and how fancy all chairs wuz. He declared if'n he'd been drunk and stumbled in there by mistake one night, he might thank he wuz in one of the smaller rooms at Miz M's house when he woke up the next mornin' with a hangover. Ain't Fern wuz, at first, a little ticked off that Cooter would talk shit 'bout her best room like he did, but when he explained 'bout Miz M and how loaded she wuz and the fact she'd jest spent $200 on a table at the swap meet, Ain't Fern felt right proud.

Now that Cooter had her ear, he kept on 'bout Miz M's house, tellin' Fern 'bout the skylight in the bedroom, the whirlpool tub in the bathroom and the nearly nekkid drawin' of a younger Miz M on one wall in the basement. From time to time he added little bits and pieces 'bout his parsonage and its aluminum railin's that looked jest like wrought iron. Ain't Fern wuz a happy listener, and Cooter jest wouldn't shut up. She wuz a-lookin' fer gossip to trade with the neighbors over the chain-link fence. The girls couldn't stand their cousin's diarrhea from the mouth another minute and started a-lookin' 'round fer somethin' to occupy their time 'til the handsome Joe Wickham came back inside with the other fellers. And when he did, Lizzy thought he looked finer 'n a frog's hair split three ways, sanded and waxed. He looked good enough to make you wanna smack yer granny. The soldiers wuz snackin' on the nabs Ain't Fern laid out, and Joe wuz cuter 'n any of 'em, even the ones chewin' with their mouths shut. They wuz all puffed up, though, walkin' like they wuz sharper 'n a hermit's toenail as they follered Uncle Phil from out back where they wuz sneakin' some white lightnin' from behind the shed.

Every eye wuz stuck on Joe like white on rice, and Lizzy wuz the lucky girl he sat next to. He started talkin' to her right away 'bout the dry weather, sayin' it wuz so dry the trees wuz beggin' the dogs fer a waterin'. Even though all the conversin' wuz 'bout the weather, Lizzy felt right certain Joe Wickham could make a conversation 'bout dog shit the most interestin' thang to listen to in the world.

With all the handsome fellers in the room, Cooter wuz plum out'a luck with the ladies, but Ain't Fern let 'im bend her ear, and she kept 'im in nabs and beer fer the time bein'. And when the card tables wuz set up, he returned the favor by playin' hearts with her while ever'body else played poker.

Joe decided against poker and sat down with Lizzy and Lydie at the coffee table where they wuz rollin' dice. Lydie wuz quick with her tongue, and she wuz happier 'n an old dog layin' on the porch chewin' on a big ol' catfish head to keep on talkin'. B'fore long, though, she got competitive with the dice and shut right up, concentratin' on winnin'. That allowed Joe and Lizzy to chew the fat a little bit, and Lizzy wuz happy to oblige. She jest hoped Joe would spill the beans on his relationship with Dutch. She didn't dare bring up the subject, but Joe started in on it without any leadin'. He asked how far Buford's place wuz from the fair grounds, and after she told 'im, he stuttered wonderin' how long Dutch'd been stayin' down there.

"I reckon 'bout a month," said Lizzy; and then, not lettin' the subject drop she said, "I hear he's shittin' in high cotton and has a farm to boot."

"He's rollin' in it. That's fer sure," Joe replied. "You ain't never gonna meet another person what can give you the low-down on Dutch better 'n me. I'm practic'lly kin to 'im. We growed up t'gether."

Lizzy's eyes flew open like two buckeyes in a barrel of buttermilk.

"They's no wonder yer surprised, Miss Lizzy, after seein' the way he snubbed me yesterd'y. I thank he's a real asshole. Are you acquainted with 'im?"

"I know 'im 'bout as much as I ever want to," cried Lizzy. "I spent four days livin' in the same house as 'im, and I thank he's 'bout as useless as a one-armed barber with a thousand skeeter bites and a case of poison ivy."

"I thank I better keep my mouth shut 'bout 'im," said Joe. "I ain't got a right to my own opinion. We go too far back, and there's too many bridges been burnt. I thank most folks wouldn't agree with what you jest said. You prob'ly wouldn't be runnin' yer mouth 'bout 'im like that, neither, less'n you wuzn't with yer kin 'round here. Other folks might talk."

"Whatever I tell you, I'd say it to anybody who'd listen, except maybe over to the doublewide near the Park N Shop. Not a soul cares fer 'im up in here. Ever'body is disgusted with his pride. Folks 'round here would rather shoot 'im as look at 'im. I'm prob'ly his best friend in this town, and that ain't sayin' much."

"Lands! And ain't I glad to hear it! What comes 'round goes 'round, and he'll git his, but not soon enough if'n you ask me. Ever'body is blinded by his fancy relations and the green in his pocket, and they's scared of 'im be'cuz he's so uppity. I thank folks jest sees 'im the way he wants 'em to."

"I thank, even fer the short time I've knowd 'im, he's mean enough to eat barbed wire and spit out the nails," she said. Joe jest nodded his head.

"I wonder," he said, "how long he's plannin' to stay 'round these parts?"

"I cain't help you there, Joe. I never heard nuthin' 'bout 'im leavin' the whole time I wuz stayin' there. I hope you won't skedattle on account of 'im hangin' 'round."

"Hell, no! I ain't gonna be driven away by no damned Dutch. If'n he ain't got a fancy to be seein' me, it's him that's gotta leave. We ain't on friendly terms, Miss Lizzy, and I hate to see 'im when I do, but I ain't got no reason to be avoidin' 'im. There never wuz a better man than Dutch's Daddy, Junior. He wuz good as gold, and I never wuz treated better by nobody in all my born days. When I'm 'round Dutch, I git all soft inside thankin' on his Daddy, and even though Dutch's been such a snake to me, a low-down snake, I thank I might could bury the hatchet on account of Junior's mem'ry."

Lizzy thought the Dutch/Joe story wuz better 'n the afternoon soap operas, but she didn't dare ask more questions on account of it jest didn't seem right.

Joe moved on to other topics, the fair grounds, the local restaurants and such. He seemed right pleased with all he'd seen, and the low rumble of his voice had gotten under Lizzy's skin in a way she liked jest fine.

"I needed to git out'a undercover work fer a while," he said. "It gits lonely, doncha know? That's why I took leave and came over to these parts. I needed to be 'round normal folks again, good people, like the soldiers. I know folks respect the National Guard, and when my buddies told me the trainin' would be at a county fair grounds, I nearly jumped at the chance. I like to be in company so close you cain't spin a cat by the tail without hittin' some friend or another. Undercover narcotics is tough on a feller. I jest got to be 'round folks. I should've been workin' security fer the gov'ner of Kentucky by now, and I would've been makin' hay while the sun shines, if'n it had pleased Dutch."

"No way."

"Yep. Junior wuz connected up there in horse country. He knew a guy who knew a guy, and he had it all set up fer me. Like I said, he wuz as good as gold, but when he passed, Dutch must've spoke against me."

"Heavens to Betsy!" cried Lizzy, "How could he do somethin' so rotten as that? You should've sued 'im right quick. It's like he stole yer lottery ticket or somethin'."

"I never got nuthin' in writin' from Junior. We had a gentleman's agreement. Junior's handshake wuz good enough fer me. And it should've been good enough fer Dutch, too. I tell you, I wuz so blue I wuz peein' ink. He said I wuz too quick with the dollar and too lazy to pick the dead lice off the gov'ner, and he wouldn't recommend me to 'em guys up there. One of 'em jobs came up a couple of years ago, and some other feller got on over me. I cain't say I done anythang to really piss off Dutch except maybe to run my mouth 'bout 'im, sometimes to his face. I never threw a punch or nuthin', but I tell you the truth, we's jest diff'rnt, Dutch and me. He hates me."

"Well, I never! He needs someone to put 'im in his place. He's gittin' too big fer his britches."

"Like I said, what comes 'round goes 'round. He'll git his, but not by me. I gots too much respect fer ol' Junior, God rest his soul."

Anybody who looked over at Lizzy could tell she wuz moonin' over Joe Wickham. He got better a-lookin' to her ever' time he said a word. "But what in the world would make 'im be so cruel to you, Joe?"

"He hates me be'cuz his Daddy liked me better. Plain as that. I thank he worried 'bout his Daddy and my Momma, if'n you git my drift. We could'a been kin; you see what I'm gittin' at?"

"Well I never! I cain't see how Dutch could be as bad as all this. I always thought he wuz disagreeable and irritatin', but I never thought he wuz as low as this. Why, he's as low as pond scum. No. I take that back. He's as low as the critters who live in the muck under the pond scum. That's how low he is. I do remember 'im braggin' one day 'bout how when he got bad blood with someone, he kept it. Dadgum!"

"I best be keepin' my thoughts to my ownself," he said.

After a bit, Lizzy continued, "And to treat poorly someone as sweet as you, his Daddy's friend and prob'ly his own playmate from childhood!"

"We went to the same little school, and we shoveled horseshit out'a barns and mended fences t'gether. Why, my family lived in a little shack on his Daddy's property. My Daddy'd been a cashier at the farm supply store and gave it all up to work fer Junior. He worked ever' day and one day jest fell down with a heart attack in the field. Junior and him wuz thick as thieves, always figurin' how to git the land to produce more crops and such. And as my Daddy lay there dyin' in Junior's arms, he made Junior promise to take right good care of me and do right by me. Junior told me so himself and said my Daddy didn't even have to ask. He owed 'im that much."

"That makes me wanna come after Dutch like a spider monkey and tear out his eyes with an ice pick. He ain't worth the powder and lead to blow himself up! You'd thank he'd use his all-fired pride to do what's right by you. I never seen a banty rooster who'd pee down yer back and tell you it's rainin', but Dutch seems like the type. I cain't stand dishonesty. It really gits my goat."

"Ever'thang he does can be tied right back to pride, Miss Lizzy. I thank his pride is his best friend and huntin' buddy."

"Havin' pride as yer best friend ain't never done nobody no good."

"That's where yer wrong. It's made 'im gen'rous with his money, right hospitable folks say. Dutch gives to his church and to missionaries over-seas. He helps the poor. I tell you, he and his sister've never had a garage sale. They give ever'thang to the Goodwill. I thank he does it all to keep up the fam'ly name, you know what I mean? He gits his name in the church bulletin, and I thank it gives 'im a rise in his Levi's to be noticed. I thank he's right good to his little sister. People say he's right attentive to her."

"What kinda girl is Miss Suzanna?"

"Folks say she's cuter 'n a bug's ear, but I thank she looks like she's been hit in the face with a bagful of nickels, so ugly she'd have to sneak up on a glass of water. She's all uppity like her brother, proud-like. When she wuz knee high to a grasshopper, she wuz jest as sweet as sugar, and hoo-wee did she take a likin' to me back in the day. We wuz close, but she ain't nuthin' to me now. She's 'bout fourteen, I'd expect. Since her Daddy died she's been livin' in Lexin'ton where she's home-schooled."

After a-tryin' everwhichway to change the subject, Lizzy couldn't help one more stab at Dutch. "I cain't figure how a fella like Dutch could be such close friends with a man as fine as Buford! That Buford drips of goodness and sunshine. Do you know 'im?"

"Nope."

"He's right charmin'. He cain't know the real Dutch!"

"Prob'ly not, but Dutch can play a good game, darlin'. He can talk right nice and show city manners if'n it suits 'im, then he can turn 'round and pois'n yer best pup. He treats his own and his betters one way, and the rest of us git the shaft. Them rich folks up in Lexin'ton jest love 'im and cain't spend enough time with 'im and those ponies he raises.

One of the soldiers at the poker table fell plum off his chair and spilled beer all over the place, so the players hopped up to avoid soilin' their britches. They circled 'round the table where Cooter and Fern wuz playin' hearts and asked 'em who wuz winnin'. Cooter admitted with a blush that he hadn't won a hand, and when Fern started to comfort 'im and offered to give 'im back some of the money she'd won off of 'im, he shoo'ed her away and said it wuzn't nuthin' but a trifle.

"Don't worry yerself one little bit, Ain't Fern. A feller knows when he sits down to a game of cards he might could lose his shirt. Fifty bucks here or there ain't no big thang fer me, I'll suwanee. I reckon there 'r those who ain't so lucky as me, but I got Prudence Majestro in my pocket, and so long as she lives, this feller will be jest fine and dandy."

The mention of the infamous Miz M caught Joe's attention, and after watchin' Cooter fer a bit, he asked Lizzy in a low voice if'n her cousin know'd the Majestro family.

"Prudence Majestro," she replied, "lines Cooter's pockets. We ain't sure why she does, but we have our ideas. It wuz Miz M who helped git 'im the preachin' job up to Knoxv'lle jest a couple of months ago. I don't know what their relations is, but it creeps me out to high heavens."

"You know Prudence and Dutch's mom, Lacy Lynn, wuz sisters. Old Miz M is Dutch's Ain't Pru."

"No way. I had no notion on it. I never knew her name b'fore yesterd'y."

"Her daughter, DeeDee, stands to inherit a bundle of money when her Momma kicks the bucket. Some folks say DeeDee and Dutch 'r kissin' cousins and might end up gittin' hitched to keep all that cash in the family, as they say."

This little tidbit made Lizzy smile, thankin' on all those missin' branches from Dutch's family tree. And poor Tammy! Lizzy wondered if'n she knew all her affection and efforts with Dutch wuz doomed from the beginnin'. She wuz always kissin' his ass twelve ways from Sund'y and askin' on Suzanna like there wuz a hope they'd all be kin.

"Cooter speaks highly of Miz M and Debbie, or DeeDee, or whatever she's called. I jest wonder if'n he's a-tryin' to hide somethin'. She's prob'ly stuck up and conceited like her nephew."

"You called it, darlin', on both counts," said Joe. "I ain't seen her in forever, but I do recall that I never liked her. She reminded me of a tomato stake, all stiff backed an full of herself. People say she's clever and has good horse sense, but I thank if'n you've got the kind of money she has, you can pay fer respect jest like you pay fer ever'thang else."

Lizzy felt Joe had been shootin' straight with her, and they had each other's ear 'til all the soldiers wuz glassy eyed and slurrin' their speech. He spent some time with the other girls in the room, flirtin' and laughin' like they wuz all old friends. Ever'body in the room liked 'im and called 'im "buddy" or "wild-man," which is what men call each other when they're too drunk to remember yer name but like you anyway.

Lizzy left fer home with her head full of Joe Wickham and of what he'd told her, but she couldn't speak a word of it on account of Cooter and Lydie never shut up the whole way back. Lydie talked 'bout ever' boy she had chatted up and her winnin's, and Cooter blabbed on and on at how his losses at hearts didn't add up to a hill of beans. Cooter worried all the way home that he wuz crowdin' his cousins, even though he pressed closer 'n they wanted. The old rust-wagon sputtered to a halt in front of their house b'fore Cooter had taken a breath, but ever'one wuz purty sure he'd broken wind.

# Chapter 17

The next day Lizzy told Janie ever' word Joe Wickham had said. Janie couldn't b'lieve her ears. She simply could not thank Dutch wuz such a rascal and that Buford could be friends with 'im. She didn't wanna say that Joe wuz talkin' with his tongue out'a his shoe. How could he have enough bb's rollin' 'round in that purty head of his to make up a story the likes of that? Thankin' on Joe's life, rougher 'n a cob, sufferin' the unkindnesses of mean ol' Dutch, she felt right tender towards 'im. Janie wuz so good-hearted, she decided there wuz a reason fer ever'thang and determined to feel sorry fer both of 'em.

"Both of those fellers have been taken fer a ride, if'n you ask me. That story could depress the devil. We have no earthly idea what really happened b'tween them two. There's two sides to every street, Liz. We need to ride the middle if'n we can."

"Hell fire and damnation, Janie! Someone's gotta be blamed!"

"You can laugh at me 'til the cows come home, but you won't change my mind one whit. Joe's story paints Dutch in the worst light, takin' a dead man's promises and throwin' 'em away like it's nothin'. It cain't be right. A man like Dutch, a real Lexin'ton gentleman, wouldn't do such a thang. Do you thank Buford would be such an idjit to be friends with a feller like that? No way."

"It's easier fer me to b'lieve Buford's bein' imposed on than Joe could've spun that yarn on his own. He had names and places, facts and ever'thang, and he spat it right out, without hesitatin'. If'n it ain't true, let Dutch say so."

"I jest don't know what to thank, Liz."

"Don't be stupid, you sweet cow! I know exactly what to b'lieve."

But Janie could thank on jest one thang-- if'n Buford'd been treated bad, he'd be embarrassed near to death if'n the gossip chain started spreadin' the story.

Lizzy and Janie wuz called from their spot behind the apple tree by the sound of four Firestone tires and a blur of red pickup. As they walked back to the house, they both wondered if'n Buford's ears wuz burnin' seein' as how they'd jest been talkin' 'bout 'im. Buford and his sisters brought flyers to the shin-dig he'd promised to throw. They wuz typed up and ever'thang. Tammy and Patty wuz right pleased to see Janie, and said it'd been an age since they seen her last. They wanted to know ever' detail of what she'd been up to. They purty much ignored ever'body else, and wouldn't give Flo the time of day. They barely grunted hello to Lizzy and kept mum with the others. Within two shakes of a lamb's tail, they wuz up and headed fer the door, surprisin' Buford who wuz jest gittin' settled in.

The idea of a throw-down wuz pleasin' to ever'body in the house, and Flo felt the entire party wuz meant fer Janie. She couldn't b'lieve Buford had come by to hand-deliver the flyer. Janie pictured herself at the party, two-steppin' with all her friends and slow-dancin' with Buford. Lizzy's thoughts wound round 'bout 'til they landed on Joe Wickham. She wanted to step out with 'im and watch Dutch's reaction. Kitty and Lydie each bet the other one that they couldn't git four boys to go out in the cornfield with 'em fer some moonin' and smoochin', and Joe wuz on the top of both of their lists of boys to tempt. Even Mary, peculiar Mary, wuz fixin' to enter into the social circle, even though she thought party dresses wuz scratchy, and she didn't like crowds of people or noise or loud music and she'd only eat cheese nabs be'cuz ever'thang else had a texture that made her wanna climb the walls.

"While I can have my mornings to myself," she said, "it is enough. I think it no sacrifice to join occasionally in evening engagements. Society has claims on us all; and I profess myself one of those who consider intervals of recreating and amusement as desirable for everybody." In plain terms, she wuz a-lookin' forward to the party as much as the rest of 'em.

Lizzy's spirits wuz so high that, though she tried to avoid talkin' to Cooter as much as possible, she couldn't help but ask 'im whether he wuz plannin' to go to the shin-dig with the family, and if'n he wuz, did he thank Miz M would approve of 'im gyrating to the devil's music. She wuz shocked as shit when Cooter said he planned to attend and gyrate with the best of 'em. He thought Miz M wouldn't mind if'n he cut a rug with his kin.

"Buford and his folks is respectable people. As long as they ain't gonna hire no pole dancers or strippers, which I'm sure they won't, Miz M would want me to celebrate with all y'all. You call it the devil's music, but I de-clare it's not at all. Maybe it's music to fall in love to. I hope to dance with all of my dear relations, and I got dibbs on you fer the first two dances. I'm guessin' Janie won't mind.

Lizzy sputtered and spat like she'd licked the wrong end of a cat. She'd been hopin' to dance all night with Joe Wickham-- and to have to dance with Cooter instead wuz enough to make her wanna puke. She wished she'd jest kept her big mouth shut. She forced a smile and said she'd dance with 'im, hopin' the songs would be a line dance or the like. And then it hit her like a ton of bricks. She'd been chosen by Cooter from among her sisters to make amends fer the family feud! Cooter had a mind to marry her. The more she thought on it, the more attention Cooter seemed to give her. He wuz holdin' open doors and laughin' at the stupidest shit she said. He threw compliments at her like nobody'd ever seen, like pitches in a batting cage with the speed turned up high. She wuz plum flabbergasted by the idea of his affection and not a little grossed out. Flo kept hintin' 'round that there might could be a weddin' to warsh all their troubles away, and Lizzy had to suck on a lollipop to keep from gaggin'.

If'n there hadn't been a dance to git ready fer, Kitty and Lydie would've driven ever'body bat-shit crazy with their boredom. It had rained straight through a week, a real gullywasher, makin' up fer the dry weather the week b'fore, and the weather kept 'em from walkin' past the fair grounds to visit Ain't Fern. No Fern. No soldiers. No gossip. The younger girls wuz a miserable pair. Even Lizzy wuz in a sour mood since the weather kept her from crossin' paths with Joe Wickham and his tight pants.

# Chapter 18

'Til Lizzy stepped onto the back patio at Buford's house the night of the party and scanned the crowd fer Joe Wickham, the inklin' that he might not be at the dance never crossed her mind. She'd taken care to iron out her hair real slow-like, and she added one of Lydie's "bump-its" to give some extra height. She'd checked her skirt to make sure it wuzn't too short when she leaned way over. When Lydie wore the same skirt, it wuz so short you could see all the way to Christmas, but Lydie liked it that way. Lizzy wuz ready to steal Joe's heart and put it in 'er pocket fer keeps, if'n she could. But at that second, she thought Joe might not've been invited on account of Dutch. When Lydie asked one of the soldiers where Joe Wickham wuz, the feller told her he'd had to run out'a town fer some reason or another, but added he didn't thank Joe's business would've been so pressin' if'n he didn't wanna avoid a certain feller who wuz jest sure to come to the party.

When Lizzy heard this, she wuz jest sure steam wuz comin' out'a her ears. Dutch wuz the reason fer Joe not bein' at the dance. She wuz mightily pissed off and could hardly keep herself from goin' over thar and tearin' 'im a new asshole. If'n she wuz nice to Dutch, it wuz akin to slappin' handsome Joe Wickham across the face. She decided she wouldn't say a word to Dutch all night, and she wuz right near perturbed at Buford fer bein' friends with 'im, so she felt she'd snub him too.

Lizzy wuzn't good at holdin' a grudge, and even though all the fun jest ran out'a her evenin' like liquor runnin' down Harley's throat, once she'd spilled her guts to Charlotte, she wuz ready to switch the conversation to talk 'bout her crazy cousin, Cooter. She pointed 'im out to Charlotte as he came towards her to claim his two dances. He stepped on her feet as often as not and didn't know the dance one bit. Standin' up with 'im wuz right near shameful- the best part 'bout dancin' with 'im wuz when it wuz over.

The next dance she spent with a soldier who smelled of pot smoke and Polo cologne, but she wuz able to talk to 'im 'bout Joe and learned that all the boys down at the fair grounds jest loved 'im. After a bit she went back to chat with Charlotte, and wouldn't you know it but Dutch came right up to Lizzy and asked her to dance. She wuz flustered, and b'fore she knew what she wuz doin', she'd said yes, and Charlotte whispered she shouldn't let thoughts of Joe Wickham drown out any possibility with a feller as hot and rich as Dutch.

Lizzy gave her a look and follered Dutch into the crush of folks. She made sure to leave room fer Jesus as they danced, even though folks wuz rubbin' up against each other like cats against a post. There wuzn't no talkin' goin' on, so Lizzy made some comment 'bout the song. Dutch said some little somethin' back, but didn't begin to carry the conversation one whit. After a while, she decided to say somethin' else.

"It's yer turn to say somethin' to me, Dutch. I said somethin' 'bout the song, now you had oughtta say somethin' 'bout the crowd of folks or the food or somethin'."

He smiled, and told her he'd say whatever she wanted 'im to say.

"I guess that works fer the time bein'. Maybe later I'll say somethin' on the twinkle lights in the trees over yonder, but fer now we can be still."

"Do you have strict rules 'bout talkin' while dancin'?"

"Well, sometimes folks should speak a little, you know. It'd look funny if'n you wuz quiet through the entire song, 'specially if'n it's a long one like *Freebird*, but fer some folks it should be fixed so's they have to say as little as possible to each other."

"Are you thankin' on yer own feelin's right now or mine?"

"Both," said Lizzy with one eyebrow raised in a challenge. "I thank there ain't two ways 'round our minds. They's the same. Both of us 'r antisocial, don't like to talk less'n we will say somethin' to make ever'body's jaw drop, and wanna go down in history as someone who had it all figured out."

"You ain't talkin' 'bout yerself. I guarantee it," he said. "And I ain't sayin' how close to the mark you came to my ownself. I'm sure you thank yer aim is right-on."

"I cain't say how I fare."

He didn't say nuthin' to that, and they wuz quiet fer a spell 'til he asked her if'n she and her sisters walked much down by the fair grounds. She said they did, and she couldn't stop herself from addin', "When you seen us down there the other day, we'd jest met a new friend."

He reacted quick as lightnin'. His eyes got deeper, and he stood up straight as an oak, but he didn't say nothin'. Lizzy couldn't keep playin' 'im like that after seein' his reaction, so she kept mum. After a bit Dutch said, controlled-like, "Joe Wickham is such a fun feller to be 'round, I'm sure he is quick to make friends-- whether he keeps any of 'em, I ain't so sure 'bout."

"Well, he ain't been so lucky as to keep yer friendship, I hear," she said, "and it seems he's payin' fer it ever' day of his life."

Dutch didn't say nuthin', and acted like he wanted to change the subject. 'Bout that time, Billy Lucas walked right by 'em and stopped to give Dutch a hearty pat on the shoulder. He wuz 'bout half drunk, and he wuz full of compliments fer Dutch and Lizzy and their dancin'.

"Y'all know how to do it, doncha Dutch? Most folks 'round here don't know a square dance from a two-step, but I can see y'all do. It don't hurt to have a partner like her," he continued, elbowin' Dutch in the ribs. "I hope to see y'all dancin' the night away. You make quite the pair, and I 'spect y'all and yer kin will have plenty of chances to dance t'gether when a certain somethin' happens." He glanced at Buford and Janie. "Won't that be a hoot? But don't let me keep ya. I can tell Lizzy is hankerin' fer me to leave. She keeps givin' me the stink eye."

Dutch barely heard the last part of what Billy wuz sayin'. He wuz glued to the spot thinkin' on the hint of a weddin' b'tween Buford and Janie and watchin' 'em with new eyes. Buford's hands wuz all over her at once. With a jolt Dutch snapped out'a it and said to Lizzy, "I'm sorry. I forgot what we wuz talkin' 'bout."

"We wuzn't sayin' anythang at all. Billy Lucas couldn't have interrupted any other folks with less to say to each other. We've been a-tryin' to find somethin' to talk 'bout, but I jest don't thank we've got much in common. I honestly don't know what the hell to say to you."

"Do you wanna talk 'bout books?" he asked, smilin'.

"Books, oh hell no. There's no way in the world we got a likin' fer the same kinds of books, I'll suwanee."

"So what? Even if'n we don't have the same opinion, at least arguin' 'bout 'em would give us somethin' to talk 'bout."

"How in the sam hill do you thank we can talk over books with all this loud music? That's too much multi-taskin' fer a Saturd'y night."

"Somehow I doubt that," he said.

She wuz quiet fer a minute, then she said, "Hey! One time I heard you say you hardly ever forgive folks and that when you hated a body, you hated 'im forever. I guess that means it takes you a while to hold that kind of grudge?"

"That's right."

"And you never let yerself be prejudiced against nobody?"

"Well, I hope not," he said.

"'B'cuz I'm thankin' if'n you make an opinion, and it never changes, well, then you better be right when you make yer opinion in the first place."

"What the hell 'r you talkin' 'bout, Miss Lizzy?"

"I'm jest a-tryin' to figure you out."

"And how's that goin' fer you?"

She shook her head. "I cain't. Ever'body has a diff'rent story to tell 'bout you. I'm jest as puzzled now as ever."

"I thank," he said serious as a heart attack, "you shouldn't rush to judge me, Miss Lizzy. You really don't know nuthin' 'bout me, and judgin' by what others say ain't a great way to form an opinion on nobody."

"But if'n I don't form an opinion on you now, I might never git the chance later."

"Whatever!" he answered cold as a flagpole in January, and they continued dancin' without talkin' to one another. At the end of the song, they both went their separate ways, both unhappy but fer diff'rent reasons. Where she burned hot as a poker with anger, Dutch wuz burnin' in another way and wanted rid of it by whatever way he could.

Not long after, Miss Tammy came walkin' up to Lizzy like she wuz 'it' on a stick. "So, Miss Lizzy, I hear you're hot fer Joe Wickham! Yer sister jest won't shut up 'bout 'im. I'd be willin' to bet money she's asked me a thousand questions. Five bucks says he didn't tell you his Daddy worked fer Dutch's Daddy. Don't b'lieve ever'thang he tells you. Whatever trash he's spreadin' 'round 'bout Dutch ain't true a lick. Dutch has always done right by Joe. I don't know the particulars, but I do know Dutch ain't to blame, and I know Dutch cain't bear to hear Joe Wickham mentioned among comp'ny. My brother thought it wouldn't be quite right to invite 'im along with the other soldiers, but he did it anyways. We wuz all sweatin' bullets, wonderin' what would happen and all, but thank the dear Lord, Joe is avoidin' Dutch and us like the plague. We wuz all jest slack-jawed that he'd even come 'round these parts at all. I feel so sorry fer you, Lizzy, fer learnin' 'bout yer sweetheart this way, but when you lay down with dogs, you git up with fleas, and Joe Wickham's been layin' down with so many diffr'ent dogs, it's a wonder he ain't covered."

"You don't know shit," Lizzy said. "Joe told me himself his Daddy worked fer Junior."

"Well, I never!" replied Tammy. "I wuz jest a-tryin' to help you. 'Scuse me fer breathin'.'"

"What a bitch," said Lizzy to herself. "Yer a-tryin' to git under my skin. You don't know nuthin' 'bout nuthin', and yer so far up Dutch's butt, you cain't see the light of day.'" Then she looked 'round fer Janie, who wuz grinnin' like the cat who had swallered the canary. She practic'ly glowed in the dark with her smiles. That very second, Dutch, Tammy and ever'thang melted away exceptin' Janie's happiness.

"What did you dig up from Buford on our friend Joe?" Lizzy asked her sister. "Maybe you wuz too busy snugglin' up against Buford to thank on anythang else."

"Naw. I ain't forgot 'im, but I don't have nuthin' good to report. Buford don't know much 'bout 'im or why Dutch is so bent out'a shape on account of 'im. He does vouch fer his buddy, though. Says Dutch is a real stand-up feller, and Joe don't deserve to stand in his shadow. Buford and his sister say Joe ain't respectable, Lizzy. He ain't done Dutch right and deserves whatever he gits."

"Buford don't know Joe personally?"

"Never laid eyes on 'im 'til the other mornin' by the fair grounds."

"So ever'thang he says comes straight from Dutch's mouth, I reckon. But I still wonder 'bout that job situation with the gov'ner's security in Kentucky."

"He ain't right sure, but he said the job wuz promised to Joe on some conditions."

"I'm sure Buford is tellin' the God's honest truth as far as he sees it," said Lizzy warmly, "but don't git yer feelin's hurt if'n I ain't convinced. Buford's only got second-hand information, and he don't even know some of the folks involved. I ain't changin' my opinion on nobody 'til I git the facts.

Then she changed the subject to avoid any arguin' with her favorite sister. Lizzy listened, smilin', as Janie told her 'bout every detail of her night so far with Buford. They had to shut up right quick when Buford, himself, swaggered up to the girls. Lizzy knew when she wuzn't wanted, and found Charlotte nearby. They hadn't said two words to each other when Cooter showed up and announced he'd jest learnt somethin' big.

"I jest found out," he said, "all on accident, you see, that at this here party there's a close relation to Miz M. I cain't b'lieve my good luck. I wuz listnin' in on a feller's conversation over yonder, and he mentioned DeeDee Majestro as his kin and her mother, too. Lawsy mercy! It's got to be fate, I tell you. Who would've thunk it, a nephew of Miz M right here? I'm jest glad I wuz listnin' over that feller's shoulder. Now I have a chance to introduce myself and tell 'im 'bout the recent plumbin' issue I had that Miz M helped me with."

"Um, Cooter. I don't thank that's such a good idea."

"Well I don't know why not. Hell, I'm embarrassed I didn't know they wuz kin in the first place. I'm sure he'll wanna know how she fared last time I seen her."

Lizzy tried her best to convince Cooter to keep his distance from Dutch. She could only imagine the impression Cooter'd give with his "plumbin' issue," and she wuz sure Dutch wouldn't wanna imagine his aunt flirtin' with the ridiculous Cooter and plungin' away at his stopped up toilet.

Once Cooter got somethin' in his head, there wuz no changin' his mind. He said, "Sugarplum, I don't doubt fer a minute a word you say when it's somethin' you understand. But this is a man thang, darlin'. I need to say howdie and shake with this feller and git on his good side fer business reasons, somethin' you cain't wrap yer purty little head 'round. I suwanee I'll foller yer lead on other stuff. I know what I'm doin' on this one, and with the tip of an invisible hat, he headed in Dutch's direction, a meetin' Lizzy couldn't help but stare at. Cooter must've led with the toilet story, be'cuz Dutch's neck and face turned bright red. She couldn't hear a word, but read on Cooter's lips the words "toilet," "Prudence Majestro," and "big clog of toilet paper and waste." She wuz ready to dig a hole and bury herself in it fer the embarrassment of her relation. Dutch looked at 'im like he escaped from the Looney Bin, and when he finally, after quite a spell, had the chance to say somethin', it wuz short and sweet. His quick reply didn't stop Cooter from goin' on and on, and the look on his face told Lizzy he thought Cooter wuzn't playin' with a full deck. At the end of the one way conversation, Dutch looked shell shocked and turned away. Cooter made his way straight back to Lizzy.

"I b'lieve Dutch liked me jest fine," he said. "He wuz so nice, and he said that Miz M wuz a good judge of character, and he never knew her to make a mistake b'fore. Ain't that nice of 'im? I right liked 'im."

Lizzy jest rolled her eyes and turned to look at Janie and Buford. They wuz standin' t'gether like two halves of a whole, holdin' hands and talkin' low to each other. Lizzy could see Janie livin' up by the Park N Shop in that nice doublewide with the new carpet and energy-efficient appliances and bein' hitched to the love of her life. She decided if'n that happened, she'd force herself to like his sisters and let bygones be bygones. She spied her Momma across the way and could tell she wuz thankin' on the same thang, so she decided to avoid her as much as possible.

When the pork wuz pulled off the spit and had cooled enough, Lizzy found the only available seat wuz one down from her Momma, so she took a load off. She carefully balanced the plate on her lap and could not help but hear her her Momma's shrill voice as she bragged to LuLu Lucas that Janie wuz 'bout to snatch up ol' Buford if'n the good Lord's willin' and the crick don't rise. And wouldn't all the girls 'round there be cryin' 'bout it. There wuz a lot fer Flo to say, apparently, and she got louder as she went. She gabbed on 'bout how nice it wuz that he lived so close, so's she could go down and visit Janie and the grandbabies any time she had the itch to see 'em. She said how lucky it wuz fer her younger girls to be exposed to a feller like Buford and how he wuz jest sure to have rich friends she could parade the girls in front of 'til they'd snagged one jest as good as him. But if'n he didn't Janie would always be there to take care of her younger sisters if'n anythang should happen to her or Benny. And with the girls hangin' out more with their sister on the other side of town, that would give her more alone time with Benny. She suggested to LuLu that someday maybe Charlotte would git lucky and find a man, though she didn't b'lieve Charlotte had a snowball's chance in hell. Lizzy could tell.

No matter what she said or did, Lizzy could not git her Momma to shut up or even lower her voice so's it wouldn't carry across the yard. She could tell most of what her Momma said had been heard by none other 'n Dutch who sat directly across from 'em. Her Momma scolded her, sayin' if'n brains wuz grease, she couldn't slick the head of a pin. Lizzy kept a-tryin' to shush her Momma.

"What is Dutch to me," she shrieked, "that I should worry one whit over what he thanks of me? This ain't none of his gol-darned beeswax."

"Oh, fer heaven's sake, Momma! Lower yer voice. What good will it do ya to make an enemy of Dutch? Ain't he the particular friend of Buford?"

Nuthin' she could say would close the floodgate that wuz her mother's mouth once it had started movin', and if'n anythang, Flo's voice got louder as she picked up steam. Lizzy's face burned hot as the hinges of hell, red as a firetruck, and she wanted to jest crawl up in a ball and die on the spot. She stole glances at Dutch from time to time, but it jest confirmed her worst fears. He wuz list'nin' all right, list'nin' to ever' word, and he wore his emotions on his sleeve, from disbelief to contempt to downright hatred.

B'fore too awful long, Flo's tirade did actually end. LuLu had been yawnin' wide as a yak through most of it and gnawed on a rib bone to suck out some of the marrow. Lizzy's fists wuz jest startin' to relax when all of the sudden somebody drug out a karaoke machine, and Mary got up to sing. Ever'body who knew Mary made faces and gestures to discourage her, but she jest couldn't read social cues to save her life. Having a chance fer a captive audience wuz too much fer her, and she began to sing. Lizzy watched in horror as Mary stumbled through line after line of the old Whitney Houston song "I Will Always Love You," with its trills and long notes lingerin' longer 'n anyone wanted in the cool night air. After the song wuz over, you could hear crickets. Not a soul clapped, but an old gal near the front (who didn't have in her hearing aids) encouraged Mary to sing another one. Lizzy wuz ready to pull her hair out and stuff 'em in her ears. Mary couldn't carry a tune in a basket. Lizzy looked at Janie fer help, but she wuz lip-locked with Buford under an oak tree. She hazarded a glance at his sisters who said all they needed to say by pretendin' to stick their fingers down their throats. Dutch jest stared off into the distance. Finally Lizzy cocked her head at Benny to git 'im to step in and do somethin'. Once Mary had finished her second song, Benny said, "That will do, Mary Lou. You need to give other folks a turn."

Mary looked down in the mouth, and Lizzy felt sorry fer her. Mary couldn't help that she wuz tone deaf and spoke with a monotone. She wuz born diff'rent, and Lizzy loved her to bits jest the way she wuz.

Cooter said, "If'n I could sing even a little bit, I'd git on up there and belt out one of them Phil Collins songs. I hear he sings and plays the drums at the same time. Once I seen a one man band, and I thought he wuz right good. Folks in the ministry, like myself, 'r usually purty good at singin', but I ain't got that gift. But if'n you got it, you should share it. I don't thank it's right to spend too much time in practice on account of there's jest so many other thangs a person's got to do of a day. Like in my case, as a preacher, I got to negotiate how much money each person oughtta give me, er, the church, based on his income and such, and I've gotta write my own sermons, though I git some of 'em off of the internet. Then there's the hospital visits to the elderly... I suwanee they's always somebody or another in the hospital these days... And the funerals... and the baptisms, why, that don't give me near 'nuff free time to make improvements to the parsonage, you cain't begrudge me that. And," he said in a much louder voice, "you cain't snub the kin folk of yer parishioners." With that he flung his arm out in Dutch's direction. Of course ever'body wuz watchin' and listnin', and most of 'em smiled, but nobody had as big a grin as Benny while Flo wuz pattin' Cooter on the back and tellin' 'im how right he wuz and how pleased she wuz to have him and his brains as a visitor to her house.

Lizzy thought her family wuz exposin' themselves like a flasher in downtown New York City, and she wuz thankin' maybe they wuz a-doin' it on purpose to embarrass her. She wuz glad Janie and Buford wuz off in the shadows swappin' spit on account of they missed most of the show, and he wouldn't like her none the less fer the display that her family had given ever'body and their brother at the party. He'd git his ear full from his sisters and Dutch, no doubt 'bout it. Lizzy didn't know which wuz worse, the wicked tongues of his sisters or Dutch's dark silence.

Nuthin' much could improve the night fer Lizzy. Cooter simply would not leave her alone. His sorry attempts at flirtin' wuz downright funny, and his breath smelled like the sulphur down at the hot springs. He stuck to her like hot chewin' gum to the bottom of a boot, and no other fellers even came close to her the rest of the night. He kept a-a-tryin' to git her to dance, but all she could see wuz the food stuck b'tween his teeth as he yammered on. She begged 'im to the point of offerin' 'im money to go two-steppin' with another girl and even offered to introduce 'im to anyone (anyone!) at the party. He told her horses couldn't drag 'im away from her and he would stick by her side come hell or high water. She knew there wuz no hope, and she wuz right grateful to her friend Charlotte fer comin' 'round and talkin' to Cooter from time to time.

With Charlotte and Cooter nearby, Lizzy didn't have to worry much 'bout Dutch comin' over to continue their grumblin' back and forth at each other. She noticed he stood fairly close, but he never came over or said a peep. She figured that wuz on the account of her mentionin' Joe Wickham earlier, and she wuz glad of it.

Benny, Flo and the girls wuz some of the last to leave Buford's house, and since Flo had accidently on purpose thrown the keys into a bush, they all had to wait 'til Benny could fish 'em out. This gave 'em a chance to see how bad ever'body wanted 'em to leave. Tammy and Patty kept yawnin' real loud and sayin' jest how tarred they wuz, and answered sharp to Flo ever' time she tried to start a conversation with 'em. The family wuz quiet exceptin' of course Cooter who wuz kissin' Buford's and his sisters asses 'bout how the music and the vittles and the neighborliness and the politeness made their shin-dig a success. Dutch said nuthin' at all. Benny seemed to be more entertained at the situation than he should've been and kept droppin' the keys back down in the bush, drunk as he wuz. Buford and Janie wuz in their own little world, only talkin' to each other and stealin' little smooches here and there. Lizzy wuz as still as Tammy and Patty; even Lydie wuz too pooped to say much more than, "Would you hurry up and find the damned keys, Daddy?"

When Benny pulled 'round in the rust-bucket Chevy, Flo went over the top sayin' how she hoped Buford and his sisters would stop by fer a visit. She held Buford's chin so's she could look straight in his eye and told 'im how her feelin's would be hurt if'n he didn't come by fer supper right soon and how he didn't need no invitation or nothin'. Buford wuz happy to oblige, jest as soon as he got back from Nashv'lle. He wuz fixin' to leave the next day.

Flo wuz tickled pink by his answer and knew deep down in her heart that it wouldn't be long b'fore her little girl would be livin' the good life. Alls she needed to do wuz git her hands on a clean, second-hand weddin' dress and a new pair of shoes, and she could be rid of one of her children in three months' time. Lizzy wuz her next thought, and she would be jest as happy to send Lizzy packin' to Knoxv'lle with Cooter after a shotgun weddin'. Lizzy wuz her least favorite daughter. The quicker and cheaper she could git rid of that one, the better.

# Chapter 19

The sun rose on the next day jest like it does ever' day, but on this particular mornin' Cooter wuz ready to make his move. He needed to close the deal with Lizzy on account of he had to be back at work the followin' Saturd'y. He practiced his speech a few times in the mirror, addin' hand motions to make it look more heart-felt. After breakfast Flo, Lizzy and one of the younger girls wuz out back chasin' the chickens that'd got loose from the coop. He said to Flo, "Do you thank you can spare Lizzy a minute? They's somethin' I've got on my mind to ask her."

B'fore Lizzy could manufacture a proper blush, Flo said, "Well, butter my butt and call me a biscuit! I'm sure I don't need Lizzy to help corral these damned chickens. Kitty and I can do it our ownselves. Come on Kitty, help me git the big brown one over yonder."

And she fluttered like one of her hens off to the other side of the chicken coop when Lizzy said, "No, Momma. I'll stay and help you. There ain't no way y'all can git that black one in there on yer own. She pecks at ever'body but me. Let me help you. Cooter can pitch in. He ain't got nuthin' to say that we all cain't hear. I'm a-comin' with ya."

"Don't you give me no lip, young lady. You stand right there and give Cooter the time o' day." And after a-lookin' at the pleadin' face of her daughter, she said through her teeth, "I'll suwanee, you could piss off the pope. If'n you don't stand right there and list'n to what Cooter has to say, I'm gonna tan yer hide with a switch and stomp a mudhole in yer back side, and I ain't foolin'."

Lizzy knew her Momma wuzn't whistlin' Dixie, so she decided to git it over quick, like pullin' off a Band-Aid. She set down on the bench under the willow tree, slumpin' her shoulders and waitin' fer it to be over with. Flo and Kitty ran off, and as soon as they wuz out'a earshot, Cooter started to talk.

"If'n I'm lyin', I'm dyin', Miss Lizzy. You're as humble as a church mouse, and it suits you jest fine. If'n you didn't play hard to git, I don't thank I would be so gosh-darned smitten with you. I'd rather do the chasin' than have a woman chasin' after me. I wuz glad to see yer Momma liked the idea of us havin' this little talk here, and I'm sure you know what I'm gittin' at. I ain't been hidin' my feelin's fer you, Lizzy. Pert near the first step I took into yer Daddy's house, I picked you out, special, to be my very own woman and the mother of my children. But b'fore I git the cart b'fore the horse, sweet darlin', maybe I should tell you my reasons fer wantin' to git hitched in the first place and why I came way in the boonies and over yonder to find me a good woman."

The idea of Cooter pourin' out his undyin' love fer her wuz nearly more 'n she could take. She had to put a finger to her mouth to keep laughter from bubblin' up out'a her. She couldn't stop 'im fer fear of laughin' in his face. He wuz jumpy as fart on a griddle.

"My reasons fer gittin' married are, first, I thank it's better fer a preacher, like my ownself, to git his milk from his own cow, if'n you know what I mean. Goin' 'bout the countryside hookin' up with women ain't the way a proper preacher oughtta act. Second, I thank havin' someone to sleep next to me and tend to my needs and warsh my clothes and fix my supper would add to my happiness. Also, and I thank I mentioned this b'fore, Miz M thanks it's the best thang fer me. Why, she wuz tellin' me so the Saturd'y b'fore I left to come over here. I wuz over to her house, playin' cards. She had me arrange a footstool fer DeeDee, and she said, 'Cooter, you must git yerself hitched. Every good preacher is married. You gotta pick jest the right kind of girl, you hear? Don't be brangin' no whores to the parsonage, fer my sake. She needs to be an active, useful sort of girl, not too big fer her britches. I don't care if'n she looks like somethin' the cat dragged in and the dog wouldn't eat, but she needs to know beyond the shadow of a doubt that she ain't got access to yer money. You're the bread-winner in the family, and she's jest hangin' in there like a tick on a dog's back. She needs to be grateful fer you. This is my advice. Find a woman like that jest as soon as you can and brang her back here. I'll visit her, and maybe I can convince her to do my laundry or weed the garden if'n she ain't got nuthin' else to do of the day.' Let me say, sweet Lizzy, that bein' noticed by a woman like Prudence Majestro is jest one of the small perks of gittin' hitched to me. She's real fancy, and they use cloth napkins at her house, and they have a generator so if'n the 'lectricity goes out, we can scoot over thar and visit 'til it comes back on.

"Now you should know that they's plenty of purty gals up to Knoxv'lle that would git on their knees ever' night of the week and twice on Sund'y to thank me fer marryin' 'em, but I'm makin' the offer to you on account of I own so much of yer Daddy's house, and if'n he kicks it any time soon (which I hope don't happen), I'd own ever'thang, and all y'all would be out on the street. This way if'n yer Daddy dies, the house will still be in the family and maybe I could jest charge 'em some kind of rent or somethin'. I don't wanna be at his funeral, like I said, I hope it don't happen fer a long, long time, and have ever'body givin' me dirty looks on account of I own ever'thang. And now I guess I come to the part where I declare my undyin' love fer you. I thank it's obvious you ain't got no money to bring to our marriage, but that's okay with me. They's no need fer you to worry yer purty little head 'bout that. I know when they's dead yer folks cain't even leave you a penny. I don't pay that no never-mind. and I'll never remind you that yer so poor you cain't afford to pay attention."

It wuz absolutely necessary fer Lizzy to stop 'im now.

"Whoa, slow down there, Cooter," she cried. "I ain't give you no answer yet. Let me git right at it without losin' no time. I appreciate yer kind offer and all, and I know what you're a-tryin' to do, but they's no way I can say yes to you."

"I seen this on one of them reality shows," replied Cooter as he scratched his head and a blizzard of dandruff landed on his shoulder. "All y'all girls turn a feller down the first time he asks. It's all the rage. I even seen one show where a girl said no half a dozen times b'fore she gave in. I want you to be sure that I ain't discouraged one whit, and I hope to watch you come down the aisle with a fistful of flowers b'fore too long."

"You'd argue with a stop sign, wouldn't you, Cooter? I ain't playin' games with you like the white trash on the tv. I'm bein' honest as the day is long. You couldn't pay me to marry you, and I am convinced that if'n I wuz the last woman on earth and you wuz the last man on earth, our species would die out. And yer sugar-Momma Miz M would no doubt find me unsuitable to do her laundry and pull her weeds. I'm the wrong person fer this job, honest Injun."

"Aw, come on, I'm sure Miz M would be happy as a clam at high tide with my union with a gal the likes of you, and I suwanee when I see her, I'm gonna tell her that even though yer country as a turnip green, yer the woman fer me."

"Boy, yer dug in like an Appalachian tick, ain't ya? There'll be no need fer you to put in a good word fer me with Miz M. I can thank fer my ownself, Cooter, and you best be believin' me the first time be'cuz I ain't wastin' my breath. I hope yer happier 'n a bumble bee in a honeysuckle patch, and I wish you more money 'n the Beverly Hillbillies, but my answer is still 'no.' By makin' yer proposal so sweet-like, you've done what you needed to do to end our family feud, and when the time comes, you can take the house and the property without no guilt or hard feelin's on my part. I thank we can shut the door on this little talk of ours."

Lizzy stood up as she wuz talkin' and would've hurried inside if'n Cooter hadn't started in again. "All right. All right. I hear what yer sayin',

Lizzy. But I want you to know that I'm hangin' in there like a hair in a biscuit, and the next time I ask ya, I'm hopin' fer a more favorable answer. I should tell ya that I feel like I've been chewed up and spit out, but I don't hold it against ya. Like I said b'fore, I know you girls like to say 'no' the first time you's asked and all, and now that the first 'no' is behind us, I'm feelin' good 'bout thangs."

"You must be dumb as a doorknob," cried Lizzy, "if'n anythang I jest said could be twisted 'round into an invitation to ask me to marry you again. I know you want what you want, but a man in hell wants a tall, cool drink of water, and he ain't gittin' that neither."

"Yakity, yakity, yak! I knows yer jest flappin' yer jaws, sweet cousin. I got reason to b'lieve yer jest messin' with me. First of all, I ain't worse lookin' 'n most of the fellers I've laid eyes on 'round these parts, plus I got a good thang goin' down in Knoxv'lle, if'n you know what I mean. Hells fire! If'n you wuz hitched to me, you might not have to work at a real job. I make a good livin', plus bein' connected with Miz M the way I am, and yer family's right fond of me. All these score points fer me. You should keep in mind that you ain't no great catch, and even though you clean up real nice, this could be the last time anyone asks you to get hitched. I'm jest sayin', Lizzy, you don't really brang nuthin' into a marriage except a nice ass and an extra pair of hands. So I knows deep down in my heart you ain't serious in yer rejection, and you wanna pull me along fer a while. That's all right."

"I don't know whether to scratch my watch or wind my butt, Cooter. Why would I wanna pull you along? Yer a good ol' boy, and I wouldn't play you like that. Why cain't you jest b'lieve what I'm sayin' to you? Like I said b'fore, I appreciate the offer, but they's no way in the world I can accept you. Ever' part of me says 'hell no.' I cain't say it any plainer. Don't thank of me as a girl a-tryin' to play you and pull you along. Thank of me as somebody in her right mind tellin' you the truth and nuthin' but the truth from her heart."

"Ain't you jest the cutest little thang!" he said. "You don't wanna look a gift-horse in the mouth. I thank yer parents might have somethin' to say 'bout all this."

Lizzy couldn't say nuthin' to someone as thick as a brick like Cooter, so she jest walked away shakin' her head. She decided that if'n he kept after her, she would go to her Daddy and give 'im a piece of her mind. She knew Benny could say 'no' in such a way as Cooter would wish he'd never asked in the first place.

# Chapter 20

Cooter didn't have to sit there alone fer long b'fore Flo hurried up the path by the chicken coop. There wuz no doubt she had watched the tail end of Cooter and Lizzy's conversation, and she slapped her knee as she congratulated 'im on his engagement. Cooter told her he wuz right pleased with what transpired, and went on to tell Flo chapter and verse of what had been said. When he got to the part 'bout Lizzy refusin' 'im, and him thankin' she wuz playin' hard to git, Flo had heard all she needed to hear. She didn't say nuthin' to Cooter, but she suspected her daughter wuzn't playin' the tomcat's kitten to increase his excitement when she'd finally give in.

"You can bet yer ass, Cooter," she said, "Lizzy will see the light of day or I'll string her up by her piggies from the laundry line. She must've put on her stupid head today. She's headstrong and foolish, that girl. I'll talk to her directly."

"Hold on jest one cotton-pickin' minute, Miss Flo," cried Cooter. "If'n she's so headstrong and foolish, she might not be the right girl fer me. I'm a-lookin' fer a woman who's gonna make me happy, not vex me. If'n she keeps on rejectin' me, maybe we shouldn't force her hand. I'm fearin' she could make my life miserable. Maybe she ain't work the buckshot it takes to shoot a fly off a horse's ass."

"Oh, Cooter! You didn't git my meanin'," said Flo all panicky. "Liz is only headstrong in situations like this. The rest of the time she's jest as pleasant as a meadow and twice as purty. I'll go to her Daddy, and we'll untangle this mess b'fore you can say 'the South shall rise again.'"

Flo didn't give 'im no time to say nuthin' else and bolted like a cannon shot to Benny who wuz lyin' down in their bedroom where he could be alone. "Oh Benny! I need yer help right now. You got to make Lizzy marry Cooter. She's sayin' she won't have 'im, and if'n you don't make her change her mind, he might could change his."

Benny raised up on one side and let out a fart. "I have no idea what yer sayin', Flo. What in the hell 'r you talkin' 'bout?"

"I'm talkin' 'bout Cooter and Lizzy. She says she won't git hitched to 'im, and now he's thankin' on changin' his mind and not wantin' her."

"What do you want me to do 'bout it, Flo?" he asked. "Seems hopeless to me."

"Talk at her, you dadburned fool! Tell her she has to marry 'im, or else."

"Tell her to come in here right now. I'll give her my two-cents worth."

Flo shouted at the top of her lungs fer Lizzy to come into the bedroom.

"Sit down here next to me on the bed, Sweet Pea," said her Daddy as she walked through the door. "I've got somethin' to say that's real important, now. Is it true that Cooter done offered his hand to you?" Lizzy said that it wuz. "All right then. And you told 'im flat out 'no?'"

"Yes, sir."

"Alrighty then. I got the picture. Yer Momma says you got to say 'yes.' Ain't that the case, Miss Flo?"

"If'n she don't, I never wanna lay eyes on her again so long as I live."

"You've got yerself in a pickle, honey. Today may be the last day you lay yer eyes on one of yer folks. Yer Momma won't see you again if'n you don't marry 'im, and I'll never see you again if'n you do."

Lizzy bit her lip to keep from smilin'. She thought she had the best Daddy who ever drew breath. But Flo, who thought she and her husband wuz on the same page, stood there catchin' flies with her open mouth.

"Are you three sheets to the wind?" she asked her husband. "You jest told me you wuz gonna say she had to marry Cooter or else."

"Flo, darlin'," said Benny, "Will you do me a favor? Let me do my own thankin' and git the hell out'a the bedroom so's I can finish my nap?"

Flo wuzn't 'bout to give up in surrender. She told Lizzy to straighten up and fly right, or she'd knock her teeth down her throat, and she'd have to spit 'em out single file. She demanded that Lizzy give up her little hissy fit and do what wuz right by her kin. Flo told her that if'n she didn't marry Cooter, she wouldn't speak to her if'n she met her in hell and Lizzy wuz carryin' an ice cube. Flo tried to pull Janie over to her side, but Janie wuzn't one to interfere. From time to time Lizzy said somethin' back to her mother fer the fun of it, but she never gave an inch.

In the meantime, Cooter wuz havin' himself a good sit down in the john, thankin' on what had happened. He thought too high on himself to thank she said 'no' be'cuz there wuz somethin' wrong with 'im, and even though he wuz low on account of the whole situation, he knew he'd be jest fine and dandy in spite of it all. He convinced himself he'd imagined any real feelin's b'tween the two of 'em and decided her Momma needed to leave her be.

While ever'thang wuz up in the air like it wuz with the family, Charlotte stopped by to visit a spell. She wuz stopped at the door by Lydie who told her what had been goin' on that mornin'. Charlotte couldn't say nuthin' b'fore Kitty ran up to her with the same story. They walked back to the kitchen where Flo wuz standin' there holdin' a fifth of Tennessee whiskey and an empty glass. Flo had already made good use of the glass and slurred as she asked Charlotte to help her make Lizzy marry Cooter. "Lord help us, Charlotte," she said chokin' back genuine tears. "Ain't nobody on my side. They treat me like shit 'round here, and nobody cares one lick 'bout what I thank."

Charlotte didn't have to answer Miss Flo on account of Lizzy and Janie walkin' in the kitchen at that very second.

"Lordy, Lordy! Here she comes," continued Flo holdin' on to the counter to keep the room from spinnin'. "She ain't even got a worry line, and here I stand with a whole face full of 'em. She acts like she didn't jest throw her en-tire family out on they's asses. But I tell you what, Miss Lizzy, if'n you go on refusin' men who wanna git hitched to ya, you'll never catch yerself a husband at all, and I ain't not sure what'll happen when yer Daddy is dead, and we ain't got nobody to support us. I know I won't be able to keep ya. I warn you, girl. I am done with you this very day. I told ya in front of yer Daddy, I'll never say a word to ya again, and if'n I'm lyin', I'm dyin'. You ain't worth my time of day, you ungrateful child. None of y'all are! I'm in a bad way 'bout this one. Nobody knows how I worry."

Her daughters listened to her slur this last part and didn't even try to pry the bottle of whiskey out'a her hand. She kept on talkin', but they could only understand half of what she said 'til Cooter came in the room standin' straight as a ram-rod. She pointed to her girls with an unsteady hand, and said, "All y'all need to jest git on out'a here so's I can have a word or two with Cooter, here."

Lizzy backed out'a the room quietly, and Janie and Kitty follered her lead, but Lydie stood her ground, wanting to be a fly on the wall. Flo started slobberin', "Oh! Cooter!"

"Ain't Flo, bless yer pea-pickin' little heart," he replied. "Let's jest pretend none of this ever happened. You can lead a horse to water, but you cain't make her drink. I got no hard feelin's against yer daughter, even though she don't want the nice home and comfortable livin' I offered her. I begin to thank me and her 'r like oil and water. We don't mix. I don't mean you or Benny or none of yer girls no disrespect, Ain't Flo, but I feel like I've been drawn through a knothole backwards, and I got no inclination to marry Lizzy no more. I've got to take Miss Lizzy at her word, ma'am. You know I mean well. My plan has always been to find a good hardworkin' woman to hook up with. I hope yer feelin's ain't too hurt, but I thank it's best if'n I look outside this house movin' forward.

# Chapter 21

The talk 'bout Cooter's marriage proposal wuz jest 'bout over, and Lizzy only had to deal with the lingerin' comments from her mother. As fer ol' Cooter, he didn't seem down in the mouth 'bout bein' rejected. He spent most of his time a-tryin' to avoid Lizzy as much as possible and switched his attention over to Charlotte fer the rest of the day. She wuz right sweet to listen to 'im and keep 'im company, and Lizzy wuz 'specially relieved.

The next day Flo wuz jest as disagreeable as she wuz the day b'fore, and Cooter kept his nose in the air with pride. Lizzy wuz hopin' his hurt feelin's would send 'im packin' sooner than later, but he stayed on. He'd planned to stay 'til Saturd'y, and he wuzn't plannin' on leavin' 'til Saturd'y. That wuz that.

After breakfast, the girls walked on down to the fair grounds to see if'n Joe wuz back from his trip. Turnin' a corner they nearly ran smack-dab into 'im, and he tagged along as they walked to Ain't Fern's house. He heard all of their moanin' and groanin' 'bout him missin' the dance at Buford's, and to Lizzy he said, right out, that skippin' the party wuz his own doin'.

"I reckoned," he said, "as Buford's party wuz gittin' closer, I'd better make myself scarce so's I wouldn't run into Dutch. Bein' in the same room at the same shin-dig as him might not end up so well. I'd have hated to smack 'im upside the head and ruin ever'body's good time."

She thought the better of 'im fer what he said, and he and another soldier walked Lizzy and her sisters all the way back home. As they walked, Joe flirted and once grabbed her 'round the waist and ran his thumb up under her shirt along the waistband of her shorts, sendin' chills up and down her back. She could not b'lieve Joe wuz goin' out'a his way and walkin' 'em home, and she wuz hopin' to show 'im off to her Momma and Daddy when they got back to the house.

They hadn't been back five minutes when the phone rang. They waited to make sure it wuzn't a bill collector then checked the message, which wuz from Tammy. Janie listened to it, then listened again. Lizzy could tell somethin' wuz wrong when Janie tried to join back in with the rest of 'em, but Janie wuzn't willin' to say nuthin' 'til the fellers had left.

Back in the lean-to, Janie spilled her guts to Lizzy. "It wuz Tammy on the phone. I'm jest beside myself. All of 'em, Tammy, Patty, Harley, Dutch and Buford, have all left fer Nashv'lle. She said they ain't got no plans to come back 'round here again. They's all goin' to stay in town at a place owned by Harley's kin. She said she don't regret nuthin' but leavin' my friendship behind, and she wants to stay in touch through email or some such thang."

Lizzy listened to ever'thang she said, but she wuzn't believin' none of it. "If'n you didn't have bad luck, I'll suwanee you wouldn't have no luck at all. He'll be back, Janie. He prob'ly went up to Nashv'lle to pick you out a genuine diamond ring. Buford will be back directly. I'm sure of it."

"Tammy said not a one of 'em will be back down here this winter. She said Buford had business in town, and they all jest up and decided to go with 'im. She wished me a Merry Christmas of all thangs, Lizzy! And she said somethin' 'bout me havin' a bunch of fellers lined up to be my beau. He ain't comin' back this winter."

"She don't want 'im to, Janie. She's fixin' to keep 'im away."

"Why on God's green earth would she wanna do that? He's a grown man. I do b'lieve he can make his own dad-gummed decisions. Plus, there's one more thang I ain't told you. Tammy says Dutch is itchin' to see his sister, Suzanna. Them girls thank she's so purty and smart, and they jest love her to pieces. Tammy says they's a hopin' to call her 'sister' b'fore long. She says Buford's always had his eye on her, and now that they'll be thrown t'gether all the time, she thanks it's a done deal. Them girls don't want me in their family, and if'n they's brother wuz partial to me, they wouldn't have said all they did 'bout Suzanna. What do you thank on it, Lizzy?"

"Here's my take on it. Tammy sees her brother moonin' over you, and she wants 'im to git hitched to Suzanna. She follers 'im to Nashv'lle, hopin' to keep 'im there and spins a yarn 'bout 'im not bein' sweet on you."

Janie shook her head.

"You had oughtta b'lieve me. Not a soul who's laid eyes on y'all can say that he ain't sweet on ya. Tammy cain't, neither. If'n she'd looked at Dutch and seen half as much love in his eyes fer her, she would've already changed her name and bought her weddin' gown. Here's the deal. We ain't rich or fine enough fer 'em, and she's anxious to git Suzanna fer her brother to give Dutch the hint that there had oughtta be another weddin' in the family. She ain't no simpleton. If'n DeeDee Majestro wuz out'a the way, it might could happen. You cain't b'lieve that jest be'cuz Tammy says somethin' 'bout Buford's feelin's, that it plum near erases the past few weeks you've spent with 'im."

"The diff'rence is, you thank Miss Tammy is a thumpin' gizzard, and she ain't never been nuthin' but nice to me. She cain't lie to my face any more 'n she could lie to her own."

"You never thank bad on nobody. Go ahead, thank she's a saint."

"Kin is kin. Even if'n Buford wuz to drive up right now in that shiny red pickup of his and git down on one knee, I don't thank I could say yes knowin' his kin wuz against it. I don't wanna be fightin' in-laws all my days."

"You got to take care of yer ownself, and stop frettin' 'bout his sisters."

"If'n he ain't comin' back anytime soon, I best should jest give up on anythang comin' of this. He might could run into one of 'em country music stars up in Nashv'lle and fall head over heels. Anythang can happen in a big city like that."

Lizzy hated the thought that Buford might not come back fer the winter. She wuz keen on the idea it wuz all Tammy's doin', and she wuz right sure Buford had a mind of his own. She spoke her mind to Janie, and soon Janie wuz hopin' fer Buford's speedy return.

The girls decided to keep most of the story from Flo and jest told her that he'd gone to Nashv'lle fer a spell. She wuzn't short on her moanin's and declared that when he came back, she wuz gonna invite 'im over to supper again, and this time put out the good plates and her prize-winnin' potato salad.

# Chapter 22

Benny and Billy Lucas dug a pit in the back yard and filled it with charcoal to slow roast one of Billy's prize pigs. Charlotte and Cooter sat out back on lawn chairs and peeled taters while the fellers worked on the hog. Lizzy wuz quick to thank her when she had a chance. "Yer keepin' Cooter in a good mood, Charlotte. I'm much obliged." Charlotte wuz quick to tell her friend she wuz happy to be useful. But Charlotte's usefulness went above and beyond the call of friendship. She wuz makin' sure Cooter wuzn't jest fallin' out'a love with Lizzy, but that he wuz fallin' in love with her ownself. Truth be told, Charlotte thought if'n Cooter didn't have to leave the next mornin' he wuz sure to propose. Her women's wiles must've been sharp on account of that next mornin' b'fore the rooster crowed, he sneaked out'a Benny's house and over to the Lucas's house to throw himself at her feet. He didn't let nobody in on his scheme, though, since his most recent proposal had fallen flat as a fritter.

Charlotte seen 'im first from the window, sneakin' through the bushes. She met 'im out by the back stoop, and in as much time as Cooter's long speeches would allow, they wuz engaged. He told her to name the day of their weddin'. He wuz jest so pleased with himself. Charlotte wuz thankin' she better strike while the iron wuz hot. This wuz her first and last marriage proposal. She wuz sick and tired of bein' the only old maid in the neighborhood, and she didn't care when she got her a husband, jest so's long as she got one and a house to boot.

Billy and LuLu soon learned the good news, and they wuz happier 'n a Momma bird in a worm farm. LuLu started calculatin' how long Benny would live, what with his eatin' habits and lack of exercise, and Billy told ol' Coot he should move in b'fore Benny wuz cold in the ground so's they could be next door neighbors. All the fat little Lucases wobbled about in celebration, and the younger girls started callin' out dibs on Charlotte's part of the bedroom they all shared t'gether. Charlotte wuz quiet as a church mouse. She had made her bed, and now she had to lay down in it. She wuz all right with it. Cooter wuz jest 'bout as sharp as a marble and not so easy to git on with. He really irked her most of the time, and he couldn't possibly be as head over heels as he said he wuz. But he would be her man, and that's all she ever wanted. A good man with a steady income and a home of her own. She so much resembled a stork that she had given up hope of ever gittin' herself hitched, so Cooter would do jest fine.

Charlotte would've rather scraped dead critters off the back stoop than tell Lizzy 'bout it, but she knew she had to give the news her ownself. Lizzy might could be mad or tell her it wuz a stupid thang to do, so she told

Cooter not to whisper a word of it back at Benny's house 'til she had a chance to spill the beans first. When he crept back through the bushes, the whole house wuz awake, and he had to dodge quite a few questions as to where he'd been out so early of the mornin'. He wanted to stand up and shout his good news from the rooftop, but showin' an unbelievable amount of self control, he kept his big mouth shut.

Since Cooter wuz leavin' b'fore dawn the next day, he said his goodbyes to his cousins the night b'fore. Flo wuz all politeness and told 'im she hoped he wouldn't be a stranger and come back soon.

"Ain't Flo," he said, "yer invitation is jest what I wuz a-hopin' fer. You can be sure as shootin' that I'll be back jest as soon as possible."

They wuz all slack-jawed, and Benny hoped it would be a long time, a real, real long time b'fore Cooter would come back. He said, "You wouldn't wanna ruffle Miz M's feathers on our account."

"No sir," answered Cooter. "I thank you kindly. I wouldn't dare do nuthin' that would stir up Miz M."

"I'd rather you stay at home than piss her off by comin' down here. Don't worry 'bout our feelin's a bit. We'll be right as rain."

"Ain't you kind, Uncle Benny! I'm gonna sit down the minute I git home and write an honest-to-goodness thank-you letter to let all y'all know how much I 'preciate yer hospitality. Now I best go and say so-long to my purty little cousins, including Lizzy."

Each of the girls gave 'im limp hugs, and ever' one of 'em wuz surprised at his sayin' he would be back lickety-split. Flo thought he wuz gonna come after one of her younger daughters and that Mary might be talked into it.

In her usual way Mary said, "I could be prevailed to accept him. I rate his abilities much higher than any of you here; there is a solidity in his reflections that often strikes me, and though he is by no means as clever as myself, I think that if encouraged to read and improve himself by such an example as mine, Cooter might become a very agreeable companion."

But the next mornin' all of Flo's hopes wuz dashed to the dirt when Charlotte came over to tell Lizzy 'bout her engagement. She'd a hunch that Cooter wuz changin' his tune in favor of Charlotte, but that her friend would opt to be hitched to Coot fer the rest of her live-long days, well, the thought didn't cross her head, not once. She hollered, "Engaged to Cooter! Hell's bells, Charlotte, what wuz you thankin'?"

Charlotte told her story, jest as calm as a sunny day, though she wuz a tiny bit nervous, wonderin' what Lizzy would say next. "Why 'r you so surprised, Lizzy? Do you thank Cooter cain't git anybody since he couldn't git you?"

Lizzy took a deep breath and said she'd throw one hell of a bachelorette party with strippers and fruity drinks with umbrellas and the whole nine-yards. She wanted her friend to be happy.

"I know yer shocked, Liz. Not two damned days ago Coot wuz proposin' to you and all. When you set down to thank on it, I hope you'll be satisfied with what I done. I ain't romantic like you. I never wuz. I jest want a home of my own where I don't have to rear the babies my Momma keeps poppin' out all the time. When you thank on Cooter's connections and his reg'lar job, I thank I can be as happy with him as any feller. At least I know what I'm gittin' myself into."

Lizzy answered, "I guess you do," and after an awkward pause, they went back in to the rest of the family. Charlotte left b'fore long, and Lizzy wuz quiet fer a peace, a-tryin' to wrap her head 'round the choice her friend had jest made. Cooter wuz such a weird feller. It wuzn't so bad that he'd made two marriage proposals in the space of three days. What wuz worse wuz one of his proposals had been accepted. She always knew she and Charlotte had diff'rent ideas 'bout marriage, but Lizzy never thought Charlotte would marry a feller fer what wuz in his wallet. It wuz bad her friend had sunk so low, but worse that she had traded in ever' chance of bein' happy. Now that wuz hard fer Lizzy to swaller.

# Chapter 23

Lizzy sat on the couch watchin' her mother trim her toenails, thankin' on what Charlotte had said and wonderin' if'n she should spill the beans or jest keep her big mouth shut when Billy Lucas walked right in like he owned the place. Charlotte had sent 'im to tell ever'body her big news. He wuz grinnin' so big you could see the chaw in his cheek, and he told 'em how happy he wuz that they wuz gonna be kin to one another. He wuz right in the middle of pattin' himself on the back when Flo interrupted, sayin' he had got his wires crossed. Lydie, who had no filter on her mouth whatsoever shouted, "Good Lord Almighty! What in the hell have you been smokin', Billy? Ain't you aware that Cooter wants to marry Lizzy?"

Anybody else on the planet would've been flustered beyond belief, but Billy held his own. He told 'em he wuz bein' honest as the day is long, and then he listened as the girls argued with 'im.

Lizzy stood up, flicked a stray toenail from her knee, and told 'em that Billy wuzn't drunk or high. He wuz tellin' the God's honest truth, and Charlotte had told her as much that very mornin'. She gave Billy a big bear hug follered by much back pattin' to try to shut the flappin' mouths of her family. Janie joined in, talkin' of Charlotte's future happiness and Cooter's good manners.

The cat had got Flo's tongue, and she couldn't say much while Billy wuz there, but the minute he left her lips started spewin' evil, and they couldn't be stopped. She insisted he couldn't help himself since he wuz dumber 'n a bag full of hammers, and his daughter wuz uglier than the northbound end of a southbound donkey. She said she hated Billy Lucas so much that she wouldn't piss down his ass if'n his guts wuz on fire. Her reasons fer not believin' 'im wuz numbered. First, he wuz the biggest liar she'd ever known. Second, the Lucases prob'ly put poor Cooter under some kind of black magic spell or somethin'. Third, She wuz sure as shootin' those two would never be happy t'gether. And fourth, the match could be called off jest as fast as could be. Flo wuz sure as she could be that Lizzy wuz to blame fer the whole situation, and she, her ownself, wuz the person who wuz goin' to suffer the most. It wuz these last two feelin's Flo kept repeatin' all day to whoever would listen. Nuthin' could console her fer days. A month of Sund'ys passed b'fore she could mention LuLu or Billy without sayin' somethin' bad 'bout 'em and longer 'n that b'fore she could forgive Charlotte.

Benny didn't give a shit 'bout the whole situation. He wuz right pleased Charlotte had landed herself a man. She always freaked Benny out with her long neck and popeyes. He'd once commented that her teeth wuz so buck, she could eat corn right off the cob through a chain-link fence. If'n she wanted to git hitched to Cooter, she wuz dumber 'n he ever gave her credit fer.

LuLu stumbled 'round drunk on whatever she could git her hands on. Celebratin' the idea of riddin' herself of one of her children. She visited Flo more often 'n usual to brag on her good fortune, and Flo gave her a look that would kill the smile right off somebody sober.

Lizzy and Charlotte didn't talk much at that point. Lizzy didn't thank they could ever be as close as they used to be, and she hung out more with Janie than b'fore. Blood's thicker 'n water, it seems. Ever' day they didn't hear from Buford brought a new worry line on Janie's face. She had tried to call Tammy several times, but they wuz screenin' their calls fer sure. She jumped a mile ever' time the phone rang, hopin' it wuz Tammy or Patty callin' her back.

A thank-you note from Cooter soon arrived, and ever' inch of the card wuz covered in his tiny little chicken scratches dronin' on and on 'bout his plans fer happiness with their beautiful neighbor. At the end he told 'em he would be back in a couple of weeks since Miz M wuz agreeable to his choice of gals and wanted 'im to git himself hitched right away.

Cooter's next visit wuzn't looked on too well by the folks in Benny's house. Flo's high-pitched whine could be heard clear up the holler as she complained 'bout havin' to move her own kids around so's to make room fer 'im when the Lucases should be takin' 'im in over thar. She wuz gonna have to warsh the sheets and clean the room on his account. She claimed she wuzn't feelin' well, and she jest knew he would sneak Charlotte over thar in the night, and they'd be doin' the nasty right there in her own house. When she wuzn't worried 'bout Cooter and Charlotte rollin' 'round on her good sheets, she worked herself up into a tizzy over Buford bein' gone so long.

Janie and Lizzy couldn't bear to listen to her squeak on 'bout the house, and ever' day that ended without a note or a phone call from Buford made life worse. When folks down by the fair grounds started sayin' Buford and them folks wouldn't be back b'fore winter, Flo wuz always correctin' 'em and callin' 'em liars. Even Lizzy started fearin' Buford's sisters could keep 'im away, but she never would say a word of her suspicion to Janie, who wuz startin' to break into the comfort food more often 'n usual. Janie wuz facin' a triple whammy-- Buford's two bitch sisters and Dutch all pullin' 'im in the same direction. And with 'im in a big city with Suzanna on his knee, he might could forgit 'bout his feelin's fer Janie.

Janie wuz purty good at hidin' her worries 'bout Buford, so's she looked like it wuzn't botherin' her much. Flo, on the other hand, didn't have no filter whatsoever, and nary an hour passed without her spewin' her impatience fer 'im to come back to their little town where, no doubt, he belonged. She started threatenin' to call 'im on the phone or send 'im a letter tellin' 'im exactly what she thought of 'im fer leavin' so long. It wuz all Janie could do to tolerate her Momma.

Cooter showed up right on time the day he promised, but he wuz 'bout as welcome as a pregnant stray dog that rolled 'round in somethin' dead and wuz covered with flies. He wuz too love drunk to notice and spent most of his time a-tryin' to cop a feel with his sweetheart as she politely shoo'ed his wanderin' hands away. He spent his days at the neighbors and returned at night with his hair all a mess and havin' to spend quite a while in the shower, runnin' out the hot water and emptyin' out all the shampoo.

Flo wuz beside herself. Any mention of the weddin' threw her into a state, and it wuz all ever'body in town wuz talkin' 'bout. She couldn't bear the sight of Charlotte and couldn't help imaginin' Charlotte turnin' 'em all out on their asses in the street. When Charlotte stopped by fer a visit, Flo wuz jest sure she wuz there to measure fer new curtains, and when she whispered in Cooter's ear, Flo knew beyond a shadow of a doubt they wuz plannin' to tear out the forsythia Flo, herself, had planted. She complained to Benny when they wuz in bed that night.

"Benny, I jest don't know what we're gonna do. That awful Charlotte Lucas will be livin' in this house, and we'll be homeless. I'll be settin' there on the sofa, cryin' my eyes out be'cuz yer dead, and she'll come over and toss out my Kleenex on the road out yonder and tell me to git out'a my own house. How will I bear it?"

"Git a hold of yerself, woman. I ain't gonna be dead fer a long time. Why is ever'body always killin' me off?"

He wuzn't makin' her feel any better, so she went on, "I cain't bear the thought of it. This is our home. Why cain't you pay Cooter back the money you owe 'im?"

"You cain't git blood from a turnip, Miss Flo," he said, then rolled over, let out a fart and started snorin'.

# Chapter 24

Another call from Tammy sealed the deal. There wuzn't no doubt that Buford and his relations wuz stayin' in Nashv'lle fer the winter. She did have the raisin' to say Buford wuz all torn up on account of he didn't git to say "so long" to his new friends.

Janie knew all her hopes wuz dashed like a cardboard box full of baby kittens on the highway, and it made her sick to hear Tammy go on 'bout how plum perfect Suzanna wuz and how close they wuz gittin' to be. She said she wuz sure 'nuff 'bout Buford's feelin's toward Suzanna that she'd already been to Kohl's twice a-lookin' fer a dress to wear fer the weddin'.

Lizzy's face looked like she wuz eatin' a persimmon as Janie told her the story. On the one hand, she wuz worried on account of her sister, but on the other, she wuz mad as a hornet's nest at Tammy and the rest of 'em. Lizzy didn't pay no nevermind to Tammy's insistin' that Buford and Suzanna wuz tight. She knew beyond the shadow of a doubt that Buford wuz smitten with Janie, but she wuz pissed he wuz lettin' his sisters push 'im 'round like some kind of a wussy. Maybe Janie wuz playin' too coy-like and didn't let 'im know how she felt. She wuzn't one of them girls who go eatin' dinner b'fore she's said grace, if'n you know what I'm talkin' 'bout. She'd been out back in the hay field a couple of times with the boys, but she wuzn't givin' out no milk fer free. Maybe she should'a let 'im git to second base so's he would know she liked 'im.

A couple of days passed b'fore Janie could work up the nerve to talk to Lizzy 'bout it, and one day Flo had been on her usual tirade 'bout Buford b'fore she left the girls to scrub the rust stains out'a the bathtub and clean the toilet. "Momma could make a preacher so mad he'd kick in a stained glass window," Janie said with her elbows deep in toilet water." I wish she'd jest shut her trap 'bout Buford. I cain't hardly stand to hear it. Her ever' word is like somebody shootin' bullets through my heart. I know she's gonna forgit 'bout 'im b'fore long, but I wish she'd hurry up."

Lizzy pushed a stray hair back from her eyes and kept scrubbin' at the rust stain in the tub.

"You thank I cain't forgit 'im? He wuz the best thang that ever happened to me, but I can see it fer what it wuz: a summer fling. I got nuthin' to hope fer. I don't hold no grudges against 'im. He didn't make me no promises. I'll git over 'im, come hell or high water, I will." She cleared her throat. "I'm torn up like a New Jersey train wreck, but it's my own doin'. If'n wishes wuz dollars, I'd be a millionaire, but that ain't gonna make a difference. The situation with Buford is like a ball in high weeds, hopeless. The sooner I git over it, the better."

"Aw, Janie!" said Lizzy. "Bless yer pea-pickin' little heart. You're jest as sweet as an angel and twice as good."

Janie started to stop her, but Lizzy went on. "I won't tell you the world ain't coated with candy. You jest thank well on ever'body. In my way of thankin', the world is covered in dog shit, and ever' day I live, I b'lieve it more. You cain't depend on nobody fer nothin'. It's like somethin' knocked the sense out'a folks. Two thangs have happened recently that I cain't explain. I plan to keep mum on one of 'em, and the other is Charlotte and Cooter. Lawsy mercy! I cain't figure that one out to beat the band."

"Liz, don't spoil yer thoughts like that. You'll poison yer mind. Folks is all diff'rent. Look at Cooter. He's all respectable-like with a good job. And Charlotte, she's been clippin' coupons and runnin' a tight ship next door since she wuz knee-high to a grasshopper. Her marriage is a chance fer her to escape that house over yonder. She's twenty-seven years old and shares a bed with three fat little sisters. Imagine what it would be like to have her own house and have to share a bed with jest one other person."

"Have mercy, Janie. Don't paint me a picture of that. Sheesh! Nobody can persuade me Charlotte likes 'im fer more 'n his steady paycheck. If'n she wuz really hot fer 'im, I would puke and then never talk to her again in all my days. Cooter's full of himself and stuck up and dumb as a stick. You know he is. Anybody who marries 'im has to be out'a her mind or a gold digger. I thank we both know which Charlotte is."

"Don't be so hard on Charlotte or Cooter," replied Janie. "They cain't help it. And what wuz it you wuz sayin' 'bout two thangs you cain't explain? You need to jest drop the thought that Buford is to blame fer my wet pillow at night. He didn't do nuthin' on purpose to hurt me. I won't deny that he wuz all over me like flies on a gut wagon, but you know as well as I do that boys 'r like that. He didn't mean nuthin' by it."

"I don't thank Buford had anythang to do with it, Janie. But other folks did, and I ain't gonna go on and on 'bout it be'cuz you's friends with them girls, and you wouldn't b'lieve me anyhow."

"You really thank his sisters boss 'im 'round?"

"Yep. And his good buddy Dutch does it too."

"There ain't no way. Why would they do such a thang? If'n they really care 'bout 'im, they should want 'im to be happy."

"That's where you're wrong, Janie. They want 'im to be rich and important, and there's one easy way to git it, marry into it."

"There ain't no doubt they want 'im to git hitched to Suzanna. But they've know'd her fer a long time, way longer than they've know'd me. But hell, why should he do what they want 'im to do? If'n we had a brother, I cain't imagine a situation where I'd tell 'im who he can marry and who he cain't. I mean, if'n she wuz a real skank, and ever'body know'd it, then maybe, but if'n his mind wuz set, I don't thank there's nuthin' we could do to stop 'im. That's what I'm a-tryin' to say. If'n Buford had his mind set on me, then his sisters couldn't have changed it, I don't reckon. I'm down right embarrassed that I wuz so sure of myself 'round 'im. I don't fault 'im or nuthin'. I gotta try to move on. Let's jest let it be."

Lizzy made a pact with her ownself to zip her lip 'bout Buford 'round Janie. Flo didn't make no such pact with herself and complained 'bout 'im 'round the clock. Her daughter tried to convince her that they wuzn't nuthin' but a summer fling, and it wuz over, but though Flo said it wuz possible, she moaned 'bout it ever' day anyway. Flo could be heard whistlin' at the dishwater, tellin' herself Buford would be back 'round when it warmed up.

Benny thought a girl oughtta have some experience b'fore she married herself off. One day he said to Lizzy, "Looks like yer sister's gone out and got her heart broke. What is it they say? It's better to git yer heart broke 'n to never git yer heart broke at all? Anyway, it gives her somethin' to thank on. I'm guessin' it's yer turn. They's fellers enough down to the fair grounds to break all the hearts in town. I thank Joe Wickham is nice enough, and he could really put a hurt on yer heart if'n you let 'im."

"I don't know 'bout that, Daddy," she replied.

"Well, I take comfort knowin' that whoever breaks yer heart, yer Momma will make the most of it."

Joe Wickham wuz 'round Benny's house more often 'n not, and it seemed to perk up the family and prevent too much snifflin'. He told ever'body who would listen 'bout how Dutch'd treated 'im. Ever'body wuz talkin' on it, and they all agreed they hated Dutch b'fore Joe had told his tale. Janie and her heart of gold always made excuses fer Dutch, but ever'body else wuz ready to hang 'im up in the oak tree the next time they laid eyes on 'im.

Chapter 25

After a week of moonin' and smoochin' with Charlotte, Cooter had to git on back home to preach a sermon and check in with Miz M, and bury a man. Leavin' wuzn't as tough as he thought it'd be. Charlotte wuzn't givin' away any milk fer free b'fore the weddin', and Cooter needed a break from their make-out sessions. The next time he laid eyes on his woman, they'd be gittin' hitched, and she wouldn't be able to git 'im off of her after that. He said "so long" to his cousins, and promised Benny another thank-you note.

On Mond'y who should pull up out front of Benny's house but Flo's brother Guthrie and his wife Matilda (Tildie) in a shiny green RV with a pull-out awnin'. They wuz plannin' to spend Christmas with Flo, Benny and the girls. As you might recall, Guthrie did well fer himself, sellin' appliances in Nashv'lle. He wuz smart as a tack and had more sense than his sisters Fern and Flo. Buford's sisters wouldn't have b'lieved 'im if'n they had seen 'im with their own eyes. He might live a stone's throw from his warehouse, but Guthrie wuz a good man, and he knew how to b'have in company. Tildie, who wuz a few years younger 'n Fern and Flo, wuz friendly and sassy, and she had it goin' on upstairs. All the girls jest loved her to pieces on account of she wuz always brangin' presents. Janie and Lizzy had a special place in their hearts fer Tildie, 'cuz she let 'em come stay with her in Nashv'lle from time to time.

Of course, the first thang Tildie did wuz start a-carryin' presents out'a the belly of the RV and tellin' the girls 'bout all the movie stars she'd seen in Nashv'lle. When she'd stopped to take a breath, Flo started in with all her grumblin' and complainin' 'bout how she'd had two daughters all but married off, but nuthin' ever came of it.

"I ain't blamin' Janie," she said. "She would've snatched up Buford if'n she could. But Lizzy, oh my word, she could've been a preacher's wife in a snap if'n she wuzn't so stubborn. He proposed to her right out there in the yard, and she flat out told 'im 'no.' And now LuLu Lucas is gonna have a daughter out'a the house b'fore I do, and her kin is gonna own this house when Benny dies. Them Lucases 'r slick as a school marm's leg. They'll take whatever they can git. I ain't talkin' out both sides of my mouth. I'm jest as nervous as a whore in church 'bout 'em takin' over my house. They don't thank on nobody but their ownselves. I'm jest so glad y'all thought to come down fer Christmas."

Ain't Tildie had heard it all b'fore since Lizzy and Janie kept in touch with her. She managed to change the subject right quick.

When she wuz alone with Lizzy later, she said, "That Buford seemed like the guy fer Janie. I'm so sorry it didn't work out fer her. This kind of thang happens all the time. A young feller like Buford falls fer a purty little thang like Janie and jest as soon forgits her."

"Yep, Ain't Tildie, I know it happens all the time, but that don't console Janie none. He ain't forgot her on accident. He had some help in that department. He wuz over the moon 'bout her, and his friend and relations dragged 'im away."

"Sayin' somebody is 'over the moon' don't tell the whole story, Lizzy. You can be over the moon 'bout somebody's peach cobbler. How far 'over the moon' wuz Buford fer Janie?"

"Let's jest say he didn't have eyes fer nobody but Janie. He ignored other folks when she wuz 'round. Ever' time they seen each other, it got worse. He ignored his own guests at his own party so's he didn't have to leave her side. I spoke to 'im twice and he didn't answer me, didn't even grunt. There wuzn't nobody else in the world fer Buford exceptin' my sister."

"Poor Janie! It does sound like he wuz hers fer the takin'. She's not one to git over this easy. It should've happened to you on account of you would've turned it into some big joke. Do you thank she'd wanna go back with us after Christmas? Maybe a change of scenery would do her good."

Lizzy thought it wuz a right fine idea and knew Janie would like it too.

"I hope she don't come with us hopin' I can hook her back up with Buford. We travel in diff'rent circles 'n he does up in Nashv'lle, and we never go out to dinner less'n it's to Bob Evans after church on Sund'y. They prob'ly wouldn't cross paths less'n he came to our place a-lookin' fer her."

"Well, that ain't gonna happen. Buford is plum hog tied by his friend, Dutch, who'd rather be run over by a coal truck than let his buddy be anywhere near Janie. Plus, Dutch wouldn't go to yer end of town if'n somebody paid 'im. Buford follers Dutch like a prize dog. He won't go no where Dutch won't go."

"That's jest fine by me. I hope they don't cross paths at all. What 'bout his sister? Doesn't Janie keep in touch with her? What if'n she calls?"

"She ain't gonna call."

Even though Lizzy felt sure Tammy wouldn't call and Buford wouldn't go out at night without Dutch, she thought there wuz hope fer Janie to see 'im. If'n he knew she wuz in town, maybe Buford would start thankin' 'bout her again. And if'n they ran into each other by accident, she wuz jest so cute, he couldn't help but fall head over heels fer her again.

When she heard the news, Janie hugged her Ain't Tildie and told her she'd love to come spend time with her in Nashv'lle. She said she didn't hope to see Buford, but maybe she and Tammy could git t'gether fer lunch somewhere.

Guthrie and Tildie stayed all of Christmas week with Benny and his kin. B'tween the Lucases, Fern and Phil and all the parties, they stayed busy as beavers ever' minute of the day. Flo made sure there wuz always somethin' to do and somewhere to go. When they ate supper at home, she made sure some of the soldiers wuz included, and Joe Wickham wuz always one of the boys she invited. Tildie watched Lizzy and Joe as they flirted and whispered to each other. She could tell they wuzn't rollin' in the hay, but she could tell they wuz sweet on each other, and it made her worry. She could tell he wuz a bad egg and decided to talk to Lizzy 'bout 'im b'fore she left. Lizzy needed to high-tail it away from that one.

B'fore gettin' hitched to Guthrie, Tildie lived in Kentucky near to the farm where Joe Wickham wuz raised. She didn't know the Wickhams, but they had folks they knew in common. She hadn't been 'round them parts in a while, but Joe might could fill her in on the local gossip seein' as how he'd been by there since she had.

Tildie wuz familiar with Pembrook Farm and had heard of Dutch's Daddy, Junior, by what other folks had said. She decided to talk to Joe 'bout the farm and Junior, two subjects they could talk 'bout fer hours. They swapped stories fer a time, and then Joe started in on his long sad tale 'bout how Dutch had ruined his life. Tildie tried to remember gossip from back in the day that would paint Dutch with mud and settled on the thought that somebody had once said Junior's boy wuz proud and 'bout as useful as a steerin' wheel on a mule.

# Chapter 26

Tildie told Lizzy to put on the brakes with Joe the first chance she got. "You're too smart to stay away from a boy jest be'cuz a body tells you to, so I'm jest gonna speak my mind. You seriously need to watch out fer Joe Wickham. He seems like a nice enough guy, but he's got a dark side, plus I don't thank he can afford his own rent. You can do better 'n him. Don't sell yerself short. You have sense, and we all expect you to use it. Don't go gittin' pregnant. Now ain't the time to disappoint yer Daddy."

"Law, Ain't Tildie! You don't need to worry 'bout me. I can take care of my ownself and Joe Wickham, too. He ain't gonna fall in love with me if'n I can keep 'im from it."

"Quit jokin' 'round, Lizzy. I'm bein' serious."

"I'm sorry, Ain't Tildie. I'm jest flirtin' with Joe, but I must say he is one fine-lookin' feller, and my Daddy likes 'im. I see what yer sayin' though. A girl can fall in love with a rich man jest as easy as she can fall in love with a poor man. I promise I'll be on my guard when I'm 'round 'im. With fellers like him, they's jest so charmin'. It's hard fer a girl to use her head. I tell you the truth, Tildie. I'll take it slow, I promise."

No sooner had the RV rolled out'a the driveway with Uncle Guthrie, Ain't Tildie and Janie than Cooter wuz back, but this time he stayed with Billy and LuLu, so Flo didn't have much to complain 'bout. Charlotte and Cooter'd planned to head on down to the courthouse on Thursd'y mornin' to seal the deal, and she stopped by Benny's to say goodbye on Wednesd'y night. Flo couldn't hardly look in her general direction and didn't squeak out one word of congratulations or nothin'. Lizzy wuz ashamed of her Momma and pulled Charlotte outside.

As they walked down the front steps t'gether, Charlotte said, "I hope you'll keep in touch, Liz."

"You know I will."

"I got a favor to ask ya. Will you come fer a visit?"

"I'm sure you'll be down here fer reg'lar visits, woncha?"

"I don't thank I'll be able to go no-where fer a while. Promise me y'all will come to Knoxv'lle."

Lizzy couldn't say "no," but the idea of stayin' with Cooter and Charlotte tasted like pine tar in the back of her throat.

"My Daddy and little Katie Jo will be up in March," added Charlotte. "I hope you'll come up with 'em. You'll be a sight fer sore eyes, I'm sure."

The weddin' went off without a hitch, and the newlyweds headed to Knoxv'lle straight away from the courthouse steps. The friends stayed in touch as often as they could, but relations wuz strained b'tween 'em. Lizzy wuzn't one to break off a friendship, so she kept it up. She wuz excited 'bout those first few phone calls. She wuz curious to know how Charlotte would like the house, how she would like Miz M, and how happy she would say she wuz, even though Lizzy knew she would be lyin' through her teeth. Charlotte said ever'thang Lizzy 'spected her to say, never once complainin'. Cooter wuz listenin' on the other line fer sure. The house, furniture, neighbors and roads wuz picture perfect, and Miz M wuz very friendly. She'd taken Cooter's version of his life and retold it, only softer, and Lizzy knew she'd have to wait fer her trip there to see the truth with her own eyes.

Janie called from Nashv'lle to say they'd gotten there all right and the traffic wuzn't as bad as she'd thought it'd be. Lizzy hoped the next call would brang news of Buford. After 'bout a week, Janie called again to say she'd seen neither hide nor hair of Buford or his sisters. She said she'd called 'em but thought their answerin' machine wuz messed up or broke. She said Tildie wuz goin' 'round their part of town the next day, and she wuz gonna go look 'em up.

Janie's next call came after she'd visited Tammy. She said, "I thank Tammy wuz feelin' poorly, but she wuz glad to see me. She wuz surprised I hadn't called her, so's I wuz right 'bout her answerin' machine bein' on the fritz. I asked after Buford, and she said he wuz always buzzin' 'bout with Dutch that she hardly ever put her eyes on 'im fer two seconds t'gether. Suzanna wuz havin' supper with 'em of the evenin', and I surely do wish I could see her. We didn't talk long on account of Patty and Tammy wuz on their way out. I'd be willin' to bet you five dollars they'll be 'round here to see me b'fore too long."

Lizzy shook her head when she hung up the phone. The only way Buford would know he wuz within fifty miles of Janie would be on accident.

After four weeks had passed, Janie still hadn't got the chance to see Buford even once. She pretended it didn't bother her none, but she wuz hurt by Tammy not callin' or stoppin' by. Fer two weeks Janie made ever' excuse she could thank of as to why Tammy wuz ignorin' her. And when Tammy finally did return a phone call she wuz right hateful over the phone and didn't stay on long.

Janie told Lizzy 'bout it. "Tammy is a two-faced hag to be sure. I hate to admit when I'm wrong 'bout a body, but in this case, I'm God's own fool. Now, don't you go a-sayin' 'I told you so.' I have no idea why she pretended to be my friend, and I'm sure if'n the same thang happened again, I'd be taken in again. Tammy never returned a single call 'til yesterd'y. When she called, it wuz to tell me to quit rangin' her up, that she wuz sorry that she wuz too busy to call ever' day and wish'd I'd git my own life. When we got off the phone, I could tell it wuz the last time she ever wanted to hear my voice. She's wrong if'n she thanks I'm hangin' on with her to try to git closer to Buford. Hell's bells, she wuz the one who started ever'thang. She has to know she's in the wrong here, and the only way I can explain it is she's bein' awful protective of her brother, which most of the time is a good quality in a friend. I don't know why she's so worried 'bout me and Buford. He knows I've been in Nashv'lle; I could tell it by somethin' she said in passin'. She seems to wanna talk herself into believin' he's sweet on Suzanna. I need to git my head on straight and quit dwellin' on bad thangs. I jest hate it when I thank bad on folks." She went on to say that Guthrie and Tildie wuz treatin' her right and she couldn't wait to talk to Lizzy again next time. "Tammy did say they wuz never comin' back to our part of the state. Buford's purty sure he's gonna give up the doublewide, but don't let it slip to nobody." Janie ended the call by urgin' Lizzy to go to Knoxv'lle fer her visit with Charlotte.

Lizzy wuz spittin' mad at the pain Janie wuz sufferin', but at least she wouldn't be fooled by Tammy again. At least Janie had turned loose of any notion Buford might be got after all. She felt as bad fer Janie as though she, herself, had been eaten by a wolf and shit over a cliff. Janie didn't wanna have nuthin' to do with any of 'em, and Lizzy hoped Buford would jest hurry on up and marry Suzanna and git it over with. After all Joe had said 'bout her, Buford would be payin' fer his mistake with the rest of his life.

The next day on the phone, Tildie called Lizzy on her promise to keep her distance from Joe. Lizzy straight up told her she could breathe easy. Joe's eye had wandered, and Lizzy'd seen it all. She wuz smitten, no doubt, and if'n she'd had two nickels to rub t'gether, he might have kept flirtin' with her, but he found himself a girl with a trust fund. Even though the dollar signs in his eyes shone jest as bright as the ones in Charlotte's, Lizzy wuz able to forgive 'im and move past it. She hoped he would be happy. She told Tildie she wuz convinced she wuz in heat rather than in love. She said, "You can put yer boots in the oven, but that don't make 'em biscuits. If'n I had really had a thang fer 'im, I'd wanna hit 'im in the Adam's apple so hard, he'd be spittin' cider fer a week, but I don't hold nuthin' against 'im. In fact, I thank his girl is right purty, and she teaches Sund'y school down at the Pentacostal Church, so she must be a good one." She continued, tellin' Tildie that Kitty and Lydie wuz angry as sprayed roaches 'bout his new love affair, but they don't know nuthin' 'bout the ways of the world and the needs of an empty wallet.

# Chapter 27

After New Year's the country ain't got much to recommend it to folks. January and February wuz spent sloshin' through the mud back and forth to the fair grounds and to Ain't Fern's house. When March rolled 'round, Charlotte started callin' with more reg'larity, a-tryin' to persuade Lizzy to make good on her promise to visit. She started to b'lieve she could make a silk purse out'a a sow's ear, even if'n the sow's ear wuz her cousin Cooter. She'd been cooped up with her Momma and sisters fer months now, and a road trip would at least give her a break from them and allow her to see Janie fer a day or two. She talked it over with Billy Lucas, and decided she would ride up with 'im and Katie Jo, and they would spend a night in Nashv'lle so's she could have a sit-down with her sister.

Bein' a Daddy's girl, it wuz hard fer Lizzy to leave Benny, 'specially since he'd have to be all alone with her Momma and sisters. He never did warm to the idea, but didn't go so far as to say she couldn't leave.

Lizzy gave a friendly hug to Joe to say "goodbye," and he gave her a little pinch on the butt to remind her that even though he wuz knee-deep in it with another girl, he still wanted to cop a feel with Lizzy. He reminded her of what she could expect up in Knoxv'lle with Miz M, and they felt assured they'd always have somethin' to talk 'bout. When she left 'im, she wuz convinced he wuz jest 'bout the friendliest feller she'd ever met, and she liked 'im all the more knowin' they'd be friends even if'n the road b'tween 'em wuz too far and snakey.

The next day she, Billy and Katie Jo hopped in his old rattletrap and started fer Nashv'lle. Lizzy spent her time thankin' on her conversation with Joe the night b'fore. Billy and Katie Jo didn't have a brain b'tween the two of 'em. Billy's head wuz as empty as a lawyer's heart, and Katie Jo wuz as useless to talk to as tits on a boar hog. They listened to the radio, but most of the time they couldn't pick up nuthin' but static.

They left early enough to be in Nashv'lle by lunch time, and as they pulled into Guthrie and Tildie's driveway, they could see Janie's face in the picture window, jest waitin' fer 'em to arrive. Lizzy bolted through the door and met her sister in a great big bear hug, so glad to see that she looked good enough to pinch. On the stairs behind Janie stood a troop of little boys and girls who wuz peekin' through the railin's to see their cousin but too shy to make a peep. They spent the day window shoppin' at the mall and that night went to the movies to see somethin' starrin' Colin Firth.

Lizzy sat next to Ain't Tildie so she could ask her 'bout Janie, and she wuz a-grieved to hear that though Janie tried to keep her chin up, she wuz reg'larly down in the mouth. Tildie told her all 'bout the phone calls and the visit that had put the last nail in the coffin of Janie's friendship with Tammy and Patty. Tildie told Lizzy how proud she wuz on how she handled Joe Wickham and that whole situation.

"Tell me 'bout Joe's girl, Lizzy. I'd hate to thank yer friend is jest after her money."

"She's a nice girl, no bigger 'n a hole in the ground, and nobody says nuthin' bad 'bout her."

"But he didn't pay her no never-mind 'til her grandaddy popped off and left her a trust fund."

"Why should he give her the time of day b'fore she had the money? He wuz flirtin' with me back then, and I don't have no money neither. Why trade one poor girl fer another?"

"But don't you thank he looks like a snake in the grass, goin' after her so soon after she inherited the money?"

"I ain't in a place to say. If'n it don't bother her, why should it bother us?"

"He's slicker 'n owl shit, and if'n she cain't see it, she must be stupid."

"Whatever you say, Ain't Tildie. He's a snake and she's an idjit. That's fer sure."

"You're twistin' my words 'round, sweet Lizzy. I cain't be sore too long with a good ol' Southern boy like Joe."

"Southern or not, some boys have shit fer brains. I'm sick of the whole lot of 'em. I'm headin' out tomorrow to visit a feller that's so dumb if'n his brains wuz turned to gas, he couldn't run a piss-ant's go-cart 'round the inside of a Cheerio. I guess stupid men 'r the only ones worth knowin', anyhow."

"You watch yer tongue, Miss Lizzy. Folks 'r gonna call you bitter."

B'fore the movie wuz over, Ain't Tildie'd  invited Lizzy to take a summer trip with her and Uncle Guthrie up to horse country in Kentucky. The thought of a summer vacation wuz better 'n shrimp and grits. She said, "Oh my goodness gracious, Ain't Tildie! I'm happier 'n a dog with two peters! I've never been out'a the state of Tennessee! I cain't wait to see it all! I'm gonna keep a journal of all the places we go and all the thangs we see so's I can always remember this trip. I'll draw maps to go along with it while we's drivin' in the car. Do you thank there really is a giant ball of twine out there somewhere off the side of the road? We're gonna have a blast! I cain't hardly stand it, I'm so excited I feel like I'm jacked up on Mountain Dew!"

Chapter 28

Ever' cotton pickin' thang on the drive the next day towards Knoxv'lle wuz new and interestin' to Lizzy. She wuz in a good mood since her visit with Janie, and the idea of a trip to Kentucky horse country wuz more than she could've hoped fer.

The minute they took their exit off the freeway into Knoxv'lle, ever' eye wuz peeled to look fer the parsonage, and ever' curve they rounded promised to show the house. A white picket fence with a jumble of rose bushes and thorns wuz their first clue they wuz close, and Lizzy grinned to herself rememberin' ever'thang she'd heard 'bout the folks that lived over yonder.

B'fore long the parsonage wuz in sight with a fence to match the one they'd jest seen. The house sat right in the middle of the lot with a garden off to one side and a wooded area behind. Mountain laurel wuz planted all 'round the house. Cooter and Charlotte wuz standin' on the stoop, wavin' like they wuz in a parade. Billy pulled the rattletrap through the gate and up the gravel driveway where it sputtered to a stop, with a tail of steam risin' from under the hood. Billy grabbed a plastic milk carton full of water, lifted the hood and poured the water while he nearly disappeared in the cloud he'd made. The girls gave hugs all 'round, and Lizzy wuz glad she'd taken the trouble to come. She could tell right away that gittin' hitched hadn't changed her cousin none. He wuz jest as stupid as b'fore, and he kept her from totin' her thangs inside while he asked 'bout every member of her family and their health. Cooter walked toward the house, quick to point out how he had hung the shutters his ownself and repaired the hand railin' jest since he'd returned with his wife. He kept callin' the house "his humble abode," which nearly made Katie Jo wanna pee her pants fer laughin'. Charlotte offered ever'body a Co'Cola and some snickerdoodles, and Coot kept repeatin' what she'd said.

Lizzy'd steadied herself fer her visit with Cooter, and she couldn't help but thank that while he wuz showin' off the size of the rooms and the view and the furniture, that he wuz talkin' to her in particular, a-tryin' to make her see what she could've had. Even though it wuz a right nice house, she couldn't give 'im the sigh he wuz a-lookin' fer. Instead she stared at her friend, wonderin' how in the world she could be so cheerful with a husband like him. If'n Cooter said somethin' to make Charlotte ashamed, she never said nuthin' 'bout it. She jest blushed.

After Billy, Katie Jo and Lizzy had the chance to see ever' piece of furniture and hear the story 'bout it, Cooter invited 'em outside to see the garden he wuz tillin', which wuz big and laid out in a perfect rectangle with strang. He wuz right proud of his little piece of land and said he planted, weeded and harvested ever'thang his ownself. He said he thought it wuz good exercise, and Charlotte agreed with 'im, sayin' she wuz glad he took such enjoyment in it, and it kept 'im outside much of the evenin' after work. She said she encouraged his gardenin' as much as she could, and Lizzy had to bite her lip to keep from laughin' out loud. He pointed out where ever' little thang wuz planted or would be planted. He discussed how he planned to keep the rabbits and deer away, and he barely gave 'em enough time to give 'im the praise he wanted b'fore he moved on to the next thang. He told 'em whose property butted up against his, and who owned each clump of trees beyond his property line. Even as briggity as he wuz 'bout his own land, he said nuthin' wuz as fine as Miz M's property and her roses and her trellises covered in Wisteria.

From his garden Cooter wanted to show 'em out beyond the shed where he kept a few rabbits and some chickens, but the girls wuz wearin' their good shoes and didn't wanna take the chance on steppin' in chicken shit. Billy went along with 'im, and Charlotte brought the girls inside to show 'em the house without Cooter and his comments. The house wuz small, but well built with cubbies everwhichway that Charlotte had filled with bins to keep ever'thang in its place. If'n you could forgit that Cooter lived there, it wuz a right nice place to live, and with him gone all the day long over to the church and in the garden 'til dusk, Lizzy imagined Charlotte could forgit 'im most of the time.

Cooter wuz all fired up that Miz M wuz still there. She had some kind of a time-share down in Florida that she liked to visit this time of year, and he wuz proud to tell 'em 'bout it at supper. "Yes, Miss Lizzy, you must be livin' right. You'll git to see Miz M at church on Sund'y, and I don't need to tell you yer gonna like her right away. I bet she'll even lower herself to come over and say howdie to you after the service. I'd be willin' to bet she'll include all y'all if'n she invites us over while yer here. She's so good to my darlin' Charlotte. We eat over thar 'bout twice a week, and she never lets us walk home even though it's not even a half a mile door to door. She carries us home in one of her cars. Yep, you heard me right. She has more 'n one car that runs, and her daughter don't even like to drive."

"Miz M has her head on straight, that's fer sure," added Charlotte. Then more quietly she said, "She comes 'round here all the time to check on us."

The rest of the evenin' wuz spent goin' over the news from back home, which Lizzy had already given to Charlotte over the phone, but she wanted to hear it again anyhow. Later that night on the blow-up mattress, Lizzy couldn't sleep on account of a fly hittin' the window screen, so she thought 'bout her friend and how well Charlotte'd handled her situation with Cooter.

The next day Lizzy wuz upstairs fixin' to go fer a walk when there wuz a loud noise downstairs, like a shout, and then she could hear footsteps runnin' up the stairs lickety-split and somebody callin' fer her. She opened the door and found Katie Jo in a tizzy, "Oh my goodness gracious. Git yer ass down here and see this. I ain't gonna tell you what it is, you jest got to see it fer yer ownself."

Lizzy asked questions as they stumbled down the stairs t'gether, but Katie Jo wuzn't talkin'. They looked out the picture window to the gate, and there sat two women sittin' there in a robin's egg blue Chrysler.

"Is this what you wuz all fired up to show me?" asked Lizzy. "Lawsy mercy! I half expected the chickens had got out, and it's nuthin' but Miz M and her daugher?"

"No, Lizzy," said Katie Jo, "it ain't Miz M. The old lady, I'm told, is Louetta Jean who lives above their garage. The other is DeeDee Majestro. Would you jest look at her? She's a tiny little thang, not even knee high to a bullfrog, and so skinny if'n she turned sideways she'd disappear. I never seen nuthin' like that. You can practic'ly see through her skin it's so white. And those fangernails! My stars! I ain't never seen nuthin' like 'em b'fore!"

"It ain't right to keep Charlotte out in that wind without a coat. I wonder why in the world she don't come inside."

"Charlotte says they almost never come inside. It's pert near a compliment if'n DeeDee Majestro comes in yer house. I don't see how she could open the car door, anyhow with her nails as long as they are."

"I like her looks," said Lizzy to herself. "She's sick and angry-lookin'. Yep, she'll be perfect fer Dutch, the perfect wife."

Cooter and Charlotte stood a little while longer at the gate talkin' to the women, and Billy stood on the front stoop, not knowin' whether it wuz proper fer 'im to stay or go, so he jest stood there and waved his arm like some kind of an idjit. A few minutes later the Chrysler peeled out, and Cooter started right in tellin' 'em how lucky they wuz, and that they all wuz invited up to Miz M's fer supper the next day.

# Chapter 29

Ol' Coot wuz beside himself with importance on havin' his guests invited over to the big house. They could hear 'im out in the garden, practicin' what he wuz goin' to say and addin' gestures fer emphasis. He wanted to show ever'body how much Miz M doted on 'im and fussed over 'im and Charlotte.

"I de-clare," said Cooter, "I wouldn't have been surprised if'n Miz M had invited us out to eat after church on Sund'y. What I mean to say is I kind of expected it, but never in a million years would I expect her to have all of us over fer supper and so soon after y'all got here, too."

"I ain't surprised at all," Billy Lucas said, "She prob'ly heard I wuz on the Sanitation Board back home and wanted to sit down with a real-life public servant."

There wuzn't two subjects to talk 'bout the next day with all of Cooter's instructions on good behavior and what to touch and what not to touch over at Miz M's house. He told 'em not say nuthin' if'n she ordered in from KFC, and put it on a family plate to make it look like home cookin', and he wuz right clear that they better not complain 'bout nuthin' while they wuz there.

When they wuz goin' off to freshen up fer supper, Coot told Lizzy she shouldn't be ashamed of her clothes, that Miz M didn't expect ever'body to look nice as her and her young 'un. He asked her to jest put on the best thang she brought along, and nobody would thank nuthin' of it.

While ever'body wuz dressin', he kept knockin' at the door, tellin' 'em to hurry it on up. Miz M didn't like to be kept waitin'. Ever' time he opened his trap 'bout Miz M, it scared Katie Jo to bits. She wuz right nervous 'bout the whole thang and kept messin' up her braids so she'd have to pull 'em out and start over.

The night wuz warm fer March, and they walked along the road and through a field to git to Miz M's house. The climbin' roses that gave the Rose House its name wuzn't bloomin' yet. The new leaves wuz startin' to reach out fer sunshine, but the thorns showed through. A few daffodils peaked out'a a whiskey barrel by the lamp post, and an empty rope swung down from a tree, its ends frayed where the tire swing'd broke away. The house wuz fancy with bevelled glass in the door and a wrap-'round porch complete with white rockin' chairs.

Ever' step they took toward the house made Katie Jo and Billy more nervous. Billy kept fidgitin' with his string tie, and Katie Jo was bitin' her fangernails clean off. Lizzy had heard so much 'bout Miz M that she wuzn't bothered by any of it, she jest wanted to have a face to put with the name.

The house had an honest-to-goodness foyer with a life-sized mirror, that made Billy nearly jump out'a his shoes when he seen himself in it, and dark paneled woodwork that positively smelled of tobacco. Lizzy recognized Louetta Jean from earlier as she let 'em in, and they follered her back to the livin' room where Miz M, and DeeDee wuz settin'. Billy's tongue wuz tied and he barely grunted his hellos. Katie Jo's eyes wuz big as saucers with her pupils goin' this way and that like one of those black cat coo-coo clocks. Lizzy had her wits 'bout her and sized up the three women she'd jest met. Miz M wuz tall and big boned. Somewhere in her jowls wuz the memory of a purty face, and she kept a look on her which sent out a warnin' to her guests that she knew she wuz better 'n them. She spoke loud, like she wuz large and in charge, and Lizzy thought 'bout Joe Wickham and all he'd said 'bout her. He hit the nail on the head with ever'thang he'd said.

After staring at the mother fer a while, who looked like a big, fat, lady version of Dutch with more chins and bushier eyebrows, she turned her eyes on the daughter. Katie Jo wuz right when she said DeeDee wuz skinny. Why, she wuz so thin you couldn't even see her shadow. A big gush of wind could jest blow her from here to kingdom come. She didn't look nuthin' like her Momma. DeeDee wuz as white as a sheet and twice as thin. She hardly had any features on her face at all, and her voice wuz as quiet as a popcorn fart. She only spoke to Louetta, who told us all what she had said like some kind of a translator, even though as far as anyone could tell, she wuz speakin' English.

Supper wuz so fancy that Katie Jo felt like she needed to hold up her pinky finger while she wuz eatin'. The food wuz put on the plate like some kind of artwork, and they didn't know if'n they should eat it or look at it. Colonial Sanders had not been involved in its preparation. Miz M put Cooter down at the end of the table where her husband would've sat if'n he'd been livin', and she reached out and patted his hand from time to time with her manicured claw. Cooter sat up straight as if'n life couldn't git any better 'n this, and he served folks as though he wuz sittin' at his own table. He complimented every dish, and stupid Billy repeated ever'thang he said like an echo. Lizzy wondered how Miz M could stand to listen to the fellers and their jabberin', but she seemed happy to have the food complimented, which wuz the only talkin' goin' on in the room. Lizzy would've started to talk, but she wuz sittin' b'tween Charlotte, who had her eyes glued on Miz M, and DeeDee who didn't say two words all during supper. Louetta spent her time watchin' ever'thang DeeDee put in her mouth, even though it wuzn't much since her fangernails kept gettin' in the way. The cat had got Katie Jo's tongue, and she jest sat there list'nin' to the fellers go on 'bout the food.

After Louetta had cleared the plates away, there wuzn't nuthin' to do but sit and listen to Miz M talk, which she did without stoppin' 'til Louetta brought her some coffee. She passed out her opinion on ever'thang like she wuz dealin' out cards. She asked Charlotte ever' question you could thank of 'bout her house and the keepin' of it, and gave her a heapin' helpin' of advice, includin' where thangs oughtta be stored and when she should put the screens in the winders and how best to keep the chickens. After she'd run out'a advice, Miz M turned to Lizzy and started in on her. She asked her how many sisters she had, if'n they wuz younger or older, if'n any of 'em wuz married or engaged, if'n they wuz purty, where they went to school, what kind of car her Daddy drove and what had been her mother's maiden name. Lizzy didn't like her nosiness, but answered her questions with all politeness.

Miz M said, "Yer Daddy owes a lot of money to Cooter, don't he?" Without waitin' fer an answer she looked at Charlotte, "Fer yer sake, I'm glad of it." Then back to Lizzy, "Do you like Karaoke?"

"Not really, but I play the fiddle a little bit."

"Well isn't that nice? Sometime you'll have to give us a little concert here. We have a hand-made violin from b'fore the War of Northern Aggression. I'm sure it's better 'n... well, you'll have to try it out sometime soon. Do yer sisters sing or have a talent? I like that tv show with the singers on it."

"One of 'em is good at fixin' hair."

"Why didn't all of you learn? Y'all all should have learnt somethin'. Folks need a particular skill to keep 'em out'a other people's pockets. Do you do hair or nails?"

"No, not at all."

"Well I wonder why not. It's not so hard. Yer Momma should take y'all up to Nashv'lle to some of the beauty schools up there."

"My Momma would like that, but my Daddy won't step foot in a big city like Nashv'lle. He says there's too many cars to run into."

"Surely yer little town has a vo-tech center."

"Our county cain't afford nuthin'. Teachers have to double up on subjects on account of the state won't give us what we need."

"How is that possible in this day and age? I've never heard of such a thang. Why, that's one step away from being a one-room schoolhouse. Yer mother must've had to help out to keep you from fallin' behind."

Lizzy tried hard not to smile as she told Miz M that hadn't been the case.

"Who helped you, then? Who taught you? Who wuz there to make sure you understood yer lessons?"

"A lot of folks up by us 'r home schooled so the classes wuzn't so full as you might thank. If'n you wanted to learn, you learned. There wuz always somethin' to read if'n you wanted to, and those who didn't wanna, they wuz jest idle."

"All of y'all should have had a better schoolin' than that. If'n I'd known yer Momma, I'd have given her the name of a tutor and twisted her arm 'til she hired 'im. I always say that you jest cain't educate a child without good teachers. Four of Louetta's nieces 'r tutors fer folks that I know. Are any of yer sisters allowed to date, Miss Lizzy?"

"Yes, ma'am, all."

"All of you. All five of you 'r allowed to go on car dates with boys? Even the younger ones? By a-lookin' at you, yer sisters must be really young!"

"Yep. My youngest is jest fifteen. I thank she's too young to be goin' out, but really, ma'am, how can you expect 'em to stay at home out in the country where we live? There's jest nuthin' at all to do on the weekends, plus it keeps the fights down b'tween us girls, I thank."

"My word! You're quick to give yer opinion. How old 'r you?"

"Do you honestly b'lieve I'm gonna tell you my age?"

Miz M couldn't b'lieve she didn't git a direct answer, and Lizzy thought she might jest be the only person on the face of the earth who didn't oblige Miz M.

"You cain't be old enough to drank, I am sure. I have no idea why you won't tell me yer age."

"I'm twenty."

Once the coffee wuz gone, Louetta brought out a card table, and Miz M, Billy, Cooter and Charlotte set down to play poker. DeeDee wanted to play Bunco, and Louetta, Katie Jo and Lizzy set down to join her. You could hear a pin drop at their table fer all the talkin' that wuz goin' on. The only time somebody said somethin' that didn't relate to the game wuz when DeeDee complained 'bout bein' too hot or too cold or that there wuz too much or not enough light. Of course she relied on Louetta to adjust the light and temperature on account of her fangernails wuz too damned long. It was a wonder whe could hold the cards with them thangs.

There wuz a lot more action at the other table where Miz M told ever'body what they wuz doin' wrong, and Cooter agreed with ever'thang she said, thanked her ever' time he won a hand, and apologized if'n he won too many in a row. Billy didn't say two words, he wuz thankin' on names to drop when he got the chance.

When Miz M and DeeDee wuz tired of playin' games, the tables wuz put away and Miz M offered to take Cooter and his guests home in one of her cars. And while Louetta went down to pull the car out'a the garage and git the heater started, they stood 'round the fire list'nin' to Miz M give 'em the weather report fer the next day. Once the car wuz ready, Cooter started thankin' Miz M and didn't stop 'til they pulled up next to the gate at his house.

Back under his own roof, Cooter wanted Lizzy to give 'im her opinion on ever'thang she'd seen. She made it sound better 'n she thought it wuz fer Charlotte's sake, but her opinions wuz not grand enough or long enough to please her cousin, so he took the job of praisin' Miz M all to his ownself.

# Chapter 30

Billy stayed on in Knoxv'lle only so long as he needed to make sure his little girl wuz settled and that Coot wuzn't smackin' her 'round. While Billy wuz there, Cooter took 'im out every mornin' down to McDonald's fer coffee and breakfast burritos, and they stayed out quite a while, which wuz fine and dandy with Lizzy. When he wuz home, Cooter spent most of his time in the garden or plannin' a sermon and a-lookin' out the window at the road so he could see if'n Miz M went out or not. Charlotte'd made herself a cozy little space on the other end of the house as far from Cooter's study as possible. If'n she'd have been any closer, he prob'ly would've asked her to make 'im snacks while he worked, and Lizzy noticed how well the set-up worked fer Charlotte.

From where Charlotte and Lizzy sat, they couldn't see the road at all, and had to depend on Cooter to shout who wuz drivin' by and how often DeeDee had Louetta take her out in her Chrysler, which happened all the time. She stopped by a lot and beeped her horn fer Charlotte to come out and speak to her, but she never once got out'a the car to come in.

The days that Cooter didn't go over to Miz M's house wuz few and far b'tween, and Lizzy couldn't thank of very many reasons he would have to go over thar so much. A couple of days a week she'd come by to visit 'em, telling Charlotte she wuz sewin' on a button wrong or suggestin' they re-arrange the furniture or pointin' out a corner that wuzn't as clean as it oughtta be. She never accepted any of Charlotte's baked goods, and when she did take somethin' it wuz tap water, which she complained wuzn't nearly as good as the bottled water she bought at Cosco.

It didn't take Lizzy long to realize Miz M had her nose in ever'body's business. She'd git wind of a fight or of somebody beatin' their wife, and she'd tell Cooter, and he'd turn it into a sermon fer Sund'y. She read and approved all his sermons b'fore Sund'y services and added promises of eternal damnation if'n it wuz fittin'.

Aside from a couple more meals at Miz M's, there wuzn't much to do, but that suited Lizzy jest fine. They couldn't afford much to go into Knoxv'lle proper fer shoppin' and the like, but she spent her time comfortable enough, talkin' with Charlotte or takin' long walks. The weather wuz unseasonably warm fer that time of year, and Lizzy took it as an opportunity to walk out along a deer path in the woods near Miz M's house.

B'fore she knew it, Easter wuz jest 'round the corner, and rumor had it that Dutch wuz comin' to spend the holiday with his aunt. Lizzy thought it'd be a real hoot to watch Tammy makin' eyes at Dutch in front of Miz M who wanted 'im fer her own daughter. Miz M talked non-stop 'bout his visit and how handsome he wuz, and she seemed a little ticked off that Charlotte and Lizzy know'd 'im already.

The day Dutch wuz due to arrive, Cooter could not stay out'a the road. He paced up one side of the two-lane highway and down the other 'til he seen the car comin' up the road and ran up to the house to tell ever'body Dutch wuz at Miz M's. The next mornin' Cooter went over to say his howdies, and when he came back home, there wuz two fellers with 'im. One wuz Dutch and the other wuz his good friend and cousin, Jake.

Charlotte seen 'em crossin' the highway from her room and ran over to where Lizzy and Katie Jo wuz to tell 'em Dutch wuz on his way. "He wouldn't have never come over here, Liz, if'n you wuzn't here."

No sooner wuz the words out'a her mouth than the doorbell rang, and the three fellers walked in the house. Jake wuz near 'bout thirty and had been hit with the ugly stick more 'n once. If'n he wuz a dog, they'd shave his butt and have 'im walk backwards ever'where. He wuz right nice, though, and he had eyes like milk chocolate, warm and smooth. Dutch looked the same and no matter what he thought of Lizzy, he wuz polite as all git-out to Charlotte. Lizzy jest nodded at 'im like a stupid bobble-head doll.

Jake started talkin' like he wuz born fer it, pleasant-like and askin' ever'body questions they'd be sure to wanna answer. Dutch, on the other hand, made a comment 'bout the new garden, then sat right down and didn't say another word 'til he asked Lizzy how her family wuz doin'.

She answered 'im in the usual way, and after a pause, she said, "My oldest sister has been in Nashv'lle fer three months. Have you run across her while y'all have been there?"

She knew he hadn't, but she wanted to see if'n he knew anythang of what'd happened b'tween Buford, his sisters and Janie. A confused look passed over his face as he said that he hadn't seen hide nor hair of Janie. Lizzy thought she prob'ly shouldn't say much more on the subject, and b'fore long Dutch and Jake went back to Miz M's house.

# Chapter 31

Jake had right nice manners, and ever'body said so at the parsonage. The girls all thought he would be fun to hang out with, but it wuz a few days b'fore they heard from the fellers again. What with all the neighbor folks comin' and goin' from the big house, they wuzn't needed much, and it wuz Easter Sund'y b'fore them boys paid the girls some attention, and then they only asked 'em to stop by Miz M's place later that night.

Cooter and Charlotte and ever'body didn't see hide nor hair of Dee Dee or Miz M fer pert near a week, neither, so they wuz happy to take them boys up on their invitation. Miz M said her howdies but purty much ignored her company, payin' more attention to Jake and Dutch than anyone else.

Jake seemed happy as a tick on a horse's ass to see 'em when they showed up. Anythang wuz better 'n hangin' out with his Ain't Pru all the time. He wuz as jumpy as a long-tailed cat in a room full of rockin' chairs, and finally he set down fer a spell next to Lizzy. They jacked their jaws 'bout the true religion of the South... football, and how the Vols would do against 'Bama in the fall. That gave way to talkin' 'bout the flood down at the Grand Ole Opry, and b'fore long they wuz debatin' the legacies of Willie Nelson, Johnny Cash and Charlie Daniels. Lizzy, not bein' one to hide it when she wuz tickled, let out a laugh and a snort that got ever'body's attention, Dutch's 'specially. He'd been sneakin' a peek at her flirtin' with Jake all night and hadn't said nothin'. Miz M wuzn't gonna miss any of the joke, so she said, "Jake, honey. You know a-tryin' to sneak a joke past me is like a-tryin' to sneak a sunbeam past a rooster in the mornin'. What is it that could have y'all so entertained over thar?"

"We's jest talkin' 'bout music, Ain't Pru."

"Music! My word! Don't keep it to yerself, son. Tell me what you said directly. There ain't nobody in the great state of Tennessee that loves honky tonk more 'n me. Folks compared me to Loretta Lynn back in the day." Dutch rolled his eyes as if sayin' "she's so full of shit her eyes 'r brown," and  he took another bite of pie.

After ever'body licked their fingers to git the pecan pie off, Jake reminded Lizzy that she'd promised to play the fiddle fer 'im. She took it out'a its case and began to pick out a purty little tune. Miz M listened fer a flea's minute and then began talkin' to Dutch. He walked away from her to stand closer to Lizzy and watch.

Lizzy seen what he wuz up to and said, "My heavenly stars, Dutch!

Yer a-tryin' to git my goose, but I ain't gonna let you. It jest dawned on me that you came over here to listen so's you could make fun of me. I know I ain't as good as yer sister, but I'm fair to middlin'. You ain't gonna give me a fright, be'cuz I ain't a-scared of you."

"I won't cross you, Miss Lizzy," he said, "on account of yer so stubborn you'd argue with a stop sign. I know you well enough to know you'd jest as soon give somebody else's opinion instead of yer own."

Lizzy slapped her knee as she laughed and said to Jake, "Yer cousin's paintin' a purty picture of me, but ever'body knows that dog won't hunt. If'n I didn't have bad luck, I'd have no luck at all, what with friends like ol' Dutch over thar. I'm workin' harder to be good than a whore at church on Sund'y, and he's come over to expose my true self to all y'all. Dutch, it ain't right of you to mention ever'thang you knew of me from back home. You're makin' me madder 'n a wet hen, and I aim to git even. I'm not so sure you want me fillin' in yer relations on yer behavior, neither."

"I ain't afraid of you," he said, smilin' like a mule eatin' briars.

"Oh, I jest got to hear this one," said Jake. "I'd love to know how he acts 'round strangers."

"You don't have to drag it out'a me. I'll tell you, but brace yerself, 'cuz it ain't purty. The first time I ever laid eyes on Dutch wuz at a hoe-down back home, and what do you thank he did all night? He leaned up against the wall and didn't cut a rug with nobody, even though we wuz short on fellers that night. If I'm lyin', I'm dyin'. Ain't that the truth, Dutch?"

"Hell's bells! I didn't know a soul there. What else wuz I s'posed to do?"

"So shy, Dutch? I'm guessin' you couldn't go up an introduce yerself to some poor gal?"

"Maybe," said Dutch, "I shouldn't ha' been so ornery, but like I said, I didn't know a soul."

"Let's ask yer kin, here. Jake, why couldn't a stand-up guy like Dutch, here, ask a girl to cut a rug at a country dance?"

"I've got yer answer. It's on account of Dutch ain't got no call to do it. He won't make the trouble to introduce himself. Laziness. That's all it is."

Dutch replied, "Jake, you've got to be pullin' my leg. I ain't good at grinnin' and shakin' and makin' small talk like most folks. I cain't pretend to be interested in all that. I'm always standin' there thankin' that the lights 'r on, but nobody's home. Most folks 'r stupid like that."

"It jest takes practice, Dutch. When I first started on the fiddle," said Lizzy, "I couldn't carry a tune in a bucket with glue on the handle. But with a little bit of practice, I got better. I cain't hold my own against some folks, but I'm better 'n others. I'd rather play fer a friend than a stranger."

Dutch winked at her. "You're right, Miss Lizzy. Nobody who listens to you play could say you're wastin' yer time. I guess neither one of us likes to show off to strangers."

They wuz cut short by Miz M who jest had to know what they wuz all talkin' 'bout. Lizzy picked up her bow again and started playin'. Miz M listened fer a bit, and said to Dutch, "Lizzy'd play better with some practice and a good teacher. I reckon DeeDee would've been a world-class fiddle player if'n her health would've allowed."

Lizzy glanced at Dutch to see how he reacted to the praise of his cousin, but she didn't see his face change one whit. He reacted to DeeDee jest as he had to Tammy. Lizzy thought either one had even chances of gittin' hitched to Dutch, even though one of 'em wuz his own kin.

Miz M continued makin' snide comments 'bout Lizzy's playin', but with urgin' from the fellers, Lizzy kept fiddlin' til the car wuz brought 'round.

# Chapter 32

Lizzy wuz usin' a free minute the next mornin' to send a quick email to Janie, seein' if she wuz keepin' her spirits up while Charlotte and Katie Jo wuz down to the Krispy Kreme. 'Bout that time somebody done dinged the dong, which nearly scared the snot out'a her since she wuzn't expectin' any visitors. She opened the door to find Dutch standin' there like hair in a biscuit.

"Well, ain't ya gonna ask me in?" he asked. He seemed surprised to find her at the house alone and said his sorries that he wuz bargin' in like that.

They each took a seat, and Lizzy asked 'im how ever'body wuz up at the big house. After he answered her, you could've heard a pin drop fer all the conversation in the room. She had to thank on somethin' to break the silence, so she decided to remind 'im of the way thangs wuz when they wuz back home. She wuz jest itchin' to find out what he would say 'bout runnin' out'a town like a scalded haint with Buford and his kin.

"All y'all left town faster 'n grass through a goose last fall, Dutch. I bet Buford wuz shocked as shit to find y'all on his heels so quick after he left fer Nashv'lle. As I recall, he left one day, and the rest of y'all left the very next day. I hope all of 'em 'r doin' well in Nashv'lle?"

"Right as rain," he said.

After a heartbeat or two, she came to the conclusion he'd said all he planned to say on the subject. She added, "I heard tell Buford ain't plannin' to return to the country any time soon. Ain't that right?"

"He ain't said a peep 'bout it to me, but I don't see 'im spendin' much time there from here on out."

"Well if'n he ain't gonna live there next to the Park N Shop, wouldn't it be best if he gave up his lease on the place so's somebody else could move in there? It's not like he's dug in there like an Appalachian tick."

"I wouldn't be bug-eyed if he gave it up b'fore his lease runs out."

Lizzy felt rougher 'n a cob fer dear Janie. Dutch'd tied her knickers in a knot fer sure, but she wuzn't goin' to let on 'bout it. If'n he wanted conversation, he wuz goin' to have to start one his ownself."

Dutch could take a hint. He said, "This is a right nice house. I thank Ain't Pru helped out with it some when Cooter first came 'round these parts."

Lizzy said, "I thank she did, and I don't doubt it that she couldn't 've found anyone happier to be on the receivin' end of that situation."

"Cooter seems to find married life satisfactual. I thank he's lucky to have snagged a girl like Charlotte."

"You ain't jokin'. She's 'bout the most sensible woman who'd have 'im, and she's no doubt got 'im happier 'n a dead hog in a mudhole. She's jest as sharp as a tack, and I have no earthly idea why she flew 'round all the purty little flowers and landed on a turd. She does seem happy, though."

"She must like bein' so close to her own folks."

"Are you drunk? Knoxv'lle is fifty miles from home!"

"It's interstate the whole way, practic'ly. If'n you've got a reliable car, you c'n be here in an hour, easy."

"I don't care what you say. It ain't that close."

"That jest proves what a homebody you are. Anythang past the fair grounds is too far from home fer you."

As he spoke a shit-eatin' grin tugged at the corners of his mouth. Lizzy wuz jest sure he wuz thankin' 'bout Janie and the doublewide she would never call her own. She blushed and said, "I ain't sayin' that a girl cain't settle too near her kin. Far and near depends on a lot of thangs. If'n a person's got a reliable vehicle, travel don't seem like that big of a deal, but when a person has to stop every five miles to put water in the radiator, then it's diff'rent. Gas is so high right now that even with Cooter's paycheck, reg'lar trips home fer Charlotte ain't in the cards. I don't thank she'd say she wuz settled close to home at half the distance."

Dutch scooted his chair a hair closer to Lizzy. "You ain't so attached to home as you let on. I've got a feelin' you've been 'round the block a time or two in yer day."

Somethin' in his tone wuz softer, Lizzy noticed. Dutch checked himself, leaned away and grabbed fer a newspaper from the table. He pretended to look over the paper as he said, "So how do you like Knoxv'lle?"

They went back and forth 'bout the attractions and the restaurants and such 'til Charlotte and Katie Jo returned with their jaws hangin' open at the sight of Dutch and Lizzy settin' t'gether. Dutch explained how he'd come to visit and found only Lizzy there. Then without much else to say, he got up and left quick as a whip.

"What the hell is goin' on here, Lizzy?" Charlotte asked as soon as Dutch wuz out'a earshot. "I thank ol' Dutch is a-tryin' to git some of that milk fer free, if you know what I mean. He would've never come 'round here like that if'n we'd been here."

Lizzy said, "Dutch is jest like a bad case of hemorroids, a pain in the butt when they come down and always a relief when they go back up. He didn't say two words to me practic'ly the whole time he wuz here. I thank he jest came over here on account of he had nuthin' else to do."

Charlotte agreed. With no football on tv, what else wuz fellers to do of the day if'n they didn't have jobs to go to? Miz M had a pool table, but a person can git tired of bein' inside all the time. He prob'ly jest needed to git away from his aunt and her daughter. From time to time Jake would come over, either with Dutch or without 'im. Lizzy liked his company and his obvious attention, which reminded her of Joe Wickham and his flirtations. Jake wuz clearly smarter and never once put a burr in her saddle the way Joe could.

Lizzy couldn't figure on why Dutch started comin' so much to the parsonage alone. He couldn't be stoppin' by fer the company since he never opened his trap to say much the whole time he wuz there. He only said somethin' if'n he had to and almost never smiled or laughed with ever'body else. Charlotte had no idea what he wuz up to, and Jake wuz always makin' some kind of fun of 'im. She watched Dutch closely to see if'n he wuz sweet on Lizzy, but she couldn't tell if'n he wuz head over heels or jest wastin' daylight. Dutch did stare at Lizzy, 'specially her legs, but most of the time it looked like he wuz starin' off into space.

Charlotte once or twice mentioned to Lizzy that Dutch might be sweet on her, but Lizzy would jest laugh and say, "You don't know shit from shinola, Charlotte!" And after that, she didn't say much on it, but she reckoned Lizzy would take a shine to 'im if'n she knew he liked her.

# Chapter 33

Often of the mornin', Lizzy wuz fond of walkin' along a little deer path through the woods out back of the parsonage. More 'n once, she ran into Dutch on her hike, which wuz weird since she wuz over yonder and back a fur piece from where anyone oughtta be. She tried to give 'im a hint to keep 'im out'a her way by sayin' that the path wuz where she liked to go and do her thankin'. The hint must'a not sunk in very far, on account of she crossed paths with 'im again! So she repeated herself, and the very next day, what do you suppose, but it happened a third time. Lizzy wuz pert-near sure he wuz meetin' up with her on purpose and it wuz pissin' her off in the biggest way. He didn't say howdie and leave, neither. Once he even did a one-eighty and hiked back with her, but he never said nuthin', and Lizzy generally thought he wuzn't worth the buckshot it'd take to shoot a fly off a horse's ass. On the third meetin', Dutch wuz actin' strange-like, soundin' like God's biggest fool, askin' a bunch of unconnected questions 'bout how she liked Knoxv'lle, if'n she liked to take walks alone (duh?) and if'n she thought Cooter and Charlotte wuz happy t'gether. He talked 'bout the big house like Lizzy, her ownself, would be stayin' there the next time she came fer a visit. She wondered if'n he supposed she and Jake wuz moonin' and smoochin'. B'fore she could figure out what in the sam hill he wuz gittin' at, they wuz back at the gate to the parsonage.

One day when it wuz finer 'n frog's hair outside, she wuz readin' over an email she'd printed out from Janie, who wuz still so down in the mouth it worried her, when instead of Dutch on the path, there stood Jake. She folded up the letter, put it in her back pocket and said, "Well, I'll be! I never knew you wuz one fer walkin' out in the woods."

"I wuz jest out here exercisin' Ain't Pru's bird dog. I have no earthly idea where in the world he's got off to. Do you mind if I walk back with you? I'm turned 'round."

T'gether they walked toward Cooter's house.

"Are y'all fixin' to leave on Saturd'y?" she asked.

"I reckon we will if'n Dutch don't put it off again. I cain't come and go as I like seein' as how I ain't got my own car with me. We'll go when he's good and ready."

"I guess Dutch likes to be in charge of thangs. That feller's on a power-trip, I'm sure."

"He likes thangs the way he likes 'em, that's fer sure, but ain't we all that way sometimes? A man with money like he has can afford to kick back now and again. With times the way they are, I'm lucky to have a steady job workin' fer 'im back home."

"My lands, Jake! You could depress the devil! You act like you ain't got the means to live right. Hell's bells! In our house, winter's 'r as cold as a banker's heart on foreclosure day at the orphans' home fer lack of heat, and I've been so hungry b'fore, my belly thought my throat'd been cut. You ain't got it bad at all. You have a family business to work fer, and with a steady paycheck you could buy jest 'bout anythang you want."

"Hah! I guess yer right, Miss Lizzy. My Daddy used to say 'I'm like the monkey makin' it with a skunk. I don't git all I want, but I guess I git all I can stand.' I git so down thankin' on the thangs I cain't have that I forgit 'bout folk less fortunate than myself."

Lizzy said, "My Momma always says it's jest as easy to fall in love with a poor man as it is to fall in love with a rich man. I'm thankin' the same is true fer rich women."

"Lawd! It ain't easy to find a rich woman who's willin' to share what's in the bank, what with pre-nuptual agreements and all. Plus, I thank a rich woman is jest out a-lookin' fer a richer man. I'll have to earn my money b'fore I can ever git hitched."

Lizzy blushed, thanking he wuz goin' 'round the barn if he wuz a-tryin' to make hints 'bout how he felt 'bout her. She said, "I'm guessin' Dutch brought you along jest fer the company. He should be the one to git hitched since he cain't stand to be alone fer two minutes t'gether. Maybe Suzanna keeps 'im company enough. Lord knows raisin' a sister on yer own must be hard."

"I've been seen puttin' a clean hippen on that poor girl in my day. We share in her raisin'. I couldn't let ol' Dutch take all that on his ownself."

"Is that right? How do y'all work it all out? Does Suzanna give y'all much trouble? I thank girls 'r tough to raise at that age. If'n she's anythang like her brother, she prob'ly likes to have her own way."

As she spoke 'bout the trouble with girls, Jake's face gave a look, and it dawned on Lizzy that she had hit pert-near close to home. Wuz it possible that Suzanna wuz wild as a March hare? She covered, "I didn't mean nuthin' by that, Jake. I suwanee. I ain't heard nary a thang 'bout her. She's liked by ever'body who knows her. I tell you, I heard Tammy and Patty singin' her praises like she hung the moon. You know Tammy and Patty, don't you?"

"I know who they are, I thank. Ain't they kin to Buford, Dutch's buddy?"

"Yep," said Lizzy. "Dutch and Buford 'r like two peas in a pod. Dutch takes such good care of Buford, you wouldn't b'lieve it if you seen it with yer own eyes."

"You know, I don't thank you're jest whistlin' Dixie 'bout that. I have seen the way Dutch watches out fer 'im. He said somethin' on the way here that makes me thank Buford owes 'im big-time, but I could jest as soon be wrong that he wuz talkin' of Buford."

"You best spill it, Jake. You've opened up a can of worms, and now I have to know what yer talkin' 'bout."

"I don't thank it's somethin' Dutch would want me waggin' my tongue 'bout on account of gossip gittin' 'round to the folks involved."

"You know I won't be goin' 'round cluckin' and tuttin' 'bout it. I don't even run in the same circles as y'all."

"Well, jest keep in mind that I'm dumber 'n a bag of hammers, and Buford might be as far from this particular situation as the north is from the south. Dutch said that he wuz bowed up like a banty rooster fer savin' a feller from a life that would've gone to hell in a handbasket. Alls I know is it had somethin' to do with a filly Buford wuz eyeballin' all last summer."

"Did Dutch say why he stuck his nose in it?"

"I thank Dutch wuz juberous 'bout whether or not this gal wuz good enough fer Buford."

"What did he do to drive a wedge b'tween 'em?"

"He didn't say how he done it, only that he wuz plum et up with relief 'bout it."

Lizzy walked on but this news wuz with her like a white elephant sittin' in somebody's lap. She couldn't thank on a thang to say, so she kept her mouth shut. After a bit, Jake asked her why she wuz so quiet all of the sudden.

"I'm thankin' yer cousin put his nose in where it don't belong. Who died and made him judge of them folks?"

"Well, ain't you jest got yer ass on yer shoulders? What makes you thank he wuz pokin' 'round where he wuzn't wanted?"

"A person cain't make decisions like that 'bout somebody else. Who in the hell does he thank he is? He prob'ly knew somethin' more 'bout the situation. Maybe the fella, whether it wuz Buford or somebody else, wuzn't smitten with the girl after all."

"Yer makin' 'ol Dutch sound lower 'n a snakes belly. I guess he shouldn't be pattin' himself on the back 'bout it."

Jake said this last part like it wuz a joke, but Lizzy thought he'd hit the nail on the head, so she jest zipped her lip on the subject and started talkin' on other thangs til they reached the parsonage. There she announced that she needed to go see a man 'bout a horse. And once the bathroom door wuz shut, she could thank on the situation without frettin' 'bout interruption. There wuz no way on God's green earth there could be two fellers that Dutch wuz leadin' 'round by a leash. And the fact that he had pulled Buford away from Janie on purpose wuz enough to gag a maggot. Lizzy'd always been sure as shootin' that Dutch'd wanted Buford fer Suzanna, but to be willfully ugly to Janie, to cause her to suffer and fret, and all on account of his own pride, well, that wuz pert near unforgivable. How could anyone mash darlin' Janie's hopes like that? She might never git over it.

Jake had said there wuz a question 'bout whether the girl wuz 'good enough' fer Buford, but Lizzy knew exactly what he meant... that her family wuzn't good enough. Flo wuz always sayin' that if'n you lay down with dogs, you git up with fleas. She wuzn't the only person who felt this way without a doubt. Janie wuz picture perfect in all ways. Hell, she could win the Miss Tennessee pageant without even a-tryin'. She's purty and smart and good as all git-out. Aside from bein' poor, a person couldn't complain 'bout Benny one lick. But when Lizzy thought on her own mother, bless her heart, she blushed quick as a duck on a junebug. Her Momma had no sense whatsoever, but that shouldn't stop Dutch from wantin' Buford to saddle up with Janie. Dutch had to be a-lookin' on it from his own designs and how it would brang 'im down in life to be associated with such folks.

Lizzy wuz fit to be tied. She holed up in her room and took more 'n a few swigs of the Peach Schnapps she'd brought along in her grip. The result wuz a quick buzz that gave way to a headache. She couldn't bear the thought of seein' Dutch that evenin' at the big house, so she told Cooter and Charlotte they should go without her. Coot wuz of course frettin' that Miz M would be ticked off 'bout it, but Charlotte convinced him it'd be all right.

# Chapter 34

Once Lizzy seen her friends turn the bend in the road, she turned on Charlotte's computer to re-read some of the emails from her sister. Janie wuzn't one to complain, but she seemed as lost as last year's Easter egg. She wuz always a 'glass half full' kind of a gal, but her letters seemed empty of any cheer. On second look Janie's words wuz filled with uneasiness, and this caused Lizzy to thank more 'bout what her sister might be goin' through. Dutch seemed so proud of himself that it made her jest sick, and she wuz never so glad in all her days that he would be out'a her sight in a day or two. She couldn't help but thank that Dutch leavin' meant Jake would be leavin' too, but since he hadn't made a move or anythang, she felt she had nuthin' to stir her stew 'bout.

At that split second, the doorbell rang and nearly scared the pee out'a Lizzy. She thought maybe it wuz Jake comin' to see how she wuz farin', and she wuz surprised as all git-out to see Dutch standin' on the stoop. She let him in, and he started askin' how she wuz feelin' and sayin' how he hoped she wuzn't too sick fer a visit. She answered with a tone colder 'n a well-digger's butt in Idaho. He seemed not to hear a word of it, but stood up and sat back down so many times Lizzy began to thank there wuz somethin' wrong with 'im.

He started to say somethin' then stopped and started again. Finally he said, "Sometimes I thank, 'Well...' and then again, I jest don't know. I've tried to stop myself. I cain't. I want you worse 'n my bitch hound dog wants a T-bone steak. The truth is, I thank I'm in love with you, Miss Lizzy."

Lizzy's jaw dropped open like she wuz a-tryin' to catch flies. She wuz all popeyed and blushin' and suddenly felt hot as blue blazes. She couldn't catch a thought in a hairnet, and Dutch took her silence as an invite to tell her all that he wanted to do to her immediately and down the road after they wuz married. Aside from the immediate needs of his pecker and his heart, Dutch had more to say. He told her how far below 'im she wuz, how cheap her Momma wuz and what skanks her younger sisters wuz. He told her how low he wuz stoopin', and even though he said it with a full heart, it didn't help 'im none.

She wuz as stuck as a duck in a dry pond. On the one hand, Lizzy liked this guy 'bout as much as taxes, but she couldn't help but be flattered that a big shot like Dutch would pay her the time of day. She didn't give his offer no nevermind, but her heart went out to 'im fer sayin' such pretties 'bout her so she couldn't be too cross with 'im. She listened to 'im in disbelief as he ended his speech by sayin' he'd tried ever' way in the world to stop wantin' her, but now alls he could do wuz be happy that they might be fumblin' 'round in the cab of his truck maybe that very night. Lizzy could tell he wuz jest as sure as he could be that she'd have 'im. He talked a good game 'bout bein' nervous as a hound dog shittin' peach pits and all, but the truth wuz, he wuz sure of himself.

When he finally quit talkin', Lizzy said, "I guess I should be thankful, but the truth is yer gittin' jest a little bit too big fer yer britches, and I'm gonna have to take you down a notch or two. You act like you're somebody. I don't mean to hurt yer feelin's, Dutch, but you must be pullin' my leg! There ain't no way in hell I could ever mess up the sheets with you, let alone marry you! Good gracious! But don't you worry yer stuck up head 'bout it. I'm sure you'll git over me b'fore long."

Dutch, who wuz leanin' against the fireplace with his eyes glued to her face looked like he'd jest tasted pine tar. His face turned white as a turnip, and his eyes said "I'm gonna skin you alive."

She waited while he picked through his thoughts, and after a spell he said, "You ain't got no call to refuse me like that. Yer Momma didn't raise you right. You could at least have been polite, but hell, I guess I jest don't give a damn now."

"I should ask why you would come courtin' me with put-downs and insults," she said. "You come over here and say you wish you didn't like me? You tell me I'm beneath you and insult my kin the way you did! How could you expect me to be on my good manners after that? Well, excuse me fer breathin'. I have other reasons why I thank you couldn't git laid in a women's prison with a handful of pardons! You cain't tell me what you want. Folks in hell want ice water, too, but they ain't gittin' it, are they? You who treated my own sister like shit? She wuz happier 'n I'd ever seen her with Buford, and you pulled that rug right out from under her feet."

As she mentioned Janie, Dutch's expression changed, but he didn't say nuthin' and let her keep talkin'.

"You thank the sun comes up jest to hear you crow, but yer as unwelcome as a skunk at a lawn party. Nuthin' you say can take away what you did to poor Janie. You cain't deny you wuz the cause of Buford's leavin' her. Now it looks like he used her fer a good time or somethin'."

She took a second to check his face fer any hint of bein' sorry, but he looked at her with a half smile like her engine wuz runnin' but ain't nobody drivin'.

"You cain't say it ain't so."

He took a deep breath and said, "I cain't say I didn't do ever'thang in my power to put miles b'tween my buddy and yer sister. I've been a better friend to him than to my ownself."

His meanin' wuzn't lost on Lizzy.

She said, "But it ain't jest the situation b'tween Buford and Janie that gits my goat. I had you figured out a long time b'fore that. From nearly the first time I laid eyes on you, I knew you thought yer shit don't stink, but it wuz Joe Wickham who filled me in on the rest. What can you say fer yerself 'bout all that business? You cain't spit shine a turd, Dutch. Of that I'd bet my last dollar."

"You've got yer head so far up Joe's ass you cain't see nuthin'," Dutch said.

"I jest feel so dagum sorry fer 'im after all he's been through. Anybody would."

"You feel sorry fer 'im!" said Dutch with venom in his voice. "Life has been hard on him? Give me a break!"

"And it's all yer fault, Dutch!" cried Lizzy. "Shit fire and save matches! You took a respectable man and ruined 'im. You know yer Daddy wanted to help 'im out, but you as much as threw his wishes out like throwin' out a baby with the bathwater. You did it all. How can you brush off his troubles and laugh at 'em? It ain't right."

"And this," Dutch shouted, "is what you thank of me? I guess I ain't the sharpest knife in the drawer that I didn't expect it. If'n yer right, I jest thank I'm it on a stick. But maybe if'n I'd been less straight with you 'bout my reasons fer a-tryin' to fergit you, I'd have gotten a Yankee dime instead of a slap across the face. I b'lieve yer gittin' bigger 'n yer raisin', Miss Lizzy. You ain't got a pot to piss in and yer judgin' me? I ain't ashamed of tellin' you my feelin's, no sirree. I'd rather be honest than proud. Do you thank I'd be happy 'bout bein' related to a family with so few branches on the family tree?"

Lizzy listened as he spoke, but felt like if he kept it up, she'd cancel his birth certificate or at least his chance of havin' children of his own. She wuz as mad as a mule chewin' on bumblebees. She forced her voice to be steady as rain and said, "Yer flat out wrong if'n you thank it wuz the way you asked me that made me refuse you. I would've felt sorry fer you if'n you'd been more polite, but my answer would've been the same."

Dutch flinched. Her voice wuz cold enough to freeze the balls off a pool table. "If'n you wuz the only crick in the dessert, and I'd been a week without water, I'd die b'fore I'd come within ten feet of you."

He kept starin' at her, sober as a Mormon preacher on Sund'y morning. He looked like he wanted to crawl into a pit and die there.

"From the very start, almost from the first minute I laid my eyes on you, I thought you didn't have the decency to die. You make me mad enough to bite nails with yer livin' high on the hog and yer fancy ways. Every minute I'm in the same room with you feels like thirty years. Git hitched to you? No way! Not fer all the tea in China."

"I thank you best shut yer trap, Missy. You've said yer peace, now I'm gonna say mine. I'm embarrassed that I ever wuz partial to you. I best leave b'fore I say somethin' I will regret. My Momma taught me that if'n you don't have nuthin' nice to say, don't say nuthin' at all."

And with that, he traveled a minute in thirty seconds and wuz out the door quick as a whip. Lizzy's mind wuz a carnival of thoughts. She sat down and cried a handful of tears fer half an hour. Ever' recollection gave her a scotch more to be surprised 'bout. That Dutch could be itchin' to git hitched to her! That he could tolerate her at all! That he wanted her in spite of all the reasons why he didn't want his best bud to marry her sister! She could've clapped her ninnies to thank that she had created feelin's so strong in any man. But his pride. Lawsy mercy, that pride! He wuz near peacock proud 'bout what he'd done to Janie and Buford, and as to poor Joe Wickham, he didn't deny a word of what she'd said. She wuz boilin' mad and went up to her room when she heard Cooter and Charlotte pull in the driveway so's not to have to answer any questions.

# Chapter 35

Lizzy slept like the dead and woke up to the same thoughts she'd had the night b'fore. No matter how hard she stared at the ceilin', she could not git over Dutch poppin' the question the way he did. After some biscuits and sausage gravy, she decided to take some air to clear her head. As she headed up the path she stopped short, rememberin' that she wuz on the path where she'd run into Dutch a few times, so she turned and walked up the lane instead. The trees wuz fillin' out but the constant Southern humidity hadn't settled down to stay jest yet. In a month the South would be hotter 'n the hinges on the gates of hell, and it'd be so dry the trees would be bribin' the dogs.

'Bout that time, Lizzy spied a feller walkin' towards her across the way, and she wuz pert near sure it wuz Dutch, so she turned on her heel and walked back the way she'd come. When she heard her name hollered out, she wuz sure it wuz Dutch, and she'd been spotted. As he caught up to her, she could see that he looked like he wuz rode hard and put up wet. He handed her a letter and said, "I've been all over hell and half acre a-lookin' fer you this mornin'. I hope you'll read this." And with that, he turned and walked away.

Lizzy looked down at the letter in her hand. Whatever Dutch had written down didn't matter a blivit to her, but she wuz curious as a nine year-old at Christmas to see what the letter said. The envelope held two sheets of paper written double sided. She sat down on a tree stump to read ever' word.

*"Don't you worry yer little head, Miss Lizzy, thankin' this letter is goin' to be a repeat of yesterd'y. We've already tilled that ground, and there ain't no use in kickin' a dead horse after rigor mortis has set in. Let's jest forgit it ever happened. You said some thangs last night that ain't true, and I ain't pickin' fly shit out'a the pepper to wanna set you straight.*

*"You accused me of two thangs last night. The first wuz to say that I put miles b'tween Buford and yer sister, and the other wuz that I wuz tighter than the bark on a tree and ruined Joe Wickham's chances of makin' somethin' of himself. You made me sound like a man who would gripe with a ham under each arm.*

*"Growin' up, Joe and I wuz like two peas in a pod. My Daddy and his Daddy wuz thick as thieves, and yer right when you say Joe wuz dependin' on us fer a job. But comparin' what happened with Joe to the situation with yer sister is like comparin' apples to oranges. It jest ain't right. Ain't nobody gonna mess on me and call it apple butter. I've got to bend yer ear so's you know the truth.*

*"With my luck I hope I don't piss you off. Some folks can fall into a barrel of assholes and come out smellin' like a rose, but lately I seem to be the*

*kind who falls into a barrel of boobies and comes out suckin' my own thumb. It's time fer me to say my peace.*

*"I hadn't been up yer way fer two shakes of a lambs tail b'fore I seen, jest like ever'body else in those parts, that Buford wuz hot and heavy with yer sister. It wuzn't 'til Buford's shin-dig that I worried that he might be smitten fer sure. I'll admit, I've seen Buford foller a girl like a hound dog after a bitch in heat more 'n once. But while I wuz dancin' with you, Billy Lucas said somethin' or 'nother 'bout Buford and Janie needin' a preacher b'fore long, and I started to worry that maybe they'd ate dinner b'fore they said grace, if you know what I'm sayin'. Now I didn't know y'all from Adam much, so I wuz kinda worried she might git herself knocked up to snag my buddy, Buford. I started watchin' 'em real close, and I could tell he wuz head over heels fer her. I watched yer sister, too. She wuz friendly but not flirtin' or moonin' over 'im. I caught 'em a time or two in a lip lock, but she never pulled 'im out into the corn field even fer a minute. I figured she wuzn't all that sweet on 'im after all. I'm not sayin' I ain't never been wrong b'fore. I'm not gonna swell up and die to admit it this time. If'n yer sister heartstrangs 'r tied up in knots over Buford, I'll admit I done put the pepper in the gumbo on that account. But you got to admit, Miss Lizzy, that nobody would've b'lieved she wuz hot fer Buford by watchin' her behave. Call me scatterbrained like a leaf in a windstorm, but I thank I seen what I wanted to see, if you catch my meanin'.*

*"I had more reasons to stop Buford than the ones I told you last night. Hell's fire and damnation, yer Momma's family ain't half so bad as yer Momma herself, yer three little sisters and even sometimes yer own Daddy, God love 'em. I sure don't wanna cause you any pain, here, and back up the truck if I do, but I don't lump you in with yer relations a bit. You and Janie've got nice manners, but watchin' the rest of yer family eat is like watchin' pigs to the slop.*

*"Anyhoo, that night at the party, ever'thang I thought 'bout yer family wuz branded true in my brain, and the next day when Buford left fer Nashv'lle, I wuz bound and determined to git the heck out'a Dodge my ownself. I know he planned on returnin' directly, but I made sure he didn't. His kin agreed with me, and you know the rest.*

*"While we wuz in Nashv'lle I took the chance to bend Buford's ear on what a bad idea it would be to git messed up with such a family, a gaumy business, I admit. I might could've pissed 'im off royally, but I made sure he seen to my way of thankin' 'bout yer sister's feelin's. He looks up to me, and well, he b'lieved what I wuz sayin'. Keepin' 'im from drivin' back out yonder wuz nothin'. I ain't got no shame 'bout none of it 'cept that I kept yer sister's bein' in Nashv'lle under my hat so's Buford wouldn't find out she wuz there. Buford's kin knew, and we wuz in kahoots to keep the information from 'im. Call me a thumpin' gizzard, but I didn't thank he wuz ready to see her yet. I wuz protectin' my friend, and I ain't got nuthin' else to say 'bout that.*

*"On yer other point, Joe, I have to say I feel like I've been chewed up and spit out. The only way I can explain what happened is to tell you the truth. You*

cain't judge a man til you've walked a mile in his moccasins, and I have no idea why he's goin' 'round tellin' folks I'm lower than a snake's belly in a wagon rut, but here's the story:

"Joe is the son of a good feller who worked at Pembrook Farm all his days. My Daddy rightly trusted 'im and stood up in church with Joe when he wuz christened, and we all wanted to say the apple didn't fall far from the tree and love Joe. Daddy paid his way through school and wanted Joe to work on the farm and manage a few other rental properties and such. This wuz all b'fore somebody throwed a clod in the churn, and Joe ended up as crooked as a barrel of snakes. He could act right fer a spell, but seein' as how I wuz 'round 'im more often than others, I could see 'im fer who he really wuz. You can lead a horse to water, but you jest cain't make 'im drank, and Joe wuz so bad he could ruin a two car funeral. It wuz a bad combination. I don't mean to be talkin' out'a school, but you need to know what happened.

"My Daddy died 'bout five years ago, and bein' the good soul that he wuz, he left somethin' fer Joe in his will and made promises to help 'im make a livin'. Joe's Daddy died b'fore mine wuz cold in the ground, and within a week after the funeral he called me up to say he didn't wanna work my land, and he wanted me to pay 'im to go away and give 'im tuition money fer law school. I thought nobody oughtta make decisions like a turpentined cat so soon after a funeral, but I wuz aggrieved fer my Daddy, so I paid 'im. I figured I'd washed my hands of 'im, and I reckollected that I wuz better off.

"I heard from some friends that Joe had no earthly intention of goin' to law school, and he wuz pissin' away my Daddy's good will and drankin' like a man fresh out'a the desert. Fer three years he lived fast and hard, and when he ran out'a money, he turned up like a bad penny, wantin' to work fer me at the farm. He wuz in a world of hurt fer cash and needed a steady job, and he reminded me of what my Daddy had once said 'bout puttin' in a good word fer 'im with the gov'ner's security detail. I, of course, said 'hell no.' I wuzn't 'bout to put myself out fer a damned drunk who couldn't even do farm work, and Joe went all 'round the Lexin'ton bad mouthin' me behind my back. He wuz diggin' his own grave, and I never had nuthin' to do with 'im after that. I have no idea how he made his money, but I b'lieve it wuz under-handed.

"Last summer I reckon he  had to go 'round his elbow to git to his thumb, and our paths crossed again. Now I'm 'bout to tell you some thangs I'm gonna regret, but you need to know what kind of a snake Joe Wickham is, so I'm gonna tell you. You cain't let on that you know this, and I'm gonna ask you to zip yer lip 'bout it.

"Suzanna is a few years younger than I am, and when my Mamma and Daddy died, Jake and me wuz told to look after her and raise her right. Last year we took her out'a reg'lar school and decided to hire a woman to home school her on account of those Kentucky schools 'r 'bout as useful as a trapdoor on a canoe. Miz Young seemed like a nice enough girl, wider than she wuz tall and quick as a whip. We hired her on the spot without knowin' she wuz kin to Joe, and instead of keepin' the fox out'a the henhouse, she wuz holdin' open the door fer 'im. He tried ever' way from Sund'y to git my sister pregnant so's she would have to marry 'im, but she, purty as she is, ain't interested in boys yet, so Joe wuzn't gittin' anywhere with her at all. One day I showed up early and caught him a-tryin' to git to second base on my Momma's sofa, and the truth came out. Joe left the house faster than a bell clapper in a goose's ass, and Miz Young could've left quicker if'n she'd have jest rolled down the driveway instead of using those stubby little legs of hers.

"There ain't no doubt Joe wuz after Suzanna's money, but I'll suwanee he wuz out to git back at me fer sendin' 'im packin'. I cain't tell nobody what happened on account of my sister's privacy and her reputation and all.

"This, Miss Lizzy, is the truth of what happened. It's no skin off my nose whether you b'lieve it or not, but I hope you won't judge me on my behavior with Joe Wickham. I know you thank he's jest the tom-cat's kitten, and I don't know what kind of lies he's been spreadin' to git yer good opinion, but he's got to be a special kind of stupid to thank that I wouldn't tell you the honest to goodness truth 'bout 'im.

"You might wonder why I didn't tell you all this last night, but I wuz too flustered and my heart wuz so heavy that it would ha' took three men and a midgit to lift it. If'n you wanna ask Jake 'bout all of it, you can. He knows all 'bout it, and I dare say you trust him more 'n me. I'm gonna try to git this letter into yer hands today.

"God bless you,
"Dutch."

# Chapter 36

Lizzy wuzn't expectin' Dutch's letter to be a re-run from the night b'fore. She knew he wuz tighter than a flea's ass over a rain barrel with his compliments, and she didn't look fer one in the letter. She wuz as anxious as a one-eyed cat watchin' two rat holes while she read. She wuz prepared to take everythang with a grain of salt. Ever' word tasted so bad if'n she wuz a dog, she'd have to lick her ass to git the taste off. He wuzn't sorry fer a thang he had done, but she expected as much. She felt so angry when she read what he wrote 'bout her sister, if'n he'd been standin' there, she would've slapped 'im to sleep and then slapped 'im fer sleepin'. Every sentence wuz full of pride, and it showed that Dutch had his ass on his shoulders fer sure.

But when she got to the part 'bout Joe Wickham, she sat up straighter and nearly tumped over a time or two. She read it quick as a hot knife through butter and read it again. By then she wuz sick at her stomach. She knew it wuz true on account of the private information Dutch had given her 'bout Suzanna, but she kept repeatin', "You lie like a rug!" and "That dog jest won't hunt." When she finished the letter, she wadded it up in a ball and stuck it in her pocket, sayin' she wouldn't let it see daylight again.

She got up and walked on a couple of steps b'fore she pulled it back out and read it again, 'specially the part 'bout Joe. Ever' word matched the stories Joe'd told her from his connection to Pembrook Farm to his bein' a favorite of the old man. The part 'bout the money didn't match up to what she b'lieved. She re-read that part a couple of more times b'fore she decided to put down the letter and let her thoughts marinate. She started to see how there could be two sides to the story and how in one of 'em, Dutch wuz blameless.

She couldn't say nuthin' 'bout Joe's bein' quick with a buck on account of she never heard tell of 'im b'fore he came 'round the fair grounds back home. He had said he wuz workin' on a drug unit, but that could've been a big fat lie. Ever'thang he said 'bout his ownself could've been made up on the spot. She thought she must not've been playin' with a full deck to have not checked up on 'im, but ever'thang 'bout 'im said he wuz exactly who he said he wuz. Lizzy tried to thank of somethin' nice maybe he did fer somebody, anythang really, to hush up the naggin' in her mind that sounded exactly like Dutch's voice, but she couldn't. She could close her eyes and see 'im standin' there in his tight jeans and cowboy boots, with his hat and his Bon Jovi good looks, but aside from bein' eye candy, she couldn't reckollect him bein' nuthin' but a bump on a log as far as offerin' a hand up or a hand out where anyone wuz concerned.

She pulled out the letter to read it again. The worst part of all wuz the way he tried to use Suzanna. This made her mad enough to tear up an anvil. She'd seen somethin' of it on Jake's face yesterd'y when they wuz talkin' 'bout Miss Suzanna, and now she had an invite in her hand to ask 'im 'bout it outright. She thought 'bout brangin' it up to Jake, but changed her mind. There really wuzn't no point in askin' 'im now since Dutch wouldn't have told her to ask Jake if'n he wuzn't sure as shootin' that his story would still hold water at the end of the day.

Lizzy felt sickly as she remembered ever' word of her first conversation with Joe Wickham. At the time she'd thought he wuz three sheets to the wind to be talkin' 'round ever'body's back like he did. He didn't know her from Adam, and he wuz spewin' garbage all over town 'bout Dutch right off the bat. She reckollected how Joe stood there grinnin' like a possum, sayin' he wouldn't budge an inch, but when it came right down to it, it wuz Joe, not Dutch, who had shied away from the cook-out that night. And she noticed he only told his sob story to her while Dutch, Buford and his kin wuz there, but when they all left fer Nashv'lle, he started spreadin' his manure to anyone who would listen. When she thought 'bout it, it puzzled her why in the world he said he wouldn't bad mouth Dutch on account of his Daddy, but turned 'round and did it anyway.

The truth dawned on her. He must've thought she had a secret trust fund or somethin'. Maybe he thought be'cuz Benny owned a repair shop that there wuz some money. Or maybe he wuz jest puffin' himself up. Whatever his reasons, Lizzy knew Joe Wickham wuz jest big hat, no cattle. Ever' point she chewed on jest made Dutch's case as strong as M'ssippi Mud. Lizzy wuz absolutely ashamed of herself. She couldn't thank on Dutch or Joe without thankin' she'd been blind and partial and lopsided and plum stupid.

"My heavenly days!" she cried. "Ain't I God's own fool. I wish I could jest dig a hole and bury myself in it fer the shame. I've been so proud of myself and briggity 'bout it. Who's got egg on her face now? I've been taken down a notch or two fer sure. I put all my money on one horse and didn't pay no nevermind to the other. 'til right this instant I never knew my ownself."

With her thoughts spinnin' from Janie to Buford to Dutch, she wuz worn to a frazzle. Dutch'd said he didn't know nuthin' 'bout Janie's feelin's fer Buford. If'n he wuz tellin' the truth 'bout Joe, surely he wuz tellin' the truth 'bout that. Even Charlotte'd said Janie wuz a little too backward with boys. Maybe if'n she'd let 'im git to third base, he would've understood she wuz hot and bothered by 'im.

The part of the letter that mentioned Lizzy's family wuz the hardest to swaller. In all her born days she'd never read nuthin' so true. She'd have to be dumber 'n a spotted dog to deny it. When Billy Lucas, drunk as a skunk, spilled his guts 'bout what ever'body expected out'a Buford and Janie, he must've had his stupid head on. That man's brain rattles 'round like a BB in a boxcar. He don't have a thought of his own. Dutch must've known he wuz jest repeatin' what Lizzy's own mother wuz spreadin'.

Dutch's words 'bout Janie and her ownself wuz fine as a frog's hair split four ways, and it soothed her like balm on a rash, but it didn't do nuthin' to ease her feelin's 'bout how the rest of her family'd behaved. She knew that her own Momma and iglant sisters had ruined Janie's hopes of gittin' hitched to Buford. On account of this, she felt lower 'n pond scum.

She wandered 'round the back of the chicken coop and through the trees fer so long she lost track of time. She figured Charlotte'd thank she'd been shell roaded, so she turned back towards the parsonage. There she found out she'd missed Dutch and Jake. Dutch had stopped by to say "so long," but Jake had stayed pert near an hour waitin' on Lizzy and almost took off after her. She wuz glad to have missed both of the fellers. All she could thank on wuz the letter in her pocket.

# Chapter 37

Dutch and Jake left Knoxv'lle with the rooster crow the next mornin', and Cooter stood out by the fence to wave like the idjit he wuz then came inside to describe what they wuz wearin'. Lizzy couldn't help but thank he had some sugar in his tank noticin' stuff like that. Cooter then sniffed his pits Once assured he smelled okay, he took off fer Miz M's house to check on 'er. He came back sayin' that Miz M wuz so bored, she'd like to have Cooter and his folks over fer fried chicken, mashed taters and collard greens.

Lizzy couldn't look on Prudence Majestro without thankin' how she could've been this lady's kin through Dutch's proposal. She grinned when she thought of the dyin' duck fit that Miz M would throw if'n all that had come to pass. What would she've said? How would she've acted? Lizzy put her mind on these thangs and entertained herself.

"Law, I'm gonna miss them boys," Miz M whined. "We're so close, like white on rice, I'll suwanee. Jake wuz purty bad 'bout leavin', but I never did see Dutch so low. He's partial to his visits here. Ever' year he's more at home here."

After they'd picked all the chicken off the bones, Miz M noticed Lizzy wuz out'a sorts and thought she wuz sore 'bout havin' to leave Knoxv'lle. She said, "Jest call yer Momma and ask her if'n you can stay a little bit longer. She won't mind, I'm sure, and Charlotte will like the comp'ny, no doubt."

"I thank you kindly," said Lizzy, "but I cain't stay. I have to be back b'fore next Saturd'y."

"You haven't been here long enough to soil the bed clothes. Yer Momma don't need you back so soon."

"My Momma needs me 'bout as much as a pocket full of paper assholes. It's my Daddy. He called last week askin' me to light a fire under myself to git home quicker. If'n I don't git home right quick, I'll feel like ten pounds of manure in a five pound sack."

"Shit fire and save matches, girl! If yer Momma can spare you, yer Daddy ain't gonna knock you into the middle of next week fer stayin' a while longer. I'll even take you to Nashv'lle my ownself when I go over later next month."

"Well, ain't you sweet as pie, Miz M, but I'm afraid I have to git the hell out'a Dodge and back to my own folks."

Turnin' to Charlotte, Miz M stomped her foot and said, "Y'all better send somebody to drive these girls. It's a fer piece to Nashv'lle fer two young uns to be out alone. They shouldn't be on the Greyhound without a feller to watch 'em with the way the world is today. It jest ain't right."

"My uncle is sendin' a feller down to carry us back. He's got a shipment comin' down to these parts."

"Gracious light! Yer uncle is sending one of his employees to git you! I'm so glad y'all have folks to thank on such thangs fer you. There's a service station down the road past the big corn maze sign if'n y'all need to fill up b'fore you hit the road."

Miz M had a list of questions as long as yer arm 'bout the trip, and she couldn't answer all of 'em fer her ownself, so Lizzy had to pay attention in case she had to say somethin'. It wuz a good thang, be'cuz if'n she didn't have nuthin' to thank on, her mind would've been wrapped 'round her own thoughts like some kind of a garden snake.

After dinner she spent time locked up in her room re-readin' Dutch's letter so much, she knew it better 'n the preacher's daughter knew a memory verse at vacation Bible school. She switched her feelin's 'bout it as often as Brett Favre decided to retire from football. When she reckollected the way Dutch wrote, she got so mad she wanted to whip 'im til he couldn't sit down fer a week. But when she thought 'bout how unfair she wuz, she got all swole up with anger at her ownself. She wuz right thankful he'd been sweet on her, but she couldn't have said yes in a million years. She didn't have no regret 'bout sendin' 'im packin' and didn't care to ever lay eyes on him again. Ever' day she wished she could kick herself in the ass with Roscoe's boot fer the way she b'haved, and rememberin' the way her kin had acted made her wanna load 'em all up on a turnip truck and send 'em to where they could learn some common sense. There wuz no help fer 'em. Her Daddy would rather scratch his butt and laugh at 'em than teach his younger girls not to chase after the fellers. And her Momma, well, there wuz no hope fer her on any account. Lizzy and Janie had tried to teach 'em some manners, but with their piss poor excuse fer a Momma goin' out at her age to enter wet t-shirt contests, they wuz fightin' an uphill battle fer sure. Kitty wuz as useful as a screen door on a submarine, a real fuss-budgit who follered her sister 'round like a lost pup after the garbage truck. Lydie wuz so purty she could make a hound dog smile, but she didn't have the sense God gave a goose. She follered her own wants and didn't have a care in the world. She thought Janie and Lizzy didn't know dip shit from apple butter. Lizzy reckoned you couldn't tell nobody nuthin' that ain't ever been nowhere, but she kept a-tryin'. Any man in a uniform wuz fair game to Lydie and Kitty, and as long as they didn't need nobody to git 'em to the fair grounds, they would go there as much as they wanted, which wuz purty much ever' day.

Lizzy frowned and fretted over Janie. In the light of Dutch's letter, Janie's loss wuz enough to drive a nun to git drunk on the communion wine. Buford wuz as good as honey biscuits at sunrise and as honest as the day is long. They would've made the cutest couple if not fer a family so stupid that it didn't git hit with the stupid stick, but wuz smacked upside the head by the whole forest!

With all these thoughts weighin' heavy as a yoke 'round Lizzy's neck, she started acting poorly as a killdee and down in the mouth. She still had to go to the big house as often as not, and in fact spent her last night in Knoxv'lle over thar where the folks wuz makin' a mess of Looziana boil with crawdads and shrimp and the whole nine yards. Miz M told Lizzy and Katie Jo how to roll her clothes in their suitcases and which rest areas wuz the cleanest so that when they made it back to the parsonage, Katie Jo undid all her packin' and started over.

Miz M put on airs when they wuz leavin'. She invited all of 'em back to Knoxv'lle the next year, and even DeeDee offered her dead fish handshake to the girls.

# Chapter 38

On Saturd'y morning, Cooter and Lizzy set down to their breakfast b'fore anyone else had hauled 'emselves out'a bed, and he decided to bend her ear b'fore she hit the road.

"I ain't got a clue, Miss Lizzy, if'n Charlotte done told you how much she 'preciates yer comin' fer a visit. They ain't much 'round these parts to recommend 'em fer a vacation. We're too far from downtown to have any tractor pulls or rodeos or even stores fer winder shoppin'. You cain't know what this has meant to Charlotte. I jest cain't... I cain't..."

"Well, Cooter, cain't never could do nothin'. Don't fret over it. I've had a knee-slappin' good time hangin' out with Charlotte. It reminds me of old times. I'm grateful fer the invitation, honest Injun."

Cooter took the compliment like a dose of salts through a widow woman and said, "I'm glad you ain't had too bad of a time down here. We did our best to 'commodate you. I know we put you in the way of better folks 'n you usually rub elbows with. I'm talkin' 'bout Miz M, of course. We's jest as lucky as a four leaf clover to have fallen in with her. Not many folks can say they keep comp'ny like her. Why, we're over thar three times a week and twice on Sund'y. Even though the parsonage can be down right lonesome, nobody can say nuthin' bad 'bout the big house."

"I'm sure you'll go right back home and tell the folks there that Charlotte is as happy as a dog with two peters. Miz M spends time with my wife and treats her like she's got some raisin'. I hope you know I don't harbor no ill will towards you, and I hope you're jest as happy as a horse in oats when you finally do git hitched. Charlotte and me wuz made fer each other 'specially when it comes to hoppin' in the sack, and I'd be willin' to swear it on a stack of Bibles."

Lizzy told 'im she wuz tickled he and Charlotte wuz happy t'gether. She jest 'bout swallered her tongue when he made hand motions and grunts which called to mind him having sex with her friend who wuz so skinny, if'n she turned sideways and stuck out her tongue, she'd look like a zipper. She wuz pleased as punch when Charlotte, her ownself, walked into the room and ended the conversation. Law she couldn't stand leavin' her friend with a husband who wuz slicker 'n owl shit, but she knew what she wuz gittin' herself into when she married 'im. When she put her mind on her house and her chickens and her garden and such, Charlotte knew there wuzn't no flies on her. She wuz right proud of how she'd come up in the world.

B'fore long a beat up delivery truck rolled to a stop out front of the parsonage, and the driver loaded up their grips into the back while a cigarette with danglin' ash bobbed along in front of 'im. He had that essential Southern skill of talkin' and holdin' a burning cigarette in his mouth at the same time. One of his elbows wuz brown from hanging it out'a the truck window fer miles on end. The rest of 'im wuz a sallow yellow color, covered in smoke and road dirt. Cooter walked out to the truck with Lizzy, askin' her to send a good word from 'im to her folks and her sisters fer their hospitality over the winter and to Guthrie and Tildie who he'd never met b'fore in his life. He helped Katie Jo in the truck with a heave and a grunt and wuz 'bout to shut the door when he realized the girls hadn't asked 'im to say anythang to the folks at the big house.

"You'll sure as shootin' want me to say 'thank you kindly' to Miz M fer all she's done fer y'all since you got here."

Lizzy and Katie Jo agreed so that Cooter would shut the damned door and they could have a minute's peace.

"Heavens to Betsy!" said Katie Jo as they made the first bend, "I feel like I've only been away from home fer a day or two, and here we're goin' home already. So much has happened, though. Wouldn't you say?"

"You ain't jest whistlin' Dixie," said Lizzy with a sigh.

"We done ate nine times at the big house, plus we went over twice fer snacks. I sure do love 'em little sandwiches she made that time. We've been eatin' high on the hog fer sure. I hope I can remember it all so's I can tell my kin when I git back."

Lizzy had been thankin' of all she had to hide from her folks but winked at Katie Jo and smiled, thankin' 'bout how very much the girl had been able to stuff in her face at each meal.

The truck engine wuz so loud they couldn't hear themselves thank, so not much talkin' took place on the trip. B'fore they know'd what happened, they wuz pullin' up in front of Guthrie and Tildie's house where they wuz to stay fer a couple of days.

Janie looked fresh as a spring flower, but Lizzy couldn't visit with her proper on account of Tildie had 'em all over hell and half acre, gittin' their nails done and their hair done and even had some glamour shots made of the girls in low cut shirts. It'd be no time at all b'fore the sisters would be back home where Lizzy could spend as much time as she cared to give watchin' her sister's expressions.

A-tryin' to keep Dutch's proposal to herself wuz like a-tryin' to stuff two angry cats in a tater sack. She wanted to see Jane's eyes pop out when she told her the news, but Lizzy worried that if'n she started to tell the story, she'd have to tell the whole damned thang. She didn't wanna say nuthin' 'bout Buford that would make her sister down in the mouth.

# Chapter 39

It wuz the second week in May when Janie, Lizzy and Katie Jo left Tildie and headed out with Guthrie to the truck stop where Benny wuz to meet 'em to carry 'em home. When they pulled in the parkin' lot of the greasy spoon where they wuz to meet up with their Daddy, the girls could see Lydie and Kitty sittin' in a booth next to the window. The girls couldn't let their Daddy leave 'em behind and had spent the last hour sashayin' 'round the place pushin' their ninnies up against the clueless fella playin' pinball in the back.

After they'd said their howdies, they wuz right proud to show their sisters the country-fried steak and gravy they'd jest ordered as a surprise.

"Ain't this a spread to beat the band? I mean to treat all of y'all," said Lydie, "but I need you to lend me some money first. I spent all mine on my new tattoo." She leaned over so her shirt would rise up above her low cut jean skirt so that Janie and Lizzy could see the sprawlin' tramp stamp on her lower back. "It's letters in Chinese. The man at the tattoo parlor told me it said 'pursuit of happiness' but I reckon I can tell folks it means whatever the hell I want it to mean that day. It ain't like I'm gonna run into anyone who can make out what it says, anyhow. I thank I'll tell the boys at school that it's somethin' dirty. Won't that be a hoot?"

When her sisters told her it jest looked like the tattoo man messed up, she said, "I'll suwanee. It looks jest xactly like the one on the wall did. They had a bunch of 'em, and I thought this one wuz the purtiest. I'm thankin' on addin' color to it later to spice it up. It's gittin' to be bathin' suit weather, and I cain't wait to show it off in my bikini. I hope the swellin' goes down soon on account of the National Guard leaves town in a couple of weeks."

"Fer real?" Lizzy asked.

"Somebody told me they wuz goin' to Myrtle Beach fer more trainin'. I been workin' on Daddy to let us go on over there this summer fer a while. We might could stay at the Hurl Rock, and I know we can afford it. We'll jest have to take some bug spray and sleepin' bags with us so's we all can fit in that room. If'n we pick up some peanut butter and bread at the Piggly Wiggly we could stay a while on the cheap. Momma is all hot to go. If'n Daddy won't let us go, we'll be a lost ball in high weeds fer sure."

"What an idjit," thought Lizzy. "I can jest see us there layin' out in the sun with our faces on, sweatin' like stuck hogs but actin' like we're jest glistenin' and set out on display fer the soldiers. Lawsy mercy! That doesn't sound like no fun at all."

"I heard somethin' through the grapevine," said Lydie as they set themselves down to eat. "What do y'all thank it is? I'll give you a hint. It's 'bout somebody y'all been droolin' over fer a while now. Any one of us would hop in the sack with 'im if'n he wuz obliged."

Lizzy and Janie took one look at each other and shoo'ed away the waiter who wuz fillin' their sweet tea. Lydie snorted and slapped her knee. "That's jest like y'all. I'll suwanee! Y'all didn't want that feller to listen in. I'd be willin' to bet my last dollar he's heard worse thangs 'n this ever day and twice on Sund'y. You might could guess it's 'bout Joe Wickham. He ain't 'bout to git tied down with Norma Lynn Hatfield. Ever'body knows he knocked her up and all, but her Daddy sent her away and came after Joe with a shotgun and told 'im to steer clear of his daughter. Joe wuz much obliged to be cut free when he thought he'd be hog-tied. He's safe fer now."

"And Norma Lynn is safe from him," said Lizzy.

"She's God's own fool fer lettin' her Daddy send her away like that, 'specially if'n she liked 'im, and how could she not like 'im with that tight little ass of his?"

"I hope neither one of 'em suffers on account of it," said Janie.

"Ha. You crack me up, Janie," said Lydie. "I know he don't have no strong feelin's fer her one way or the other. He never cared three straws 'bout her. She's as country as a turnip green and red on the head like a dick on a dog. Y'all know what *that* means. Law! She's uglier 'n a mud fence! It'd be a dark night at the well b'fore she'd git a drank. I have no earthly idea why he wuz dippin' his wick in *that*!"

Lizzy turned beet red as she listened. Poor Norma Lynn wuz knocked up, and here wuz Lydie pilin' on the insults like corn in the crib.

As soon as they'd all filled their bellies, the older girls paid, and the truck wuz brought 'round. Lord only knows how they got all their grips and five girls plus Benny in the cab of that truck, but after they moved Benny's guns and liquor bottles out'a the back seat they wuz able to squeeze in.

"Well, ain't this nice?" said Lydie, scootin' down so her new tattoo wouldn't rub up against the seat. "I'm so glad I got this tattoo. It gives me somethin' interestin' to talk 'bout and show off to folks. Now let us be snug as bugs in a rug and talk and tell dirty jokes all the way home. Y'all have to go first since y'all have been away so long. Did you meet any fellers? I bet there wuz so many you couldn't stir 'em with a stick. Hear tell, did y'all do much flirtin'? I wuz jest sure as all git-out that one of y'all would come back with a big ol' diamond on yer fanger. Janie, you're gittin' so old yer 'bout to dry up, I reckon. I'd be ashamed if'n I wuz twenty-one years-old and not married already. Some girls yer age 'r on their second ball 'n chain with two kids from the first and a bun in the oven from the second. D'y'all know how much gob'ment money you git fer three babies? Ain't Fern says Lizzy should've snatched up Cooter while she could, but I thank his nekkid body could gag a maggot. Lordy! I'll prob'ly git married b'fore all y'all, then I'll have to give up my fellers to you. We had so much fun with Lieutenant Dan the other day. Kitty and me hung out with 'im down at the bar. The two Adkins girls wuz s'posed to be there, but Sissy wuz sick with her allergies, and May-Bell had to come alone. It wuz a hoot. Y'all never b'lieve what we done. We dressed up Seth Jackson in drag. He's got sugar in his tank, and ever'body knows it. Anyway, not a soul knew it wuz Seth 'cept Lieutentant Dan and Kitty and me and Ain't Fern on account of we had to borrow some of her duds. I laughed so hard I nearly peed my pants. Some of the boys came in, and they wuz checkin' 'im out like he wuz fresh meat. I couldn't keep a straight face, and so the boys all knew somethin' wuz up. All of 'em acted like they know'd, but I could tell by the way they'd been checkin' out Seth's ass that they wuz hot fer 'im b'fore they wuz wise to it."

All the way home Lydie and Kitty told their stories of parties and practical jokes. Lizzy tried to ignore their reg'lar mentions of Joe Wickham, but that wuz impossible. She wuz jest relieved when her Daddy pulled up the dirt road and said, "Home again, home again, jiggity jog."

Flo wuz standin' at the door when they pulled up, and b'fore the dirt settled, she'd told Janie how purty she looked. When they set down to supper, Benny patted Lizzy's leg and said, "I'm glad y'all 'r back."

Supper that night spilled out from the kitchen, down the back stoop and out into the yard since all the Lucases, big as all daylights, came to bring Katie Joe home and hear the news of Charlotte and her chickens. Flo wuz as busy as a one-armed barber with hives, askin' Janie 'bout ever' little thang 'bout Nashv'lle and then repeatin' it out the window so the Lucas girls could hear. And with Lydie repeatin' the story of her tattoo to anyone who would listen, it wuz so loud you couldn't hear yerself thank.

"Oh, Mary," said Lydie, "You should've tagged along with us. We had a rip-roarin' time. Kitty and me sat in the back seat of the pickup and flashed the truck drivers as they went past, and a few of 'em honked at us. I would've done it the whole way if Kitty hadn't flashed that state trooper. We wuz scared after that. Once we got settled at the truck stop we treated the girls to a right nice lunch, and if'n you had come along, we would've bought yers, too. And on the way back, Lord have mercy, we like to never crammed all of us in that truck. I wuz ready to die laughin'. I know folks in the other cars wuz wonderin' what kind of weed we wuz smokin'."

Mary, as usual, wuz serious as a heart attack. "Far be it from me, my dear sister, to depreciate such pleasures. They would doubtless be congenial with the generality of female minds. But I confess they would have no charms for me. I should infinitely prefer a book."

Lydie didn't understand a word of it, as usual, but she couldn't pay attention if'n it wuz free anyhow.

Lydie wuz hot to go down to the fair grounds after their supper had settled a bit. Some of the other girls wanted to go, but Lizzy kept tellin' 'em the skeeters wuz already out, and they'd git et alive. She told them folks would be talkin' if'n Benny's girls couldn't be home half a day without trailin' after them soldiers. Her real reason wuz puttin' off a meetin' with Joe fer as long as possible. She wuz tickled pink that the National Guard wuz headin' out to South Carolina in two weeks, and to her way of thankin', time couldn't fly fast enough.

She had jest stepped away fer a cold drink from the ice box when she overheard Benny and Flo talkin' over the trip to Myrtle Beach that Lydie wuz so on fire to take. She could see her father had dug in like a tick and wouldn't budge, but Flo got stuck behind the door when they wuz givin' out brains so she kept after 'im 'bout it.

# Chapter 40

Lizzy wuz as jumpy as a fart on a griddle to tell Janie 'bout her letter from Dutch. She'd already decided to keep mum on the parts that would upset her sister. So the next day she spilled her guts 'bout what happened b'tween herself and Dutch.

At first Janie couldn't do nuthin' to hide the shock, but she could always make a silk purse out'a a sow's ear, and turned it all 'round to be a huge-ass compliment to her sister. She thought Dutch wuz a dick to have proposed to Lizzy in such a way as without gittin' down on one knee with a ring box and with vinegar on his tongue. And her heart bled jest a little bit to thank on how low he must've been when she said "no."

"He shouldn't've been so dadgum sure of himself," she said. "I'll bet it made yer pill that much harder to swaller."

"Ain't that the truth?" replied Lizzy. "I do feel right sorry fer 'im on that account. I'm sure he's got other thangs to thank on, though. He won't be sorry fer long. You cain't blame me fer turnin' 'im down, though, can you?"

"Blame you? Oh Lawd no!"

"But I can tell you're pissed 'bout me thankin' Joe wuz so high and mighty."

"Naw, I cain't say as I am. I don't thank you wuz wrong a bit," said Janie.

"You'll know it when I tell you the rest of it. I ain't told ya what happened the very next day."

She told Janie all 'bout the letter and all it said 'bout Joe Wickham. Half way through Janie started fannin' herself with a scrap piece of cardboard from one of Benny's six packs, and she had to set down. She might could've lived the rest of her natural born days without knowin' the particulars of all Joe'd done. She'd known from watchin' her afternoon stories that some of what Lizzy said took place, but she never would've guessed someone she knew, herself, could be guilty of it. She wuz glad to hear that Dutch wuz shootin' straight, but it didn't make up fer the crooked road Joe'd taken. She wanted to b'lieve both of the boys wuz without blame.

"Yer so country, you've got corn growin' up b'tween yer toes if'n you thank both of them fellers can behave right. Take yer pick, but only one of 'em can be a good ol' boy this time 'round. Maybe if'n you mixed both of 'em t'gether you might could git one decent man, but I doubt it. As fer me, I thank Dutch is the winner this time, but you can have yer own opinion."

Janie set there a spell, thankin'.

"I cain't tell you when I've been more surprised," she said. "Joe is as crooked as the hind leg of a dog! I cain't hardly b'lieve it. And Dutch! Woo-wee! Jest thank on it a second. First you pulled the rug out from under 'im with yer refusal, then you gave 'im a pile-driver to the go-nads when you told 'im jest what kind of a dog you thought he wuz. And then havin' to talk out'a school 'bout his own sister. Law, child! It's too much to reckon on."

"I ain't got to feel too bad 'bout it all seein' as how yer feelin' bad enough fer both of us. If'n you keep it up, my mind will be clear of it by mornin'."

"Joe needs to paint his butt white and run with the antelope. He seemed like a right nice feller."

Lizzy said, "How two fellers from the same neck of the woods could've turned out so diff'rent is beyond me. One of 'em is as good as gold, and the other looks like he is."

"Come on, you cain't tell me you thank Dutch is painful on the eyes."

"I thought I wuz smart as a tack fer decidin' to hate 'im right away without any cause fer it. It makes me feel dumb as a stick."

Janie said, "I feel fer you. You said nice thangs 'bout Joe to Dutch, and now after the letter he gave you, he prob'ly thanks you're not the sharpest tool in the shed."

"Law, don't I know it! I guess the only thang left fer us to figure is whether to let the news 'bout Joe slip to Miz Pritchett or Ain't Fern. If'n either one gits wind of it, the whole town will know overnight. They's more reliable than the weather service. If'n they find out, folks'll be sayin' it's comin' up a cloud against poor Joe Wickham."

Janie returned a long string of chewin' gum she'd pulled out'a her mouth, blew a bubble and sucked it back in with a snap and said, "We best not be spreadin' rumors, Lizzy."

"Yer right, yer right. Plus, Dutch didn't give me no permission to be talkin' 'bout this out'a school, 'specially the parts 'bout his sister. Who in the hell would b'lieve me anyway? Joe has ever'body snowed, and Dutch is the devil.  It might could kill half of the old folks in town if'n they had to change their opinion 'bout Dutch like that. Joe is fixin' to leave with the National Guard soon, and b'fore long, he'll be fergotten like a sock out'a the laundry. Ever' snake comes out'a the grass sometime, and we can jest wait patient-like 'til the truth 'bout Joe dawns on folks, then we can say we knowed it all along."

"Yep. I agree with you. We don't wanna call 'im out. He might could go down to Daddy's garage and key up some of his customer's cars or take out the spark plugs or ciphon the gas out'a the tanks or some such nonsense.  We don't wanna piss 'im off."

Lizzy's mind wuz put at ease after her visit with Janie. She'd unloaded a barrel of secrets, and it felt good to git 'em off her chest. But the truth 'bout what'd happened with Buford still hung in the air b'tween 'em like a puff of school bus exhaust. She knew she couldn't say nuthin' at present and wondered if'n there'd be a time when she could tell Janie when it wouldn't matter one whit.

Now that Lizzy wuz back under her Daddy's roof, she had time to watch Janie to see how her spirits wuz. Truth wuz, she wuz low most of the time. She stared off into space and sighed so often Flo threatened to backhand her once or twice. Janie had a bad case of first love, and ever' thought of Buford wuz put through the same pair of rose-colored glasses. Janie wuz lucky the country music stations played gracious plenty of songs 'bout lost loves on account of she could relate to ever' last one of 'em.

"Well, Lizzy," said Flo. "Do you thank Janie will ever quit mopin' 'round? Heavens to Betsy! Somebody oughtta tell her they's other fish in the sea.  I told Fern jest this mornin' that I don't thank Janie seen hide nor hair of 'im in Nashv'lle. He don't deserve her, and when I see 'im again, I'll say it to his face. Rumor has it he ain't comin' back 'round this way, and I done asked ever'body who might could know."

"He ain't comin' back, Momma."

"I guess he'll do as he pleases. Nobody wants 'im 'round here anyhow. If'n I wuz Janie I wouldn't put up with it. I'd git back at 'im somehow. If'n she dies of a broken heart, I reckon he'll regret what he done."

Lizzy couldn't see how that would help none, so she didn't say nuthin'.

"I hear tell that Cooter and Charlotte have a nice little love nest over to Knoxv'lle way. I jest hope they can stay t'gether. I wonder if'n she can cook at all. Why, she's so skinny if'n she turns sideways, you cain't see her shadow, and Cooter's so fat, I reckon he might could eat jest 'bout anythang she set in front of 'im. They'll make it with a wing and a prayer."

"Yes, ma'am."

"I reckon they talk 'bout when yer Daddy dies and what all they'll do with our house. I hope they have a celebration dinner and choke on their fried okra."

"I never heard either of 'em say a word on it, Momma. I suwanee."

"No, I reckon they didn't say nuthin' in front of you, Lizzie, but I'd bet the farm they talk 'bout it when folks ain't 'round. If'n I wuz them, I'd be ashamed to take property from a widow woman."

# Chapter 41

The first week went by like water through a sieve. At the start of the second week, the National Guard wuz fixin' to leave the fair grounds, and the girls all had their panties in a wad 'bout it. Ever' girl in town wuz laid low. Janie and Lizzy wuz still able to act right, which their little sisters thought wuz down right rude to the rest of 'em.

"My heavenly stars! What 'r we goin' to do fer fun now?" they'd whine. "Stop yer grinnin' Lizzy!"

'Course Flo wuz jest beside herself and liked to tell how the same 'zact thang happened to her twenty-five years ago.

"I'm sure as shootin' I cried fer two days t'gether when them soldiers left us. I thank it done broke my heart," she said.

"They ain't no fixin' mine. It's broke fer sure," said Lydie.

"If'n we could all load ourselves up and take a roadtrip up to Myrtle Beach, we'd be all set," Flo said.

"Hell, yeah. But Daddy's so tight, he wouldn't give us a nickel to save a dime. He won't have none of it."

"It's been so hot out that you could fry eggs on the hood of the truck. A dip in the ocean is what all of us need 'bout now."

"Ain't Fern done tole me that all's I need to do to clear up all these zits is take a swim in the ocean," added Kitty.

Benny's girls made 'bout as much noise as a teapot fussin' on the stove. Lizzy knew her family wuzn't nuthin' she could dress up, no matter how hard she tried. Ever' time she thought on Dutch, she felt he wuz down right justified in what he done fer Buford.

Lydie's troubles went away with a wing and a prayer one day when Lieutenant Dan's gal invited her to go to Myrtle Beach with her and the Guard. Dixie wuz young, but she'd been 'round the block a time or two. She liked to have a good time and sometimes made a little cash on the side pole dancin' at one of 'em gent's clubs down off the highway. She and Lydie had become friends what with all the time Lydie'd spent down by the fairgrounds. They'd shared a bottle of Boone's Farm more 'n once while waitin' on the fellers to stop marchin' 'round.

Lydie jumped 'round like a popcorn kernel in hot kettle grease all day. She and Flo couldn't say enough nice thangs 'bout sweet Dixie. Kitty wuz fit to be tied, though. She acted like she didn't have a pot to piss in, ner a window to throw it out'a. Lydie picked right up on it and teased her so bad if'n she'd been hair, she wouldn't have needed a spray of Aqua Net. Kitty set on the sofa fightin' back tears like they wuz a rotten turnip.

"I don't see why Dixie didn't ask me to tag along with y'all," she said. "Me and her ain't tight or nuthin', but I got jest as much right to go as Lydie does. Hell, I'm almost two whole years older 'n she is."

Lizzy and Janie tried to calm her, sayin' if'n she kept up her worryin', she'd have so many lines in her face, she'd look like a roadmap. Lizzy thought the idea wuz plumb stupid and figured Lydie wuz goin' to hell in a handbasket fer all of her floozey ways. She bent their Daddy's ear 'bout it, explainin' how Dixie had a reputation and how Lydie didn't have no willpower at all when it came to boys. Fer all they could tell, Lydie would go skinny dippin' at night in one of them hotel swimmin' pools and end up with some kind of coochie disease. Her Daddy listened to her and then said, "Lydie ain't never gonna be happy til she's exposin' herself in some public place or another. This, here, trip is 'bout the cheapest way I can see her gittin' to go anywhere, and Lord knows she's more trouble 'n she's worth."

"Law, Daddy. Y'alls always sayin' how if you lay down with dogs, you'll git up with fleas. Don't you see what yer doin' to all of us? Folks do talk, y'know. There's so many of us girls in this family, folks is bound to confuse one of us with the other. If Lydie's marked as cheap, we'll all be cheap. I'm sure tongues've been waggin' 'bout her hangin' down by the fair grounds already."

"Already!" he repeated. "Has Lydie been frightenin' away any of the dogs sniffin' 'round fer you? Poor Lizzy! Let's all have a pity party fer ya. Where's this long list of fellers yer baby sister has run off. I'd like to take a gander at it."

"Don't be an asshole, Daddy. I ain't talkin' 'bout any one person, but jest in general. She gits the rumor mill started sure enough. I got to shoot straight with you, Daddy. If'n you don't put her hormones in check, and teach her that chasin' after the fellers the way she does ain't right, she's gonna git herself in a heap of trouble all on her own. She'll be the one of yer daughters who got herself knocked up at age fifteen, and she'll never live it down. She's such an airhead, I'll suwanee. Alls she'll be good fer is a roll in the hay while she's young and purty. Then after that, what? She'll be old and used up b'fore she's twenty-five with an armload of kids and no way to feed 'em. Kitty won't be any better. She follers Lydie's lead. Why look at that ridiculous perm she got jest be'cuz Lydie got one. Neither one of 'em can barely read a job application, and they don't do nuthin' all day but stuff their ninnies so they look big busted. Them boys 'r gonna be real surprised when they unhook those girls' bras and two rolls of toilet paper come out. I cain't hardly stand it. Janie and I git the raw end of it on account of we're their kin."

Benny could see Lizzy wuz serious as a heart attack. He elbowed her in the arm and said, "Don't you worry yer purty little head 'bout it, Liz. Wherever you and Janie go, folks know you got yer heads on straight. You won't look like a slut even though two of yer sisters are. I'm in a mind to let her go. If'n I don't, she'll be blubberin' and spewin' her evil tongue all 'round. Lieutenant Dan is a good military man. He'll make sure she don't git herself into trouble. Alls she'll be doin' is sun bathin'. She ain't got no money to go to the carnival or out any place. I bet them soldiers'll find 'em some real women with big titties and the knowledge of what to do with 'em. Lydie's jest a little girl. She'll end up bein' left behind, and that will give her a heapin' spoonful of reality."

Even though Lizzy didn't agree with her Daddy, she felt she'd said her peace and decided not to be a worry wart 'bout the situation with Lydie. If'n Flo or Lydie had known that Lizzy'd tried to keep her little sister at home, smoke would've poured out'a their ears and their words would've been venom. In Lydie's imagination, the streets of Myrtle Beach wuz paved with soldiers all makin' eyes at her. She seen the tents pitched in the sand and boys swimmin' in the ocean without their drawers on. She imagined herself in her smokin' hot red bikini, swimmin' out to the boys and flirtin' with 'em 'til they'd have to stay in the water a little while to hide their attraction.

Lizzy had been stirrin' so many pots that when the day fer her to say "so long" to Joe Wickham fer the last time dawned, well, it pert near snuck up on 'er. They'd kept company ever' day since she'd gotten back to town, so seein' his face didn't make her wanna slap 'im quite so hard any more. He wuz right friendly toward her and tried to flirt with her like b'fore, but she wuzn't havin' none of it. He wuz of the mind that she'd cozy right back up to 'im and lap it all up like a dry speckled pup jest like she'd done b'fore.

The last day the soldiers all ate t'gether at the Golden Corral, and Benny, Flo and them happened to be there fillin' up on steak and yeast rolls. Lizzy wuz spit on a griddle and had no mind to leave 'im without takin' 'im down a few notches. He asked her if'n she'd heard from her good friend Charlotte, and she let slip that Jake and Dutch had spent three weeks up there, and then asked if'n he heard tell of Jake b'fore.

Joe looked jest like he'd swallered a hair ball, shocked, mad as a wet hen and not a little bit worried. He caught himself after a bit and smoothed his face into a slick smile, sayin' he used to see Jake all the time back in the day, and he thought Jake wuz a real stand-up kind of a guy. He asked Lizzy how she liked 'im. She said she liked 'im jest fine. Later on, pretendin' he didn't care all that much, Joe asked "How long did you say Jake wuz up there?"

"Three weeks."

"And did you cross paths with 'im frequent-like?"

"Pert near ever' day."

"He ain't nuthin' like his cousin, I'd say."

She said, "He's diff'rent. But I thank Dutch is somebody who could grow on you."

"You don't say!" cried Joe with eyes as big as milk saucers. "What the hell...," but he caught himself and said like a joke, "Did he learn some kind of comedy routine or somethin'? Did he learn himself some manners? I cain't b'lieve he, his ownself, has got better."

"Well, I declare, I thank he's the same as he ever' wuz."

Joe didn't know how to take what she said. It seemed to him that Lizzy had a bee in her bonnet, and she wuzn't gonna be happy til she let it loose in his boxers. He perked up his ears when she said, "When I said he could grow on you, I didn't mean that his jokes or manners got better. I wuz jest sayin' that once you git to know Dutch, you can see where he's comin' from, if you know what I mean."

Joe had been holdin' a bag of chaw in his hands, and Lizzy noticed he'd done wrung it so hard that tobacco wuz fallin' on his boots. He started to say somethin' once or twice, but jest looked like a fish out'a water, openin' and shuttin' his mouth like that. Finally he said, "You know how I feel 'bout ol' Dutch, so I got to say how glad I am to hear he's behavin' himself better. I thank he must've been on his best behavior on account of his Ain't Pru wuz there, and he stands in respect of her and all. He's got his eyes on DeeDee, that's fer sure. He prob'ly stood up straight to make a good impression."

Lizzy let out a snort and slapped her knee. She could tell Joe wanted to jump back on that old horse, to tell 'bout all the ways Dutch had wronged 'im, but she wuzn't havin' it. The rest of the time they didn't say a word to each other and chewed their food with the rest of 'em. When they wuz leavin', neither Lizzy nor Joe had any thought of seein' the other one again.

Benny dropped Lydie off at Dixie and Lieutenant Dan's apartment on account of they wuz fixin' to leave at sunrise the next day. Kitty made an awful fool of herself, cryin' the way she did, not fer the thought of missin' her sister, but fer the fact that she had to stay back home. Flo gave gracious plenty advice so that ever'body else's goodbyes couldn't be heard at all.

# Chapter 42

If'n Lizzy had looked 'round herself to find out what marriage wuz like, she would've run hollerin' to the hills. Her Daddy'd been drawn like a horse to water to her Momma one night at a Sizzler Steakhouse. Flo wuz workin' the table in a skirt that wuz so short you could see all the way to Christmas, and her ninnies wuz on display fer the world to see. Of course she got herself in the family way after she found out he'd been to the county vo-tech and could fix cars. Once they wuz hitched, he found out real quick that he couldn't stand bein' in the same room with her 'cept fer at night when the lights wuz out. That's how they ended up with five mouths to feed. The yellin' and hollerin' didn't make comin' home much fun, so he spent as much time at the garage as he could. His Momma and Daddy taught 'im that good Christians git married and stay married. "It's a life sentence," his Daddy used to say, so Benny found thangs to keep 'im busy and out'a the house. He wuz religious 'bout every kind of huntin' and fishin'. He had poker night once a week, and he never turned down an offer to go down to Davis's Bar fer a shot of whiskey or a cold one. He'd learned to use Flo as his very own form of entertainment, and he laughed with his friends 'bout how plum stupid she wuz.

Lizzy wuzn't blind. She could see what her Daddy wuz up to. She hated the way he and her Momma treated each other, but she wuz grateful to be her Daddy's favorite. She overlooked his glazed eyes and the lipstick on his collar after a night out and tried to forgit how he'd made his wife the butt of every joke in the family. But lately she'd been thankin' on how his bein' horny that night at the Sizzler had been a wreckin' ball to his whole damned life and now to hers, too. If'n he wuz a stronger person, he could've brought all of 'em up instead of lettin' her Momma bring 'em all down.

Even though Lizzy wuz real excited that Joe Wickham wuz gone, it didn't do much fer her social life. The soldiers wuz a big part of the social scene, and without 'em the parties wuz dull. She found that the thang she'd been a-hopin' fer didn't bring her as much happiness as she thought it would. She put her mind toward her trip to Lexin'ton with her kin and took to thankin' on it when her Momma and Kitty had their knickers in a twist over Lydie bein' gone. If'n she could somehow git Janie included in the invite, she could've shared her plans with somebody.

When Lydie left, she swore on ever'thang holy that she'd call or email ever' day to her Momma and Kitty. She wuz always in a hurry to git off the phone, but she seemed to have time to tell 'em 'bout her new jeans with the holes already in 'em and the store that only sold skivvies. Emails to Kitty wuzn't much better. She wuz always typin' in all caps and spellin' ever'thang wrong, and some of the thangs she wrote couldn't be shared in mixed company.

After a spell, life wuz back to normal at Benny and Flo's house, and Lizzy started to git ready fer her trip up north. A call from Tildie let her know that the trip'd be shorter 'n they'd hoped on account of Guthrie needed to be back to work earlier 'n he thought. Also, she told Lizzy they'd spend a few days in Lost Crick, a little town where Tildie had lived as a girl.

Lizzy wuz down in the mouth 'bout the trip bein' shorter 'n expected, but after a while she decided to be happy, and she wuz. Ever' time somebody mentioned Lexin'ton, she always thought on Dutch and Pembrook Farm. She wondered if'n she could be in his part of the country without him knowin' it.

Time passed like molasses in January 'til Guthrie and Tildie pulled up in the RV with their four kids, two girls and two boys, who wuz to be looked after by Janie. The RV leaked oil fer jest one night in Benny's driveway, and the next day they wuz pullin' out in a cloud of blue fumes. Guthrie had the soundtrack to Talledega Nights turned up full blast on the stereo, and Tildie'd brought along her scrapbook scissors and colored paper to keep her occupied fer the drive.

I ain't gonna tell y'all what Kentucky is like. Fer one thang, it's so far north, them folks 'r practic'ly Yankees, and fer another thang, this ain't a tour book from the Triple A. If'n yer interested in Kentucky, y'all can go look it up fer yer ownselves. All y'all need to know is it's purty country up there with all them horse farms and fences and green hills. All y'all need to worry 'bout is one little town, called Lost Crick, which is where Tildie spent a few years when she wuz knee-high to a grasshopper.

Once they'd said their howdies to all the folks Tildie knew up to Lost Crick, they told Lizzy that Lexin'ton wuzn't but a few miles away, and they should stop in at Pembrook Farm on account of it wuz really somethin' to see.

"I'm sure we might could make a stop over to take a gander at it. Surely you wanna see a place you heard so much 'bout." said her aunt. "So many folks you know grew up over thar. I thank Joe Wickham even grew up at Pembrook."

Lizzy bit at a hangnail. She'd rather be caught dead 'n be seen at Pembrook Farm. She told 'em "once you've seen one chicken coop, you've seen 'em all."

Tildie started in on her, "If'n it wuz jest a chicken coop, I wouldn't care much fer it myself, but it's an honest-to-goodness horse farm, smack-dab in the middle of horse country."

Lizzy kept mum, hopin' they would change the subject. The thought of runnin' into Dutch while she wuz checkin' out his very own farm wuz akin to bein' caught with yer pants down in public. She blushed at the very idea, and thought she should talk straight with her aunt than to risk it. Tildie wouldn't hear none of it.

They stopped at an RV park jest down the road from the farm to stay the night. Lizzy caught the manager's attention and asked if Pembrook Farm wuz a nice place, who owned it and if'n the owners wuz in town. The manager said the owner'd been out'a town at some races somewhere and wuzn't due back fer some time. So the next day when the gravel rumbled under the RVs tires as they made their way back out to the big road, Lizzy wuz cool as a cucumber 'bout goin' to Dutch's farm.

# Chapter 43

Lizzy wuz wound up like a top when they pulled in beside the Pembrook Farm sign. There wuz trees ever' which way you looked, so she couldn't see much. The road cut up a holler with trees leanin' in on both sides, so it seemed to Lizzy she wuz goin' through a tunnel. After 'bout half a mile the woods thinned out, and Lizzy could see the farm house over on the next ridge with the road snakin' back to where they wuz. The house wuz three stories high if it wuz an inch and made in the old-fashioned Southern way with a wrap-'round porch on the first floor and a balcony on the second. Behind the house wuz a little groupin' of trees on a hillside, and off to the left and down a slope wuz the biggest horse barn Lizzy'd ever seen. A ramblin' crick made its way past the long side of the barn and 'round the front of the house b'fore runnin' down the hill with a little waterfall here and there under the shade. She could've swore that God, himself, put that house on top of that ridge and built the world 'round it, and she wondered what it would've been like to live there with Dutch and look out at all of nature ever' day.

Guthrie wondered whether the RV would make it up the hill to the horse barn, but he didn't have to worry none. He pulled that metal monster right up past the front door and stopped by the barn. Lizzy wuz nervous as a fawn on the first day of huntin' season as they drove past. She seen a shadow move past the curtain in the house, and she said a little prayer that the manager at the RV park hadn't been wrong 'bout Dutch bein' at the races.

'Bout that time a spindly feller, skinny as a bean pole, walked out'a the barn wavin' howdie to 'em. He slapped Guthrie on the back like they wuz old pals and invited 'em into the whitewashed barn. Lizzy immediately drew in her breath. Four of her Daddy's houses could fit end to end inside, and the ceilin' wuz as tall as the farm house. The floor wuz so clean, a person could eat right off of it. Instead of ladders leadin' up to a loft, there wuz a solid staircase, shiny with polish, that led to offices and a sittin' room where folks could look out on the horses. Ever' stall wuz filled with a velvet nose or a big butt swishin' flies with its tail. Whinnies sounded out here and there, and the air hinted at the sweet smell of hay and horse shit.

The manager's name wuz Mr. Brown, and he wuz all jacked up on coffee and glazed doughnuts, but he wuz proud to show 'em 'round. The offices upstairs with their leather davenports and framed pictures of horses, made Lizzy thank of how it would be to keep all of this clean. Dutch didn't have it fancy with a lot of dust-catchers layin' 'round. It wuz simple and manly and smelled of saddle leather and lemon Pledge.

"All this could've been mine," she thought. "I might've been in this office brangin' Dutch a cup of coffee and dustin' off them frames. Instead of bein' a stranger to this place, I could be livin' here in this little bit of heaven on earth. I'd be showin' Guthrie and Tildie 'round, knowin' the names of them beautiful creatures down there. But no," she thought, "I wouldn't 've been allowed to invite my own kin."

This wuz a lucky recollection. It kept her from havin' any regrets.

She wanted to ask Mr. Brown if'n the owner wuz expected back any time soon, but didn't have the guts. After a while Guthrie asked, and Mr. Brown told 'im Dutch wuz at the races, but they expected 'im back in the next day or two, and he wuz brangin' some friends to stay with 'im fer a spell. Lizzy thanked her lucky stars they'd come when they did.

Tildie hollered over to her to take a look at a picture in a frame near the bookshelf, and Lizzy seen Joe Wickham a-lookin' back at her from the photo. Her aunt asked her how she liked the picture, grinnin' all the while. Mr. Brown told 'em it wuz the son of one of the hands that used to work the farm, and that old Junior had practic'ly raised 'im. "Folks say he's in the army now," he said, "but I thank he's turned out wild as a March hare."

"And that," said scrawney Mr. Brown, pointin' to a large picture over the mantle piece, is the boss-man. It wuz taken 'bout the same time as the other one, eight years ago."

"I heard the owner of Pembrook Farm is a hottie," said Tildie, "but I had no idea how good a-lookin' he really wuz. Does he still look like that, Lizzy?"

Mr. Brown took a long look at Lizzy. "Do y'all know Dutch?"

Lizzy turned red as a beet. "A little."

"Well, he don't have trouble gittin' dates, if'n y'all know what I mean."

"He is handsome," Lizzy said under her breath.

"There's another one over to the house that I'll show you. It's more recent. This wuz Junior's office, so thangs in here 'r jest like they wuz b'fore he died."

This explained to Lizzy why the photo of Joe wuz still hangin' on the wall. Mr. Brown then pointed to one of Suzanna taken when she wuz no more 'n five years old.

"Gosh, that must be Dutch's sister. I can see the resemblance," said Guthrie.

"Gosh, she's the purtiest little girl I ever laid my eyes on. She can play the fiddle and sing like a lark. The boss man jest bought her a new fiddle. It's over to the house. She's comin' home tomorrow with Dutch."

Guthrie wuz a natural salesman and could git folks talkin'. B'fore long he'd gotten Mr. Brown to open up 'bout Dutch and Suzanna.

"Does Dutch help train these here horses?"

"He ain't here enough to help train 'em, I'm afraid. Horses need somebody who's 'round all the time. He's here 'bout half the time, and Suzanna's here more 'n she used to be, what with the home schoolin' and all."

"Maybe if Dutch'd find himself a fine little lady and settle down, he'd spend more time at home."

"Ain't that the truth? But ain't nobody know when that's gonna be exceptin' the good Lord, himself. I reckon there ain't a girl out there good enough fer ol' Dutch."

Lizzy said, "That says a lot 'bout Dutch, comin' from somebody who works fer 'im."

"If I'm lyin', I'm dyin'. You can go ask anybody 'round these parts," he said, takin' off his ballcap and rubbin' his bald spot. Lizzy thought there wuz no point in Mr. Brown kissin' Dutch's ass when he wuzn't even 'round to hear it. He added, "I've been 'round 'im since he wuz too young fer Popeye's but could suck on a biscuit, and he's never raised his voice to me in all that time."

Lizzy stood there slack-jawed and catchin' flies. She wuz jest sure Dutch wuz somebody only a Momma could love. Uncle Guthrie said, "There ain't too many folks can say that 'bout their bosses, I'll suwanee."

"I always b'lieved that if'n folks 'r good when they're little, they'll be good when they're grown. Dutch wuz always a good little feller, nice to the animals and always givin' his toys away. Good-hearted, Dutch is."

Lizzy couldn't b'lieve they wuz talkin' 'bout the same Dutch.

"His Daddy wuz a good man, I hear," said Tildie, fannin' herself with a scrap of paper.

"There wuzn't none better. His son'll be jest the same, jest as good to the poor."

Lizzy listened and wondered and doubted and wanted to hear more. Mr. Brown showed 'em every corner of the barn and every bridle and halter, but all Lizzy wanted to hear wuz more 'bout Dutch. Guthrie brought 'im back to the subject as they walked to the farm house.

"He owns 'bout half this part of town, I'd say. He's a good landlord. I rent from 'im, myself. He ain't like young folks these days who thank on nuthin' but themselves. You could ask anybody who rents from 'im or the store owners who set up shop in his business properties, and they'll all give 'im a good word. Some folks call 'im 'proud,' but I never seen none of it. He's jest quiet and keeps to his ownself."

"This paints 'im a purty picture," thought Lizzy.

"He sounds like quite the catch," whispered Tildie. "Too bad our good buddy Joe has another story to tell."

"What if we're wrong 'bout Joe?"

"We ain't wrong. Y'all seen it with yer own eyes."

Once they wuz inside the house, Mr. Brown took off his boots and put 'em on the mat next to the door. Lizzy couldn't help notice his dirty toenail peeking out from the hole in his sock. He showed 'em into a sun room set up like a schoolhouse and told 'em Dutch had jest re-painted the room and bought new furniture fer Suzanna. He said, "The boss-man did this room up right fer his sister while she wuz gone. That's the way he is with her. He goes over the top to make her happy. There ain't nuthin' that boy wouldn't do fer his little sister."

The house had store-bought pillows that Lizzy thought she seen on a Target commercial, and none of the furniture looked like it had been picked up at a yard sale. The bookshelves wuz made of wood instead of cinder blocks and two-by-fours like back home. Ever'thang wuz jest-so, right down to the pictures hung on the walls. She walked over to one of 'em and found Dutch's face grinnin' back at her like the cat that'd swallered the canary. She remembered 'im a-lookin' at her like that from time to time, and she stood there like a bump on a log starin' at the photo. Mr. Brown said it'd been taken back when Junior wuz alive.

Lookin' at Dutch's face like she did, Lizzy felt warm in the middle, in a way she'd never felt when a-lookin' at Dutch in the flesh. Mr. Brown's kind words came back to her, and she reckoned they wuz more powerful on account of Mr. Brown wuz Dutch's employee and all. She thought 'bout all the folks who depended on Dutch: his sister, his employees, his tenants. He had to juggle it all. She let out a long sigh and realized she had a soft spot fer Dutch.

As they left the house and headed over to the crick to see if'n there wuz any fish in it, Guthrie started askin' questions 'bout the age of the house and barn. And right there, out'a the blue, came Dutch his ownself, pullin' into the driveway.

Lizzy wuz jest a stone's throw from 'im, so she couldn't avoid 'im one whit. Their eyes locked on, and both of 'em turned red as a balloon at the county fair. They both stood in their spot, frozen and starin'. Dutch moved first and said his howdies.

Well, Lizzy jest wanted to crawl up under a rock and die of embarrassment. The others figured out who he wuz soon enough since they'd jest been a-lookin' at his picture not five minutes ago. They watched 'im as he spoke to Lizzy, who absolutely could not look 'im in the eye fer nuthin'. Her mind wuz swirlin' 'round what happened the last time they'd seen each other, and the very idea of him findin' her snoopin' 'round his farm wuz jest 'bout the worst thang in the whole wide world to her. He wuz nervous as a whore in church and kept stammerin' away 'bout Knoxv'lle and her folks back home and anythang else that popped into his mind. After a bit he couldn't thank on anythang else to say, so he turned away and walked off toward the house. With his back to her, Lizzy wuz brave and checked out his butt as he walked away.

Guthrie came over and said somethin' 'bout Dutch must lift weights, and Tildie said she thought he had the tightest little ass she'd ever seen in all her days. (Tildie wuz an expert of sorts on tight asses, so this wuz a high compliment comin' from her.) Lizzy wuz overpowered by shame and vexation. If she could, she would kick her ownself in the ass fer havin' come to Dutch's house at all. She couldn't imagine what he could be thankin' 'bout her. It probl'y looked like she'd thrown herself in his path. Lord, Almighty, why in the world had she come, and why did he show up a day b'fore he wuz wanted? Why didn't they leave ten minutes earlier? They might've passed 'im on the road without a second look. And he wuz sweet as a Georgia peach 'bout ever'thang, askin' after her kin and all. He wuz downright changed since he'd given her the letter down to Charlotte's house. Lizzy didn't know what to thank.

They walked along the crick fer a bit and into the woods b'fore Lizzy paid much attention to the dirt under her feet or the trees above her head. She answered questions that her aunt and uncle asked, but she felt like she wuz on autopilot. All she could put her thoughts on wuz the farmhouse where Dutch wuz and what in the world wuz goin' on in his noggin'. She wondered to herself whether he wuz still sweet on her or if he wuz jest usin' his best manners on account of folks wuz 'round. He wuz usually slicker 'n snot on a doorknob 'round her, but there wuz somethin' in his voice. His feathers wuz ruffled, of that she wuz sure.

They walked along a horse path through the woods and up to a clearin' at the top of one of Kentucky's rollin' hills. There they could see they wuz standin' in God's country, and Mr. Brown told 'em that Dutch owned ever'thang fer three miles. After goin' over yonder and 'round a fer piece, they passed over a little stone bridge and stopped to rest. Tildie wuz jest 'bout as big 'round as she wuz tall, and her shirt wuz near soaked through with sweat. Guthrie's face lit up like a Christmas tree when he seen fish in the crick and said he wished he'd brought his pole along so's he could catch some supper. Lizzy wuz kickin' some dried deer turds when she heard a rustlin' through the trees and seen Dutch walkin' their way. If'n she'd been alone, she would've taken off on a path to avoid 'im, but there wuz no movin' fast while Tildie wuz 'round. She couldn't thank on nuthin' to say, but he wuz right nice 'bout it. She started in with some compliments on his property but stopped fast when she thought 'bout how it prob'ly sounded to 'im.

Tildie stood close by fannin' herself like she meant it, and Dutch asked Lizzy if'n she'd introduce 'im to her kin. She wuz as prepared fer that as George Bush wuz prepared fer Hurricane Katrina and couldn't help but smile at 'im wantin' to be acquainted with somebody she knew he'd looked down his nose at not but a few months ago. "He'll be fit to be tied when I tell 'im who they are," she thought. "He thanks they're somebody worth knowin' since they're wearin' nice clothes and all."

She made the introduction and watched out'a the corner of her eye fer him to squirm. He looked surprised, but he didn't make an excuse to stomp off like she wuz expectin'. He simply walked over to Guthrie and started talkin' 'bout fishin'. Since Tildie wuz still fannin' away and catchin' her breath, Lizzy had a chance to listen to Guthrie and Dutch, and she wuz thrilled to pieces that her uncle stood up straight, looked Dutch in the eye and didn't scratch anywhere he shouldn't. Guthrie knew what he wuz talkin' 'bout when it came to huntin' and fishin', and Lizzy could tell Dutch wuz impressed with what he knew. B'fore long, Dutch invited Uncle Guthrie to stop by and fish while he wuz in these parts and even offered to lend 'im a rod and reel. To this, Tildie's eyes flew open wide and she gave Lizzy a look. Lizzy said nuthin', but she couldn't figure why he wuz so changed. "Could he be actin' nice fer my sake? There ain't no way he could still be sweet on me after ever'thang I said to 'im back at Cooter and Charlotte's," she thought.

They walked back towards the horse barn on the path by two's. Lizzy and Tildie walked in front, and Guthrie and Dutch walked behind. Mr. Brown'd stayed behind to move a branch that had fallen across the path. After a spell, Tildie said she needed to lean on Guthrie on account of her dogs wuz barkin', so Dutch moved up next to Lizzy, and they walked ahead a little faster since they didn't have Tildie slowin' 'em down. After they wuz out'a ear-shot, Lizzy wuz quick to tell 'im that she wuz as sure as a pregnant rabbit that he wuz out'a town when they decided to stop by to see his farm. "Even yer man, there, told us that you wuzn't due back til tomorrow."

He said he'd planned to come back the next day with some other folks, but he decided not to stop along the Bourbon Trail with the rest of 'em. He'd been there and done that already. He said, "They'll be along directly, and Buford and his sisters 'r with 'em."

Lizzy nodded. The last time she and Dutch had mentioned Buford shot through her mind like a semi-automatic rifle with its sites on a deer in season. By the look on his face, she could tell Dutch wuz a-thankin' on the same thang.

"My sister, Suzanna, is with 'em, and she told me she fancies meetin' you. Would that be all right? Would you give 'er the time of day while yer in town?"

She wuz caught off guard by the question. The only way Suzanna would've heard 'bout her wuz through her brother, and she wuz happy to know that even though she'd pissed him off royally, he hadn't been spewin' gossip 'bout her to his sister. They walked along without makin' a peep 'til they wuz standin' in front of the RV. Tildie and Guthrie wuz a fer piece behind, so he asked her if she wanted to go inside fer some sweet tea. She said her no thank you's and couldn't thank on nuthin' else to say at all. Finally it dawned on her that she'd been travelin', so she started talkin' 'bout Bowling Green and Frankfort. Ever' second wuz a lifetime, and Tildie seemed to be slowin' down the closer she got to 'em. Lizzy nearly ran out'a thangs to say 'bout Kentucky b'fore her aunt and uncle finally made it back. Dutch offered fer 'em to come in fer a cold drink, but Guthrie told 'im he'd put a six pack on ice, and it wuz callin' his name. Dutch helped the girls up into the RV and walked slowly back into the house.

Guthrie and Tildie started in talkin' 'bout Dutch b'fore they wuz out'a his damned driveway. "He's a stand-up guy fer sure," said Guthrie.

"He walks like he's got a rod up his ass, so I can see how some folks would say he's full of himself, but I don't thank he's overly proud."

"I wouldn't 've been more surprised if'n a haint had jumped out to spook me 'n I wuz when he wuz so nice. It had to be on account of Lizzy. He don't know us from Adam," her uncle said.

Tildie said, "Well, he ain't the hottie that Joe Wickham is, that's fer sure, but you wouldn't have to dip 'im in tuna to git the cat to look at 'im. How come you said he wuz such a pain in the ass, Lizzy?"

Lizzy said she'd never seen 'im so agreeable as he wuz there at his farm, and she thought he wuz never as nice as he'd jest been that mornin'.

"Well, jest in case he's wishy-washy with his invites, I thank I'll skip his offer to fish at his place. He might change his mind and come after me with a shot gun."

"From a-lookin' at 'im," continued Tildie, "a person wouldn't thank he could be such a jerk as he wuz to poor Joe. They's somethin' 'bout the way Dutch holds his mouth that makes me thank he's not as good as he lets on. Mr. Brown surely had good words fer 'im, but he knows who butters his bread."

Lizzy defended Dutch as best she could and told the short version of what she'd heard 'bout Joe without givin' away any names. Tildie jest shook her head, and Lizzy couldn't tell what she wuz thankin' b'fore they rolled into Lost Crick. Once Tildie seen her old stompin' grounds, she couldn't do nuthin' but remember. She showed Guthrie all her old haunts and the field where she and her beau used to go make out. Lizzy could barely hear Tildie's stories fer the thoughts runnin' like a freight train through her head. Why in the world would Dutch be sweet as sugar, and why did he want her to meet Suzanna so much?

# Chapter 44

Lizzy figured Dutch'd bring his sister 'round once she and the others had a chance to settle in a bit. She wuz surprised to find 'em waitin' fer her the very day they showed up at Pembrook Farm. Lizzy and her kin'd been visitin' some folks Tildie knew from back in the day and planned to eat lunch with 'em when Dutch pulled up in a shiny silver Mercedes. Guthrie and Tildie thought somethin' must be up b'tween their niece and Dutch, 'specially when they seen Lizzy fidgit with her hair the way a girl does when she's nervous 'bout how she'll look to a feller. While these new idears wuz swirlin' in their heads, Lizzy stepped back from the window to keep from bein' seen. She paced a worn spot in the rug while she waited on Dutch and his sister to come inside, and Guthrie and Tildie asked why she wuz so nervous, which jest made thangs worse.

Dutch and Suzanna turned the corner 'bout that time, and the girls howdied and shook. Lizzy could see Suzanna wuz jest as shy 'bout the meetin' as she wuz, herself. Folks had said Dutch's sister wuz too big fer her britches, but Lizzy could tell right away she wuz jest as shy as a polecat that'd been kicked a few times. She wuz a low-talker, that's fer sure, and Lizzy could barely make out a word she said.

Suzanna wuz tall fer her age, and she had a pair of ninnies on her that you might find in a nudey magazine. She tried to cover 'em up, but they wuz burstin' out ever'which way. She wuzn't a looker, but her smile told Lizzy that she liked a good joke and knew how to have a good time with her friends. She wuz glad to see that Suzanna might look like a grown-up, but she wuz jest a girl in a woman's body. All the butterflies she'd felt on bein' judged by Suzanna soon flew out the window.

After 'bout five minutes of chit chat, Dutch told Lizzy that Buford wuz plannin' to stop by, and no sooner wuz the words out'a his mouth, than Buford, himself, swaggered through the door wearin' cowboy boots and tight jeans. She'd done shoved her anger toward Buford in her back pocket months ago, but even if'n she hadn't, he would've won her good feelin's back in a heartbeat. He wuz the same sweet-hearted Buford they'd all come to know and love. He asked 'bout her family and grinned that boy-next-door grin he always used to give her.

Guthrie and Tildie wuz tongue-tied at meetin' the man they'd heard so much 'bout from Janie. They watched Dutch as Lizzy talked to Buford, and though no words passed, both wuz sure that Dutch wuz head-over-heels fer her. They couldn't make hide nor hare 'bout whether she felt the same way 'bout 'im.

Lizzy's mind was jumpin' like crickets in the pantry. On the one hand she wanted to know where she stood with Dutch and Suzanna, and on the other hand, she wanted to find out all she could from Buford. She wanted to know how he felt 'bout Janie so bad she could taste it. He stared at her face, which wuz a bit off-puttin', 'til she thought that maybe he wuz a-tryin' to find a resemblance b'tween her and Janie. One thang wuz clear as a bell, Buford and Suzanna wuz not a match, and that kind of pissed Lizzy off be'cuz Buford's sister had drawn such a purty picture of 'em bein' meant fer each other. It wuz all bullshit as far as Lizzy could tell. She thought Buford paid closer attention to what she said when she talked 'bout home. Once he even said, "It's been more 'n eight months since I've seen y'all. It wuz November 26th when we wuz all dancin' t'gether back at my place."

Lizzy wuz pleased as punch to hear he remembered the exact date he last saw Janie, and when no one else could hear, he asked her if ALL her sisters wuz at home again. The question, itself, wuzn't what caught Lizzy's attention, but it wuz the way he said it that made all the difference.

She didn't often steal a glance at Dutch, but when she did, she seen the same "Dutch" she'd spied yesterd'y at the farm. She wuz glad his good manners had lasted longer 'n one day but didn't expect 'em to live long. He wuz laughin' and talkin' with folks he would've looked down his nose at jest a few months ago. She remembered their argument at Cooter and Charlotte's, and the change in him wuz wider 'n the Miss'ippi River is long. She had never seen 'im so happy to oblige when he wuz 'round his kin or his friends as he wuz now with her Aunt Tildie and Uncle Guthrie, and if'n Tammy and Patty wuz here, they'd be havin' a big ol' time makin' fun of ever'body.

After 'bout a half hour, Dutch, Suzanna and Buford got up to leave, but not b'fore Dutch invited 'em all to Pembrook Farm fer a sit-down dinner. Tildie looked at Lizzy fer some sign that she wuz game but couldn't catch her eye, and Guthrie said they'd be free in two days. Buford seemed a little overly happy at the idea of supper with Lizzy, and said he had so much he wanted to ask her 'bout her family and their friends. She took this to mean he wanted to hear more 'bout Janie and reckoned this wuz a good sign.

Lizzy needed a minute to rub two thoughts t'gether without her aunt and uncle askin' too many questions. Not long after Dutch and them had left, she snuck away to shower b'fore dinner. She didn't have to worry 'bout Guthrie and Tildie, though. They wuzn't folks to pry. There wuz no doubt in their minds that Lizzy knew Dutch better 'n she let on, and Guthrie would've bet a store full of name-brand appliances that Dutch wuz smitten. They decided that if'n you set up the Dutch they'd heard 'bout against the Dutch they'd actually met, they'd rather b'lieve he wuz a stand-up guy. Rumors wuz rumors, after all.

The stories told 'bout Joe Wickham 'round those parts wuz that he left Kentucky with more gamblin' debts 'n he could pay, and Dutch went 'round and settled up with folks usin' his own money.

Lyin' in bed that night, Lizzy's thoughts wuz on Pembrook farm and its owner. She stared at the ceilin' fer two hours a-tryin' to figure on how she felt 'bout 'im. She couldn't say she hated 'im. Naw, that wuz long gone, and now all that wuz left wuz shame fer ever feelin' bad towards 'im in the first place. Now that she'd heard so many stories 'bout 'im as a boy and of how he wuz quick to help the poor and all, she felt a kind of respect fer 'im. And yesterd'y! He had been so friendly to her kin that she could only call what she felt "gratitude." She wuz thankful he'd proposed to her and fer forgivin' her fer the smack-down she gave 'im when she told 'im where he could stick his proposal.  He could've been a real ass 'bout ever'thang, but he wuzn't. He pretended like nuthin' ever happened b'tween 'em to spoil thangs and went on to introduce her to his sister and show respect to her kin. Ever' path her mind took led her back to one spot. Could he still be so much in love with her that he'd look past his intolerable pride to try to make up with her? She thought maybe, if'n he wanted her to, she could stand to flirt with 'im a little bit to see where it would take 'em. Maybe he'd ask her to marry him again.

The next day Tildie suggested they meet up with Suzanna since she'd stopped by on the very day she returned to Pembrook Farm to see 'em. Lizzy wuz happy to oblige her aunt, but she couldn't say whether she wuz excited to see Suzanna or whether she hoped to run into Dutch at the farm. Guthrie didn't need much of a nudge to git 'im to go fishin', and he decided to tag along.

Chapter 45


Convinced as she wuz that Tammy's hatred of her wuz jealousy, Lizzy wuzn't so sure how welcome she'd be at Pembrook Farm with Buford's sisters. She smiled to herself when she thought of how they'd treat her.

On pullin' up into the driveway, Lizzy and them wuz invited back to the glassed-in patio room, which wuz a little too warm from the sun but had a nice view. Suzanna, Tammy and Patty wuz all there cluckin' and tuttin' over the humidity. Suzanna wuz as shy as a virgin at a wet t-shirt contest when she spoke to Tildie and Lizzy, but they understood she wuzn't puttin' on airs or nothin'. Tammy and Patty barely spoke to 'em at all. Nobody said a peep fer what felt like a long wet week 'til a woman barreled through the door with a tray of iced glasses and a sweatin' pitcher of pink lemonade with honest-to-goodness slices of actual lemon floatin' 'round inside. The woman wuz cute as a button but she needed to touch up her roots real bad, and anybody could tell she wuz the housekeeper or some such help as that.

She introduced herself as Tracy and started to fill up the silence with her own idea of what passed fer conversation. Her attempts to be nice showed she wuz better raised than either of Buford's stuck up sisters, and she and Tildie hit it off right away talkin' 'bout recipes fer cornbread and sweet-cakes. Suzanna looked once or twice like she wanted to join in the conversation, but she didn't know nuthin' 'bout cookin', so she jest agreed when Tracy said hers wuz the best cornbread in four counties.

Lizzy couldn't help but notice that Tammy wuz practic'ly burnin' holes in her with her stares. Honestly, if'n Tammy had taken a picture it would've lasted longer. Lizzy couldn't say a word that wuzn't bein' criticized with Tammy's overdone eyes, and she hoped ever' minute that one of the fellers would come in the room to spice up the talk a little bit. She didn't know whether she hoped for or feared that Dutch would poke his head in fer a howdie. After a full fifteen minutes of recipe swappin', Tildie and Tracy scooted off to the kitchen to git some cucumber sandwiches and fruit salad with Jell-o.

When they finally made it back with the food, ever'body got real busy chewin', but they wuz all glad of somethin' to do. This also gave Lizzy the chance to thank on whether she really wanted to see Dutch or not, and she'd jest 'bout decided when he walked through the damned door.

Dutch had been out gittin' Guthrie and some other boys settled down by the crick when he heard the girls had stopped by to see Suzanna. Lizzy pretended not to care whether he stopped in or not, but ever'body else in the room must've picked up on the vibe b'tween the two of 'em, be'cuz glances wuz flyin' fast as pinballs 'round the room. Tammy's antenny wuz up, and the smile that spread across her powdered face didn't make it all the way to her eyes, if'n you git my drift. She wuz jealous, that's fer sure, but she wuzn't desperate yet.

Once her brother wuz in the room, Suzanna tried harder to join in the conversation, and Lizzy could see Dutch wuz anxious to git talk started b'tween her and his sister. Tammy seen the whole thang and with a shot of piss and vinegar said to Lizzy, "So, I hear the National Guard has left yer little part of the world, Miss Lizzy. Yer kin must be beside yerselves fer the loss of 'em."

Lizzy knew Tammy wuz talkin' 'bout Joe but didn't have the balls to mention his name in front of Dutch. Jest the thought of Joe wuz enough to turn Lizzy seven diff'rent shades of red, but she answered Tammy in a bored kind of way. Dutch gave Lizzy a thankful kind of look, and Suzanna kept her eyeballs glued to a spot on the carpet. If Tammy'd known what thin ice she wuz skatin' on, she wouldn't have said nuthin' 'bout it. All she wuz a-tryin' to do wuz to confound Lizzy by brangin' up a feller she thought she wuz sweet on to try to hurt her in Dutch's eyes. Tammy also wanted to knock Lizzy down a few rungs on the social ladder by mentionin' how important the military boys wuz to countrified folk. Of course Tammy wuz ignor'nt of what happened with Joe and Suzanna, and Lizzy'd put the whole sad tale in the vault and thrown away the key.

Dutch looked a little worried Lizzy might could let somethin' slip, but after a bit he relaxed. Suzanna didn't, though, and kept her lips zipped the rest of the visit. While Dutch wuz leadin' Lizzy and Tildie out to the RV, Tammy let loose a dam of nastiness 'bout Lizzy, but Suzanna didn't join in one whit. When Dutch came back in, Tammy felt she had to spew some more venom so's he could hear it.

"Damn! She looks like shit! I'll suwanee I ain't never seen nobody so changed since the last time I laid eyes on her. I thank she's been in the fake bake or somethin'. Patty and me wuz jest sayin' how we might not have recognized her if'n we passed her on the street."

As you might imagine, there wuz 'bout a million thangs Dutch could've said back, but instead he jest commented that Lizzy'd been travelin' and on vacation, so of course she'd have a nice tan.

Tammy continued, "I, my-ownself, never seen nuthin' in that girl. Why, I thank she's so ugly she'd make a freight train take a dirt road. She jest sets there, grinnin' like a 'possum with them teeth of hers, and don't y'all thank her eyes 'r jest too far apart? Creeps me out, it does. I've heard tell folks thank she has right purty eyes, but I never could see it. I thank she looks like a doe in the headlights. Makes me wanna shoot Bambi, it does. She has a look 'bout her, like she can take care of her ownself, but not in a good way. I cain't stand her."

Seein' as how Tammy thought Dutch wuz sweet on Lizzy, her approach prob'ly wuzn't the best, but she wuz as hot as fire and thought her own feet didn't stank, so she said it anyway. When she seen Dutch looked like somethin' wuz stankin' to high heaven, she waited to hear what he would say. When he didn't say nuthin', she said, "I do recall when we first met her, we wuz all surprised to hear that she wuz one of the purtiest girls in that part of the country. You said, "She's purty? I thank I'd rather call her Momma smart." But later she seemed to grow on you, and you thought she wuz good-a-lookin' at one time, didn't you?"

"You got that right," said Dutch who wuz done bitin' his tongue,"but that wuz b'fore I got to know her. Now that we're acquainted, I'd say she's one of the most beautiful girls I ever laid my eyes on."

With that, he turned and walked plum out'a the room, leavin' Tammy with what she had been dreadin' all along. The worst part wuz, she brought it on her ownself.

The afternoon with Buford's sisters and Suzanna wuz all Tildie and Lizzy could talk 'bout on the way back. Both of 'em wanted to air out Dutch's behavior and the particular way he wuz with Lizzy. They circled 'round it with talk of Suzanna and the sandwiches and fruit and lemonade but never landed on Dutch and what Tildie thought of 'im. Truth wuz, Tildie didn't know how to start talkin' 'bout it and wished Lizzy would've said somethin'.

# Chapter 46

Every dad-blammed day when Lizzy got back to the RV park, she half-expected to git an email from Janie, but she didn't have any luck 'til three popped up the same day. They'd been fixin' to take a walk when the manager stopped by to tell 'em the wifi was fixed, and Tildie and Guthrie had the good sense to take their walk, jest the two of 'em and leave Lizzy to her readin'.

She opened the one that looked like it'd been sent first, and appeared to be 'bout five days old. The first part of the letter said how Janie wished Lizzy was havin' a good time in Kentucky, and how she wished Lizzy had a cell phone with her so that she didn't have to write damned letters, and how when they wuz both married with a couple of kids, they might could git cell phones of their own and talk whenever they wanted with the "friends and family plan." The second letter wuz written a day later than the first, and Janie's typin' didn't look like much more 'n chicken scratches at first. Here's what it said:

*"Since I started writin' this letter, somethin' serious as a heart attack has happened, but I don't want you to fret 'bout it none. It's Lydie. Last night the phone rang right 'round midnight when we wuz already in bed fer the night. It wuz Lieutenant Dan callin' to tell us Lydie had run off to Dollywood with one of the men, and she's most likely in the family way. I hate to tell you who, but it wuz Joe Wickham. Ever'body wuz surprised except Kitty.*
*"I'm hopin' fer the best. Maybe they'll git hitched, and folks won't hear 'bout his past. He ain't the sharpest knife in the drawer; we all know, but he must have a gold nuggit in his heart fer her be'cuz he knew straight out that our Daddy couldn't afford to give 'em anythang to live on. Momma is jest beside herself, but Daddy seems calm 'bout it. I've been thankin' my lucky stars we never let on what we knew 'bout 'im. We've got to jest put it out'a our heads. They'll prob'ly be by here in a day or two. Lydie left Dixie a note when she left sayin' as much. I've gotta go fer now since Momma can hardly wipe her own ass by herself these days. Sorry 'bout my typin'. J."*

Like a drunk with an empty bottle in one hand and a full one in the other, Lizzy clicked open the third letter and started to read. It'd been written the day after the second letter.

*"By this time you've read my first two letters. I hope you can read this one better, but I doubt it since I'm as anxious as a one-eyed cat watchin' two rat holes. I don't know what to say to sweeten this, so I'll jest say it. As bad as it is with Lydie prob'ly knocked up at fifteen and all, there's a chance Joe ain't gonna marry her after-all. In fact, he might be tradin' her 'round like a hooker fer some*

*extra cash. We thank she and Joe never went to Dollywood at all. Lieutenant Dan came by yesterd'y, drove straight all the way from Myrtle Beach. Lydie's letter to Dixie said they wuz goin' to Pigeon Forge to git married and to Dollywood fer their honeymoon, but Dan heard it from one of the boys that Joe didn't plan on goin' back through Tennessee at all and that he might be fixin' to git Lydie into some kind of dirty pictures in Las Vegas.*

*"Lieutenant Dan tried to figure what route they'd take, but he didn't know if'n they'd stole a car or wuz plannin' to take the Greyhound bus. Somebody said they'd seen 'em at the bus station, but it could've been jest 'bout anybody. Lieutenant Dan contacted the South Carolina state police, and they sent out photos of Lydie to ever' hotel and motel and police station b'tween here and Nevada. Oh, he's lower 'n a Bassett Hound's belly 'bout it all. He and Dixie 'r real torn up 'bout it, but you cain't blame 'em. Momma and Daddy 'r hotter 'n a goat's ass in a pepper patch, but I cain't hardly b'lieve Joe would do somethin' like that. We'll find her, and then Daddy'll put a leash on her fer good.*

*"Lieutenant Dan b'lieves the worst. I can tell. He even said he didn't trust Joe as far as he could throw 'im. Momma's jest as useless as tits on a boar-hog. She stays in her room all the time and wants us to wait on her. Daddy is busy doin' nuthin', like a one-legged cat in a sandbox. I've never seen 'im like this b'fore. Kitty is spit-fire mad fer not tellin' folks they wuz foolin' 'round, and I'm jest glad you've been with Tildie and Guthrie and had to miss all the drama. I wish you wuz here, though. Law knows there's enough of Momma to go 'round.*

*"I hate to ask, but could you please come home? I know Guthrie won't mind, plus, Daddy is fixin' to go off to Las Vegas a-lookin' fer Joe and Lydie, and I know he ain't got the cash. Lieutenant Dan has to git back to Myrtle Beach by tomorrow night, but they wuz goin' to head to Pigeon Forge and look 'round b'fore Dan had to git back. Guthrie's help and deep pockets sure would be a comfort right 'bout now. J."*

"Uncle Guthrie!" Lizzy called as soon as she finished the letter. She stood up and moved to the door of the RV. Jest as she touched the knob, the door opened, and there stood Dutch. Well, she wuz jest white as a sheet, and it made 'im stop right there in his tracks. B'fore he could git a word out, she said, "I'm sorry, but I need to find Guthrie right away. I ain't got time fer a visit, Dutch."

"My God, Miss Lizzy! What's the matter?" he cried. "I won't keep you, but why don't you set down a minute and I'll go find Guthrie fer you? Or I could send Mr. Brown. He's in the truck outside."

Lizzy felt her knees turn to butter, and she set down in the tiny kitchen booth. She agreed to let Mr. Brown fetch Tildie and Guthrie fer her. Dutch set down next to her. She wuz the picture of misery, and he couldn't leave her. "Is there somethin' I can git you? A cold drank?"

"No, thanks," she said, "There ain't nuthin' wrong with me. I'm jest vexed by some news from back home."

And 'bout that time she broke into a sobbin' fit and couldn't say another word. Dutch tried to say somethin' that would make her feel better, then patted her back in silence while she cried a river. She wiped her nose on her sleeve and said, "I jest read a letter from Janie with the worst news. I feel like an episode of Jerry Springer. I cain't keep it from anyone. My littlest sister has run off with Joe. She might be pregnant, and she might be workin' as part of a porn ring in Las Vegas. They took off from Myrtle Beach. You know 'im too well to wonder if'n it's true. She ain't got a cent of money on her. She don't know a soul. B'fore this summer she'd never even been out'a the state of Tennessee. Findin' her is gonna be like a-tryin' to find a needle in a haystack."

The look on Dutch's face said it all.

"And when I thank that I could've stopped it," she said, "On account of I knew what kind of feller he wuz. If'n I had told anybody, even part of it, then none of this would've happened. It's too late now."

"I'm so sorry," Dutch said. "This is eggregious. I cain't b'lieve it. Are you sure 'bout all of this?"

"Oh, yes. They left Myrtle Beach t'gether on Sund'y night, and folks thought they seen 'em at the Greyhound Station after that."

"What is bein' done to find her?"

"My Daddy went to Pigeon Forge to see if'n he could spot 'em out there, and Janie wrote us to see if'n Uncle Guthrie might could help. I'm hopin' we can unhook and drive out'a here right quick. I cain't thank on what can be done to find 'em. I ain't got no hope. How could they even be found? This really sucks."

Dutch shook his head in agreement.

"When I opened my eyes and seen what he wuz, whoo-whee! I should ha' done somethin', but I wuz afraid. I didn't know what to do. What a horrible, damned mistake!"

Dutch didn't say nuthin' and seemed like he couldn't hear a word she wuz sayin'. He wuz pacin' back and forth like a horned bull at the rodeo. He had an aggravated look on his face, and his eyebrows wuz all scrunched up like he wuz in pain. Lizzy knew in a minute she didn't have a snowball's chance in hell with Dutch. And it wuzn't 'til that very minute that she realized she wuz sweet on 'im; the minute she realized she could never have 'im.

She couldn't thank on her own loss very long. The thought of Lydie, the humiliation, the misery she had brought on her own kin, brought on another bucket full of tears. After a bit, Dutch said quietly "I thank you've been hopin' I would leave, and I cain't thank of any reason to stay except concern. I wish to heaven there wuz somethin' I could do to make you feel better. I'm sure y'all won't be able to set down with Suzanna fer dinner tonight. I'll tell her family business calls y'all away. I'll keep it from her as long as I can. I thank the truth will git out b'fore long, though. It might even make the news."

He promised her, again, he wouldn't spread it 'round and told her he hoped thangs would resolve themselves on her family's account. He asked her to tell her aunt and uncle "so long" fer 'im, and with one serious look he opened the door to the RV and wuz gone. As he walked down the gravel path looking fer Mr. Brown and his truck, Lizzy thought fer sure she'd never lay eyes on 'im again in all her days. She thought on how many times over the past months she'd wished to never see 'im again, and now that she felt diff'rent, her wish had come true. She thought 'bout how she'd hated Dutch at first sight and loved Joe Wickham at first sight, and how she wuz wrong in both cases. She decided not to make opinions of folks 'til she knew 'em better from here on out.

Ever since she read Janie's third letter, she wuz sure that Joe didn't plan on marryin' her little sister. Why in the world would he? She's a minor, fer one thang, and would need her Daddy to sign a letter. Clearly Lydie had no money to her name. She couldn't support 'im; she wuz all of fifteen years old, fer heaven's sake! She wouldn't have left Myrtle Beach fer "Dollywood" if'n she didn't thank Joe wuz plannin' to git hitched. She wuz too young and stupid not to be easy pickin's fer Joe Wickham.

When she thought back on it, she couldn't tell that Lydie had a crush on Joe, but all Lydie needed to fall in love wuz a pat on the ass as an invitation, and Joe passed 'em out like a new Daddy with cigars in the maternity ward. She wuz always flittin' from one feller to the next. If'n she'd been reeled in a little bit, she might could've been controlled, and this never would've happened. A thimble-full of parentin' could've stopped it all.

Lizzy wuz beside herself to be home with her family, Janie in particular. With their Daddy out a-lookin' under every rock fer Lydie and their Momma watchin' re-runs of "My Name is Earl" while locked up in her room, Janie'd be needin' some help takin' care of the house and Benny's store, not to mention Mary and Kitty and Guthrie's kids.

Tildie and Guthrie hurried back as fast as Tildie could waddle, and Lizzy told 'em the whole story and read both letters to 'em. Although Lydie wuz not their favorite niece, they wuz concerned anyway, and Guthrie said he'd do ever'thang he could to find her. Lizzy, expectin' nuthin' less from her uncle, said her thank you's through her own tears. Guthrie set out to empty the chemical toilet while Tildie unhooked the RV from the electric and pulled in the extended bay window with the flick of a switch on the dashboard. Lizzy unhooked the awnin', and they wuz ready to roll.

# Chapter 47

"I've been thankin' on it, Lizzy," Guthrie said as they drove along, "I thank Janie's right. I thank this boy'll do what's right with Lydie. Who in the world would make up a plan like this with a teenage girl who has friends and kin to come a-lookin' after her? I mean to say, she wuz livin' with a damned officer in the National Guard. We ain't in some God-forsaken third world country where girls git carried off in the middle of the night. Did he thank he could jest git away with it? Did he thank the National Guard wouldn't come a-lookin' fer his ass? His action ain't worth the risk."

"Do you really thank so?" Lizzy asked.

"Land-sakes-alive!" said Tildie, "I thank yer uncle's right. What can he git 'cept fer a few bucks in his pocket that won't last but a day or two in Las Vegas. There's weddin' chapels all over the place in Nevada. Jest be'cuz it looks like they've gone off to Vegas, doesn't mean he's plannin' to take nude photos of her and sell her off like a piece of meat. I cain't thank bad on Joe. I cain't. Can you, Lizzy?"

"If'n he wuz plannin' to do what's right, why didn't he call Momma and Daddy fer permission? Why didn't he go to Dollywood instead of takin' a bus out to Vegas?"

"There ain't no proof they've gone off to Las Vegas," said Tildie.

"Well, I thank we ain't gonna find hide nor hair of 'em in the state of Tennessee."

"They could very well be in Nashv'lle at a concert or on their way back home by now. Neither one of 'em has any money to speak of, so I reckon they'll be home b'fore long, married or not."

"Aw, that dog won't hunt. Why keep a concert a secret? Why worry 'bout who wuz gonna find out? Why wouldn't Lydie be braggin' 'bout the trip to Dixie instead of writin' that confounded note 'bout Pigeon Forge? It ain't likely. Janie done said his good buddy already admitted to hearin' that Joe wuz plannin' to take her off and sell her to folks that take nude photos of girls. Naw. Joe ain't run off to marry Lydie. He's too proud to be poor. He'll find himself a girl with a trust fund and then work his hardest to empty it out fer her."

"Why in the world would Lydie go off with him if'n she knew what he wuz up to?"

"She's an idjit," said Lizzy with tears in her eyes. "I don't know what to tell you. Fer a year now she's been spendin' more time shakin' her ass at anythang with a uniform down at the fair grounds. Momma and Daddy haven't reined her in a bit. Since the National Guard first set up their camp, nuthin' but boys and uniforms and makin' out behind the grandstands has been in her head. It's all she talks 'bout day and night. She's wild as a March hare, and we all know Joe's tight jeans and smooth talk could turn a nun's head even if'n it hairlipped the Pope."

"Now, Lizzy, you need to calm yerself down. Janie doesn't thank ill on Joe, so how can we?" asked her aunt.

"Who the hell does Janie ever thank bad on? Tell me that! It don't matter what a feller's done in the past, she cain't help but expect 'im to be better. It's her way. But deep down Janie knows what Joe really is. He ain't got an honest bone in his entire body. He's a cheat and a liar, and I'd tell 'im to his face if'n he wuz standin' here."

Tildie loved the taste of gossip in her mouth almost as much as a gooey pound cake, and she wuz startin' to figure that Lizzy had some information she wuzn't sharin'. She said, "Do you know all this fer sure?"

"Hell yeah," said Lizzy, turnin' red in the face. "I done told you the other day 'bout how he treated Dutch, and you, yer ownself, heard Joe spreadin' lies 'bout 'im, bold-faced lies. There's other stuff, too, but I cain't tell you, be'cuz it ain't worth tellin', really. The lies he's told jest 'bout the folks livin' at Pembrook Farm could go on fer a hundred miles of country road. Ever'thang he said 'bout Suzanna, I wuz expectin' a real snobby bitch, but he knew she wuz sweet as sugar. He knew she wuz, but he made it up anyway."

"If'n he's such a damned liar, why ain't Lydie wise to it?"

"That's the worst part, Ain't Tildie. It wuzn't 'til I wuz in Knoxv'lle that I had the chance to visit with Dutch and his cousin Jake and learn the truth. When I got home, the National Guard wuz already packin' to head out to the beach. Since Joe wuz plannin' to leave with the troops, Janie and I decided to keep mum on the subject. We didn't thank there wuz any call fer spreadin' shit 'bout folks who wuz 'bout to skedaddle fer good. Even when the plan fer Lydie to go stay with Dixie and Dan sprung up, I never dreamed I'd need to spill the beans on Joe. I mean, she's FIFTEEN fer heaven's sake! I didn't thank she wuz in his sites."

"When they all left fer Myrtle Beach, I reckon you had no gumption that they wuz sweet on each other?"

"Not at all. Not from either of 'em. Ever'body knows the kind of family I've got. If a nice word passes b'tween one of my sisters and a feller, my Momma jumps on it faster 'n a duck on a junebug. Of course when he first came to town, she wuz checkin' out his butt jest like ever'body else. Ever' girl in three counties wuz plum head over heels fer 'im fer the first couple of months, but he never so much as winked at her. She wuz behind the grandstands with half the troop after that."

Y'all might imagine the subject would begin to wear on folks if'n it wuz repeated enough, but durin' the long ride home in the back of the RV, the girls kept bouncin' back to it. The thought sat in Lizzy's head like a burr under her saddle. The guilt she felt nearly wore her to a frazzle.

They drove straight through, usin' the RV's chemical toilet when somebody had to "go" and eatin' sandwiches and pickles out'a the on-board fridge. Guthrie and Tildie's kids wuz settin' on the porch swing watchin' cars go by when they spotted the huge, shiny RV kickin' up dust along the road. They whooped and hollered and jumped up and down like fatback bacon on a hot griddle.

Lizzy hopped down from the top step of the RV, mussed up the hair of a couple of smaller versions of Guthrie on the stoop and ran into the house. Janie came runnin' from her Momma's room, and they met in a bear hug. Both girls wuz wore slap out from worryin'.

"I ain't heard nuthin' from Daddy," said Janie. "But now that y'all 'r here, and Uncle Guthrie is fixin' to go help, I have a good feelin'.

"Is Daddy still in Tennessee?"

"Yep. He went off to Pigeon Forge the day I wrote you."

"Have you heard from 'im at all?"

"He called on Wednesd'y to say that he wuz there safe. He said he reckoned he wouldn't waste any more money on long-distance calls 'til he had somethin' to tell us."

"How's Momma? How 'r all y'all?"

"Momma is fair to middlin'. She'll git a lift out'a layin' her eyes on you and Tildie. 'Course she ain't leavin' her room fer nuthin'. Mary and Kitty 'r doin' fine as a frog's hair split three ways. I thank they're likin' the attention from the neighbors."

"But you-- how 'r you?" asked Lizzy. "You look like you've been cooked in the squat."

Janie said she wuz fine and dandy, and their little visit wuz ended when Guthrie and Tildie had finally pried the last of their kid's dirty little fingers from their arms and legs and kicked open the screen door. Janie gave 'em both a hug and kiss b'fore they headed to the family room. There Janie ran over the same ground she'd jest covered with Lizzy in the hallway, and they figured she didn't know any more 'n they did already. She still thought there'd be a phone call from Lydie or Benny any minute, explainin' what happened.

They tiptoed down the hallway to Benny and Flo's room, careful not to wake her up. Lizzy could hear her shoutin' letters at the contestants on the gameshow she wuz watchin' from the bed. Of course when she heard a knock at the door, she switched off the tv and started sniffin' like she'd been cryin' fer a spell. She started in on Joe, sayin' if'n he wuz here, she'd slap 'im to sleep, then slap 'im fer sleepin'. After she wuz through with 'im, he'd run out'a town like a turpentined cat. She blamed ever'body fer what happened to Lydie, exceptin', of course, her ownself.

"If'n that damned Benny had let me carry my own family down to Myrtle Beach, this wouldn't 've happened," she said. "Poor Lydie didn't have a soul to take care of her. Why did Dan and Dixie ever let her out'a their sight? That's what I wanna know. I have a reason to b'lieve they didn't watch her like they should. She ain't the kind of girl who would go off on her own like that. I suwanee, I thought Dixie wuz too young to have watch over her, but Benny rules 'round here with a strong hand. My poor baby! And now Benny has run off a-lookin' fer her, and he took the pistol out'a the bedside table, and I jest know he's gonna try to kill Joe Wickham. Then what in the world will happen to us? Benny'll be dead, or worse, and Cooter'll come to town and throw us out in the street on our asses b'fore his body gits cold in the ground. Lawsy mercy! I don't know what we'll do."

Ever'body told her she wuz so full of shit, she wuz turnin' brown, and Guthrie said he would take off in Benny's direction at first light, and she shouldn't worry. "They ain't been gone but a week," he said. "I'll fetch Benny and take 'im back home with me so's we can make a plan. I'll even buy plane tickets if'n I have to."

"Oh, Guthrie!" said Flo pushin' aside empty plates nearly licked clean. "That's 'bout the best thang I could hope fer. When you find 'em, if'n they ain't hitched already, you walk 'em to the chapel and see it done yerself. If Lydie's worried 'bout a weddin' dress, y'all tell her she can rent one from 'em places in Las Vegas. And tell her when she gits home, if'n she's knocked up, we can go down to the Goodwill and find some real cute maternity clothes fer her, and if'n we cain't find cute maternity clothes, I'll bet you a dollar I can find cute fat lady clothes down there. I'll suwanee, they have jest 'bout ever'thang you could ever want down there.

"Oh, and make Benny unload that gun and put it away. He don't have a license to carry a concealed weapon, and I ain't gonna have 'im shoot nobody. He'd git caught fer sure. Tell 'im I cain't even leave my room fer the worry. I cain't eat nor sleep, and I thank I might have a cadillac arrest. I got pains in my side and a headache that's bigger 'n the state of Texas. I'm jest scared out'a my wits, and I'm shakin' all over. Oh, and tell Lydie not to be payin' no retail prices fer first-hand clothes. She'll see all them stores out there and start buyin' on credit. Oh, Guthrie! Yer the best brother in the whole world!"

Guthrie said he'd do his best and told her to stay calm fer her girls' sake. 'Bout that time Janie had some country fried steak and gravy with all the fixin's ready fer supper, and her company left her to tell her worries to the dog, who sat sheddin' and bitin' at a flea at the foot of her bed.

Guthrie and Tildie thought she wuz plum stupid fer hibernatin' in her room like that. The house wuz filthy and needed a bug bomb. The least she could do is carry her plates to the kitchen so's one of the girls could warsh 'em and put 'em away. They didn't say nuthin' to the girls on it, though, since havin' Flo hidin' in the bedroom kept her out'a Janie and Lizzy's hair of the day.

In the kitchen they found Kitty and Mary already bent over their plates shovelin' fork-fulls of mashed taters and canned peas into their open and meat-filled mouths. One of 'em had a book open at the table; the other's lips wuz painted as red as bird shit at pokeberry time.

When her sister sat next to her at the table, Mary whispered, "This is a most unfortunate affair; and will probably be much talked of. But we must stem the tide of malice, and pour into the wounded bosoms of each other, the balm of sisterly consolation."

When Lizzy jest blinked at her, Mary added, "Unhappy as the event must be for Lydie, we may draw from it this useful lesson; that loss of virtue in a female is irretrievable-- that one false step involves her in endless ruin-- that her reputation is no less brittle than it is beautiful-- and that she cannot be too much guarded in her behavior towards the undeserving of the other sex."

Lizzy lifted up her eyes in amazement but couldn't thank of anythang to say back to her sister. Mary continued to make her ownself feel better with her moral jibber-jabber that not a soul at the table could figure out.

Later that night Lizzy and Janie had half an hour to themselves, and Lizzy used it as a chance to learn more 'bout what happened with Joe and Lydie. "Spill it, Janie," she said. "I need to know ever'thang 'bout it that I ain't heard already. What did Lieutenant Dan say? Didn't they pick up a whiff of somethin'? They must've seen Joe and Lydie t'gether."

"Lieutenant Dan said he had a hunch they wuz up to somethin', 'specially with all of Lydie's talk. You know how she is. There wuzn't nuthin' that set off his alarm bells, though. I feel sorry fer 'im. He's a good egg, and he wuz good to Lydie, lettin' her live with 'im fer the summer. He wuz on his way here to tell us they'd run off to Pigeon Forge when he learned that somethin' else wuz goin' on."

"And Joe's buddy, wuz he sure Joe had bad connections out west? Did he know Lydie is under-age? Did Dan speak with this feller face to face?"

"Yep; but the funny thang is, when Lieutenant Dan asked the feller if'n he knew anythang 'bout their plan, he wouldn't say nuthin' to nobody. Not one word. I sure hope he wuz drunk when he said the part 'bout the nekkid photos to his buddies."

"So what yer sayin' is that none of y'all had an inklin' that somethin' wuz up 'til Lieutenant Dan knocked on that door over yonder?"

"Heavens to Betsy, Lizzy! How wuz I to dream up the thought that somethin' like this would happen? 'Course when we thought they wuz gittin' married, I wuz a bit worried 'bout our little sis. She ain't old enough to git married and keep a house. Hell, have you looked at her side of the bedroom in there? I knew he wuz always a-lookin' at the little girls 'round town, but I didn't dream he wuz a creep. Momma and Daddy didn't know nuthin' 'bout none of that, neither. They jest knew she wuz practic'ly a baby, but Momma wuz fifteen when she had me, so what can they say?"

Kitty admitted that Lydie had emailed her some pictures Joe had taken of her. She said they wuz fer her to git jobs modelin'. Lizzy asked if any of the pictures wuz taken here or if they wuz all taken at the beach, and Kitty said they wuz all shot in a bikini on the beach.

Lizzy asked Janie, "Did Lieutenant Dan thank high on Joe? Did he know anythang 'bout 'im?"

"He wuz trash-talkin' Joe. He thought Joe wuz livin' high on the hog fer somebody who'd needed a job so bad at the first. And since he skipped out with Lydie, Dan's had reports that Joe left debts all over the place. I hope it ain't true, though."

"Oh, Janie! If'n we'd spilled our guts 'bout Joe back when we first caught wind of it, this mess would never've happened!"

"Would'a, could'a, should'a," said Janie. "The Good Lord tells us to forgive and forget. We cain't go spreadin' rumors 'bout a feller's past without knowin' what's in his heart right then and there. We did what we thought wuz right."

"Did Dan tell you what the note to Dixie said?"

"He brought it with 'im, and I have it here." She reached into her bra and pulled out a folded sheet of paper and handed it to her sister.

*"Dear Dixie-- Y'all 'r gonna plum crack up when y'all know where I am. My side hurts from laughin' at all y'all's faces when you wake up in the mornin' and find me gone. I'm off to Pigeon Forge, and if'n y'all cain't guess with who, then yer dumber 'n I give you credit fer. There ain't but one feller fer me, and he is sexier 'n Brad Pitt back in the Thelma and Louise days. We've been doin' the sweaty bop fer a few weeks now, and I'm purty sure there's a bun in the oven, if'n you catch my drift. I figure this is my chance to git my hooks into 'im.*
*"Y'all don't need to tell my folks or nuthin', be'cuz I'm real excited to send 'em a postcard from Dollywood and sign my name Lydie Wickham'. It tickles me to thank on it. I cain't hardly write fer laughin'. Tell Leroy I'm sorry I cain't dance with 'im tonight at the bonfire, and explain why. Tell 'im I'll take a rain check fer the next one, will ya?*
*"I left my bathin' suit hangin' on the peg in the bathroom. I'll call you when I git home so's you can send it to me. You can wear it if'n you want.*
*"Yer BFF, Lydie."*

"She's an airhead. That's all I can say," said Lizzy. "It does show she thought she wuz 'bout to git married. Whatever ends up happenin', she wuzn't plannin' on workin' at a peep show. Can you imagine our Daddy readin' this? I know he must've been mad enough to spit nails."

"I never seen nobody speechless like that. He didn't say nary a word fer ten minutes, at least. Momma looked green in the gills, but I'll suwanee she wuz swallerin' a grin. Then she broke into craziness like I've never seen b'fore."

"The way you've been waitin' on her hand and foot, feedin' and takin' care of the girls and the chickens and the house and all, it's too much fer you, Janie. I'm sorry as shit I wuzn't here to help."

"Mary and Kitty have been real good with the dishes and feedin' the dogs and the cats. I didn't want 'em out there with them chickens, and havin' 'em cook is 'bout the same as burnin' the house down, so I wuzn't havin' any of that. Kitty's been spendin' her time coverin' up all them zits of hers with makeup, and Mary keeps her nose in a book nearly all the time, so they ain't been much trouble. Fern came by on Tuesd'y after Daddy left and stayed a couple of nights with us. She made a few casseroles and stuck 'em in the deep freeze. LuLu Lucas stopped by with fried okra and red beans and rice, and she asked if I wanted her to pick up the dog shit in the yard, but we never do that, anyway, so what's the point, right? She sent over a couple of her girls to see if'n we needed anythang from the Winn Dixie, but since we don't shop there, I didn't ask fer nuthin'."

"I wish she'd keep her nose out'a it," cried Lizzy. "She probl'y meant well, but I'm inclined to b'lieve she wuz fishin' fer gossip. There's not one thang she could do to help us. If'n she wants to rub our noses in it, she can do it from the other side of the fence."

Lizzy asked what their Daddy wuz plannin' to do to find Joe and Lydie.

"I thank," said Janie, "he wuz takin' recent pictures of Lydie down to the Greyhound station. He thought he'd find out the number of the busses goin' to Las Vegas and maybe git a lead that way. I thank he wuz gonna try to make a report with the state police b'fore he left Tennessee. I don't know what else he's doin', and he wuz so low when he left, Lizzy, that I barely got this much out'a 'im."

## Chapter 48

The whole house wuz hopin' fer a call from Benny the next day, but Judge Judy reruns came on the tv, and they still hadn't heard a peep from 'im. He wuzn't much on waggin' his tongue, even on his best day, but they'd hoped he'd make the call on account of ever'body wuz settin' on pins and needles waitin'. Even if'n he'd called to say he didn't have nuthin' to say, the folks back home would've been right pleased to hear it.

Guthrie pulled out'a the driveway, promisin' to call the minute he laid eyes on Benny. Uncle Guthrie had his orders to send Benny back home as soon as he could since it wuz the only way to git Flo to shut up 'bout how he wuz sure to git shot or be in a wreck or git mugged in a big city like Las Vegas.

Tildie stayed behind with all her kids to help out with the chores and wait on Miss Flo when she wuz needed. Janie and Lizzy wuz right thankful fer the break from their Momma. Fern dropped by more reg'lar 'n usual with high hopes of brangin' cheer, but she never darkened the door without some new story 'bout Joe's debts or his wild ways that left 'em feelin' lower 'n a snake's belly when she left.

Ever'body in town wuz givin' old Joe a tongue-lashin', fergittin' that he wuz the bee's knees jest three months b'fore. Folks wuz sayin' that he owed money to ever' Mom 'n Pop shop down the main drag. Ever' girl he ever two-stepped with wuz callin' it a seduction, and folks loudly declared he wuz the wickedest young man that'd ever been through these parts. As a matter of fact, they said they'd distrusted the look of 'im from the git-go. Lizzy didn't b'lieve half of what she heard, but the half she did b'lieve made her sure Lydie wuz in a heap of trouble. Even Janie, who could sing the praises of jest 'bout any livin' thang, started to doubt that they'd gone off to git hitched, sayin' that if'n they'd gotten married, Lydie would've called 'em to brag 'bout it by then.

Guthrie'd left town on Sund'y, and Tildie didn't hear from 'im 'til Tuesd'y. He said he'd found Benny and convinced 'im to head on up to Nashv'lle where they could be comfortable at Guthrie's house and make some calls to the motels in Las Vegas. Guthrie didn't expect to git anywhere on the phone, but he thought they could at least be close to an airport with direct flights jest in case the police got a lead on the case. In any event, his wuz a better plan than drivin' all over God's creation and bein' without a phone.

When he called Tildie, he said, "I called and left a message fer Lieutenant Dan to see if'n he can find out whether Joe has any relations or buddies who might know where the hell he is. If'n we could find anybody, jest one person, who had any information, it would sure help 'bout right now. We ain't got nuthin' but hunches. Dan best be helpin' us seein' as how he is partly responsible fer this mess. But maybe Lizzy knows somethin'. She wuz as close to Joe as anybody."

Lizzy wuz quick as a duck on a junebug to say she didn't know nothin'. He'd never mentioned any kin except his Momma and Daddy who wuz both dead and gone, but there had to be a buddy in the National Guard who knew more 'bout 'im.

Ever' day wuz long as a wet week while they waited fer word from Guthrie or Benny. They listened fer the phone and nearly jumped out'a their socks when it did ring. Their habit of lettin' it go to message wuz gone with Lydie, and where they used to hope the phone wouldn't sound at all, now all they wished wuz that it would ring.

One mild night when they wuz all out on the stoop drankin' Jack 'n Coke, the phone rang but nobody heard it. When Lizzy seen the light flashin' on the machine, her heart jumped up in her throat, but it wuz jest Cooter's flea-bitin' voice on the message.

*"Benny. This is Cooter. I jest caught wind of yer troubles from my wife's kin. LuLu called Charlotte yesterd'y and told her all 'bout it. I want you to know from the horse's mouth that Charlotte and me, well, we feel fer you, and fer yer girls and yer wife. I b'lieve y'all must be wrangin' yer hands night and day with worry over little Lydie. Folks say time heals all wounds, but I reckon nuthin' can heal what's bein' done to her. I spent most of the day yesterd'y figurin' out what to say to make y'all feel better, but seein' as how I ain't a parent myself, I couldn't thank on..."*

Here the machine cut off, and a second message started. *"Like I wuz sayin', I couldn't thank on nuthin' of comfort to say except I 'spect hearin' she wuz dead would prob'ly be better 'n this. If'n she died of the whoopin' cough or some kind of infection, y'all wouldn't blame yerselves fer what happened. Charlotte told me y'all 'r partly to blame fer it all on account of she wuz runnin' all over the country with her skirt so short y'all oughtta call it a shirt. As parents, y'all should've reigned her in a little bit more. All y'all should jest feel right proud that none of the other girls have turned out to be..."*

The machine stopped again, and a third message continued Cooter's thoughts. *"Well, the other girls ain't so wild, so she must've been a bad apple to start with. Laws! I pity y'all!, and Charlotte says she does, too. And of course when we told Miz M and DeeDee, they said one bad apple spoils the whole peck and that all of the girls would be considered floosies from here on out. Miz M says fellers will look at them pictures of Lydie and decide that the other sisters must be jest as cheap, and not a good man in the great state of Tennessee will look twice at the girls. So's I wuz settin' and thankin' on it, I thought 'bout that certain somethin' that almost happened last fall, and how if'n it had happened, I would've been as mixed up in this mess as the rest of y'all, and I wuz so very thankful..."*

The final message began, *"So, anyways, I thank y'all should consider disownin' Lydie. She made her bed, and now she needs to lay down in it. That's my advice. I'll talk to y'all later."* And he hung up.

Guthrie didn't call again 'til he had heard from Lieutenant Dan, who said Joe didn't have one relation that he kept in contact with, and the boys who knew Joe thought he wuz alone in this world. Plenty of folks knew who he wuz, but nobody claimed to be his close friend, and that meant that nobody could give Guthrie any news 'bout where he might've gone. The one thang ever'body said wuz that he didn't leave a forwardin' address since he owed jest 'bout ever'body money and prob'ly didn't wanna be found. Lieutenant Dan said he owed twenty thousand dollars in gamblin' debts jest in the Myrtle Beach area, and he prob'ly had left a few illegitimate babies on the way, as well. Guthrie didn't try to hide anythang from Benny's girls, and Janie seemed horrified to hear it all.

On another call, Guthrie said Benny had spent most of his time in Nashv'lle sitting drunk or passed out on the davenport, so he'd sobered up their father and would send 'im home the next day. Guthrie said he reckoned he could git more done without Benny hangin' 'round anyhow. When Flo heard that Benny would be home the next day, she didn't go off in raptures like her children thought she would, 'specially considerin' the fact that she'd been so worried he'd git shot or arrested.

"What? Is he coming home without poor Lydie?" she cried. "I'm sure he won't leave Nashv'lle b'fore he's found those kids. Who will beat the livin' shit out'a Joe and force 'im to do right by her if'n they ain't already hitched?"

Tildie and the kids wuz wishin' fer home 'bout that time, and the girls thought it would be okay fer her to head on out. Guthrie had a delivery truck from the appliance store come to brang Benny back and carry 'em home. Tildie spent a good chunk of her time in the truck thankin' on Lizzy and her friend from Lexin'ton. She'd half-expected a call or somethin' from 'im or fer Lizzy to at least have mentioned his name since they seen 'im last, but there wuz nuthin'. Lizzy didn't seem much bothered by it, but there wuz so much hullabaloo 'bout Lydie that Lizzy prob'ly didn't have time to thank on it.

When Benny walked through his own front door, he plopped on the couch, grabbed the remote control and started flippin' through channels like nuthin' had happened. He didn't say much less'n it wuz askin' one of the girls to fix 'im a sandwich or pop open a cold beer. He didn't say a word 'bout Lydie, and the girls took a while musterin' up the courage to ask.

Later that night, over peach cobbler, Lizzy decided to bring it up, sayin' how sorry she wuz fer the trouble he'd been to. He said, "Save yer sorries, Lizzy. I reckon I got a right to feel bad, seein' as how it's all my fault."

"Don't be hard on yerself, Daddy," she replied.

"Hell-fire and damnation! I don't take responsibility fer nuthin' 'round here, and it's time I start. Probl'y won't last long, though."

"Do you thank they're in Tennessee, Daddy?"

"Naw. I thank they've gone off to Nevada, Sweetie."

"Lydie and me used to watch them Las Vegas dancers on the internet," Kitty added. "They wuz real glamorous, they wuz."

"See, she's happy, then," said Benny with sarcasm. "She'll prob'ly git herself a nice job givin' lap dances to bored Wall Street types. She's set fer life."

He wuz silent fer a minute, then said to Lizzy, "You wuz right to warn me 'bout her goin' off to the beach like she did with them folks. You can say 'I told you so,' and I wouldn't care a bit. You wuz one-hundred percent right."

The conversation stopped when Janie came in to git a couple of pills and a bottle of Mad Dog fer her mother.

"This is jest fine, ain't it? It's like the St. Patrick's Day parade in Jackson Miss'ippi," he said. "We're all here gittin' liquored up to dull the worry. I thank I'll do the same thang tomorrow. I'll set here on the couch in my underwear, and y'all can brang me stuff to eat and drink. I'll set here 'til Kitty decides to run off."

"I ain't gonna run away, Daddy," Kitty said. "If'n you ever let me go off to Myrtle Beach, I'll behave way better than Lydie did, I'll suwanee!"

"You!? go to Myrtle Beach!? I wouldn't trust you to the Tennessee border, missy. No, Kitty, I've learnt my lesson. No fellers 'r gonna cross through that doorway, and none of y'all 'r goin' out to another hoe-down if'n I've got anythang to say on the matter. You and yer sisters cain't even step outside in the sunshine 'til you can show me you've got some sense in yer head."

Kitty started to cry.

"Don't you worry yer purty little head over it, Kitty. If'n you're a good girl fer the next ten years, I might could change my mind."

# Chapter 49

Two days after Benny'd come home, a feller from the FedEx pulled up in front of the house with an overnight package in his hands. Lizzy and Janie wuz outside with the dogs at the time.

"I got a package here fer a Benny Ledbetter. Do y'all know where he lives? There ain't no house numbers up in here."

Lizzy said, "This is where he lives. Who's that package from?"

"It's an overnight from Las Vegas."

"I'll take it into our Daddy," Lizzy said as she signed fer the package. The return address wuz in Guthrie's handwritin'.

Benny wuz asleep on the couch with the top button of his jeans open fer comfort. The girls poked at 'im, but when that didn't work, they nearly pushed 'im onto the floor b'fore he snorted awake. Janie stayed back a bit on account of Benny wuz famous fer rippin' out a big fart on wakin' up, but Lizzy got right in his face and handed 'im the envelope.

"Open it, quick. Tell us what it says."

Benny fumbled with the envelope, stopped to wipe the sleepers out'a his eyes b'fore handin' it to Lizzy. "I left my readin' glasses back in the bedroom." This wuz a reg'lar occurrence, and the girls knew he wuzn't a good reader. He asked Lizzy to read it to 'im.

*"Dear Benny. I'm  happier 'n a hog in slop to be able to send you this note. I tried to call, but yer phone's been turned off again, I reckon. After you left me on Saturd'y, I got a call from the state police. They had put out an Amber Alert fer Lydie, and one of the casinos sent footage from their security cameras of two people who looked an awful lot like Joe and Lydie.*
*"I flew out to Vegas on the very next flight, and I won't tell you how they wuz livin' 'til I see you face to face. You don't wanna know. But I found 'em, and I have laid eyes on both of 'em. They ain't married, and Lydie says she's sure she's in the family way, but she hasn't even taken a pee test yet. She pats her belly like she's real proud of herself. Joe ain't got no mind to make her an honest woman, but I thank I can twist his arm if'n you can promise to help 'em out at least fer the first year.*
*"Joe ain't as bad off as we first thought. He knows a thang or two 'bout cards and made some money in the past two days, at least that's where he said he got his money. I looked 'round where they 'r livin', and I didn't see no dirty*

*pictures or nothin'. Let me know what y'all want me to do. I can carry 'em to the*
*chapel, and they'll be hitched in a flash if'n that's what you want.*

*"Call me at my hotel from the garage or from the Lucas's if'n yer*
*phone's still shut off. I'll write to you again if'n I cain't reach you.*

*"Yer brother-in-law, Guthrie."*

"Do we want her to marry that asshole?" Lizzy asked.

"He ain't so bad as all that," Janie said.

"Well, do we? We should jest brang her home, shouldn't we?"

"I s'pose I should go next door and see if'n they'll let me borry their
phone."

"Don't let grass grow under yer feet," Lizzy said.

He said, "I don't like it, but I thank I've got to make 'im marry her. It's
the right thang to do, and gittin' hitched lets Lydie save face. I'd hate it fer her
to start high school all knocked up and without a man. Plus, if'n he has to take
care of her, then I don't have to listen to her squawkin' voice any more, and
we can do a better job with Kitty if Lydie ain't 'round. I jest wonder how much
Guthrie has laid down to make this happen, and how in the world I am ever
gonna pay 'im back."

"What the sam hill 'r you talkin' 'bout, Daddy?" Janie asked.

"No man in his right mind is gonna volunteer to git hitched to Lydie
after havin' spent more 'n a day with her."

"Yer right," said Lizzy. "Plus, somebody has to pay off his debts. I
know he didn't make that money gamblin'. He's already proved he sucks at it.
I'd be willin' to bet Guthrie laid down that money. What a sweetheart he is.
God bless 'im. He ain't got that kind of money."

Ever'body wuz quiet fer a spell 'til Benny grunted as he hauled
himself off the couch so he could borrow the phone next door to call Guthrie.

"They're really gonna tie the knot!" said Lizzy when she wuz alone
with Janie. "I declare! I cain't b'lieve we're s'posed to be happy 'bout this.
They're bound to make each other miserable. Poor Lydie!"

"I like to thank he won't really marry her if'n he doesn't love her,
Lizzy. Uncle Guthrie has helped 'em out, I'm sure, but I don't thank he's bailed

'em out completely. Guthrie has a family of his own to support. He cain't afford to lend out as much as Joe owes."

"If'n we can ever learn what Joe owes, then we will know what Guthrie's done fer our sister, be'cuz Joe Wickham doesn't have a cent to his name. We will never be able to repay his kindness. He prob'ly took out a second mortgage on their house or somethin'. He might could've used up his life's savin's. Can you imagine how Lydie must feel 'bout robbin' children of their summer vacations and Christmases? If'n I wuz her, I could never look Ain't Tildie in the eye again."

"Once they're married, we've got to git in our heads to forgit all this business," Janie said. "I thank they can be happy with each other. Agreein' to git married is a big step fer 'im, 'specially considerin' her age and all. If'n they work hard and live within their means, they'll be okay, I 'spect."

"How can you be such a knucklehead? We'll never be able to forgit this. It ain't worth the breath to consider."

Jest at that minute, it dawned on the girls that their Momma prob'ly didn't have an inklin' 'bout what wuz goin' on. As Benny walked out the back door, they opened the kitchen window and yelled out to ask their Daddy if'n they should tell their Momma.

"I don't give a shit," wuz his reply.

Janie and Lizzy ran back to Flo's room with the letter. Mary and Kitty wuz both there with Flo watchin' Wheel of Fertune re-runs, so one readin' of the letter would take care of the whole rest of the family.

As soon as Flo heard Lydie would prob'ly be married right soon, she jumped up on her knees on the bed and bounced, shoutin' "Halleluia!" Every sentence created more bouncin' and shoutin', 'til Flo wuz beside herself with happiness. She didn't worry one whit 'bout whether Lydie would be happy, and she seemed to have forgotten the bad behavior that'd led 'em into this pickle in the first place.

"My dear, dear Lydie!" she cried. "Ain't this jest the best news in the whole wide world! She's tyin' the knot with Joe effin' Wickham! Married in high school! My brother is the best! I knew he'd find her and manage it all! I cain't wait to lay eyes on my beautiful girl! Oh, Lordy! I cain't wait to see that handsome Joe Wickham! Lawsy mercy! She's gonna need some bedroom clothes. Somethin' skimpy and sexy fer that Joe. I'll ask Tildie what she thanks. Lizzy, go downstairs right this instant and ask yer Daddy how much money he will give her. Oh, wait! I'll go down my ownself! I don't reckon I need to put on any britches fer yer Daddy. That Lydie! How much fun we're gonna have at them adult stores. I cain't wait!"

Janie tried to calm her Momma by tellin' her that Guthrie no doubt laid down a load of cash to git Joe to agree to the weddin', She told her that the happy endin' to this long tale wuz all thanks to Uncle Guthrie.

"Well," cried Flo, "Who should help her but her own uncle? If'n he and Tildie hadn't've popped out so many kids, I reckon he might could've given all his money to y'all. And this is the first time he's ever done anythang fer any of y'all except brang presents. Nuthin' can spoil my happiness. I am the damned mother-of-the-bride! Mrs. Lydie Wickham! Sounds good, don't it? Look at this, my hands 'r shakin'. Janie, help me out with one of them catalogues. I wanna order a few thangs b'fore I ask yer Daddy how much he's willin' to part with."

She wuz comparin' the benefits of cotton to satin or spandex and would've ordered, too, if'n Janie hadn't convinced her to wait 'til Benny could be asked. With the quick-as-lightnin' shippin', one day wouldn't make a big difference, anyhow. Flo wuz in too good of a mood to be stubborn 'bout it, and thangs kept poppin' up in her head.

"I'm fixin' to go into town as soon as I can git myself dressed," said Flo, "and tell Fern the good, good news. When I git back from there, I can go rub it in the face of LuLu next door. Kitty, run down and fire up the truck. Girls, do y'all need anythang from the store?" 'Bout that time one of the cats jumped up on the bed. Flo rubbed her ears and said in a voice she saved fer babies and small animals, "Did you hear, Boots? Yer Lydie is gittin' married. I'll give you a saucer of milk to celebrate."

Poor Lydie wuz gonna have it rough if Joe kept livin' the life he'd been used to up to now. Knowin' what Lizzy knew 'bout Joe's dark side, she wuz thankful he hadn't sold her sister into porn or worse. She couldn't expect Lydie to live a happy life with him runnin' 'round on her, dippin' his wick in anythang that moved, but compared to her worst fears, Lydie wuz lucky.

# Chapter 50

Sometimes when he wuz under the hood of a car, elbow-deep in grease, Benny wished he'd set aside some money fer the girls and Flo in case anythang ever happened to 'im. He wished it more 'n ever now. If'n he had put aside jest a little bit, Lydie and them wouldn't be in debt to Guthrie fer however much it cost 'im. He promised himself to find out how much the whole mess had set his brother-in-law back and try to pay it back as soon as he could.

When Benny and Flo first got hitched, he didn't thank 'bout savin' be'cuz he knew deep down in his heart that he would have a son, who'd take over the garage fer Benny when he couldn't fix cars any more. He imagined the sign over the door readin' "Benny & Son." With two of 'em workin' on cars, they'd make double what Benny made on his own, and they'd be shittin' in high cotton then. Even after Lydie, the fifth daughter, had come along, Flo wuz jest sure a boy would be born, but none ever came. By that time, the idea of savin' money seemed ridiculous. Flo wuz addicted to other people's yard sales, and Benny wuz always fixin' up a friend's rust bucket at no charge.

Once years ago he'd saved 'bout five thousand dollars, hopin' to give some to the girls when they got married, but how would he divide it, 'specially now that Lydie had gotten herself in so deep? His little nest egg was long gone now. He owed Guthrie so much fer his kindness, and without a doubt he owed 'im money he didn't have. Benny figured he'd spend less time at the bar and more time in the shop. He could take in dirtbikes and four-wheelers to fix to help pay Guthrie back. The truth of the matter wuz, he'd never be able to buy back his own piece of shit house from Cooter.

Benny wuz surprised Lydie's mess had been patched up without 'im havin' to lift so much as a finger, and he carried 'round some guilt fer it. When his anger at Joe fer havin' taken off with his baby girl started to wane, he turned back into the lazy man he'd always been. He wished he knew how much he owed Guthrie, but he wuz too pissed at Lydie to try to contact her to see what she knew.

Ever'body in town knew Lydie had gone missin', thanks to Kitty and the rumor mill. So when news spread like maple syrup in July that she really had run off to git hitched, it wuz all anybody could talk 'bout. The excitement would've been more juberous if'n she had rolled into town her ownself and spread the news, but there wuz plenty to talk 'bout anyway. Every busy-body who'd been whisperin' over the laundry lines out back 'bout Lydie clucked 'bout how they jest knew she wuz run off to tie the knot. They wuzn't any less excited 'bout the fact that she wuz marryin' the sorry bastard they'd all been gossipin' 'bout jest five minutes b'fore.

It'd been two weeks since Flo'd come out'a her room except to go stink up the bathroom, but on this happy day, she came down to sit at the table fer supper with her family. She wuzn't ashamed a bit. Havin' a daughter married-off wuz her birthday wish fer every one of her girls since Janie had turned fifteen, and now at least one of her wishes had been granted. She didn't have an unspoken thought during dinner, and most of those had to do with weddin' nights and lingerie and maybe baby clothes, if'n they wuz lucky. She tried to recollect on if'n there wuz any empty trailers or houses to rent 'round the neighborhood fer Lydie and Joe to move into, not thankin' they wouldn't be able to afford anythang but a hole somewhere.

"I thank Millie's place would be right nice if'n she could git her do-less nephew out'a there. Then there's that little speck of a house down by the sludge pond, but it has such a little back yard on account of the sink hole. She cain't go to Mossy Glen! That's jest too far! And I heard tell there wuz a whole attic full of bats at that abandoned house down on Wolf Creek. Alls it needs is some windows and somebody to git those bats out'a there."

Benny let her talk a spell, and then he said, "Flo, b'fore you go traipsin' off a-lookin' at houses fer Joe and yer daughter, you need to git one thang through yer thick skull. There's one house they'll never come into, and that's mine."

After Benny spit out them words, Flo went into a full-blown conniption fit, but Benny didn't budge an inch. And after that Flo found out Benny wuzn't givin' a nickel to buy clothes fer his daughter. He said he wouldn't give Lydie a pat on the ass fer the occasion, and that wuz that. Flo couldn't b'lieve her own ears! She couldn't imagine he could be so angry with Lydie that he could ignore the most important day of her life! Flo wuz more ashamed that Lydie would start her new life with old underclothes than the fact that Lydie had run off to Vegas at fifteen doin' God-knows-what with with a grown man.

Lizzy wuz now very sorry that she'd, in the distress of the moment, shared with Dutch an iota of what wuz goin' on in her family. There wuz no doubt Dutch would've found out 'bout the weddin', and if'n she'd jest kept her big trap shut, she could've hidden what really happened from ever'body who didn't already know.

She knew he wouldn't go spreadin' it 'round ever'where. There wuzn't nobody she could trust not to gossip more 'n Dutch. Afterall, she had some shit on his family, too, but there wuz no one on earth she'd rather keep the information from than him. She didn't thank he'd ever take a likin' to her again. Naw, that wuzn't it. Even if Lydie'd waited 'til she wuz of age and married Joe in a church weddin' with a preacher and three bridesmaids, she knew Dutch'd never stoop so low as to be connected to somebody who'd tried to snatch the virginity of his one and only sister.

Lizzy figured he'd washed his hands of her. How could he wanna be with a girl who had such a white trash family? She wanted to curl up into a ball, and roll into a pile of horse shit and disappear. Now that she couldn't hope to have 'im, she wanted 'im to still like her. She wanted to know where he wuz and what he wuz doin' and who he wuz runnin' with. She jest knew she could've been happy with 'im, but by then it wuz too late.

He'd be too big fer his britches fer sure if'n he knew his hand would be snatched up like the last barbeque rib at the church picnic if'n he wuz to repeat the offer. He wuz a good man, but he'd be struttin', that's fer sure. And now she started to figure that he wuz exactly the man fer her. They would've been good fer each other. Two halves of a whole wuz what they wuz.

It wuz jest too bad their match made in heaven would never end in a hook up. Instead, all Lizzy had to look forward to wuz a match made in hell b'tween Joe and her little sister. How in the world they could live on their own wuz beyond Lizzy. And how could they be happy t'gether when they wuz basically bein' forced to git hitched to cover up their own mistakes?

The next they heard from Guthrie wuz in an email he sent to Benny. He talked on a few of the thangs Benny had asked when he'd called Guthrie from the Lucas's house b'fore. The phone bill still hadn't been paid, but the girls could check their email at the public library, which had faster internet than the dial-up they had at home...when the phone wuz turned on. Guthrie said he wuz happy to help out his nieces, and he hoped Benny wouldn't speak on the money again. The main reason fer his email wuz to tell 'im that Joe had decided to quit the military. Kitty printed out the email from Guthrie and brought it home to her Daddy.

It read:

*"I told Joe he best be gittin' out'a the military jest as soon as the marriage wuz fixed on. I thank it's best seein' as how he would've gotten in some deep shit fer havin' run off with a minor and made them fellers look bad. Plus, with Joe under Lydie's thumb, he won't be populatin' half the world like some kind of a horny honeybee. Joe plans to be a security guard somewheres, prob'ly at some kind of a mall, but 'ventually he wants to git trainin' to sell real estate. There's a feller outside of Atlanta who is willin' to give 'im a job at a strip mall, and I thank it's a good idea to git 'im as far away from Tennessee as he can git.*

*I thank if'n he can git out from under all his own bullshit, he and Lydie can try to make a respectable life t'gether. I emailed Lieutenant Dan to tell 'im all 'bout my plan, and to ask 'im to let all the folks that Joe owes money, that they'll be gittin' theirs b'fore long directly from my ownself. I hope you'll let folks know the same 'round yer parts. They'll all be paid, and I've attached a list that Joe made of folks he owes. I'm sure they'll be comin' out from under rocks to git money. I hope to hell he ain't lyin' 'bout any of it. I thank I can have 'em set up in Atlanta in 'bout a week, and they can leave here directly less'n y'all want 'em over fer a visit b'fore they go. I heard tell from Tildie that Lydie is fit to be tied she wants to see y'all so bad. -- Uncle Guthrie."*

Benny and the girls all thought Joe's leavin' the military wuz a good idea. Flo thought it wuz the stupidest thang she'd ever heard tell of. Havin' Lydie so far off didn't fit into her plan, and she thought Lydie would miss all her old beaus from the neighborhood.

Lydie's askin' to visit her kin b'fore movin' away wuz shot down the first go-round. But Janie and Lizzy didn't wanna hurt Lydie's feelin's and thought her family should git to say a proper "so-long" to their sister, so they begged Benny to let her and Joe come as soon as the ink on the marriage certificate wuz dry. He gave in, and Flo wuz beside herself with happiness to be able to show off her married daughter to the neighbors. Benny called Guthrie later that day from Billy Lucas's house and told 'im Joe and Lydie could come as soon as the deal wuz done. Lizzy couldn't b'lieve Joe would show his face 'round town, and she didn't thank she could look at 'im without hockin' a goober on 'im.

# Chapter 51


The day of their sister's weddin' came, and Janie and Lizzy prob'ly felt more fer Lydie than she felt fer her own self. By late afternoon the newlyweds landed in Nashv'lle, and Guthrie carried 'em up home in time fer supper. The older girls dreaded seeing both of 'em. The family peeked through the sheers in the front room to catch the first sight, and Flo started hoppin' up and down when she seen the truck pull down the dirt road and into the driveway. Benny looked pissed, and his daughters wuz clearly on edge.

Lydie's voice could be heard b'fore she'd even stepped out onto the gravel. She ran up the stoop, threw open the door and sashayed into the room. Flo wrapped her up in a bear hug that lifted Lydie's feet off the floor then adjusted her bra and did the same thang to Joe. Benny barely smiled at 'em and hardly said a word. He wuz no doubt thankin' on the amount of money these kids had jest cost 'im, and they didn't seem worried 'bout it one whit.

Lydie wuz Lydie; still the same, untamed, unashamed, loud, wild and without the good sense to be afraid of nothin'. She moved from sister to sister, like some kind of a celebrity, waitin' to be congratulated. When they all took a seat, she noticed a new ballcap hangin' on one of the taxidermied deer heads and said with a laugh that she'd been gone so long and so much had changed.

Joe stretched out on the couch with one arm behind Lydie and one behind Flo. He kicked his feet up on the coffee table and made himself right at home. He acted jest exactly like he'd done b'fore, and if'n they all didn't know what kind of a low-life he actually wuz, they would've been happier to visit with 'im fer a spell. Lizzy couldn't b'lieve he didn't say he wuz sorry fer all the trouble. He acted like nuthin' out'a the ordinary had happened.

The bride and her Momma couldn't talk fast enough; and Joe switched seats so's they could set next to each other. He leaned in toward Lizzy and started askin' 'bout folks in the neighborhood that he knew. He wuz down-right at ease with himself, and Lizzy wuz short with her answers. Both Joe and Lydie seemed to be happy as two peas in a pod. There wuzn't no talk of what wuz happenin' in Vegas or the fact that Joe's arm had to be twisted to git 'im to marry little Lydie. And Lydie felt like she needed to go into detail 'bout her flexibility and gymnastics in the sack.

"Can y'all imagine it's only been three months since I went away to the beach? It seems like jest a couple of weeks, I'll suwanee! So much has happened, though. Good Lord! When I went to the beach, I never dreamed in a million years I'd come home an old married lady, but I thought it'd be hilarious if'n I did."

Benny, Janie and Lizzy exchanged looks. Lizzy shot daggars at Lydie, but she didn't pick up on any of it on account of she wuz dumb as a stick.

"Oh, Momma! Does ever'body in town know I got hitched? I wuz worried nobody would've caught wind of it yet. We passed by Vern Snodgrass on our way into town. We wuz at a red light, so I rolled down my window and set my hand on the door of the truck so's he could see my ring better. Then I waved at 'im jest like always."

Lizzy couldn't take it another minute. She stood up and walked back to her room and slammed the door. When she heard 'em in the kitchen, she came back out jest in time to see Lydie take Janie's spot at the table, which she'd eyed since she wuz out'a a high chair. Lydie said, "I don't live here anymore. That makes me a guest, and Momma always says guests can set wherever they want. I'll be settin' here next to Momma when I come fer a visit. You can set in my old seat."

Nobody in the whole world ate as fast as Lydie did that night. She wuz hell-bent on goin' visitin' to see Ain't Flo and the Lucases and all the other neighbors. She wanted 'em to call her "Mrs. Wickham" and throw fits over her ring. After dinner she said, "Well, Momma, what do you thank of my husband? He's got a six pack and he's funny as all git-out. I bet my sisters 'r jealous fer sure. All of y'all need to go up to Myrtle Beach next summer. It's the place to find husbands, I'll suwanee. It's a cryin' shame all of us didn't go this summer."

"You ain't jest whistlin' Dixie! If'n I'd had my way, we would've all gone. But Lydie, darlin', I don't like the idea of y'all goin' all the way to Atlanta to set up house. Do y'all have to go so far?"

"Laws, yes. There ain't a thang I can change 'bout that. All of y'all must come fer a visit. Our new address is on Beaverbrook Drive, and I swear on the Bible we'll be havin' some throw-down parties. I'll make sure there's plenty of fellers to go 'round."

"I'd like that better 'n anythang," said her mother.

"And when y'all come back, you can leave one or two of my sisters behind, and I'll git 'em hitched b'fore the winter is over."

"Wow, Lydie. Thank you kindly fer the offer," said Lizzy, "but I don't particularly like yer way of gittin' husbands."

The happy couple stayed with her kin less 'n a week b'fore they had to head out fer Atlanta. Joe had to go to some trainin' b'fore they'd let 'im use the taser at his new job. He had to be there or he could lose the chance, and then he could only carry a big flashlight, which obviously wuzn't as cool as the taser.

Flo wuz the only member of the family who wuz sad to see 'em go. She spent the week invitin' folks over fer crackers and her pineapple cheeseball, and when she wuzn't drunk from one of her parties, she wuz out visitin' with Lydie to nearly ever' house in town. Lydie wanted to say 'so-long' to her teachers and friends from school. She promised 'em she'd git her GED sometime down the road.

Where Lydie always had a hand somewhere on Joe, twistin' a hair 'round her finger or leanin' over 'im, pressin' her boobs against 'im, Joe seemed less lovin' to Lydie. Lizzy could tell Joe had been caught in Lydie's cross-hairs, and their hook-up and its results wuz more from her skills at man-catchin' than his love fer her little sister. She wondered why he would've run off with her like that less'n he had to leave fer financial reasons, and she tagged along fer company.

Lydie wuz love-struck with 'im. She called 'im her "dear Joe-Joe" ever' time she talked 'bout 'im. Nobody wuz better 'n 'im at anythang, and he wuz the best husband that'd ever walked the face of the earth. She wuz sure, come huntin' season, that he would brang home more meat to the deep freeze 'n anybody else in the South.

One mornin' not long after she'd got there as she wuz settin' with Janie and Lizzy, Lydie said, "Lizzy, I never told you nuthin' 'bout my weddin'. You wuzn't in the family room when I wuz tellin' Momma all 'bout it. Ain't you curious 'bout it?"

"Not really," said Lizzy. "I don't really care, to be honest."

"Yer as strange as a Yankee! I've got to tell you how it went off. We wuz married at the Las Vegas Weddin' Chapel. It's diff'rent from the Little White Weddin' Chapel. We couldn't git it on account of we didn't have time. Anyway, the chapel we went to wuz in a strip mall, which is purty funny now considerin' Joe will be a security guard fer a place jest like that when we git to Atlanta. We wuz s'posed to be there first thang in the mornin', and Ain't Tildie and Uncle Guthrie wuz both there. Tildie flew out special, and that jest touched my heart. I wuz worried that Joe wouldn't show up on account of he wuz purty drunk the night b'fore. If'n he'd left me at the altar, I would've been pissed. Anyhoo, Ain't Tildie wuz there while I wuz puttin' on the rental dress at the chapel, and she wuz jest preachin' to me like she wuz some kind of a evangelist or somethin'. I barely heard a word she said on account of my mind wuz on Joe-Joe, and I wuz wonderin' what he'd be wearin'.

"Tildie and Guthrie wuz jest plain awful the whole time. They didn't let me out'a their sight fer one second. I didn't git to have a bachelorette party or put one nickel in a slot machine or even see the sights. They let me go down to the all-you-can-eat buffet at the hotel where we stayed, and I didn't even have one single, solitary drank be'cuz one of 'em wuz always with me like stink on a dog.

"Jest when I had the dress all zipped up, Uncle Guthrie wuz called outside, and I wuz pissed as hell be'cuz he wuz s'posed to give me away, and I wuz ready to go. We only had the chapel fer fifteen minutes, so ever' minute counted, if'n you know what I'm sayin'. But as luck'd have it, Guthrie came back, and ever'thang worked out jest fine. Now that I'm thankin' on it, if'n Guthrie hadn't come back, I reckon Dutch could've given me away jest the same."

"Dutch!" said Lizzy with amazement.

"Oh, yeah. He wuz to bring Joe-Joe to the chapel. Oh, Lord! I forgot! I wuzn't s'posed to say nuthin' 'bout Dutch bein' there. I promised 'em and swore on the Bible. What will Joe-Joe say? It wuz s'posed to be a secret."

"If you wuz s'posed to keep yer mouth shut, why didn't you do it?" asked Janie.

"Seriously," said Lizzy, but her mind wuz spinnin'.

"All right," said Lydie, "be'cuz if'n y'all wanted to know, I'd tell you, and then Joe-Joe would be mad at me."

Lizzy walked away from 'em burnin' up with questions. She wanted answers. Dutch'd been at her sister's weddin'. Why would he be there? It wuz the last place on earth he'd wanna be. Ideas swirled 'round but none of 'em made any sense to her. She took off fer the library to email Ain't Tildie to find out the particulars.

She wrote:

*"Ain't Tildie. I heard tell that a certain person, who ain't related to none of us and is practic'ly a stranger, wuz at my sister's weddin'. Please fill me*

*in on why he wuz there and what happened. I'll understand if'n you cain't say nuthin', but I'm beside myself with curiosity."*

# Chapter 52

Lizzy didn't have to wait long fer her answer from Tildie. Almost as soon as it wuz sent, an email came back from her aunt.

*"Dear Lizzy. I jest got yer email, and I wanna tell you ever'thang I know, which is quite a bit. I have to tell you I'm as shocked as I can be at yer askin'. I thought you of all people would know ever'thang there wuz to tell. If'n you don't catch my drift, then jest forgit I said anythang. Guthrie is as shocked as I am, and he wouldn't have done none of what I'm 'bout to tell you if'n he didn't thank it could help you, sweet Lizzy.*

*"The day I came home from up at y'all's house, Dutch called yer Uncle Guthrie, and they wuz on the phone fer pert near two hours, accordin' to Guthrie. Dutch told 'im he'd found yer sister and Joe Wickham and talked to both of 'em. He'd bent Joe's ear a few times, and Lydie's jest once. From what I can tell, he left Kentucky the day after we did and flew straight to Las Vegas to hunt fer 'em. He said he done it on account of he thought it wuz all part his own fault fer not lettin' folks in on what kind of a feller Joe really wuz. He said any respectable girl wouldn't fall fer Joe's act if'n she didn't know what she wuz gittin' herself into. He said he'd kept secrets out'a his own pride, and there wuz thangs he didn't want the world to know. He stepped up to fix thangs.*

*"He wuz in Vegas a few days b'fore he caught wind of 'em. Dutch'd a lead that none of the rest of us had. There wuz a woman that used to work fer him watchin' Suzanna. I b'lieve her name wuz Miz Young, and she wuz fired fer her part in some scandal, but he didn't say what. Well, this Miz Young rents a big house a couple of blocks from the old strip, and they ain't no question what kind of business she's runnin' in that place. There's creepy-lookin' older men and girls painted up like street walkers runnin' all over the place. There's even a place where the customers can buy candy fer the girls. It's all disgustin' and shameful. Dutch knew that Joe and Miz Young wuz tight, and he went straight there from the airport. But it wuz two or three days, as I said, b'fore he could git anythang out'a her. She wuz not gonna give 'em up fer nuthin'. I reckon Lydie wuz worth a bundle, and Miz Young wuzn't stupid.*

*"As it turns out, Joe and Lydie wuz stayin' in the attic of that very same house, and Dutch had to pay a purty penny fer that little bit of information. He seen Joe and then threatened 'im with the Law 'til Joe let 'im see Lydie. Dutch tried at first to git her to leave that awful place and jest go home. He offered to pay the plane fare and ever'thang. She didn't want none of it. Joe'd promised her she could be a model, she wanted Joe Wickham, and she thought they'd git hitched at some point. She really didn't care when it happened but she hoped it would happen soon since they'd been at it like rabbits since they left the beach, and she knew if'n she wuz anythang like her Momma, she'd be knocked up b'fore you know it.*

"Dutch then went to Joe to try to git 'im to stand up with Lydie, but he said flat out that he never planned to marry her. She wuz a business partner. Joe said he'd had to leave the Guard on account of he owed so much money to the other soldiers and to the back-door bookies in Myrtle Beach that he wuz worried fer his own safety. Also there wuz some high school girls he'd been friendly with, and their daddies had found out and wuz after 'im. He left and Lydie tagged along. He knew he had to go somewhere, but he didn't know where, and he didn't have nuthin' to live on. Dutch asked 'im what he'd planned to do with Lydie, and Joe didn't have an answer fer 'im. With ever'thang pilin' up against Joe, he wuz at the end of his rope and desperate.

"Dutch offered to help 'im, and they met several times to discuss how it could work. Joe wanted more 'n he deserved, of course. Once ever'thang wuz settled, Dutch let Guthrie in on the scheme. Yer Daddy wuz still there at the time, and Dutch didn't want Benny to catch wind of what he wuz doin', so Guthrie sent Benny home. The next time Dutch called I wuz there, and I answered the phone myself. He wuz very stubborn, I must confess. Ever'thang that wuz to be done, he wanted to do it his ownself. This is his true fault, Liz. Guthrie would've done all of it, I'll suwanee. He would've taken food out'a his own kids' mouths to help y'all out. He and Dutch went back and forth fer a while on it b'fore Guthrie gave in. Dutch gave all the money and did all the work, and Guthrie got the credit fer it. I didn't thank it wuz right to do it that way, but who am I to judge?

"Guthrie wuz pleased as punch when I read 'im yer email today. It let 'im take off his borrowed feathers and let the praise fall where it oughtta. But, Lizzy, you cain't tell a soul 'bout this. You might could tell Janie, but that's it. Y'all know what's been done fer those idjits. All Joe's debts will be paid, their house and his job have all been set up through Dutch's property and contacts in Atlanta. Dutch is even gonna pay fer Joe to take some classes at some point.

"Dutch stayed in Vegas 'til he seen them married and on a plane with us to Nashv'lle. I declare, back at home Lydie wuz jest as briggity as if she wuz the queen of England. Joe wuz jest like he used to be, pleasant and handsome. Lydie couldn't've been more annoyin', but I understand from an email Janie sent me that she wuz twice as bad when she wuz at y'all's house. I tried to tell her, seriously, how bad she wuz bein', and how much trouble she'd caused and shame. I don't thank she heard a word of it. There wuz a time or two I wanted to slap her into next week, but then I thought on you and Janie, and I took a deep breath.

"I cain't keep it in any more, Lizzy. That Dutch is jest 'bout the finest man I ever met in my whole damned life. He's so kind to me and Guthrie, jest like when we wuz up to his house in Lexin'ton. He's so smart, and his shoulders 'r so broad! The only thang lackin' is a good sense of humor, but I'm sure the right woman could help 'im with that. He almost never mentioned yer name at all, but I know as well as I know my own hand that someday you'll invite yer old aunt up to the farm and give me the insider's tour. I cain't wait to bring the kids to the farm when the mares 'r foalin'. I better go fer now. These kids is wantin' their lunch. Much love, Tildie."

The contents of the email threw Lizzy into a tizzy. She couldn't tell if she wuz happy or upset. She'd feared Dutch'd been workin' behind the scenes somehow, and now that she knew the long and short of it, she didn't know how she could ever repay 'im fer all he'd done. He'd taken it all on his own shoulders. He follered 'em to Vegas, found 'em in a whore house, bribed the madam fer information, repeatedly met with Joe (who he couldn't stand) to come to some agreement 'bout money, and stood by to make sure everythang wuz legal. He had done all this fer a little tramp who didn't deserve the time of day from 'im. Lizzy's heart did hope that he might've done it all fer her, but she quickly remembered how cold she'd been to 'im, and now she wuz sister-in-law to a child molester.

Dutch'd given his reasons fer helpin'. He felt he wuz to blame fer keepin' Joe's past a secret. He'd made up fer his sins, fer sure-- many times over. She felt sorry she couldn't thank 'im or do anythang fer 'im as a thank you. She could kick herself when she thought on all the mean thangs she'd said to 'im and ever' speech she'd ever given 'im. She wuz humbled by his goodness, and she wuz proud to know 'im. She read the email over a few more times. She loved readin' the good thangs Tildie'd said 'bout 'im, and she laughed at how sure they wuz that somethin' wuz goin' on b'tween her and Dutch.

She walked home slowly, rememberin' ever' thang Dutch'd done. 'Bout a half mile from home, she seen Joe comin' across the field towards her.

"I hope you wuzn't wantin' to be alone," he said as he walked up.

"Not 'specially," she answered.

"I'm sorry if'n you wuz. I hope we can be as close as friends as we used to be," he said, touchin' her arm, "maybe closer."

"Where is ever'body?" she asked, changin' the subject.

"Hell if I know. Flo and Lydie went into town. I hear from Guthrie and Tildie that you've been to Pembrook Farm."

She said that she had.

"I'm jealous, but I thank it would be too much fer me. I guess y'all met Mr. Brown? He always liked me, but I'm sure he didn't mention me to y'all."

"Actually, he did."

"What did he say?"

"He said that you wuz in the service, and he wuz afraid you hadn't turned out so well. I'm sure he's heard rumors."

"I reckon he has," he said, bitin' his lip. Lizzy hoped she'd put a cork in 'im, but he kept talkin'. "I wuz surprised to see Dutch the other day. We crossed paths in Vegas when I wuz out there with Lydie. I wonder what he's doin' in Sin City."

"Maybe he wuz havin' a bachelor party fer himself, gittin' ready fer his big day with DeeDee Majestro?" said Lizzy. "Somethin' important must've taken 'im out there. He doesn't seem like a Vegas kind of guy."

"Without a doubt. Did y'all see 'im when you wuz in Lexin'ton? I thought Tildie said y'all did."

"Yes. He introduced us to his sister."

"Did you like her?"

"Why, sure!"

"I hear tell that she's growin' into a fine young lady since I last laid eyes on her. I'm glad she's doin' well. I hope she turns out all right."

"I don't doubt that she will. She's gittin' over the worst of her growin' pains."

"I sure am gonna miss that part of the country. I'm afraid Atlanta is too big a city fer me. I like the quiet, rolling Kentucky hills. A man could be happy livin' among the horses and the distilleries up there-- a simple life. Too bad it wuzn't in the cards fer me. Did you ever hear tell of the life I wuz s'posed to live?"

"I heard a diff'rent story 'n you told me b'fore. I hear tell that the job wuz yers only if Dutch felt you wuz gonna work hard and pull yer own weight."

"Yes, I do recall somethin' like that bein' said."

They wuz almost at the door of the house. Lizzy had been practic'ly runnin' to git rid of 'im, and unwillin' to piss 'im off royally fer her sister's sake when he grabbed her 'round the waist and pulled her up tight against 'im. Her quick knee ended the embrace, and she leaned down to whisper in his ear while he wuz doubled over. "We're family now, Joe. You keep yer dirty little paws off of me and Lydie's other sisters, and we'll be jest fine, you hear?"

And with that, she walked inside the house.

# Chapter 53

Joe wuz a quick learner. He understood what Lizzy wuz sayin' so well that she didn't have to repeat it even once. Time ticked by, as it does, and b'fore long the day came where Lydie would have to say goodbye to her kin and head on out to Atlanta with Joe. Flo, of course, wanted the lot of 'em to follow her there and help set up house, but Benny wuz havin' none of it.

"Hell's bells, Lydie!" she said, "When'll I ever lay eyes on you again?"

"Laws, Momma, I surely don't know."

"You'll have to call me ever' day. Do you hear me?"

"I'll call as often as I can, Momma, but you know I'll be so busy with Joe. Maybe my sisters can send me an email from time to time. Lord knows they ain't got nuthin' else to do."

And with that, she and Joe piled into the truck and drove away.

Benny said, "Ain't he somethin'? He rolls into town unashamed of himself, kisses our asses fer a week and rolls out. Reminds me of Billy Lucas's son-in-law if'n you ask me."

Flo wuz down in the dumps fer a while after Lydie left. "I miss Lydie so much I cain't hardly stand it. Good gracious heavenly days, it's boring as hell 'round here without her."

"I reckon this is what happens when you marry off yer daughters, Momma," Lizzy said. "Now you can count yer lucky stars that the rest of us ain't married and don't have any prospects."

"Aww, nonsense. Lydie didn't leave me on account of she wuz married. She left be'cuz Joe's job takes 'im so far away. If'n he'd found work close by, she'd still be here.

All of Flo's sighs and moans wuz put to rest when the gossip mill spewed out a mighty tasty morsel fer her to chew on fer a bit. Rumor had it the little girl who cleaned Buford's doublewide had got a call that she needed to git her ass over thar and run the Hoover and clean the toilets. Buford wuz comin' to town fer some huntin' and fishin'. Flo wuz beside herself and kept a-lookin' at Janie and smilin'.

"Well, well, well, and so Buford is comin' to pay us a visit," she said to Fern who had brought the news from town. "Ain't that jest fine and dandy? I don't give a rat's ass where he does his huntin', and you know it. He ain't nuthin' to us now, and I can guarantee you that I never hope to see 'im again in all my born days. Ain't nuthin' that I can do to keep 'im from his doublewide. It's a free country. I thought we decided not to talk 'bout 'im no more, didn't we? Are you sure he's comin'?"

"I'm jest as sure as I can be, Flo. I wuz down at the Park N Shop on account of they had their cream corn on special fer thirty-five cents a can, and Lord, you know I make the best corn puddin' in the whole world. Anyhow, I seen the little cleanin' girl in the aisle gittin' herself some PineSol and toilet cleaner. She wuz in line ahead of me, and I heard it from her own lips. She told Marge at the check out that Buford wuz comin' on Thursd'y, but she wuz to have the place spit-shined by Wednesd'y afternoon at the latest in case he came early. She had groceries in her cart, too. Now I cain't say whether they wuz fer her or if'n she'd bought a few thangs to put in Buford's icebox, but I'd bet they wuz fer him."

Janie turned fify shades of red when she heard 'em talkin' on Buford. It'd been quite a while since she'd said anythang 'bout 'im, even to Lizzy, but the minute they wuz alone, Janie said, "I seen you a-lookin' at me when Ain't Fern started talkin' 'bout Buford. I know I must've looked funny to you, but don't imagine fer a second that I still have feelin's fer 'im. I felt like ever'body wuz a-lookin' at me, and I wuz bashful fer a second. I don't really care if'n he comes or not. What's it to me, right? I'm jest glad he ain't brangin' some girl with 'im on account of folks would talk.

Lizzy didn't know what to make of Buford's visit. If'n she hadn't seen 'im in Lexin'ton, she might could've supposed that he'd come down here to shoot jest like ever'body said. But after seein' 'im, she could tell he still wuz sweet on Janie, and she wondered if'n Dutch approved of 'im comin' to their little part of the world or if Dutch even knew anythang 'bout it.

"I feel fer Buford," Lizzy thought. "He cain't even come to his own house, that he's rented with his own money, without makin' a stir. I thank I'll leave 'im to his huntin'."

Even though Janie said she didn't care one way or the other that Buford wuz comin' to town, Lizzy could see she wuz on edge and nervous as all git-out.

Their parents had the same damned conversation they'd had a year ago 'bout Buford and settin' up visits.

"Jest as soon as Buford rolls into town, you git yer ass down there and offer to lend 'im the four wheeler fer huntin'," Flo said.

"Hell, no, woman! You forced me into goin' over thar last year, and said if'n I did, we could unload us one of these girls on 'im. It didn't happen, and I ain't goin' again."

Flo told 'im he really needed to do it to be neighborly, and how else wuz Buford gonna git them animals back so's he could skin 'em?

"Why don't you bake 'im a pie or somethin', Flo? If'n he wants to borrow my four-wheeler, I'm sure he'll ask me or stop in to the garage. He knows where we are, and he knows I have a four-wheeler. I ain't goin' runnin' 'round after 'im fer nuthin'."

"Well, alls I know is you ain't bein' neighborly at all. I guess I'll have to ask 'im over fer dinner after church. I'm fryin' up some chicken and makin' a mess of beans fer the preacher and his wife and the Millers, and I thank with the six of us, that would mean we'd have thirteen total. I reckon I could ask 'im since I'm makin' so much anyhow."

Flo wuz right proud of herself fer comin' up with the idea, but she wuz still bummed that other folks in the neighborhood would git to lay eyes on 'im first.

The closer the day came fer 'im to roll into town, the more nervous Janie got. "I'm sorry he's comin'. I can bear havin' 'im close by, really I can, but I cain't stand that he's all ever'body wants to talk 'bout. Momma means well, but ever word she says 'bout 'im feels like a knife in my gut. I'll be happy as a clam when he's gone."

"I wish there wuz somethin' I could say to make you feel better, Janie, but I know there ain't. You have more patience 'n I do. I thank I'd jest tell Momma to shut the hell up."

Buford showed up, and Flo knew 'bout it the minute he did on account of she called Marge down at the Park N Shop three times a day to git an update. She wondered how she could plan to run into 'im so's she could invite 'im to dinner on Sund'y. After he'd been in town three days, Flo looked out the window and seen 'im walkin' up the driveway. She called back to the girls so they could know they wuz 'bout to have comp'ny. Janie stayed put at the kitchen table shellin' pecans, but Lizzy went to the window to satisfy her Momma. She looked, and she seen Dutch walkin' alongside 'im. She turned quicker 'n lightnin' and sat down at the table with her sister to help.

"Hey, there's a feller with 'im, Momma," said Kitty. "I wonder who it could be."

"It's prob'ly somebody he's been huntin' with, I suppose."

Kitty said, "It looks jest like that feller that used to hang 'round 'im. What's his name? That tall, stuck-up feller."

"Lord have mercy!" said their Momma. "It's Dutch! I'll suwanee, any friend of Buford's is welcome here, but I declare I cain't stand the sight of 'im."

Janie looked at Lizzy with worry lines b'tween her eyes. She didn't know much 'bout what happened in Lexin'ton, and she knew that Lizzy must be nervous as a wet cat to see Dutch face-to-face after the letter he'd given her when she wuz in Knoxv'lle. Each of the girls worried 'bout the other one, and Flo kept on with her list of ever' reason she hated Dutch. She swore she'd only be nice to 'im since he wuz buddies with Buford.

Lizzy had more reasons 'n she let on fer bein' nervous 'round Dutch. She'd never told Janie 'bout what Ain't Tildie had said. To Janie he wuz jest some feller who used to be sweet on her and who she'd turned down. But to her, she knew her entire family owed 'im so much fer bailin' 'em out'a the mess Lydie'd made. Though she didn't thank her feelin's fer Dutch held a candle to Janie's fer Buford, they wuz pert near the same. She could've fallen down dead with shock seein' 'im back in town like he wuz. The fact that he'd come to see her again made her weak in the knees.

When she first laid eyes on 'im comin' up the driveway, her face had gone white as a sheet, but the color came back, and her eyes sparkled like a Christmas tree with the hope that he still wuz sweet on her. She couldn't be sure, but she could hope.

She set with a bowl of pecans on one side and a grocery bag of shells in the other, keepin' her eyes on her work as Flo let the boys in the house. Janie seemed cool as a cucumber, but her hands wuz shakin' on the nut cracker. When the boys set down next to her at the table, she kept workin' like nuthin' wuz goin' on. Janie wuzn't cold, but she wuzn't starin' at Buford, neither.

Lizzy didn't say much, but kept workin' like them pecans wuz the most interestin' thang in the whole damned world. She snuck one look at Dutch, who looked serious as a heart attack, more like he did last year 'n when he wuz home at Pembrook Farm. But maybe he couldn't be relaxed like he wuz with Tildie and Guthrie while her Momma wuz 'round.

Buford looked happy and embarrassed. Flo heaped so much love on 'im that it wuz shameful, 'specially considerin' how short she wuz with

Dutch. Lizzy wuz awful ashamed on account of she knew how much her Momma owed Dutch fer his kindness to Lydie and Joe.

Dutch asked Flo how Guthrie and Tildie wuz, and she looked as confounded as Benny always did when he wuz puttin' t'gether furniture out'a a box from Walmart. Dutch didn't say nuthin' to Lizzy, but that might've been on account of he wuzn't very close to her. But when they wuz in Lexin'ton, he'd talk to her kin if'n she wuzn't sittin' close by. It seemed like a month of Sund'ys b'fore Lizzy could look up at 'im, and when she did, he wuz a-lookin' at Janie as often as not. He seemed lost in thought and not so eager to please as he'd been last time they laid eyes on each other. She wuz mad at herself fer hopin' fer anythang more.

"What did I expect?" she thought. "But why the hell did he come?"

She wuz not in the mood to talk to anybody but him, and she didn't have the guts to say nuthin' to 'im. She asked after Suzanna but couldn't say more.

"Buford, it's been a long time since you went away," said Flo.

"Yep."

"I wuz worried y'all might not come back. Folks said you wuz gone fer good, and that you wuzn't gonna renew yer lease, but I hope it ain't true. Lots has been happenin' 'round these parts since y'all left. Charlotte Lucas is married, and one of my girls, too. I'm sure you prob'ly seen it in the papers. It wuz in The Tennessean and the Courier, but not as long as it should've been since Benny is so cheap. All it said wuz that they'd got hitched, Lydie and Joe Wickham, and not a peep wuz said 'bout who her family wuz or where she came from or nothin'. Guthrie sent it in fer us, and I have no idea why he didn't do a better job. Did y'all see it?"

Buford said he'd seen somethin', but Lizzy didn't dare look up at him or at Dutch.

"I thank it's the best thang in the whole world to have one of yer daughters married off," said Flo. "I miss her somethin' awful, though. They live down in Atlanta, a fer piece, if I do say so myself. I have no idea how long they'll stay down there. Joe's job is there, but Lydie tells us he wants to git trainin' to sell folk's houses or some such business. As it turns out, Joe has loads of friends, but I reckon he deserves more 'n he has."

Lizzy knew her Momma had shot that arrow right at Dutch, and she could've crawled under the table fer shame and misery. She could barely sit there. It did force her to say somethin', which she couldn't do b'fore, and she asked Buford if he meant to stay long. He said he thought they'd be there a few weeks at least.

"Well, when you've killed all the animals you want fer food, you can brang the rest over here. We have a deep freeze, and we'll eat 'em if'n y'all cain't. Plus, Benny's an amateur taxidermist. He can stuff a head like nobody's business."

Lizzy wuz drownin' in her own misery. She knew that if'n the fellers fell fer her and Janie again, like they'd done last year, the end result would be the same, broken hearts. Nuthin' in the world could make her feel better at that second in time.

She said to herself, "If'n I jest had one wish, it would be to never have to be humiliated in front of these fellers again. I'd rather never see 'em again than have to live with the shame of this big-mouthed witch."

Her wish wuz not granted, though. One look at Buford showed her he wuz love struck with Janie again. When he first walked in, he didn't say much to her, but now he seemed to pay her more attention ever' minute. He thought she wuz as purty as when he last seen her, jest as sweet natured, but a little quiet. Janie wuz hopin' he wouldn't be able to see a difference in her at all, and when he said she wuz bein' shy, she said she wuz talkin' as much as ever. Lizzy could tell her mind wuz goin' a mile a minute, and sometimes she didn't know she wuzn't sayin' much.

When the boys got up to leave, Flo asked 'em to stop by fer dinner after church on Sund'y. "Y'all owe me, Buford. When y'all left town last winter, you'd promise you'd come fer dinner as soon as you came back. I didn't forget."

Buford said somethin' 'bout havin' to be in Nashv'lle last time, and his voice trailed off, then they left.

Flo'd wanted to ask 'em to set down to dinner with 'em that very day, but alls she wuz havin' fer dinner wuz heated up fish sticks and tater tots. She figured that wuzn't good enough fer a future son-in-law or his hoity-toity friend.

# Chapter 54

The minute them fellers wuz out the door, Lizzy went out fer some fresh air and to thank on what the hell wuz goin' on with Dutch. He wuz actin' mighty strange.

"Why in the world did he come if'n he wuz fixin' to jest stand there and look good?" she asked herself. She couldn't come up with an answer. "He wuz right friendly to my aunt and uncle when he wuz with 'em the other day. Why couldn't he be like that with me today? If'n he don't like me, why did he come 'round? And if'n he does, why didn't he say nuthin'? He's jest a big ol' tease, that's what he is. I ain't gonna waste any more time thankin' on 'im."

She wuz able to keep her word at least fer a little bit on account of Janie walked up, grinnin' like the cat who'd swallered the canary. She seemed happier with the boys' visit than Lizzy did.

"Now that we've got that over with, I feel jest fine and dandy. I thank I handled myself purty well, and I feel sure I won't make a fool of myself again. I'm glad he's comin' to eat with us. Then ever'body in town'll know that we're jest friends. Miz Miller is the worst gossip in town, and she'll spread it 'round faster 'n grass through a goose," said Janie.

"Oh yeah, jest friends! I can see that. Keep tellin' yerself that, sister."

"You cain't possibly thank I've got my hopes up fer Buford now."

"I seen the way he wuz a-lookin' at you."

They didn't see the boys again 'til Sund'y, and in the meantime Flo wuz hummin' "Here Comes the Bride" after jest that short little visit b'tween Janie and Buford.

On Sund'y Benny's little house wuz packed to the gills with folks. B'tween Benny's own family, the Millers, the preacher and his wife, Buford and Dutch, there wuz hardly any room to turn 'round. Lizzy watched to see if Buford took the seat next to Janie, where he'd always sat b'fore. Flo wuz caught behind Elsie Miller, who could hardly make it through the door she wuz so fat, so she couldn't lead Buford over to her oldest girl. Buford looked 'round like he didn't know what to do, but 'bout that time Janie set her eyes on 'im and smiled purty like she does, and it wuz settled. He pulled out the chair next to her and sat down.

The moment his butt hit the chair, he looked up at Dutch, who jest looked bored standin' there watchin'. Lizzy might could've b'lieved that Buford had cleared it with Dutch ahead of time if'n Buford didn't have a look of worry when he looked at his buddy.

Buford paid close attention to Janie during dinner, and Lizzy could tell if'n he got his own way, both he and Janie would hookup b'fore long. Watchin' 'em cheered her up as much as she could be cheered on account of she wuz in a piss-poor mood. Dutch wuz jest 'bout as far away from her as he could be, settin' next to her Momma of all people. Neither one of 'em looked to be too happy 'bout it. She wuz too far away to hear what they wuz sayin' to each other, but she could see it wuzn't much. Flo wuz purty much a bitch to 'im, and Lizzy wished she could pull Dutch aside and tell 'im how grateful she wuz for the kindness he'd showed her family, even though they didn't know a thang 'bout what he'd done.

Lizzy hoped some time after dinner they'd have a chance to talk fer a minute, and while she and the girls wuz cleanin' off the table, all she could thank on wuz what she'd say when she went back in the family room where the fellers wuz watchin' tv.

"If'n he don't come up to me when I'm in there with ever'body, I'm gonna give up on 'im," she thought as she carried two plates of pie in fer the men.

As she wuz walkin' toward Dutch, Elsie Miller moved right into her way and took both of the plates of pie from her and said, "I love pie." From that point Elsie explained in horrifyin' detail why she loved pie so much, and there wuz no way in the world Lizzy could've gotten 'round her, what with the deer heads pokin' out from the wall like they did. She could only watch as Dutch took a plate of pie from Kitty and talked to Benny and the preacher. She had to go back in the kitchen to git two more pieces of pie and wanted to kick herself fer bein' so silly.

"Lordy, Lordy!" she thought. "I done turned that feller down once. Why in the world would he wanna git kicked in the teeth again? Nobody'd do that to themselves twice."

She felt better when he brought his empty plate to her. She said, "Is Suzanna still at Pembrook Farm?"

"Yes. She plans to stay put fer a while."

"Does she have any friends to keep her company, besides the horses, of course."

"Her tutor is there, and Mr. Brown and the other folks that help with the horses 'r 'round. We're so far back in the country that her little friends don't come by. I thank they text and video chat on the computer."

She couldn't thank of another thang to say to 'im, but he stood next to her fer a few minutes without sayin' nuthin', and when Elsie came back with two more empty plates, he walked away.

When dessert wuz all cleaned up, the boys set down to watch football. Lizzy wuz hopin' Dutch'd come over to set by her, but he wuz stuck on the couch next to the preacher who wouldn't stop talkin' to 'im. She knew he'd be there all night since the preacher never shut up. She did notice 'im look over toward her ever' once in a while, but she wuz settin' next to the tv, so she couldn't be sure if'n he wuz a-lookin' at her or at the game.

Flo had high hopes of Buford and Dutch stayin' fer supper, but their car wuz last in the driveway, so when the preacher's wife wuz ready to go, they decided to jest go, too.

"Well, girls," Flo said once ever'body wuz gone, "how do y'all thank it went today? I thank it came off right nice. I do b'lieve that wuz the best chicken I ever fried up. LuLu told me to try the cornflakes as the breadin', but I'll suwanee I thought she wuz crazy. I never in all my days seen so much cornbread ate up so fast, and I have to brag on my green beans. They wuz fifty times better 'n LuLu's last time she made 'em. Even Dutch said the gravy wuz the best he'd ever had, and I reckon he's eaten himself some gravy in his day. And Janie, you looked so purty settin' over thar in yer blue sweater. Even the preacher's wife said you and Buford made the cutest couple!"

Flo wuz in a great mood fer the rest of the day. She'd seen Buford makin' eyes at Janie, and she knew Janie would git 'im fer sure, which could only help her find husbands fer the rest of her girls. She wuz so sure of it that she wuz downright disappointed the next day when Buford didn't come over with an engagement ring and git down on one knee.

"This has been the best day I can remember," Flo said. "Ever'body seemed to git along and mix well. We wuz all rootin' fer the same team on account of nobody likes the Patriots since they's all Yankees up there. I thank we should do it again real soon."

Lizzy smiled.

"Now Lizzy! Don't you be suspectin' me of makin' a plan," Flo said. "I'd be ashamed! I have learnt to talk to a hottie like Buford 'bout football and such without hopin' fer more. I'm happy as all git-out with 'im bein' friendly the way we all are. I thank he's jest the sweetest young man in all the world, that's all."

"Yer so cruel, Momma," said Janie. "You won't let her smile a bit, but yer makin' me almost snort laughin'."

# Chapter 55

A couple of days passed, and Buford showed up alone fer another visit. He said Dutch had to go out'a town on some business but would be back in 'bout a week or so. He sat there fer over an hour and looked happier 'n a hound dog in a sunbeam. Flo invited 'im to eat with 'em, but he said he wuz s'posed to eat someplace else.

"Maybe another time," Flo said.

He said he'd love a rain check and how obliged he wuz fer her kindness, and he said he'd stop back by in a day or two.

"Can you come tomorrow fer breakfast?"

Yes, he said he didn't have any plans fer tomorrow, and he wuz happy to come.

The next day dawned bright and sunny. Flo wuz up early makin' monkey bread, biscuits with gravy and a sausage and cheese breakfast casserole with fresh eggs from her own chickens. Buford came early while the deer wuz still out in the field, and none of the girls had their faces on yet. Flo shouted back to the girls, "Janie! Hurry it up and git down there. He's here. Buford is here. I jest heard 'im knock at the screen door. Lizzy, help her git her hair jest right. Nevermind yer own."

"We'll be out as soon as we can," said Janie, "Kitty is all but ready. I'll send her out to open the door."

"Oh, hang, Kitty! What the hell does she have to do with any of it? Put on some lip gloss and git out here."

Janie wouldn't leave the lean-to without Lizzy. Anybody could see she wuz nervous as a long-tailed cat in a room full of rockin' chairs.

After breakfast Flo tried ever' way in the world to git Buford and Janie to be alone. As usual, Benny took a mug of coffee out on the porch with a cigarette to read the paper b'fore headin' off to the garage. Mary went out to the shed to practice her fiddle, and Flo set there winkin' at Lizzy and Kitty fer a while without 'em takin' notice at all. Finally Kitty asked, "What's the matter, Momma? Do you have somethin' in yer eye or 'r you winkin' at me? Are you a-tryin' to tell me somethin'?"

"Nuthin', baby. I wuzn't winkin' at you. I must have some mascara floatin' 'round in my eye." She waited five more minutes and couldn't wait another second. She said to Kitty, "Come out to the kitchen with me so's I can show you somethin'," and she practic'ly pulled Kitty out'a the room.

Janie gave Lizzy the look that says "don't you dare leave me alone," but in half a minute Flo peeked her head in the room and said, "Lizzy, git in here. I got somethin' I need to tell you."

Lizzy had to go.

"We might as well let 'em alone, you know," Flo said as soon as she wuz in the kitchen. "Kitty and me 'r goin' out to stack firewood. Why don't you make yerself useful and help?"

Lizzy waited in the kitchen 'til they wuz gone and then slipped back in the family room with Janie and Buford.

Flo's plans fer the day wuz all shot to hell. Buford wuz ever'thang she wanted 'im to be except her daughter's fiance. He stayed with 'em a good part of the day, and all the time he wuz funny and flirty. He listened to Flo's talk with smiles and patience, which Janie wuz grateful for. He stayed fer lunch, and on his way out the door, he promised to come over to hunt with Benny the next day.

After spendin' half the day with Buford, Janie kept her mouth shut 'bout how she thought she and Buford wuz jest friends. Lizzy fell asleep with a smile on her face, thankin' that her sister might could git her hooks in Buford if'n Dutch didn't come back too early. On the other hand, she thought there wuz no way that all of this moonin' and smoochin' could've happened without Dutch sayin' it wuz all right with him.

Buford showed up right on time fer his huntin' date with Benny. They loaded up their cooler full of beer and nearly left their guns behind. After Benny'd thrown down a couple, he wuz jest as much fun as any huntin' buddy could be, and Buford had a good ol' time even though nobody shot nuthin' but the bull. Buford wuz happy, after a long day in the woods, to eat supper with Flo and the rest of 'em, and she wuz workin' hard to git Buford and Janie alone t'gether. Lizzy discovered a dial tone on the phone in the hall and sat down to write an email to send Charlotte while they had service, and the rest of the family wuz playin' cards at the kitchen table to see who had to shovel out the chicken shit the next day.

When Lizzy'd sent the email, she went into the family room. Jest as soon as she opened the door, Janie and Buford jumped up from where they wuz layin' on the couch, guilty as sin. They jumped away from each other like somethin' wuz catchin', and Buford quickly adjusted himself and said he needed to talk to a man 'bout a horse.

Janie couldn't keep nuthin' from Lizzy, and ran up to her and hugged her, sayin' that she wuz the happiest girl in the world. Buford'd been rubbin' up against her, and when she told 'im she wuzn't that kind of a girl, he asked her to marry 'im right there on the spot.

"It's too much!" she said. "I jest cain't b'lieve it! I don't deserve a feller like Buford! Ever'body should be so happy as I am right this minute."

Lizzy patted her on the back and said her "congratulations" with a heart full of tenderness fer her sister. Janie wuz beside herself and couldn't find half the words she needed to say how smack-down excited she wuz.

"I gotta go right away to Momma," she said. "She needs to hear it from the horse's mouth. She's gonna shit bricks; she'll be so happy."

She then ran back into her Momma's room, who'd cheated at cards to avoid the poop clean-up and wuz consoling Kitty who had lost fer the fourth week in a row.

Lizzy smiled to herself at how fast ever'thang had been settled this go-round. She remembered the worryin' she'd done over the past months. "And this," she thought, "is the end of all of Buford's friend's meddlin' and his sister's bad-mouthin'. It's the happiest, best possible end to it all."

In a few minutes, Buford came back from the john. "Where's yer sister?" he asked.

"She went back to talk to Momma. She'll be back in a little bit."

"I guess she told you, then?"

"Yeah, I'm as lost as a June-bug in July to find words to say how much y'all's news tickles me." She gave 'im two big pats on the back, and after Janie came back in, he told Lizzy jest how happy they wuz, and how perfect and purty Janie wuz, and how he wanted to have a live Lynard Skynard cover band at their weddin' reception. Janie said how she wanted to have some of them tiny little bottles of soap bubbles that folks can blow instead of throwin' bird seed ever'where. She wanted to wear a white weddin' dress and white cowboy boots underneath. Buford thought they could find a plastic deer's head to put on top of the cake instead of a bride and groom. Janie seemed too love struck to tell 'im what a completely stupid idea that wuz.

That night nobody could find fault with anybody else in the house. Flo wuz so pleased with herself fer gittin' rid of another daughter, and to somebody like Buford, that she glowed like it wuz her own weddin' she wuz plannin'. She looked twenty years younger. Kitty giggled and smiled and hoped maybe her day wuz comin' soon. Benny wuz on his very best behavior. He didn't fart or burp or scratch his butt the whole evenin'. He didn't say nuthin' 'bout the weddin' while Buford wuz still there, but once he left, Benny said to his daughter, "Janie, I congratulate you. Yer gonna be a very happy woman."

Janie went to 'im and sat on his lap, kissed 'im and thanked 'im fer bein' such a good Daddy.

"You're a good girl, Janie," he said. "It eases my mind to know you'll be taken care of so good. There ain't a doubt y'all will git along right well t'gether. Both of y'all 'r so laid back that you'll never make a decision. Folks'll cheat you out'a house and home, and you'll be takin' in yer sisters so much that y'all will never have a minute to yerselves or a nickel to put away fer yer retirement."

"Oh, Daddy! I hope not. I got a head fer money. I do. Haven't you seen me clippin' coupons fer Momma out'a the Sund'y paper?"

"You thank jest be'cuz you cain't seem to make ends meet fer yer family that Buford and Janie will be poor as dirt?" said Flo. "He's got plenty of money rollin' in ever' month. More 'n you have.." Then turnin' to Janie, "Oh! My Janie! I jest don't know what to do with myself. I'm so happy fer y'all! I know I ain't gonna sleep a wink all night. I jest knew you wuzn't so purty fer nuthin'. I remember the first time I laid eyes on that Buford, I had 'im picked out special jest fer you. Lawsy! He's the hottest feller I've ever seen in all my days."

Joe and Lydie had slipped Flo's mind, and Janie wuz winnin' the trophy fer favorite daughter. Flo didn't give a rat's ass 'bout anybody else in the family. Janie's little sisters wuz already makin' lists of thangs Janie would git fer 'em once she wuz married off and had her hands on some of Buford's money.

Mary wuz jest sure that she'd be gittin' one of them fancy Kindle machines fer readin' her books, and Kitty wanted 'em to throw big parties and invite all the cutest boys fer her to dance with.

After that of course, Buford wuz over to Benny's all the time. He showed up sometime b'fore breakfast and hung 'round 'til after supper. From time to time one of his backwoods neighbors'd give 'im an invite to come over that he thought he had to accept.

Lizzy didn't spend all that much time with her sister since Buford wuz over so much. They wuz allowed to go back in the lean-to, and Lizzy didn't wanna go back in there and interrupt whatever it wuz that wuz goin' on. If'n Janie had chores to do, she'd come out'a there all rumpled with her face red from Buford's beard, and he'd find Lizzy and hang with her 'til Janie wuz finished and ready to go back in the bedroom. And when Buford had to run out on an errand, Lizzy wuz always there fer Janie to talk to.

"He's made me so happy," said Janie one night. "He didn't have no idea I wuz in Nashv'lle the same time he wuz. I find that hard to b'lieve, but he swears on it."

"I had a hunch," said Lizzy. "What did he say 'bout it?"

"I reckon it wuz his sister's doin'. They wuzn't too happy that he wuz sweet on me, which I can understand since there 'r so many other purty girls out there. But I'd be willin' to bet when they see me and see how happy Buford is with me, that they'll start to treat me like kin. I cain't never trust 'em as far as I can throw 'em, though."

"That's the meanest damned thang I ever heard you say," said Lizzy. "Good girl! I'd be fit to be tied if'n I seen you fooled by that Two-faced Tammy."

"Can you b'lieve it, Lizzy? When he left fer Nashv'lle last year, he wuz head over heels in love with me, and nuthin' but him thankin' that I didn't like 'im kept 'im away. Laws!"

"He made a mistake with that one, but I'm sure it wuz on account of he's a humble kind of a feller."

Lizzy wuz happier 'n a hungry baby in a barrel of boobs that Buford hadn't let on that Dutch wuz the one who'd convinced 'im Janie didn't have feelin's fer 'im. Even though Janie had the most forgivin' heart in the whole wide world, Lizzy knew she'd have hard feelin's on that one.

"Oh, Lizzy!" Janie said, "I'm the luckiest girl who ever walked the face of the earth. I have no idea what I ever did to deserve a man like Buford. I'm the happiest and most blessed of all God's creatures. If'n only there wuz another man like Buford fer you, then I'd be happy as a stud horse with two peters."

"If'n you found forty fellers like Buford fer me, I'd never be as happy as you are. I'm not the Southern belle you 'r with all yer sweetness and good manners. I'd be lucky if'n another Cooter came by and took an interest in me."

The engagement couldn't be kept under a bushel fer long. Flo whispered the news to Fern over the phone, and Fern wuz obliged to tell ever' person she knew. Janie wuz called the luckiest girl in town, even though jest a few weeks b'fore, Lydie'd been called the same thang.

# Chapter 56

One mornin' 'bout a week after Janie's engagement, Buford and the girls wuz settin' down at the kitchen table makin' signs fer the church bazaar, and they seen a fancy car drivin' real slow down the dirt road. When it turned and pulled up into the grass in front of their house, they tried to figure who would be out visitin' in a car like that. Nobody they knew could afford nuthin' so nice. There wuz no doubt that somebody wuz comin', so Buford took Janie by the hand and scooted out the back door and into the bushes. They wuz like rabbits, those two. Anyway, the three sisters who wuz left watched to see who would git out, and it wuz none other than Mrs. Prudence Majestro, Miz M!

Well, they couldn't 've been more surprised if'n it'd been the Pope. Flo and Kitty wuz 'specially shocked, prob'ly even more 'n Lizzy wuz.

She walked right in the house without knockin', like she owned the damned place. She didn't make a peep when Lizzy said her hello's and set herself down without sayin' a word. Flo didn't know what to do with herself at all. She wuz tongue-tied at havin' somebody so uppity right there in her very own kitchen. After settin' there a minute or two like she had a rod up her butt, she said to Lizzy, "I hope you 'r doin' all right, Miss Lizzy. I'm guessin' that lady is yer mother?"

Lizzy said that she wuz.

"And that, I suppose, is one of yer sisters?"

"Yes, ma'am," said Flo, pleased as punch to have somethin' to say. "She's the kneebaby of the family. My youngest girl has jest been married off, and my oldest girl is wanderin' somewhere outside with her beau."

"You have a very small house," said Miz M after a bit.

"It ain't nuthin' like I've heard tell of yer place, but it's bigger 'n the Lucas's house next door."

"This kitchen must git awful hot in the summer since the windows face west."

Flo told her they put up a piece of cardboard in the summer time to keep out the heat, and then added, "I hope Cooter and Charlotte 'r doin' well."

"Yes. I seen 'em night b'fore last, and they wuz jest fine."

Lizzy thought maybe Miz M would have a package or somethin' from Charlotte on account of she couldn't thank on any other reason fer her to 've come, but no package wuz given or hinted at. Lizzy wuz puzzled.

Flo begged Miz M to take a glass of sweet tea or a Co-Cola, but Miz M looked 'round the kitchen with an eye like she wuz gonna vomit, and with a nasty tone, said she wuz fine.

She then stood up and said to Lizzy, "Miss Lizzy, there seemed to be a right nice magnolia tree over yonder. I'd like to go take a gander at it if'n you'll go with me."

"Go on," said Flo, "and show her the little flower bed we put in over thar with the old tires from Daddy's shop. Them white-walls make a good little border, I'll suwanee."

Lizzy put on her overboots, and they walked without talkin' to the magnolia tree. She couldn't thank on nuthin' to say to somebody bein' so disagreeable as Miz M.

As soon as they wuz out'a earshot of the house, Miz M started. "I'm sure you know why I've come all this way to talk at you. Yer not stupid, so I know in yer heart you know."

Lizzy's mouth dropped open. "Well, yer wrong. I cain't imagine a reason why you'd wanna bend my ear."

"Miss Lizzy," said Miz M with an angry tone, "you should know already that I ain't somebody who wants to play games. Even though you 'r hell-bent on pretendin' I am. I've got a reputation fer tellin' thangs as they are, and at a time like this I won't stray from it. I heard tell of some news two days ago that set my pants on fire. I wuz told yer sister wuz fixin' to git hitched, and that you wuzn't far behind her, and you wuz plannin' on gittin' yer claws into my nephew, Dutch. I know it must be a big fat lie, and I know my nephew has better sense than that, but I wanted to look you in the eye and tell you it ain't never gonna happen."

"If'n you thank it's so impossible," said Lizzy turnin' almost purple in the face, "I wonder why you came all the way out here from Knoxv'lle. What 'r you a-tryin' to git me to say?"

"I'm here to hear with my own ears that it ain't true."

"You comin' all this way to see me and my kin seems to prove yer rumor, if there's even a rumor to gossip 'bout."

"If?! Are you sayin' that you've never caught wind of it? Haven't y'all been the ones spreadin' it 'round ever'where?"

"I'll suwanee I never heard tell of no such story."

"And will you swear there's no reason fer you to thank a rumor like that is true?"

"I ain't gonna pretend I'm an open book like you are, Miz M. You can ask as many questions as you want, but I might decide not to spill the beans on any of it."

"I ain't gonna take this backsass from you, Miss Lizzy. You best jest tell me now. Has he, my nephew, asked you to marry 'im?"

"You said it cain't be true yer ownself. Why should you have to ask me?"

"Well, it had oughtta be a lie if'n that boy still has his head on his shoulders right. Who knows what kind of spell you've put on 'im? He might be followin' yer short little skirt and forgit 'bout his own kin."

"If'n I've snagged 'im, I'd be the last girl to say so."

"Miss Lizzy, do you know who I am? Didn't yer Momma teach you to respect yer elders? I ain't used to folks talkin' to me like this. Now I am jest 'bout Dutch's closest relation in this world, and I have a right to know what's goin' on with 'im."

"That may be, Miz M, but you ain't got no rights when it comes to me. And the way yer goin' on, I don't thank I feel obliged to tell you."

"Let me git this clear. This match, which you hope to make with Dutch, cain't never happen. Not in a million years. Dutch is engaged to my daughter, so what do you have to say 'bout that?"

"Only that if'n he's engaged to yer daughter, you ain't got cause to thank he's engaged to me, now do you?"

Miz M thought fer a second and said, "Well, he might've forgot he wuz engaged to her on account of they've been promised to each other since they wuz babies. This wuz what his Momma and I wanted. We'd planned it while we wuz rockin' 'em in their cradles. We both thought if'n they'd git hitched to each other, then we could prevent 'em from marryin' beneath 'em. Don't you care what his family wants fer 'im? Don't you care 'bout his engagement to DeeDee? Don't you see what kind of mess yer makin'? Ain't you heard me say from day one that DeeDee had dibs on 'im?"

"Yep. I heard it all b'fore, but why should I care one whit? If'n you ain't got any other objection to me marryin' yer nephew than a plan laid down all those years ago b'tween two hens, then y'all cain't hold me to it. Whether he marries his own cousin or not really depends on him, doncha thank? It's his choice to make, and if'n I'm his choice, why shouldn't I jump at the chance?"

"But, but my daughter has dibs on 'im. You cain't go against his kin. Ever'body in this family will hate you, and we won't invite you to family reunions or weddin's or nuthin'."

"Wow! Not sure how I can stand not bein' invited to yer reunions or weddin's," said Lizzy with a heavy dose of sarcasm. "I'm guessin' any wife of Dutch's might could have other thangs to keep her happy. I don't thank I'll mind missin' yer reunions, Miz M."

"You headstrong bitch! I cain't b'lieve you! Is this the way you thank me fer bein' so kind to y'all last spring? Don't you owe me nuthin' fer that? You need to git it through yer pea-pickin' little brain that I came here with a purpose, and not a soul can keep me from it. You can try to brush me off, but I won't be disappointed."

"I feel sorry fer you, then."

"Don't interrupt me, Missy. You shut yer trap fer a minute. DeeDee and Dutch wuz made fer each other. They come from a long line of American patriots. I am a member of the Colonial Dames and the Daughters of the American Revolution. A member of our family has served in every American war, and during the War of Northern Aggression, some of 'em fought their own kin to preserve their way of life. Both DeeDee and Dutch have a good education and money in the bank. Do you thank you can wave yer high school diploma under his nose and git his attention? He has it all, and you ain't nuthin' but trailer trash. I cain't take it! This cain't and won't happen. If'n you knew what wuz good fer you, you'd stay back here with yer own folks."

"When I marry yer nephew, I won't be gittin' away from my raisin', if'n that's what yer gittin' at. He's a businessman, and I'm a businessman's daughter."

"Well, I'll give you that. Dutch owns property and a horse farm, and yer Daddy owns a grease pit where he fixes cars and cain't make enough money to pay his own mortgage. And look at yer Momma! She's a high school drop-out. Yer aunts and uncles ain't much better. You don't thank I'm stupid do you? I know who they are."

"If'n Dutch don't object to my kin, why should you?"

"Tell me right now. Are y'all engaged?"

Lizzy tried to thank on a way to git 'round the question, but she couldn't. She said, "No, we ain't."

Miz M seemed tickled pink.

"Will you promise me you won't never git engaged to 'im?"

"Nope."

"Miss Lizzy, I cain't b'lieve you! I thought you wuz more respectable than other folks. You best git used to me, then, be'cuz I ain't gonna leave you alone til you tell me what I wanna hear."

"You best git comfortable, then, be'cuz I'll never say what you want. Jest be'cuz you want yer daughter to git married to Dutch, you want me to say I won't never do it. But my promise won't make yer wishes come true. If'n he walked up to me tomorrow and got down on one knee to propose, and I said "no," do you thank fer a minute that'd mean that he'd suddenly fall fer DeeDee? Truth is, I thank yer a couple of cards short of a full deck if'n you thank you can come here and git me to do what you want. I jest wonder what Dutch'd thank of you gittin' mixed up in his business like this. Alls I know is, you ain't got no call to be mixed up in mine, so I thank it's time fer you to hit the road."

"Hold on one cotton-pickin' minute. I ain't done here. You've got a lot of nerve! You thank yer good enough fer 'im? You with yer sister who's some kind of an internet porn star? You thank I don't know all 'bout it? Ever'body knows she run off with that horrible Joe Wickham to star in nekkid movies with 'im. How's that gonna go over at Christmas git-t'gethers? Are all of y'all gonna sit 'round the Christmas tree at Pembrook Farm and watch their movies t'gether? I cain't imagine!"

"You don't know what yer talkin' 'bout, and you cain't have nuthin' else to say, Miz M," Lizzy said. "You've said enough to make my blood curdle. I'm goin' on inside now."

"You selfish bitch! You don't thank 'bout anybody but yerself."

"This is me walkin' away from you. You can kiss my white trash ass."

"You plan to marry 'im, I guess?"

She looked over her shoulder at Miz M. "I ain't said nuthin' of the kind. Alls I'm sayin' is I'll do whatever makes me happy without one single, solitary thought of you or anybody else."

"That's it? That's what yer leavin' me with? I'll have my way, Missy. You can mark my words. You will marry Dutch over my dead body."

Miz M continued to mutter threats as she got back in the car and pulled away. Lizzy walked in the house and slammed the front door so hard that dust tumbled off one of the deer heads hangin' on the walls. She then went back into her bedroom, which wuz empty fer once, and slammed that door too. Flo knocked on the door, peeked her head inside and said, "Why didn't you offer Miz M a Co-Cola or some sweet tea?"

"She didn't want it, Momma. She needed to git goin'."

"She looks great fer her age! I bet she's been to one of them plastic surgeons to git her face lifted and some Botox. I guess she came by on her way somewheres else to tell us how Cooter and Charlotte 'r doin'. Did she say anythang else, Lizzy?"

"Nope," Lizzy lied.

# Chapter 57

Well, the visit with Miz M put Lizzy in a piss-poor mood, and it wuz a while b'fore she could thank on anythang else. She couldn't b'lieve the old biddy'd drive all the way from Knoxv'lle to confront her. Miz M must've heard from Charlotte that one of Benny's girls wuz gittin' hitched and had a conniption fit. Or maybe she thought since Lizzy would be 'round Janie and Buford so much that Liz wuz hopin' fer a double weddin' or somethin'. She wuz bound and determined to stop anythang from happenin', and Lizzy could only imagine the nasty thangs Miz M would say to Dutch 'bout her and her kin. She didn't know how close he wuz with his aunt or if he'd even listen to her at all.

If'n Dutch'd been on the fence 'bout Lizzy at all, it wuz possible his nasty aunt might could push 'im over to the wrong side.

"If'n Dutch don't come to visit Buford directly like he said he would, I'll know she's had her hand in it," thought Lizzy. "If'n he's swayed so easy by a bitch like Miz M, then he's not the feller I thank he is. I'll quit moonin' over 'im."

The next morning as she wuz lettin' the dogs back in, Lizzy heard her Daddy callin' fer her from the family room. As she walked in the room, her Daddy wuz hangin' up the telephone. She set herself down on the couch and laid her head on his shoulder. She wuz sure he wanted to talk to her 'bout somethin' somebody had said over the phone jest then, and it hit her that Miz M might could've called her Daddy on her.

He said, "I got a call jest now that knocked my socks off. I'll suwanee I feel like a doe in the headlights. I didn't know I had two girls who wuz fixin' to git 'emselves hitched."

Heat rushed into Lizzy's face and she started to sweat, thankin' it wuz a call from Dutch instead of his aunt. Then she wondered why Dutch would talk to her Daddy and not ask to talk to her personal-like.

Benny said, "You look worried. I'm guessin' you're a-tryin' to figure out which of yer fellers have been callin' me. I'll tell you, it's Cooter."

"Cooter! Why in the world would he ring us up?"

"He started by congratulatin' me on Janie's engagement to Buford. Seems he heard tell of it from LuLu and her gossipin'. Of course I set here fer half an hour with my ear gittin' all hot with the phone pressed against it while he wuz talkin' on like he does. Then he switched the subject to you, and he said you wuz fixin' to git hitched to somebody real important. You'll never guess who he thanks you've got yer eyes on. He started in on all the feller's good manners and how much money he has and how he owns his own property and has a right nice horse farm. He sounded so sold on the feller, I wondered why Cooter didn't marry 'im, his-own-damned self. Then he went on to tell me that the feller's family didn't like the idea of you marryin' 'im. You won't b'lieve it, Lizzy, but he thought you wuz engaged to Dutch. I thought Cooter wuz ig'lant, but I had no idea he wuz stupid, too. I set right there holdin' the phone and imagined Dutch bein' the last man on earth, and you tellin' 'im he needed to go take care of his own damned needs. He never even looks at a girl fer any reason other than to find somethin' wrong with her, and he prob'ly never really ever laid eyes on you b'fore in his life. I took it as a compliment."

Lizzy couldn't join in with her Daddy, even though he wuz havin' a good time. She gave 'im a little smile, but she felt a little sick at her stomach fer the way he wuz talkin'.

"So anyhoo, Cooter told me he let word slip to Miz M that folks wuz talkin' 'bout y'all hookin' up, and she told ol' Coot she would never allow it. Can you imagine anyone talkin' like that? Well, Coot wanted us to know what folks wuz sayin' behind our backs, and fer that I'm obliged to 'im, I reckon. He said he wuz real happy thangs worked out quiet-like fer Lydie and Joe, and he jest hopes someone don't run across some pictures of her on the internet and recognize her as his kin. He thought I shouldn't've let 'em back in the house so soon. He said I had oughtta forgive 'em fer all of it, but not look on 'em again. He don't have an unspoken thought, I'll suwanee. He ended his little speech by sayin' how swell he and Charlotte wuz doin', and... Why, Lizzy, you don't look like you're enjoyin' Cooter's comedy as much as I am. What is there to live fer if'n you cain't make fun of yer neighbors and kin?"

"I jest thank it's all strange, Daddy."

"But that's the best part, Liz. If'n they'd picked another feller to tease us 'bout, the story might have stuck. He's such a snob to ever'body, and you clearly hate 'im worse 'n jest 'bout anybody. Makes it funnier, don't you thank? I'm so glad we've mended our fences with Cooter. He cracks me up ever' time I hear 'im talk. By the way, what did Miz M say when she stopped by the other day? Did she tell you not to marry her nephew?"

To this question, Lizzy jest laughed, but she felt a lump in her throat. He asked her again, but she still jest laughed at his question. She felt kicked in the gut that her own Daddy thought it wuz such a joke that Dutch would be sweet on her.

# Chapter 58

Not too many days passed after Miz M's visit b'fore Buford brought his buddy, Dutch, to visit the girls. The fellers got there bright and early, and b'fore Flo could say anythang 'bout his aunt's visit, the young folks went outside fer a walk down past the silo and around the rusty car graveyard. Flo and Benny hurried back to their bedroom, and Mary sat with a notebook open, practicin' her school work or other such nonsense.

Headed down the road, Janie and Buford wuz up front a ways b'fore the others passed 'em by. Dutch, Lizzy and Kitty walked ahead, but Kitty wuz so scared of Dutch that she didn't say a word, which wuz unusual for her. When they made it to the Lucas's driveway, Kitty said she needed to talk with Katie Jo, and left Lizzy and Dutch alone t'gether. Lizzy's stomach wuz in knots. She felt like she wuz walkin' to her own funeral.

"Dutch, I've got to say somethin'. I cain't help but tell you how much obliged I am, we, my family, all are fer you steppin' up to help my sister. Ever since I caught wind of it, I've been wantin' to say how grateful I feel. If'n my folks knew what you done, I thank they'd be doin' the same."

"I'm sorry you found out. I thought I could trust yer Ain't Tildie," he said.

"Don't be thankin' ill of her. Lydie said somethin' first, bein' careless like she is, and then I couldn't sleep 'til I knew what'd happened. I jest don't know what to say to thank you enough fer my whole family."

"Yer thanks is enough fer me, Miss Lizzy," Dutch said. "I did it to make you happy, I'll admit. But yer family don't owe me nuthin'. I didn't do it fer 'em, jest fer you."

Well, the cat had Lizzy's tongue after he'd said what he did, and she couldn't say nuthin'. He continued, "You shoot straight with me, and I like that 'bout you. Don't play with me. If you still feel the same way you did last April, let me know. I feel exactly the same way. I thank you hung the moon, and I wanna wake up ever' mornin' a-lookin' at yer purty face, but jest say the word, and I'll never say nuthin' 'bout it again."

At this, Lizzy had to say somethin'. She told 'im her feelin's had done a one-eighty since last spring, and that she wuz his fer the takin'.

At her words, he leaned down and kissed her so hard that they had to steady themselves against a tree. She couldn't see what wuz goin' on since her eyes wuz closed with the kissin', but it seemed like he had eight hands, and they wuz all over her at once. As he kissed her neck, he whispered to her how he felt 'bout her and how important she wuz to 'im. Ever' word made her love 'im more.

The ground wuz still wet from the frost, so after they worked themselves into a tizzy, they jest had to calm themselves back down. They walked hand-in-hand through the woods, and she found out that all her happiness wuz on account of his Ain't Pru (Miz M) who visited 'im when he wuz in Nashv'lle and told 'im 'bout her trip to see Lizzy. She repeated ever' word Lizzy had said to her, hopin' to piss Dutch off, but it jest made 'im wanna come back quicker.

"I started to hope like I'd never let myself hope b'fore," he said. "I knew you enough to know that if'n you wuz hell-bent against me, you would've said so to Ain't Pru right then and there."

She said, "Yer right 'bout that. After bein' such a bitch to you to yer face, you know I'd bash you to all yer kin."

"You didn't say nuthin' I didn't deserve. Even though you wuz wrong 'bout some of it, you wuz right that I wuz bein' an ass. I hate to thank on it."

"I didn't know I'd made such an impression on you."

"You thought I wuz some kind of a robot without feelin's at all. What wuz it you said 'bout there not bein' any way I could've asked you that you would've said 'yes' to. Ouch. Now, that hurt."

"Lawsy! Don't repeat what I said back to me. I'll have to crawl under a rock and die."

Dutch started talkin' 'bout his letter. "Did it make you thank better on me? Did you b'lieve any of what I wrote to you?"

She told 'im how it had made her feel and how she started a-lookin' at thangs from another angle after she'd read it.

He said, "I knew that some of it would hurt when you read it, but I had to say it. I hope you threw it out after you read it. There's one or two parts at the beginnin' that I know prob'ly pissed you off."

"I can burn it if'n you want me to."

"When I wrote that letter," said Dutch, "I thought I wuz calm, cool and collected, but the truth is I wuz angry as bed bug on sheet washin' day."

"Well, now, the letter started angry-like, but it ended nice. Let's not talk 'bout it any more. The feller who wrote it and the gal who read it 'r both diff'rent people now. Let's only thank on thangs in the past that make us smile."

"I'm the kind of guy who needs to learn from his past. I've been selfish, I'll admit. My folks taught me right, but I wuz an only child fer so long, I didn't learn how to hold my temper. I've been uppity, and you taught me that. It wuz a hard pill to swaller, but I'm the better fer it. You took me down a notch when I needed it the most, sweet Lizzy. You showed me how far I needed to go 'til I could deserve someone as good as you are."

"You must have hated me after I turned you down that night."

"Hate you? Naw. I wuz angry at first, but then I took a good hard look at myself."

"I'm afraid to ask you what you thought when you seen me at Pembrook Farm. Did you thank I wuz scopin' out the place?"

"No. I sure wuz surprised, though."

"You couldn't have been half as surprised as I wuz. We wuz told that y'all wouldn't be back fer another day, and we wanted to snoop 'round a little bit. And then you drove up and wuz sweet as all git-out to us. I didn't thank you'd have a nice thang to say, but you wuz over-the-top to both me and my kin."

"I wuz a-tryin' to show you that I wuzn't such a bad guy. I hoped to git you to forgive me and make you see I could be a good boy when I wanted to be. More 'n that, though, I wanted you to see what you said to me that night had stuck, and I wuz attemptin' to make amends."

Then he told her of how much Suzanna loved her and how sad she wuz when Lizzy had to leave town so soon. They wandered along the deer path fer so long, talkin', 'til they realized they should be headin' back to the house or folks would start to worry 'bout 'em.

As they walked back home, Lizzy asked if'n Dutch wuz surprised at all by Janie and Buford's engagement.

"Oh, hell no. When I left fer Nashv'lle, I thought he would pop the question."

"Does that mean you told 'im it would be okay? Did you give 'im some kind of permission to marry her?" Dutch over-acted his shock, which told Lizzy she'd hit the nail on the head.

"The night b'fore I left fer Nashv'lle, I told 'im what'd happened when we left town last time. I should've told 'im long b'fore then. He wuz surprised and fairly pissed at me fer thankin' yer sister didn't care fer 'im none. I could tell right away he wuz as smitten with her as ever and that they could be happy t'gether. Plus, I'd watched her since we came back to town, and I could tell she wuz nuts 'bout 'im."

"So when you wuz sure of it, you told 'im and he b'lieved you?"

"Purty much. Buford's a great guy, but sometimes he needs somebody to give 'im a nudge in the right direction. The one thang that got under his skin, and he's still kind of sore 'bout it, is that I knew Janie wuz in Nashv'lle last winter visitin' with her Ain't Tildie and didn't say nuthin' to 'im 'bout it. But now that he's spendin' so much time back in the lean-to, I thank he's forgiven me."

Lizzy wanted to say that Buford wuz a great friend to be so easily pushed 'round, but she stopped herself. Dutch didn't know how to be the butt of a joke, and she thought it wuz too early to start teachin' 'im now. They kept talkin' on Buford and Janie and how happy they wuz 'til they reached the house. Once they wuz inside, they sat across the room from each other.

# Chapter 59

"Good Lord, Lizzy! Where have y'all been? We thought you'd been done et up by a bear or somethin'," said Janie as soon as they sat down. All Lizzy said wuz that they had follered a deer path, and even though she wuz blushin' like a whore in church, nobody thought nuthin' of it.

The evenin' passed quietly watchin' wrastlin' on tv. Janie and Buford did God-knows-what under a thick blanket they'd brought in from the bedroom, and Dutch and Lizzy jest kept a-lookin' over at each other. Dutch wuzn't one to show his feelin's outright, and Lizzy knew she wuz happy, but she wuz all mixed up inside 'bout what her folks would thank when they knew she wuz engaged to Dutch. Not a soul in her family liked 'im exceptin' Janie, and she didn't even thank all his money could convince 'em to like 'im at all.

That night she spilled her guts to Janie, who didn't b'lieve a word of it. "You're kiddin', Lizzy. This cain't be. I won't fall fer another one of yer practical jokes. It ain't happenin' this time, Sister."

"Gracious goodness, Janie. I wuz dependin' on you to b'lieve me. I know nobody else will. If I'm lyin', I'm dyin'. I swear on a stack of Bibles. He loves me, and we're engaged."

"But you hate 'im. I know it."

"You don't know shit from shinola. That's all in the past. Maybe I didn't love 'im so much b'fore as I do right now, but I plan on puttin' all them feelin's behind me."

Janie still couldn't b'lieve her. "Gracious goodness, Lizzy! Is it possible? I reckon I oughtta b'lieve you. I guess I should give you a pat on the back to congratulate you, but 'r you right sure 'bout it? Do you thank you can really live with 'im ever' day fer the rest of yer life?"

"No doubt. We already decided we're gonna be as happy as two drunks in a river of whiskey. Ain't you happy fer me, Janie? Doncha thank he's got the cutest little ass you've ever seen?"

"There ain't two opinions b'tween us 'bout his ass. You know that. And as fer Buford and me, well, we couldn't be happier fer y'all. We talked on it jest yesterd'y, and both of us said it wuz impossible fer y'all to come t'gether. Seriously, though, Lizzy! Do you really love 'im enough to git hitched? Don't hook up with 'im on account of he's loaded. Make sure you love 'im fer his ownself instead of his bank account."

"He's mine, come hell or high water. You'll understand better when I tell you ever'thang."

"Be serious, Liz. Tell me ever'thang slow-like so's I can understand how this happened. You best tell me right now how long this has been comin' and how I didn't see none of it."

"Welp, these feelin's snuck up on me when I wuz at Pembrook Farm up to Lexin'ton. Ambushed me from out'a the horse barn. Nearly knocked me down, they did."

Janie wuz gittin' pissed be'cuz Lizzy wuz teasin', and once she'd turned her back on Lizzy and picked up a People Magazine, Lizzy knew she wuzn't jokin' 'round. She told Janie ever'thang there wuz to tell, and Janie wuz satisfied that her sister wuz plum et up with love fer Dutch.

Lizzy told her of Dutch's part in Lydie's situation, and the sisters spent the rest of the night talkin' 'bout ever'thang and plannin' each other's weddin's.

"Heavens. To. Betsy!" cried Flo as she looked out the kitchen window the next mornin'. "I wish that horrible Dutch would quit follerin' sweet Buford over here ever' single day. Don't he have nuthin' else to do? He wears me out, I'll suwanee. Why don't he go huntin' or fishin' or somethin'? Lizzy, why don't you take 'im out fer a walk like you did the other day so's he won't be botherin' Janie and Buford and keepin' 'em from their business."

The ground had dried up a bit more, and Lizzy'd already spied an old picnic blanket that could be put to good use if they took another "walk." She almost laughed out loud at how convenient her Momma's ideas wuz fittin' into her own plans.

As soon as the boys wuz through the front door, Buford caught Lizzy up in a big bear hug and swirled her 'round. There wuz no doubt he knew her good news. When Benny walked through the room with his paper, Buford said, "Hey there, Benny. Do you know of any good deer paths Lizzy can git lost on today?"

Flo piped up. "I thank they might oughtta head out past the Boy Scout camp. There won't be no hunters out that way, and it's a nice looong walk. I reckon Dutch ain't never been out them parts."

I thank Lizzy and Dutch could handle a long walk like that, Miz Flo," said Buford, "but it might be too fur a piece fer Kitty."

Kitty admitted that she'd rather stay at home, and Dutch said he'd always wanted to go down past the Boy Scout camp. He'd heard it had a really nice view. Lizzy couldn't look up from her shoes. As she went back to her room to grab a sweatshirt, Flo follered her. "I sure am awful sorry, Lizzy, that yer havin' to keep comp'ny with that horrible man all by yerself. I hope you don't mind it. It's all fer Janie, you know. Don't feel you have to say much to 'im, darlin'. Jest nod and point out the sights. Don't put yerself out."

When they'd reached the camp, Dutch found a stack of dry wood under a tarp and made a fire in the clearin' where little boys had been buildin' fires fer a hundred years. He and Lizzy spread out the blanket and got busy right there in the outdoors in broad daylight.

They'd decided on the walk that Dutch would talk to Benny that night, and Lizzy would let her Momma know they wuz engaged. She wuzn't sure jest how her Momma would take it, wonderin' if'n his deep pockets wuz enough to make Flo forgit how much she hated Dutch. Lizzy wuz sure of one thang, she'd tell her Momma in private, so's to keep her first reaction from Dutch. It could go one of two ways, and Lizzy didn't want Dutch to see either one.

That night after the supper dishes wuz put away, Benny went off to the family room to see what wuz on tv. Dutch got up and follered 'im in there, and Lizzy thought she'd throw up right there on the linoleum. She didn't worry 'bout her Daddy sayin' he didn't have enough money fer two weddin's. She didn't want nuthin' fancy like Janie would have. She wuz worried that he'd be upset with her fer her choice, and since she wuz by far and away his favorite, she didn't like to do nuthin' to change that. She set there nervous as a turkey the day b'fore Thanksgivin' 'til Dutch came back in the kitchen with a grin the size of Texas on his face. He walked up behind her at the sink, and whispered, "Go on in to yer Daddy. He wants to bend yer ear a minute." She scooted past 'im and went to Benny.

Benny wuz sittin' there on the couch without the tv on, which wuz unusual fer him. He looked old 'round the eyes. He said, "Liz, my God! What in the hell 'r you doin'? Have you lost yer damned mind to marry this guy? I thought you hated 'im!"

She wished more 'n anythang that she'd kept her opinions 'bout Dutch to her ownself early on. It would've kept her from havin' to do so much explainin' to her Daddy, which wuz tough at this point, 'specially considerin' the thoughts that kept swirlin' 'round in her head 'bout what they'd been up to at the Boy Scout camp that day. She made it through and convinced her Daddy of how much she loved Dutch.

Benny said, "What yer sayin' is you 'r bound and determined to git hitched to 'im. He's loaded. I cain't deny that. You'll have finer clothes and better cars than even Janie will, but will all them possessions make you happy?"

"Do you really thank I don't love 'im, Daddy?"

"I might could git past 'im bein' proud and puffed up and hard to git-along with, if'n I wuz sure you really loved 'im, sweet Lizzy."

"Aw, Daddy! Don't say such thangs 'bout 'im," said Lizzy with tears in her eyes. "Y'all jest don't know 'im the way I do. Y'all don't know what he's like. I jest, I jest love 'im to pieces."

"He says he wants to throw you the biggest weddin' we've ever seen in these parts, and he wants to pay fer the whole thang, dress and all. I told 'im I'd be obliged to let 'im. I don't thank I could tell 'im he couldn't do a damned thang anyhow. Jest promise me, girlie, that this is what you want. I'd hate to see you married off to a man you couldn't stand. Yer my girl, Lizzy."

She made sure her Daddy knew how much she loved Dutch, and told 'im how her thoughts had warmed to 'im over time. She told 'im she'd built on her feelin's fer 'im fer so long, and they wuz stronger than the Tennessee Vol's front line. Eventually, he made peace with the idea.

"Well, Lizzy," Benny said, "He seems like quite the catch. I don't thank I could've let you go to anybody less deservin' of you. I'm gonna miss havin' you 'round."

She then told 'im ever'thang Dutch had done fer Lydie, and he listened slack-jawed at the whole story.

"You mean to say Dutch did ever'thang? He found the two of 'em, made sure they wuz married, paid Joe's debts and got 'im a job in Atlanta? Laws! And I wuz feelin' low on account of I thought yer uncle had taken money from his own family to bail out those two good-fer-nuthin' brats. And you say Dutch don't want paid back? I would pay 'im back if he wanted, a little at a time, but I would've paid 'im back. I'll visit with 'im 'bout a payment plan tomorrow, and he'll tell me not to be stupid, and that'll be the end of it."

He remembered how embarrassed she'd been when he'd told her 'bout Cooter's phone call and laughed himself into a coughing fit. As she wuz leavin' to head back into the kitchen, he said, "If'n any fellers is out there waitin' to git hitched to Mary or Kitty, send 'em on back. I ain't got nuthin' else to do but git rid of me some daughters."

Later that night when Flo wuz tuckin' Lizzy into bed, Lizzy told her Momma 'bout Dutch. When the words first hit Flo's ears, she stood still as a statue, starin' at the wall, unable to say a word. She set down slow-like, and Lizzy started to git worried 'bout her. Finally Flo started fidgitin' and poppin' her knuckles. She stood up and set back down, and then did it all over again.

"Good gracious! Lord bless me! Jest thank on it! Dutch! Who would've thunk it? Is it really true? Oh! Sweet, sweet Lizzy! You're gonna be rich! You're gonna live in a big farm house with horses and prob'ly a housekeeper. I bet you'll have yer own car, and it won't break down all the time, and if'n it does, Dutch will send it out to be fixed instead of a-tryin' to fix it his ownself. I am so happy! Dutch is such a hottie! Way hotter 'n Buford, I always thought. My, oh, my! He's so tall, and he has such large hands. My, my! Oh, Lizzy, I'm so sorry fer havin' hated 'im so much b'fore. I hope he don't know 'bout it. I cain't b'lieve this is happenin' to me! Three daughters married off! This house jest got a lot bigger! I wonder what I'll do with all the room."

Flo gave her kisses to the girls and headed out into the hall, but then turned right 'round and came back in. "Sweetie!" she cried, "I cain't thank on nuthin' else. He's the richest man I ever did meet in all my days. He's practic'ly one of them Rockefellers or Kennedys. What does he like to eat? I'll make it special fer 'im tomorrow."

Lizzy wuz worried 'bout how much attention her Momma would give Dutch the next day, but she needn't have worried. Flo wuz so much flustered by the idea that Dutch wuz fixin' to marry her daughter, that she didn't say nuthin' less'n it wuz to offer 'im somethin' cold to drink. Benny made an effort to git to know Dutch a little better, and Lizzy could tell Benny liked 'im more ever' second they spent t'gether.

"I like all my new sons-in-law," he said later. "Joe is my least favorite, but I thank I'll like yer husband as much as I like Janie's."

# Chapter 60

Lizzy wuz in a playful mood these days, and she wanted Dutch to tell her exactly how he fell in love with her. "How did it all git started?" she asked. "I can understand how once you'd gotten started, you could go along without a push, but what started you off in the first place?"

"I cain't tell you the hour or the spot or the look or the words that sparked it all. It wuz too long ago, plus I wuz already in love with ya b'fore I realized anythang."

"Well, clearly it wuzn't my good looks. You made that clear early on. I wuz mean as a hornet to you most of the time, hopin' to give you a little sting here and there. You must have liked me fer bein' such a bitch to you."

"Well, I guess it wuz on account of what wuz goin' on b'tween yer ears."

"I thank it wuz be'cuz I never gave you no nevermind. You wuz used to all these high-falutin' gals who paid so much attention to you. I thank you wuz sick of all them girls who wuz always sayin' stuff so's you'd hear it and gittin' all dolled up jest fer you. You took notice of me on account of I wuz jest the opposite of 'em. That's it. That's the reason. Now you can save yer breath. I'll suwanee you didn't see nuthin' good in me at all."

"Now, hold on a minute, little darlin'. You wuz so sweet to Janie when she wuz sick up to Buford's. What 'bout that?"

"Ah, but that's Janie. Law! Who could do any less fer her? But if'n you wanna say I'm good fer that little ol' thang, go right ahead. You can blow it right out'a proportion, and as a trade, I can pick on you alls I want. I'll start straight away by askin' you why you didn't let on that you wuz sweet on me when you first came by here this time and when we all ate t'gether? You looked like you didn't care 'bout me one whit."

"Hell's fire, Lizzy! You wuz all quiet and always a-lookin' down at yer shoes! I didn't thank you wanted the attention."

"I wuz embarrassed, you turd!"

"So wuz I."

"You could've said more to me when y'all came to supper."

"Hey, I had a lot on my mind, all right. If'n I didn't care so much, I might 've run on at the mouth like yer cousin Cooter."

"I jest wonder when you'd have loosened yer lips if'n I hadn't thanked you fer ever'thang you did fer Lydie. To thank that us pairin' off like we 'r is thanks to Lydie and Joe behavin' like they didn't have no raisin' at all. It gits my goat. I wish'd I never brought it up."

"Don't worry yer purty little head 'bout it, Lizzy. It wuzn't yer bein' grateful 'bout Lydie that got me started. When Ain't Pru came down here to try to separate us, that's when I wuz sure 'bout you. I heard all 'bout it, and then I started to hope."

"Well, when 'r you fixin' to tell yer Ain't Pru the good news?"

"Hand me the phone, and I'll tell her d'rectly."

"Git it yerself. I've got an email to send to my own aunt b'fore our phone gits shut off again."

Lizzy hadn't answered Ain't Tildie's last email on account of she wuz embarrassed that Tildie and them thought she wuz tight with Dutch when she wuzn't, but now she wuz over the moon to tell her aunt ever'thang. She wrote:

*"Tildie, I should've written you back earlier fer ever'thang you told me 'bout the situation with Lydie, but I wuz confounded. You thought Dutch and me wuz tight, but we wuzn't. Now y'all can thank whatever in the hell you want. We ain't hitched yet, but we've done ever'thang else, if'n you know what I mean. I cain't thank y'all enough fer cuttin' our trip short and fer stoppin' by Pembrook Farm fer a peek. Next time y'all come, you can bring the kids, and they can ride them ponies like you said. I gotta admit, I'm happier 'n even Janie. She walks 'round here with a shit-eatin' grin on her face, but I cain't stop laughin'. Dutch says 'hi,' and he wants y'all to come at Christmas fer a visit. Much love, Lizzy."*

Dutch's phone call to Miz M wuz short and sweet, and Benny's email to Cooter wuz best of all. It read:

*"Cooter, I reckon you should pat me on the back again. Lizzy is gittin' hitched to Dutch, so do what you can to help Miz M with the news. I hear there's a sale on Kleenex at the Dollar General. If'n I wuz you, I'd put my money on Dutch instead of the old biddy. Uncle Benny."*

Tammy seemed happy enough that her brother wuz fixin' to marry Janie. She sent a sweet email to her with a smiley-face emoticon, but Janie seen right through it. Suzanna wuz so darned excited 'bout the news that she spent two hours on long-distance switchin' b'tween Dutch and Lizzy, tellin' 'em how she wuz beside herself with joy, and how she'd always wanted a sister.

B'fore Benny got any kind of email back from Cooter or b'fore his wife could congratulate Lizzy, they caught wind from next door that they wuz on their way to the Lucas's that same day. The reason fer this nearly caused Lizzy to pee in her pants fer laughin'. Miz M had been so pissed off by the phone call with Dutch, and Charlotte'd been so happy 'bout it, that they wanted to git away 'til the storm that wuz Miz M passed over. Lizzy wuz tickled to death that her friend wuz comin', but she felt bad fer Dutch who had to spend time with that banty rooster of a cousin of hers. To Dutch's credit, he held his patience with all of 'em over at the Lucas's, and only managed to sneak a couple of pointed looks at Lizzy that clearly said "git me the hell out'a here."

Even tho' Dutch wuz bein' patient with the Lucases, he couldn't brang himself to be in the same room with Ain't Fern. Both Flo and Fern wuz too scared to say "boo" when he wuz 'round, so that made it a little better fer 'im. But when they did open their mouths, it wuz to say somethin' that would hairlip the Pope. Lizzy tried to keep Dutch away from her Momma and Ain't Fern so's he wouldn't have to hear all their plans fer a bachelorette party, complete with candy underpants and vibrating door prizes. Honestly Lizzy couldn't wait to git 'im home to Pembrook Farm where they could start bein' a family t'gether with his sister.

# Chapter 61

The happiest damned day of Flo's life wuz when she got rid of her two best daughters. She wuz jest proud as a peacock to go to Janie and Bufords to visit of a Sund'y, and she couldn't say nuthin' but good thangs 'bout Dutch and Lizzy while she wuz there. I wished I could say the new inlaws inspired Flo to improve herself so's she wouldn't be so hard to be around, but I reckon Benny wuz used to her enterin' in ever' wet t-shirt contest in town and flirtin' with the fellers who brought their cars down to the garage. He wouldn't know what to do with himself if'n his wife had started to behave herself.

Benny missed Lizzy somethin' awful. He never wuz one fer travelin' north of the Mason-Dixon line, but he liked makin' surprise visits to Kentucky to see his girl.

Buford and Janie, even as sweet-tempered as they wuz, could only take livin' close to Flo and them fer a year, then they had to git the hell out'a Dodge. Both sisters wuz beside themselves with happiness when Buford bought a little house with a stable in Kentucky, not twenty minutes from Lizzy and Dutch.

Kitty lucked out big time. She spent a lot of her time with her married sisters, and gittin' away from her wild-ass Momma wuz good fer her. Kitty had rules to follow and chores to do. Janie and Lizzy didn't let her watch reality tv or soap operas or Jerry Springer. They also kept her from goin' off to Atlanta to visit Lydie, even though she emailed her ever' single day, askin' her to come, sayin' she had a line of fellers jest waitin' on her older sister. Sometimes Lydie sent photos, but Lizzy knew Kitty's password and erased most of 'em.

Mary wuz the only daughter who stayed home with the folks. Even though she'd rather read or research topics fer discussion, she started spendin' more time with her parents. Flo couldn't stand to watch tv or go out alone, so Mary had to mix more with the neighbors. She still looked down her nose at 'em fer bein' so crude and immoral, but now that ever'body wuz gone, she wuz the purtiest sister left, and she didn't mind the change none.

Joe and Lydie proved that leopards cain't change their spots. Joe purty much gave up the idea that Dutch wouldn't fill Lizzy in on what he wuz really like. But in spite of it all, he wuz hopin' Dutch would still let 'im come home to work fer 'im after all. Once Dutch and Lizzy wuz settled in Kentucky, Lydie left this message on Lizzy's new cell phone:

*"Hey, there, Lizzy. I hope y'all 'r happier 'n two flies on a gut wagon. If'n you love Dutch half as much as I love Joe-Joe, y'all be all right. I'm glad you caught yerself such a rich feller, and when you ain't got nuthin' else to do, I hope you'll give me a call. Joe-Joe is always tellin' stories 'bout his time up at yer farm. I thank he'd like to come back there to work at some point if'n thangs don't work out fer 'im down here. I don't thank we're gonna have enough to live on without some help from somewheres. But don't whisper a word of it to Dutch if'n you don't wanna. Talk to ya later."*

As it turns out, Lizzy didn't wanna mention it to Dutch and the next time she spoke with Lydie, she let her know it. On birthdays and at Christmas Lizzy send gift cards to Lydie, but she wuz real particular 'bout where she bought the gift cards, makin' sure the places didn't sell liquor and such. Joe and Lydie moved 'round a lot, never stayin' in one place long enough to let the bills pile up too high. Sure they had wide-screen tvs and an X-box and Lydie wore rings from Home Shopping Network on every fanger, but somehow they couldn't manage to pay the electric on time. After a spell, his eye started wanderin', and she tried to overlook it, but eventually she started spendin' too much time down at the pool hall with the biker boys.

Dutch never could stand the thought of Joe Wickham in his house, but he did help Joe find work. A couple of times Lydie came fer a visit to Pembrook Farm when Joe wuz in rehab. And once or twice when Joe wuz out'a work, Lydie stayed with Buford and Janie, but she wore out her welcome when she wuz drinkin' whiskey out'a a baby bottle fer fun and spilled some of it on the rug next to the fireplace and didn't bother to clean it up. Buford actually had to ask her to leave.

Tammy wuz embarrassed to death that Dutch had up and married Lizzy, but she wanted to stay in good with 'im so's she could git invitations to his parties and such, so she kissed Lizzy's and Suzanna's asses thoroughly and reg'larly.

Suzanna and Lizzy wuz thick as thieves. They wuz always t'gether, and the only thang they ever fought over wuz who loved the other one best. It took Suzanna a while to git used to the way Lizzy teased her brother, but she learned that a husband will take a load of shit from his wife that he absolutely won't take from his little sister.

Miz M wuz so thoroughly pissed off that Dutch had actually married Lizzy she cussed 'im up one side and down the other. He wouldn't have nuthin' to do with her after that 'til Lizzy convinced 'im to be sweet to her. He didn't wanna, but Lizzy had whispered promises into his ear that made 'im eager to make up with his Ain't Pru. It took a while, but finally she got over herself and came 'round. She drove up from Knoxv'lle fer a visit even though Lizzy wuz expectin' a visit from Tildie and Guthrie, who Miz M continued to call 'the appliance man' fer the rest of her life.

Dutch and Lizzy wuz close with Guthrie and Tildie as the years went by. They loved each other to pieces, and Dutch wuz grateful that they'd brought Lizzy to Kentucky and made 'im the happiest man on earth.

## Acknowledgements

Thanks to my earliest readers, Laura Cummings, Tracy Gwinn, Rebecca Meek, Tracy McComas, Lois Merritt and Julie Winn. Every edit made it better. Huge, giant thanks to my fabulous editor Allyson Ey, who is so talented THAT I wish everyone could know her. To Jane Austen... you rock! Big hug to my sister, Amy Jenkins, for her help with the title. A delicious glass of Sangria to my book club buddies for being awesome. Thanks to my best friends Julia Thompson Bryan and Tracy McComas and Jillian Kendall for being wonderful and supportive and for encouraging me and feeding me cupcakes. Special thanks to my mother, Louetta Hale Jimison, for always believing in me and for making me a quilt when I needed it the most. Love and hugs to my sons, William, Harrison and Dewey. No, I do not expect you to read this book, but you get extra points if you do. And to Cam, my very own Mr. Darcy... there are no words sufficient to express my love and gratitude, and no, you don't have to read it either.

I want to give the biggest thank you to the Holy Spirit, who fills me with life and love and laughter.

Authors

Jane Austen is famous for her quick wit and
her unmatched contributions to the literary world.
Her novels include Pride & Prejudice, Emma, Sense & Sensibility,
Mansfield Park, Persuasion, and Northanger Abbey.

Mary Calhoun Brown is famous for making delicious brownies
and occasionally sticking her foot in her mouth.
Her debut novel, There Are No Words, won 11 literary awards.

www.ingramcontent.com/pod-product-compliance
Lightning Source LLC
Chambersburg PA
CBHW060546260626
47161CB00003B/1070